In the absurd morning light of 3 A.M. while the plane sleeps, I think of my writing. Flights are a time of summary, an occasion for sweating palms. If I should die, what would I make of my life? Was it whole, or just beginning? I used to write miniature novels, vividly imagined, set anywhere my imagination moved me. Then something slipped. I started writing only of myself. . . . That visionary gleam; India may restore it, or destroy it completely. We will set down an hour in London, in Paris, in Frankfurt, and even Kuwait—what does this do to the old perspectives? Europe is just a stop-over, Cokes in a transit room on the way to something bigger and darker than I'd ever imagined.

—From Clark Blaise's
"Going to India"

RL 6, IL 7-up

MODERN CANADIAN STORIES
A Bantam Book | November 1975
2nd printing .... August 1976
Seal edition | September 1978
3 printings through February 1980

COPYRIGHT NOTICES AND ACKNOWLEDGMENTS

MODERN CANADIAN STORIES

Edited by John Stevens

SEAL BOOKS
McClelland and Stewart-Bantam Limited
Toronto

TABLE OF CONTENTS

INTRODUCTION

All the stories in this book were written in the period between the 1930s and the 1970s, and all the writers except one are still alive and creatively active. In fact, three of the eldest—Callaghan, Garner and Ross—have published new novels within the past year. The exception is Malcolm Lowry, but he left behind such a mass of manuscripts for enterprising editors to work on that he has become a phoenix of Canadian letters, re-arising into publication every few years with yet another novel or story. "Ghostkeeper" in the present collection first appeared in print in 1973, sixteen years after Lowry's death, and no doubt more of his work is to come.

The image of the phoenix might almost apply to the Canadian short story itself in the latter part of this period. After World War II, with the advent of television as the primary medium of entertainment, the recreational reading of short stories went into steep decline. But since the late 1960s there has been a resurgent interest in them. I do not mean to suggest that the short story is re-asserting the hypnotic dominance that printed fiction once exerted over readers like the young Nellie McClung, who tells us in her autobiography, *Clearing in the West*, that as a farm girl in the pioneer days of Manitoba she would go to the neighboring village to pick up the latest issue of the *Family Herald and Weekly Star* and trudge home through the prairie snow-drifts engrossed in reading *Saved, or the Bride's Sacrifice*, oblivious of the shouts of the other members of her family urging her to hurry. Today most mass circulation papers and magazines no longer print serials and short stories. The great majority of readers whose story hunger could be appeased by uncomplicated characters in continual danger have long since defected to television, which offers a daily schedule of formula plots and stereotyped characters. But a growing number of people find their imaginations undernourished by television's ordinary fictions. The Nellie McClungs of the 1970s (and their boyfriends) are spending hours before the TV set, to be sure, but with increasing frequency the CBC is varying television's routine blancmange with dramatizations of significant stories like "Flying a Red Kite," "How I Met My Husband," and "The Wedding Gift." Some of these young viewers are also listening to CBC radio's weekly short story readings and a few of their older brothers and sisters, who have now reached Canadian universities by the hundreds of thousands, are even dipping into middlebrow periodicals like *Canadian Forum*, *Tamarack Review* *Queen's Quarterly*, and *Fiddlehead*, all of which have printed quality stories for years.

So strong is this resurgence of the short story that the older literary periodicals have been augmented since 1972 by a hardy new one, *The Journal of Canadian Fiction*, whose every issue contains half a dozen or more short stories as well as critical essays and reviews. A further heartening sign is that *Chatelaine*, which has never abandoned fiction, is growing in popularity, and the recently revived octogenarian, *Saturday Night*, has returned to the practice of its youthful heyday by once again soliciting short stories from writers both new and established.

Still other evidence of the short story's renewal of life is literally before my eyes at this moment. Facing my desk is a bookshelf where I can count more than thirty short story collections by individual Canadian authors—all published within the past five years. On a lower shelf there are five regional anthologies published within the last three years and next to them four annual anthologies of stories by new writers, the earliest bearing the publication date of 1971. Opening a collection of Morley Callaghan's stories that first appeared in 1959, I see that it has gone through three reprintings since 1967. And when I recall ~~my~~ problems last month of getting temporary possession of three of the story collections listed in the card catalogue of the local public library, I am delighted to conclude that Canadians' thirst for buying and borrowing books of stories by their own countrymen is growing.

What dampens my pleasure in the new interest that Canadians show in reading their own writers is the persistent though now somewhat lessening division between the two dominant cultures—the English and the French. Three stories in this collection are by French Canadians, Jean-Guy Carrier, Claire Martin, and Jacques Ferron, whose linguistic and cultural background stands quite apart from that of English Canada. To illustrate the separateness of the two literatures in Canada let me mention the case of Jacques Ferron. The author's note on page 286 explains his significance in Quebec politics and culture; it is enough to say here that he is an enormously important Quebec writer, a prolific creator of stories, novels, and plays. And yet it was not until 1972 that a single book by him was available in English translation, *Tales from the Uncertain Country*, from his *Contes du pays incertain* which had won a Governor General's Award ten years earlier. The "two solitudes" of French and English Canada which Hugh MacLennan described in 1945 in his novel of that title, retain much of their traditional insulation from each other. Paradoxically, MacLennan borrowed his title from a poem by Rilke which speaks of solitude as a condition of love:

> Love consists in this,
> that two solitudes protect,
> and touch, and greet each other.

Unhappily, the English and French solitudes did not originate as a function of love and have not developed so, but several events signal that at least the touching and greeting has begun. Since Ferron first appeared in English translation in 1972, three more of his books have become available in English. At least one publishing house is now specializing in such works in translation, and several others are bringing out English versions of French-Canadian writers as part of their regular publication schedule. Jean-Guy Carrier, a bilingual journalist now working in Ottawa, embodies this literary rapprochement. His story, "He Had a Dog Once," is one of a cycle of related stories entitled *My Father's House*, which takes its inspiration from the author's French-Canadian background and experience; but Carrier wrote the book first in English and has just completed a French translation of it for publication in Quebec.

The touching of the two solitudes may further be exemplified in the present anthology by a certain similarity of tone and idea between two of the French-Canadian stories and two stories by English-language Canadians. Those by Claire Martin and Jacques Ferron are examples of the "conte," the brief symbolic tale or fable that has been a common feature of French-Canadian literature since the nineteenth century. The older tales of this type were parables upholding traditional customs and values against the incursions of North American secular progress. As late as 1944 Felix Leclerc published *Allegro*, a book of such fables. In one of them, "The Patriot," a giant moose presides over an unchanging and harmonious woodland community, until one day a telephone wire is strung through the middle of the forest. The rest of the animals admire it and begin imitating the ways of men, heedless of the moose's warning:

> Don't believe in easy paradises. Let's remain ourselves. . . . Don't let yourselves be corrupted by the gaudiness and trumpet blasts, and the great voices that announce great voids.

Finally, since the animals continue to ignore him, he attacks the wire and pulls it down, electrocuting himself and dying in the act of redeeming his people. The latter day "conteurs" Ferron and Martin have abandoned that kind of tragic idealism and, as "The Flood" and "Springtime" attest, write bleakly satirical commentaries on the disruptive influences on society and negative aspects of human interaction. "The Cure" and "Heil!," two stories from English Canada resemble them in their effect on the reader. It does not require a distorting squint to detect similarities between the tyrannical wife in "The Cure" by E.G. Perrault (who is an English Canadian, the Gallic flavor of his name notwithstanding) and the sour autumn bride in Martin's "Springtime." And the compressed symbolism that marks Ferron's parable, "The Flood," finds an echo in Randy Brown's more nightmarish "Heil!"

However, the resonantly laconic parable, for generations a staple of French-Canadian short fiction, is less common among English-Canadian writers who, from Callaghan and Garner to Lowry and Atwood, have favored a more complexly developed realism. Which is not to say that they preoccupy themselves recording physical minutiae of characters and places. In fact, their quarry is almost always psychological and philosophical truth. But they work from plausibly detailed human beings perceived in a full context of sights, tastes, and smells. The surface reality of people and place is secured before the interior reality of their psychological and spiritual tensions is attempted. Even such subtle writers as Lowry and Atwood, whose stories in this collection probe the various and contradictory facets of human personality, set their characters in a sharply drawn here and now—a tired writer on the seashore of Vancouver's Stanley Park, lifting his head to the noisy pines on a mild, windy February afternoon; a cynical young woman nibbling on a bit of currant cake after midnight in a musty Welsh Bed-and-Breakfast while her lover sleeps—the launching dock for the voyage into metaphysical speculation or mythic fantasy is concrete reality, the signals systems of syntax, symbol, and metaphor are coherent and functioning before lift-off. Most short story writers of note in English Canada today work from the assumption that to achieve a symbolic "everywhere" they must start with a recognizable "somewhere" and that no character can be

xiii

"everyman" without first being given the physical and psychological particularities of a distinctive human being.

Since the mid 1960s some writers have departed from those principles and from the associated traditional view that a short story should move a protagonist through a series of related incidents to a climax of victory or defeat, and instead have flirted with the surreal and absurdist visions that have had some vogue in modern theater and film. Two of the best of these, Ray Smith and Matt Cohen, have each published a collection of such innovative stories, and dozens of lesser writers working the same vein have managed to get published in literary journals and anthologies which specialize in iconoclastic short fiction. In exuberant word hashes and melanges of discontinuous incident they explore alienation, fragmented identities, rootlessness, generational conflicts, and the new sexual freedom. The results tend to be absurd in the common understanding of the term rather than in the technical sense intended by the authors. The worst among them remind you of those chlorinated cake and pudding ready-mixes that food companies try out on volunteer housewives before risking the stuff in the supermarket chains. The best, like the stories by Cohen and Smith, have the merit of artfully concocted Singapore slings and Vienna sachertortes; they provide an amusing fillip to the palate before and after dinner, but make weak substitutes for the main course.

One final comment regarding themes. I selected the stories that appear in this book because I felt that they represented the best Canadian writing available today. A secondary reason was that they also represented the main geographical regions of Canada. I did not concern myself with themes since I was confident that twenty-five different writers from widely separated parts of the country would be bound to reflect and interpret the typical concerns of their society and times. And the themes that you might expect do turn up: the problems of growing up, the continuing quest for identity, the problems of moral behavior in times of transition, modern man's alienation from traditional beliefs and institutions, and the dynamic tensions between men and women. What surprised me when I looked over my final choice was the number of times the world's oldest theme appeared, the troubled relations between men and women. In three stories, "Springtime," "The Cure," and "After Dinner Butterflies," a comic role reversal makes the woman the oppressor, but in the stories by Alice Munro, Hugh Garner, Sinclair Ross, Morley Callaghan, Margaret Atwood, and Beth Harvor it is the man who dominates and victimizes. He may regret his cruelty, as does Ross's distraught farmer and Callaghan's numbed piano player, or he may be insensitively unaware, as Atwood's nameless man is unaware of the pain and ennui he is inflicting on his companion, but oppressor he is, regardless of whether the narrative point of view is masculine or feminine. I am not sure what the frequent appearance of this theme in our contemporary short stories may mean, unless it is that the world's oldest relational problem is seen by Canadian writers as still the most interesting one.

John Stevens

HOW I MET MY HUSBAND

by *Alice Munro*

We heard the plane come over at noon, roaring
through the radio news, and we were sure it was going
to hit the house, so we all ran out into the yard. We
saw it come in over the treetops, all red and silver, the
first close-up plane I ever saw. Mrs. Peebles screamed.

"Crash landing," their little boy said. Joey was his
name.

"It's okay," said Dr. Peebles. "He knows what he's
doing." Dr. Peebles was only an animal doctor, but had
a calming way of talking, like any doctor.

This was my first job—working for Dr. and Mrs.
Peebles, who had bought an old house out on the Fifth
Line, about five miles out of town. It was just when the
trend was starting of town people buying up old farms,
not to work them but to live on them.

We watched the plane land across the road, where
the fairgrounds used to be. It did make a good landing
field, nice and level for the old race track, and the
barns and display sheds torn down now for scrap lumber so there was nothing in the way. Even the old
grandstand bays had burned.

"All right," said Mrs. Peebles, snappy as she always was when she got over her nerves. "Let's go back in the house. Let's not stand here gawking like a set of farmers."

She didn't say that to hurt my feelings. It never occurred to her.

I was just setting the dessert down when Loretta Bird arrived, out of breath, at the screen door.

"I thought it was going to crash into the house and kill youse all!"

She lived on the next place and the Peebleses thought she was a countrywoman, they didn't know the difference. She and her husband didn't farm, he worked on the roads and had a bad name for drinking. They had seven children and couldn't get credit at the Hi-Way Grocery. The Peebleses made her welcome, not knowing any better, as I say, and offered her dessert.

Dessert was never anything to write home about, at their place. A dish of Jell-O or sliced bananas or fruit out of a tin. "Have a house without a pie, be ashamed until you die," my mother used to say, but Mrs. Peebles operated differently.

Loretta Bird saw me getting the can of peaches.

"Oh, never mind," she said. "I haven't got the right kind of a stomach to trust what comes out of those tins, I can only eat home canning."

I could have slapped her. I bet she never put down fruit in her life.

"I know what he's landed here for," she said. "He's got permission to use the fairgrounds and take people up for rides. It costs a dollar. It's the same fellow who was over at Palmerston last week and was up the lake-shore before that. I wouldn't go up, if you paid me."

"I'd jump at the chance," Dr. Peebles said. "I'd like to see this neighborhood from the air."

Mrs. Peebles said she would just as soon see it from the ground. Joey said he wanted to go and Heather did, too. Joey was nine and Heather was seven.

"Would you, Edie?" Heather said.

I said I didn't know. I was scared, but I never admitted that, especially in front of children I was taking care of.

"People are going to be coming out here in their cars raising dust and trampling your property, if I was you I would complain," Loretta said. She hooked her legs around the chair rung and I knew we were in for a lengthy visit. After Dr. Peebles went back to his office or out on his next call and Mrs. Peebles went for her nap, she would hang around me while I was trying to do the dishes. She would pass remarks about the Peebleses in their own house.

"She wouldn't find time to lay down in the middle of the day, if she had seven kids like I got."

She asked me did they fight and did they keep things in the dresser drawer not to have babies with. She said it was a sin if they did. I pretended I didn't know what she was talking about.

I was fifteen and away from home for the first time. My parents had made the effort and sent me to high school for a year, but I didn't like it. I was shy of strangers and the work was hard, they didn't make it nice for you or explain the way they do now. At the end of the year the averages were published in the paper, and mine came out at the very bottom, 37 percent. My father said that's enough and I didn't blame him. The last thing I wanted, anyway, was to go on and end up teaching school. It happened the very day the paper came out with my disgrace in it, Dr. Peebles was staying at our place for dinner, having just helped one of our cows have twins, and he said I looked smart to him and his wife was looking for a girl to help. He said she felt tied down, with the two children, out in the country. I guess she would, my mother said, being polite, though I could tell from her face she was wondering what on earth it would be like to have only two children and no barn work, and then to be complaining.

When I went home I would describe to them the work I had to do, and it made everybody laugh. Mrs. Peebles had an automatic washer and dryer, the first I ever saw. I have had those in my own home for such a long time now it's hard to remember how much of a miracle it was to me, not having to struggle with the wringer and hang up and haul down. Let alone not having to heat water. Then there was practically no baking. Mrs. Peebles said she couldn't make pie crust, the most amazing thing I ever heard a woman admit. I could, of course, and I could make light biscuits and a white cake and dark cake, but they didn't want it, she said they watched their figures. The only thing I didn't like about working there, in fact, was feeling half hungry a lot of the time. I used to bring back a box of doughnuts made out at home, and hide them under my bed. The children found out, and I didn't mind sharing, but I thought I better bind them to secrecy.

The day after the plane landed Mrs. Peebles put both children in the car and drove over to Chesley, to get their hair cut. There was a good woman then at Chesley for doing hair. She got hers done at the same place, Mrs. Peebles did, and that meant they would be gone a good while. She had to pick a day Dr. Peebles wasn't going out into the country, she didn't have her own car. Cars were still in short supply then, after the war.

I loved being left in the house alone, to do my work at leisure. The kitchen was all white and bright yellow, with fluorescent lights. That was before they ever thought of making the appliances all different colors and doing the cupboards like dark old wood and hiding the lighting. I loved light. I loved the double sink. So would anybody new-come from washing dishes in a dishpan with a rag-plugged hole on an oilcloth-covered table by light of a coal-oil lamp. I kept everything shining.

The bathroom too. I had a bath in there once a week. They wouldn't have minded if I took one oftener, but to me it seemed like asking too much, or maybe risking making it less wonderful. The basin and the tub and the toilet were all pink, and there were glass doors with flamingoes painted on them, to shut off the tub. The light had a rosy cast and the mat sank under your feet like snow, except that it was warm. The mirror was three-way. With the mirror all steamed up and the air like a perfume cloud, from things I was allowed to use, I stood up on the side of the tub and admired myself naked, from three directions. Sometimes I thought about the way we lived out at home and the way we lived here and how one way was so hard to imagine when you were living the other way. But I thought it was still a lot easier, living the way we lived at home, to picture something like this, the painted flamingoes and the warmth and the soft mat, than it was for anybody knowing only things like this to picture how it was the other way. And why was that?

I was through my jobs in no time, and had the vegetables peeled for supper and sitting in cold water besides. Then I went into Mrs. Peebles' bedroom. I had been in there plenty of times, cleaning, and I always took a good look in her closet, at the clothes she had hanging there. I wouldn't have looked in her drawers, but a closet is open to anybody. That's a lie. I would have looked in drawers, but I would have felt worse doing it and been more scared she could tell.

Some clothes in her closet she wore all the time, I was quite familiar with them. Others she never put on, they were pushed to the back. I was disappointed to see no wedding dress. But there was one long dress I could just see the skirt of, and I was hungering to see the rest. Now I took note of where it hung and lifted it out. It was satin, a lovely weight on my arm, light bluish-green in color, almost silvery. It had a fitted, pointed waist and a full skirt and an off-the-shoulder fold hiding the little sleeves.

Next thing was easy. I got out of my own things and slipped it on. I was slimmer at fifteen than anybody would believe who knows me now and the fit was beautiful. I didn't, of course, have a strapless bra on, which was what it needed, I just had to slide my straps down my arms under the material. Then I tried pinning up my hair, to get the effect. One thing led to another. I put on rouge and lipstick and eyebrow pencil from her dresser. The heat of the day and the weight of the satin and all the excitement made me thirsty, and I went out to the kitchen, got-up as I was, to get a glass of ginger ale with ice cubes from the refrigerator. The Peebleses drank ginger ale, or fruit drinks, all day, like water, and I was getting so I did too. Also there was no limit on ice cubes, which I was so fond of I would even put them in a glass of milk.

I turned from putting the ice tray back and saw a man watching me through the screen. It was the luckiest thing in the world I didn't spill the ginger ale down the front of me then and there.

"I never meant to scare you. I knocked but you were getting the ice out, you didn't hear me."

I couldn't see what he looked like, he was dark the way somebody is pressed up against a screen door with the bright daylight behind them. I only knew he wasn't from around here.

"I'm from the plane over there. My name is Chris Watters and what I was wondering was if I could use that pump."

There was a pump in the yard. That was the way the people used to get their water. Now I noticed he was carrying a pail.

"You're welcome," I said. "I can get it from the tap and save you pumping." I guess I wanted him to know we had piped water, didn't pump ourselves.

"I don't mind the exercise." He didn't move, though, and finally he said, "Were you going to a dance?"

Seeing a stranger there had made me entirely forget how I was dressed.

"Or is that the way ladies around here generally get dressed up in the afternoon?"

I didn't know how to joke back then. I was too embarrassed.

"You live here? Are you the lady of the house?"

"I'm the hired girl."

Some people change when they find that out, their whole way of looking at you and speaking to you changes, but his didn't.

"Well, I just wanted to tell you you look very nice. I was so surprised when I looked in the door and saw you. Just because you looked so nice and beautiful."

I wasn't even old enough then to realize how out of the common it is, for a man to say something like that to a woman, or somebody he is treating like a woman. For a man to say a word like *beautiful*. I wasn't old enough to realize or to say anything back, or in fact to do anything but wish he would go away. Not that I didn't like him, but just that it upset me so, having him look at me, and me trying to think of something to say.

He must have understood. He said good-bye, and thanked me, and went and started filling his pail from the pump. I stood behind the Venetian blinds in the dining room, watching him. When he had gone, I went into the bedroom and took the dress off and put it back in the same place. I dressed in my own clothes and took my hair down and washed my face, wiping it on Kleenex, which I threw in the wastebasket.

The Peebleses asked me what kind of man he was. Young, middle-aged, short, tall? I couldn't say.

"Good-looking?" Dr. Peebles teased me.

I couldn't think a thing but that he would be coming to get his water again, he would be talking to Dr. or Mrs. Peebles, making friends with them, and he would mention seeing me that first afternoon, dressed up. Why not mention it? He would think it was funny. And no idea of the trouble it would get me into.

After supper the Peebleses drove into town to go to a movie. She wanted to go somewhere with her hair fresh done. I sat in my bright kitchen wondering what to do, knowing I would never sleep. Mrs. Peebles might not fire me, when she found out, but it would give her a different feeling about me altogether. This was the first place I ever worked but I already had picked up things about the way people feel when you are working for them. They like to think you aren't curious. Not just that you aren't dishonest, that isn't enough. They like to feel you don't notice things, that you don't think or wonder about anything but what they liked to eat and how they liked things ironed, and so on. I don't mean they weren't kind to me, because they were. They had me eat my meals with them (to tell the truth I expected

to, I didn't know there were families who don't) and
sometimes they took me along in the car. But all the
same.

I went up and checked on the children being asleep
and then I went out. I had to do it. I crossed the road
and went in the old fairgrounds gate. The plane looked
unnatural sitting there, and shining with the moon. Off
at the far side of the fairgrounds, where the bush was
taking over, I saw his tent.

He was sitting outside it smoking a cigarette. He saw
me coming.

"Hello, were you looking for a plane ride? I don't
start taking people up till tomorrow." Then he looked
again and said, "Oh, it's you. I didn't know you without your long dress on."

My heart was knocking away, my tongue was dried
up. I had to say something. But I couldn't. My throat
was closed and I was like a deaf-and-dumb.

"Did you want a ride? Sit down. Have a cigarette."

I couldn't even shake my head to say no, so he gave
me one.

"Put it in your mouth or I can't light it. It's a good
thing I'm used to shy ladies."

I did. It wasn't the first time I had smoked a cigarette, actually. My girl friend out home, Muriel Lower,
used to steal them from her brother.

"Look at your hand shaking. Did you just want to
have a chat, or what?"

In one burst I said, "I wisht you wouldn't say anything about that dress."

"What dress? Oh, the long dress."

"It's Mrs. Peebles'."

"Whose? Oh, the lady you work for? Is that it? She
wasn't home so you got dressed up in her dress, eh?
You got dressed up and played queen. I don't blame
you. You're not smoking that cigarette right. Don't just
puff. Draw it in. Did nobody ever show you how to in-
hale? Are you scared I'll tell on you? Is that it?"

I was so ashamed at having to ask him to connive
this way I couldn't nod. I just looked at him and he
saw *yes*.

"Well I won't. I won't in the slightest way mention it or embarrass you. I give you my word of honor."

Then he changed the subject, to help me out, seeing I couldn't even thank him.

"What do you think of this sign?"

It was a board sign lying practically at my feet.

SEE THE WORLD FROM THE SKY. ADULTS $1.00, CHILDREN 50¢. QUALIFIED PILOT.

"My old sign was getting pretty beat up, I thought I'd make a new one. That's what I've been doing with my time today."

The lettering wasn't all that handsome, I thought. I could have done a better one in half an hour.

"I'm not an expert at sign making."

"It's very good," I said.

"I don't need it for publicity, word of mouth is usually enough. I turned away two carloads tonight. I felt like taking it easy. I didn't tell them ladies were dropping in to visit me."

Now I remembered the children and I was scared again, in case one of them had waked up and called me and I wasn't there.

"Do you have to go so soon?"

I remembered some manners. "Thank you for the cigarette."

"Don't forget. You have my word of honor."

I tore off across the fairgrounds, scared I'd see the car heading home from town. My sense of time was mixed up, I didn't know how long I'd been out of the house. But it was all right, it wasn't late, the children were asleep. I got in bed myself and lay thinking what a lucky end to the day, after all, and among things to be grateful for I could be grateful Loretta Bird hadn't been the one who caught me.

The yard and borders didn't get trampled, it wasn't as bad as that. All the same it seemed very public, around the house. The sign was on the fairgrounds gate. People came mostly after supper but a good many in the afternoon, too. The Bird children all came without fifty cents between them and hung on the gate. We got used to the excitement of the plane coming in and taking off, it wasn't excitement anymore. I never went over, after that one time, but would see him when he came to get his water. I would be out on the steps doing sitting-down work, like preparing vegetables, if I could.

"Why don't you come over? I'll take you up in my plane."

"I'm saving my money," I said, because I couldn't think of anything else.

"For what? For getting married?"

I shook my head.

"I'll take you up for free if you come sometime when it's slack. I thought you would come, and have another cigarette."

I made a face to hush him, because you never could tell when the children would be sneaking around the porch, or Mrs. Peebles herself listening in the house. Sometimes she came out and had a conversation with him. He told her things he hadn't bothered to tell me. But then I hadn't thought to ask. He told her he had been in the war, that was where he learned to fly a plane, and now he couldn't settle down to ordinary life, this was what he liked. She said she couldn't imagine anybody liking such a thing. Though sometimes, she said, she was almost bored enough to try anything herself, she wasn't brought up to living in the country. It's all my husband's idea, she said. This was news to me.

"Maybe you ought to give flying lessons," she said.

"Would you take them?"

She just laughed.

Sunday was a busy flying day in spite of it being preached against from two pulpits. We were all sitting out watching. Joey and Heather were over on the fence with the Bird kids. Their father had said they could go, after their mother saying all week they couldn't.

A car came down the road past the parked cars and pulled up right in the drive. It was Loretta Bird who got out, all importance, and on the driver's side another woman got out, more sedately. She was wearing sunglasses.

"This is a lady looking for the man that flies the plane," Loretta Bird said. "I heard her inquire in the hotel coffee shop where I was having a Coke and I brought her out."

"I'm sorry to bother you," the lady said. "I'm Alice Kelling, Mr. Watters' fiancée."

This Alice Kelling had on a pair of brown and white checked slacks and a yellow top. Her bust looked to me rather low and bumpy. She had a worried face. Her hair had had a permanent, but had grown out, and she wore a yellow band to keep it off her face. Nothing in the least pretty or even young-looking about her. But you could tell from how she talked she was from the city, or educated, or both.

Dr. Peebles stood up and introduced himself and his wife and me and asked her to be seated.

"He's up in the air right now, but you're welcome to sit and wait. He gets his water here and he hasn't been yet. He'll probably take his break about five."

"That is him, then?" said Alice Kelling, wrinkling and straining at the sky.

"He's not in the habit of running out on you, taking a different name?" Dr. Peebles laughed. He was the one, not his wife, to offer iced tea. Then she sent me into the kitchen to fix it. She smiled. She was wearing sunglasses too.

"He never mentioned his fiancée," she said.

I loved fixing iced tea with lots of ice and slices of lemon in tall glasses. I ought to have mentioned before, Dr. Peebles was an abstainer, at least around the house, or I wouldn't have been allowed to take the place. I had to fix a glass for Loretta Bird too, though it galled me, and when I went out she had settled in my lawn chair, leaving me the steps.

"I knew you was a nurse when I first heard you in that coffee shop."

"How would you know a thing like that?"

"I get my hunches about people. Was that how you met him, nursing?"

"Chris? Well yes. Yes, it was."

"Oh, were you overseas?" said Mrs. Peebles.

"No, it was before he went overseas. I nursed him when he was stationed at Centralia and had a ruptured appendix. We got engaged and then he went overseas. My, this is refreshing, after a long drive."

"He'll be glad to see you," Dr. Peebles said. "It's a rackety kind of life, isn't it, not staying one place long enough to really make friends."

"Youse've had a long engagement," Loretta Bird said.

Alice Kelling passed that over. "I was going to get a room at the hotel, but when I was offered directions I came on out. Do you think I could phone them?"

"No need," Dr. Peebles said. "You're five miles away from him if you stay at the hotel. Here, you're right across the road. Stay with us. We've got rooms on rooms, look at this big house."

Asking people to stay, just like that, is certainly a country thing, and maybe seemed natural to him now, but not to Mrs. Peebles, from the way she said, oh yes, we have plenty of room. Or to Alice Kelling, who kept protesting, but let herself be worn down. I got the feeling it was a temptation to her, to be that close. I was trying for a look at her ring. Her nails were painted red, her fingers were freckled and wrinkled. It was a tiny stone. Muriel Lowe's cousin had one twice as big.

Chris came to get his water, late in the afternoon just as Dr. Peebles had predicted. He must have recognized the car from a way off. He came smiling.

"Here I am chasing after you to see what you're up to," called Alice Kelling. She got up and went to meet him and they kissed, just touched, in front of us.

"You're going to spend a lot on gas that way," Chris said.

Dr. Peebles invited Chris to stay for supper, since he had already put up the sign that said: NO MORE RIDES TILL 7 P.M. Mrs. Peebles wanted it served in the yard, in spite of the bugs. One thing strange to anybody from the country is this eating outside. I had made a potato salad earlier and she had made a jellied salad, that was one thing she could do, so it was just a matter of getting those out, and some sliced meat and cucumbers and fresh leaf lettuce. Loretta Bird hung around for some time saying, "Oh, well, I guess I better get home to those yappers," and, "It's so nice just sitting here, I sure hate to get up," but nobody invited her, I was relieved to see, and finally she had to go.

That night after rides were finished Alice Kelling and Chris went off somewhere in her car. I lay awake till they got back. When I saw the car lights sweep my ceiling I got up to look down on them through the slats of my blind. I don't know what I thought I was going to see. Muriel Lowe and I used to sleep on her front veranda and watch her sister and her sister's boy friend saying good night. Afterward we couldn't get to sleep, for longing for somebody to kiss us and rub up against us and we would talk about suppose you were out in a boat with a boy and he wouldn't bring you in to shore unless you did it, or what if somebody got you trapped in a barn, you would have to, wouldn't you, it wouldn't be your fault. Muriel said her two girl cousins used to try with a toilet paper roll that one of them was the boy. We wouldn't do anything like that; just lay and wondered.

All that happened was that Chris got out of the car on one side and she got out on the other and they walked off separately—him toward the fairgrounds and her toward the house. I got back in bed and imagined about me coming home with him, not like that.

Next morning Alice Kelling got up late and I fixed a grapefruit for her the way I had learned and Mrs. Peebles sat down with her to visit and have another cup of coffee. Mrs. Peebles seemed pleased enough now, having company. Alice Kelling said she guessed she better get used to putting in a day just watching Chris take off and come down, and Mrs. Peebles said she didn't know if she should suggest it because Alice Kelling was the one with the car, but the lake was only twenty-five miles away and what a good day for a picnic.

Alice Kelling took her up on the idea and by eleven

o'clock they were in the car, with Joey and Heather and a sandwich lunch I had made. The only thing was that Chris hadn't come down, and she wanted to tell him where they were going.

"Edie'll go over and tell him," Mrs. Peebles said. "There's no problem."

Alice Kelling wrinkled her face and agreed.

"Be sure and tell him we'll be back by five!"

I didn't see that he would be concerned about knowing this right away, and I thought of him eating whatever he ate over there, alone, cooking on his camp stove, so I got to work and mixed up a crumb cake and baked it, in between the other work I had to do; then, when it was a bit cooled, wrapped it in a tea towel. I didn't do anything to myself but take off my apron and comb my hair. I would like to have put some makeup on, but I was too afraid it would remind him of the way he first saw me, and that would humiliate me all over again.

He had come and put another sign on the gate: NO RIDES THIS P.M. APOLOGIES. I worried that he wasn't feeling well. No sign of him outside and the tent flap was down. I knocked on the pole.

"Come in," he said, in a voice that would just as soon have said *Stay out*.

I lifted the flap.

"Oh, it's you. I'm sorry. I didn't know it was you."

He had been just sitting on the side of the bed, smoking. Why not at least sit and smoke in the fresh air?

"I brought a cake and hope you're not sick," I said.

"Why would I be sick? Oh—that sign. That's all right. I'm just tired of talking to people. I don't mean you. Have a seat." He pinned back the tent flap. "Get some fresh air in here."

I sat on the edge of the bed, there was no place else. It was one of those fold-up cots, really: I remembered and gave him his fiancée's message.

He ate some of the cake. "Good."

"Put the rest away for when you're hungry later."

"I'll tell you a secret. I won't be around here much longer."

"Are you getting married?"

"Ha ha. What time did you say they'd be back?"

"Five o'clock."

"Well, by that time this place will have seen the last of me. A plane can get further than a car." He unwrapped the cake and ate another piece of it, absentmindedly.

"Now you'll be thirsty."

"There's some water in the pail."

"It won't be very cold. I could bring some fresh. I could bring some ice from the refrigerator."

"No," he said. "I don't want you to go. I want a nice long time of saying good-bye to you."

He put the cake away carefully and sat beside me and started those little kisses, so soft, I can't ever let myself think about them, all over my eyelids and neck and ears, all over, then me kissing back as well as I could (I had only kissed a boy on a dare before, and kissed my own arms for practice) and we lay back on the cot and pressed together, just gently, and he did some other things, not bad things or not in a bad way. It was lovely in the tent, that smell of grass and hot tent cloth with the sun beating down on it, and he said, "I wouldn't do you any harm for the world." Once, when he had rolled on top of me and we were sort of rocking together on the cot, he said softly, "Oh, no," and freed himself and jumped up and got the water pail. He splashed some of it on his neck and face, and the little bit left, on me lying there.

"That's to cool us off, miss."

When we said good-bye I wasn't at all sad, because he held my face and said "I'm going to write you a letter. I'll tell you where I am and maybe you can come and see me. Would you like that? Okay then. You wait." I was really glad I think to get away from him, it was like he was piling presents on me I couldn't get the pleasure of till I considered them alone.

No consternation at first about the plane being gone. They thought he had taken somebody up, and I didn't enlighten them. Dr. Peebles had phoned he had to go to the country, so there was just us having supper, and then Loretta Bird thrusting her head in the door and saying, "I see he's took off."

"What?" said Alice Kelling, and pushed back her chair.

"The kids come and told me this afternoon he was taking down his tent. Did he think he'd run through all the business there was around here? He didn't take off without letting you know, did he?"

"He'll send me word," Alice Kelling said. "He'll probably phone tonight. He's terribly restless, since the war."

"Edie, he didn't mention to you, did he?" Mrs. Peebles said. "When you took over the message?"

"Yes," I said. So far so true.

"Well why didn't you say?" All of them were looking at me. "Did he say where he was going?"

"He said he might try Bayfield," I said. What made me tell such a lie? I didn't intend it.

"Bayfield, how far is that?" said Alice Kelling.

Mrs. Peebles said, "Thirty, thirty-five miles."

"That's not far. Oh, well, that's really not far at all. It's on the lake, isn't it?"

You'd think I'd be ashamed of myself, setting her on the wrong track. I did it to give him more time, whatever time he needed. I lied for him, and also, I have to admit, for me. Women should stick together and not do things like that. I see that now, but didn't then. I never thought of myself as being in any way like her, or coming to the same troubles, ever.

She hadn't taken her eyes off me. I thought she suspected my lie.

"When did he mention this to you?"

"Earlier."

"When you were over at the plane?"

"Yes."

"You must've stayed and had a chat." She smiled at

me, not a nice smile. "You must've stayed and had a little visit with him."

"I took a cake," I said, thinking that telling some truth would spare me telling the rest.

"We didn't have a cake," said Mrs. Peebles rather sharply.

"I baked one."

Alice Kelling said, "That was very friendly of you."

"Did you get permission," said Loretta Bird. "You never know what these girls'll do next," she said. "It's not they mean harm so much, as they're ignorant."

"The cake is neither here nor there," Mrs. Peebles broke in. "Edie, I wasn't aware you knew Chris that well."

I didn't know what to say.

"I'm not surprised," Alice Kelling said in a high voice. "I knew by the look of her as soon as I saw her. We get them at the hospital all the time." She looked hard at me with her stretched smile. "Having their babies. We have to put them in a special ward because of their diseases. Little country tramps. Fourteen and fifteen years old. You should see the babies they have, too."

"There was a bad woman here in town had a baby that pus was running out of its eyes," Loretta Bird put in.

"Wait a minute," said Mrs. Peebles. "What is this talk? Edie. What about you and Mr. Watters? Were you intimate with him?"

"Yes," I said. I was thinking of us lying on the cot and kissing, wasn't that intimate? And I would never deny it.

They were all one minute quiet, even Loretta Bird.

"Well," said Mrs. Peebles. "I am surprised. I think I need a cigarette. This is the first of any such tendencies I've seen in her," she said, speaking to Alice Kelling, but Alice Kelling was looking at me.

"Loose little bitch." Tears ran down her face. "Loose little bitch, aren't you? I knew as soon as I saw you. Men despise girls like you. He just made use of you and went off, you know that, don't you? Girls like you are just nothing, they're just public conveniences, just filthy little rags!"

"Oh, now," said Mrs. Peebles.

"Filthy," Alice Kelling sobbed. "Filthy little rag!"

"Don't get yourself upset," Loretta Bird said. She was swollen up with pleasure at being in on this scene. "Men are all the same."

"Edie, I'm very surprised," Mrs. Peebles said. "I thought your parents were so strict. You don't want to have a baby, do you?"

I'm still ashamed of what happened next. I lost control, just like a six-year-old, I started howling. "You don't get a baby from just doing that!"

"You see. Some of them are that ignorant," Loretta Bird said.

But Mrs. Peebles jumped up and caught my arms and shook me.

"Calm down. Don't get hysterical. Calm down. Stop crying. Listen to me. Listen. I'm wondering, if you know what being intimate means. Now tell me. What did you think it meant?"

"Kissing," I howled.

She let go. "Oh, Edie. Stop it. Don't be silly. It's all right. It's all a misunderstanding. Being intimate means a lot more than that. Oh, I *wondered*."

"She's trying to cover up, now," said Alice Kelling. "Yes. She's not so stupid. She sees she got herself in trouble."

"I believe her," Mrs. Peebles said. "This is an awful scene."

"Well there is one way to find out," said Alice Kelling, getting up. "After all, I am a nurse."

Mrs. Peebles drew a breath and said, "No. No. Go to your room, Edie. And stop that noise. That is too disgusting."

I heard the car start in a little while. I tried to stop crying, pulling back each wave as it started over me. Finally I succeeded, and lay heaving on the bed.

Mrs. Peebles came and stood in the doorway.

"She's gone," she said. "That Bird woman too. Of course, you know you should never have gone near that man and that is the cause of all this trouble. I have a headache. As soon as you can, go and wash your face in cold water and get at the dishes and we will not say anymore about this."

Nor we didn't. I didn't figure out till years later the extent of what I had been saved from. Mrs. Peebles was not very friendly to me afterward, but she was fair. Not very friendly is the wrong way of describing what she was. She had never been very friendly. It was just that now she had to see me all the time and it got on her nerves, a little.

As for me, I put it all out of my mind like a bad dream and concentrated on waiting for my letter. The mail came every day except Sunday, between one-thirty and two in the afternoon, a good time for me because Mrs. Peebles was always having her nap. I would get the kitchen all cleaned and then go up to the mailbox and sit in the grass, waiting. I was perfectly happy, waiting, I forgot all about Alice Kelling and her misery and awful talk and Mrs. Peebles and her chilliness and the embarrassment of whether she had told Dr. Peebles and the face of Loretta Bird, getting her fill of other people's troubles. I was always smiling when the mailman got there, and continued smiling even after he gave me the mail and I saw today wasn't the day. The mailman was a Carmichael. I knew by his face because there are a lot of Carmichaels living out by us and so many of them have a sort of sticking-out top lip. So I asked his name (he was a young man, shy, but good-humored, anybody could ask him anything) and then I said, "I knew by your face!" He was pleased by that and always glad to see me and got a little less shy. "You've got the smile I've been waiting on all day!" he used to holler out the car window.

It never crossed my mind for a long time a letter might not come. I believed in it coming just like I believed the sun would rise in the morning. I just put off my hope from day to day, and there was the goldenrod out around the mailbox and the children gone back to school, and the leaves turning, and I was wearing a sweater when I went to wait. One day walking back with the hydro bill stuck in my hand, that was all, looking across at the fairgrounds with the full-blown milkweed and dark teasels, so much like fall, it just struck me: *No letter was ever going to come.* It was an impossible idea to get used to. No, not impossible. If I thought about Chris's face when he said he was going to write to me, it was impossible, but if I forgot that and thought about the actual tin mailbox, empty, it was plain and true. I kept on going to meet the mail, but my heart was heavy now like a lump of lead. I only smiled because I thought of the mailman counting on it, and he didn't have an easy life, with the winter driving ahead.

Till it came to me one day there were women doing this with their lives, all over. There were women just waiting and waiting by mailboxes for one letter or another. I imagined me making this journey day after day and year after year, and my hair starting to go gray, and I thought, I was never made to go on like that. So I stopped meeting the mail. If there were women all through life waiting, and women busy and not waiting, I knew which I had to be. Even though there might be things the second kind of women have to pass up and never know about, it still is better.

I was surprised when the mailman phoned the Peebleses' place in the evening and asked for me. He said he missed me. He asked if I would like to go to Goderich, where some well-known movie was on, I forget now what. So I said yes, and I went out with him for two years and he asked me to marry him, and we were engaged a year more while I got my things together, and then we did marry. He always tells the children the story of how I went after him by sitting by the mailbox every day, and naturally I laugh and let him, because I like for people to think what pleases them and makes them happy.

GOING TO INDIA

by *Clark Blaise*

1

A month before we left I read a horror story in the papers. A boy had stepped on a raft, the raft had drifted into the river. The river was the Niagara. Screaming, with the rescuers not daring to follow, pursued only by an amateur photographer on shore, he was carried over the Falls.

It isn't death, I thought, it's watching it arrive, this terrible omniscience that makes it not just death, but an execution. The next day, as they must, they carried the photos. Six panels of a boy waving ashore, the waters eddying, then boiling, around his raft. The boy wore a T-shirt and cut-off khakis. He fell off several feet before the Falls. Who would leave a raft, what kind of madman builds a raft in Niagara country? Children in Niagara country must have nightmares of the Falls, must feel the earth rumbling beneath them, their pillows turning to water.

I was raised in Florida. Tidal waves frightened me as a child. So did "Silver Springs," those underground rivers that converge to feed it. Blind white catfish. I could hear them as a child, giant turtles snorting and grinding under my pillow.

My son is three years old, almost four. He will be four in India. Born in Indiana, raised in Montreal—what possible fears could he have? He finds the paper, the six pictures of the boy on a raft. He inspects the pictures and I grieve for him. I am death-driven. I feel compassion, grief, regret, only in the face of death. I was slow, fat and asthmatic, prone to sunburn, hook-worms, and chronic nosebleeds. My son is lean and handsome, a tennis star of the future, and I've tried to keep things from him.

"What is that boy doing, Daddy?"

"I think he's riding a raft."

"But how come he's waving like that?"

"He's frightened, I think."

"Look—he felled off it, Daddy."

"I know, darling."

"And there's a water hill there, Daddy. Everything went over the hill."

"Yes, dear. The boy went over the water hill."

"And now he knows one thing, doesn't he, Daddy?"

"What does he know?"

"Now he knows what being dead is like."

2

A month from now we'll be in India. I've begun to feel it, I've been floating for a week now, afraid to start anything new. Friends say to me, "You still here?" not just in disappointment, more in amazement. They've already discarded the Old Me. "Weren't you going to India? What happened—chicken out?" They expect transmutation. "I *said* June," I tell them, but they'd heard April. "I'd be afraid to go," one friend, an artist, tells me. "There are some things a man can't take. Some changes are too great." I tell him I *am* afraid, but that I have to go.

I never cared for India. My only interest in the woman I married was sexual; that she was Indian did not excite me, nor was I frightened. Convent-trained, Brahmanical, well-to-do, Orthodox and Westernized at once, Calcutta-born, speaker of eight languages, she had simply overwhelmed me. We met in graduate school at Indiana. Both of us were in comparative liter-ature, and she was returning to Calcutta to marry a forty-year-old research chemist selected by her father. Will you marry him? I asked. Yes, she said. Will you be happy? Who can say, she said. Probably not. Can you refuse? I asked. It would be bad for my father, she said. Will you marry me? I asked, and she said, "Yes, of course."

It was Europe that drove me mad.

Five years ago I threw myself at Europe. For two summers I did things I'll never do again, living without money enough for trolley fare, wakening beside new women, wondering where I'd be spending the next night, with whom, how I'd get there, who would take me, and finally not caring. Coming close, those short Swedish nights, those fetid Roman nights, those long Paris nights when the *auberge* closed before I got back and I would walk through the rain dodging the Arabs and queers and drunken soldiers who would take me for an Arab, coming close to saying that life was passionate and palpable and worth the pain and effort and whoever I was and whatever I was destined to be didn't matter. Only living for the moment mattered and even the hunger and the insults and the occasional jab in the kidneys didn't matter. It all reminded me that I was young and alive, a hitchhiker over borders, heedless of languages, speaking just enough of everything to cover my needs, and feeling responsible to no one but myself for any jam I got into.

I would have given anything to stay and I planned my life so that I could come back.

Not once did I think of India. Missionary ladies from Wichita, Kansas, went to India. Retired buyers for Montgomery Ward took around-the-world flights and got heart attacks in Delhi bazaars. I was only interested in Europe.

At graduate school in Indiana I was doing well, a Fulbright was in the works, my languages were improving, and a lifetime in Europe was drawing closer. Then I met the most lushly sexual woman I had ever seen. Reserved and intelligent, she confirmed in all ways my belief that perfection could not be found in anything American.

But even then India failed to interest me. I married Anjali Chatterjee, not a culture, not a subcontinent.

3

When we married, the Indian community of Indiana disowned her. Indian girls were considered too innocent to meet or marry Western boys, although hip Indian boys always married American girls. Anjali was dropped from the Indian Society, and only one Indian, a Christian dietician from Goa, attended our wedding. So the break was clean, my obligations minimal. I had her to myself.

Her parents were hesitant, but cordial. Also helpless. They had my horoscope cast after the marriage, but never told us the result. They asked about my family, and we lied. To say the least, I come from uncertain stock. My parents had been twice-divorced before divorcing each other. Four of the five languages I speak are rooted in my family, each grandparent speaking something different, and the fifth, Russian, reflects a secret sympathy that would destroy her parents if they knew. I have scores of half brothers and sisters, cousins-in-law, aunts and uncles known by the cars they drive, or by the rackets they operate. My family is broad and fluid and, though corrupt, fabulously unsuccessful. Like gypsies they cover the continent, elevating a son or two into law (a sensible precaution), some into the civil service, others into the army and only one into the university. My instructions for this trip are simple: do not mention divorce. My parents are retired, somewhat infirm, and comfortably off. After a while we can let one die (when we need the sympathy), and a few months later the second can die of grief. They will leave their fortune to charity.

4

E. M. Forster, you ruined everything. Why must every visitor to India, every well-read tourist, expect a sudden transformation? I, too, feel that if nothing amazing happens, the trip will be a waste. I've done nothing these past two months. I'm afraid to start anything new in case I'll be a different person when I return. And what if this lassitude continues? Two fallow months before the flight, three months of visiting, then what? What the hell is India like anyway?

I remember my Florida childhood and the trips to Nassau and Havana, the bugs and heat and the quiver of joy in a simple cold Coca-Cola, and the pastel, rusted, rotting concrete, the stench of purple muck too rank to grow a thing, to ever be charmed by the posters of palms and white sand beaches. Jellyfish, sting rays, sand sharks, and tidal waves. Roaches as long as my finger, scorpions in my shoe, worms in my feet. Still, it wasn't India. Country of my wife, heredity of my son.

Will *his* children speak of their lone white grandfather as they settle back to brown-ness, or will it be their legendary Hindu grandmother, as staggering to them as Pushkin's grandfather must have been to him? Appalling, that I, a comparatist who needs five languages, should be mute and illiterate in my wife's own tongue! And worse, not to care, not for Bengali or Hindi or even Sanskrit.

I thought you were going to India—

I am, I am.

But—

Next week. Next week.

And don't forget those pills, man. Take those little pills.

5

We are going by charter, which still sets us back two thousand dollars. Two thousand dollars just on kerosene! Another two thousand for a three-month stay; hundreds more in preparation, in drip-dry shirts, in bras and lipsticks for the flocks of cousins; bottles of after-shave and Samsonite briefcases for their husbands. A complete set of the novels of William Faulkner for a cousin writing her dissertation. Oh, weird, weird, what kind of country am I visiting? To prepare myself I read. *Nothing could prepare me for Calcutta,* writes a well-traveled Indian on his return. City of squalor, city of dreadful night, of riots and stabbings, bombings added to pestilence and corruption. Somewhere in Calcutta, squatting or dying, two aged grandmothers are waiting to see my wife, to meet her *mlechha* husband, to peer and poke at her outcaste child. In Calcutta I can meet my death quite by accident, swept into a corridor of history for which I have no feeling. I can believe that for being white and American and somewhat pudgy I deserve to die— somewhere, at least—but not in Calcutta. Receptacle of the world's grief, Calcutta. *Indians, even the richest, are corrupted by poverty;* Americans, even the poorest (I add), are corrupted by wealth. How will I react to beggars? To servants? Worse: how will my wife?

6

I know from experience that when Anjali dabs the red *teep* on her forehead, when the gold earrings are brought out, when the miniskirts are put away and the gold necklace and bracelets are fastened to her neck and arms (how beautiful, how inevitable, gold against Indian skin), when the good silk saris with the golden threads are unfolded from the suitcases, that I have lost my wife to India. Usually it's just for an evening, in the homes of McGill colleagues in hydraulics or genetics, or visitors to our home from Calcutta, who stay with us for a night or two. And I fade away those evenings, along with English and other familiar references. Nothing to tell me that the beautiful woman in the pink sari is my wife except the odd wink during the evening, a gratuitous reference to my few accomplishments. The familiar mixture of shame and gratitude; that she was born and nurtured for someone better than I, richer, at least, who would wrap her in servants, a house of her own, a life of privilege that only an impoverished country can provide. One evening I can take. But three months?

7

Our plane will leave from New York. We go down two days early to visit our friends, the Gangulis. To spend some money, buy the last-minute gifts, another suitcase, enjoy the air-conditioning, and eat our last rare steaks. I've just turned twenty-seven; at that age, one can say of one's friends that none are accidental, they all fulfill a need. In New York three circles of friends almost coincide; the writers I know, the friends I've taught with or gone to various schools with, and the third, the special ones, the Indo-Americans, the American girls and their Indian husbands.

Deepak is an architect; Susan was a nurse. Deepak, years before in India, was matched to marry my wife. She was still in Calcutta, he was at Yale, and he approved of her picture sent by his father. One formality remained—the matching of their horoscopes. And they clashed. Marriage would invite disaster, deformed children most likely. He didn't meet her until his next trip to India when he'd gone to look over some new selections. Alas, none were beautiful enough and he returned to New York to marry the American girl he'd been living with all along.

Deepak's life is ruled by his profound good taste, his perfect, daring taste. Like a prodigy in chess or music he is disciplined by a Platonic conception of a yet-higher order, one that he alone can bring into existence. Their apartment in the East Seventies was once used as a movie set. It is subtly Indian, yet nothing specifically Indian strikes the eye. One must sit a moment, sipping a gin, before the underlying Eastern-ness erupts from the steel and glass and leather. The rug is Kashmiri, the tables teak, the walls are hung with Saurashtrian tapestries—what's so Western about it? The lamps are stone-based, chromium-necked, arching halfway across the room, the chairs are stainless steel and white leather, adorned with Indian pillows. It is a room in perfect balance, like Deepak; like his marriage, per-

haps. So unlike ours, so unlike us. Our apartment in
Montreal is furnished in Universal Academic, with
Danish sofas and farm antiques, everything sacrificed
to hold more books. The Who's-Afraid-of-Virginia-
Woolf style.

But he didn't marry Anjali. I did. He married Susan,
and Susan, though uncomplaining and competent, is
also plain and somewhat stupid. Very pale, a near-
natural blond, but prone to varicosed chubbiness. An
Indian's dream of the American girl. And so lacking in
Deepak's exquisite taste that I can walk into their place
and in thirty seconds *feel* where she had been sitting,
where she'd walked from, everything she'd rearranged
or brushed against. Where she's messed up the Platonic
harmony even while keeping it clean. Still, Deepak
doesn't mind. He cooks the fancy meals, does the gour-
met shopping: knows where to find mangoes in the
dead of winter, where the firmest cauliflower, the fresh-
est *al dente* shrimp, the rarest spices, are sold. When
Deepak shops he returns with twenty small packages
individually wrapped and nothing frozen. When Susan
returns it's with an A&P bag, wet at the bottom.

When the four of us are dining out, the spectators
(for we are always on view) try to rearrange us:
Deepak and Anjali, Susan and me. Deepak is tall for a
Bengali—six-two perhaps—and impressively bearded
now that it's the style. He could be an actor. A friend
once described him as the perfect extra for a Monte
Carlo scene, the Indian prince throwing away his mil-
lions, missing only a turban with a jewel in the center.

How could he and Anjali have a deformed child?

I'm being unfair. He is rich and generous, and there
is another Deepak behind the man of perfect taste. He
told me once when our wives were out shopping, that
he'd tried to commit suicide, back in India. The Central Bank had refused him foreign exchange, even after
he'd been accepted at Yale. He'd had to wait a year
while an uncle arranged the necessary bribes, spending
the time working on the uncle's tea estate in Assam.
The uncle tried to keep him on a second year, claiming
he had to wait until a certain bureaucrat retired;

Deepak threw himself into a river. A villager lost his life in saving him, the uncle relented, a larger bribe was successful and Deepak the architect was sprung on the West. He despises India, even while sending fifty dollars a month to the family of his rescuer.

But his natural gift, so resonant in itself, extends exactly nowhere. He rarely reads, and when he does he confines himself to English murder mysteries. He is a man trapped in certain talents, incapable of growth, yet I envy him. They eat well, live well, and save thousands every year. They have no children, despite Susan's pleading, and they will have none until the child's full tuition from kindergarten through university is in the bank. While we empty our savings to make this trip to India. We'll hunt through bazaars and come up with nothing for our house. There is malevolence in our friendship; he enjoys showing me his New York, making the city bend to his wishes, extracting from it its most delicate juices. We discuss India this last night in America; aside from trips to land a wife, he's never been back. And he won't go back, despite more pleading from Susan, until his parents die.

8

None of Deepak's restaurants tonight: it is steak, broiled at home. Thick steak, bought and cut and aged especially, but revered mainly for wet red beefiness. "Your meat *chagla*," he calls out from the kitchen, spearing it on his fork and holding it in the doorway, while Anjali, Susan, and I drink our gin and our son sips his Coke. A *chagla* is a side of beef. "Normally I use an onion, mushroom, and wine sauce, but don't worry—not tonight. Onions you will be having—bloody American steak you won't."

The time is near; two hours to lift-off. Then Deepak drives us to the airport because he says he enjoys the International Lounge, especially the Air-India lounge where anytime, any season, he can find a friend or two whose names he's forgotten, either going back or seeing off, and he, Deepak, can have a drink and reflect on his own good fortune, namely not having to fly twenty four hours in a plane full of squalling infants, to arrive in Bombay at four in the morning.

And so now we are sitting upstairs sipping more gin with Susan and Deepak, and of course two young men run over to shake his hand and to be introduced, leaving their wives, who are chatting and who don't look up. . . .

"Summer ritual," he explains. "Packing the wife and kids off to India. That way they can get a vacation and the parents are satisfied and the wives can boss the servants around. No wonder they're smiling. . . ." Looking around the waiting room he squints with disgust. "You'll have a full plane."

No Americans tonight, the lounge is dark with Indians. We're still in New York, but we've already left. "At least be glad of one thing," Deepak says. "What's that?" I ask. He looks around the lounge and winks at us. "No cows," he says.

No, *please,* I want to say, don't laugh at India. This trip is serious, for me at least. "Don't ruin it for me, Deepak," I finally say. "I may never go over again." "You might never come back either," he says. We are filing out of the lounge, down a corridor, and up a flight of stairs. Anjali and Deepak are in good spirits. Susan is holding our son, who wants another Coke.

". . . and the beggars," Deepak is saying, "*Memsahib,* take my fans, my toys, my flowers, my youngest daughter—"

"—then suddenly a leprous stump, stuck in the middle of the flowers and fans," says Anjali.

"Maybe that's India," I say, "in an image, I mean."

Deepak and Anjali both smile, as if to say, *yes, perhaps it is. Then again, perhaps it isn't. Maybe you should keep your eyes open and your mouth shut.* And then we are saying good-bye, *namaste*-ing to the hostess, and taking our three adjoining seats. India is still a day away.

9

"Listen for the captain's name," says Anjali. Need I ask why? Anjali's erstwhile intendeds staff the banks, the hospitals, the courts, the airlines, the tea estates of Assam and West Bengal. They are all well-placed, middle-aged, fair-complected, and well-educated Brahmins.

"D'Souza," we hear. An Anglo-Indian, not a chance.

"I heard that Captain Mukherjee is flying for Air-India now," she tells me. "He was very dashing at Darjeeling in '58, flying for the Air Force." Another ruptured arrangement.

There are times when I look at her and think: She, who had no men before me will have many, and I, who had those girls here and there and everywhere even up to the day I married but none after, will have no more, ever. All of this is somehow ordained, our orbits are conflicting, hers ever wider, mine ever tighter.

This will be a short night, the shortest night of my life. Leaving New York at nine o'clock, to arrive six hours later in London's bright morning light, the sunrise will catch us east of Newfoundland around midnight New York time. During the brief, east-running night two businessmen behind me debate the coming British elections. Both, as Indians, feel sentimental toward Labour. As businessmen they feel compromised. They've never been treated badly. Both, in fact, agree that too many bloody Moslems have been admitted, and that parts of England are stinking worse than the slums of Karachi or Bombay. Both will be voting Tory.

In the absurd morning light of 3 A.M. while the plane sleeps and the four surly sari-clad hostesses smoke their cigarettes in the rear, I think of my writing. Flights are a time of summary, an occasion for sweating palms. If I should die, what would I make of my life? Was it whole, or just beginning? I used to write miniature novels, vividly imagined, set anywhere my imagination moved me. Then something slipped. I started writing

only of myself and these vivid moments in a confusing
flux. That visionary gleam; India may restore it, or destroy it completely. We will set down an hour in London, in Paris, in Frankfurt, and even Kuwait—what
does this do to the old perspectives? Europe is just a
stopover, Cokes in a transit room on the way to something bigger and darker than I'd ever imagined. Paris,
where I survived two months without a job; Frankfurt,
where six years ago I learned my first German—*wo
kann man hier pissen?* How will I ever return to Europe and feel that I've even left home? India has already ruined Europe for me.

10

From London we have a new crew and a new captain: His name is Mukherjee. Anjali scribbles a note to
a steward, who carries it forward. Minutes later he returns, inviting Anjali to follow him through the tiny
door and down the gangway to the cockpit. Jealous Indians stare at her, then at me. And I, a jealous American, try to picture our dashing little captain, mustached
and heavy-lidded, courting my wife when he should be
attending to other things.

She stays up front until we land in Paris. My son
and I file into the transit room of Orly, and there in a
corner I spot Anjali and the captain, a small, dark,
heavy-lidded fellow with chevroned sleeves a mite too
long for his delicate hands.

"Hello, sir," he says, not reaching for my hand. He
holds a Coke in one, a cigarette in the other. "Your
wife's note was a very pleasant distraction."

"Nice landing," I say, not knowing the etiquette.

"Considering I couldn't find the bloody runway, I
thought it was. They switched numbers on us."

"So," I say. "You're the fam—"

"No, no—I was just telling your wife: you think that
I am Captain *Govind* Mukherjee formerly Group Captain Mukherjee of the IAF. But I am Sujit Mukherjee—regrettably a distant cousin—or else I would have

met this charming lady years ago. I was just telling your wife that Govind is married now with three children and he flies out of Calcutta to Tokyo. I *knew* she was not referring to me in the chit she sent forward and I confess to a small deception, sir—I hope I am forgiven—"

"Of course, of course. It must have been exciting for her—"

"Oh, exciting I do not know. But disappointing, *yes*, decidedly. You should have seen the face she pulled spotting Sujit Mukherjee and not Govind—" Then suddenly he breaks into loud, heavy-lidded laughter, joined by Anjali and a gray-haired crew member standing to one side.

"This is my navigator, Mr. Misra," says the captain. "Blame him if we go astray."

"And this is our son, Ananda," I say.

"*Very* nice name, Ananda. Ananda means happiness."

"Are you the driver?" Ananda asks.

"Yes, yes, I am the *driver*." The captain bursts into laughter. "And Misra here is my wiper." And Misra breaks into high-pitched giggles. "Tell me, Ananda, would you like to sit with us up front and help drive the plane?"

"Would I have to go through that little door?"

"Yes."

"No," he says decisively. He holds my hand tightly, the captain and navigator bow and depart, and then we go for a Coke.

Somewhere out there, I remind myself, is Paris.

11

Back in the plane the purser invites me forward; Captain Mukherjee points to the seat behind him, the rest of the crew introduce themselves, a steward brings me lemonade, and the plane is cleared for leaving the terminal. Then an Indian woman clutching a baby bursts from the building, dashes across the runway waving frantically.

"Air-India 112—you have a passenger—"

"Stupid bloody woman," the captain says under his breath. "Air-India 112 returning for boarding," he says, then turns to me: "Can you imagine when we're flying the jumbo? Indians weren't meant for the jumbo jets."

Then the steward comes forward, explaining that the woman doesn't speak Hindi, English, or Tamil and that she doesn't have a ticket and refuses to take a seat. The only word they can understand is "husband." The captain nods, heavy-lidded, smiling faintly. "I think I should like a glass of cold water," he says, "and one for our passenger." He takes off his headphone, lights a cigarette. Turning fully around he says to me: "We have dietary problems. We have religious problems and we have linguistic problems. All of these things we prepare for. But these village women, they marry and their husband goes off to Europe and a few years later he sends for them. But they can't read their tickets and they won't eat what we give them and they sit strapped in their seats, terrified, for the whole trip. Then they fall asleep and we can't wake them. When they wake up themselves they think they're on a tram and they've missed their stop, so they tell us to turn around. London, Paris, Rome—these are just words to them. The husband says he will meet her in Paris—how is she to know she must go through customs? She can't even read her own language let alone *douane*. So she goes to the transit room and sits down and the husband she's probably forgotten except for one old photograph is tapping madly on the glass and when the flight re-boards she dutifully follows all the people—"

"Captain, someone is talking to her."

"Fine, fine."

"She is to meet her husband in Paris."

"Did you tell her this is Paris?"

"She won't believe *me*, Captain. She wants you to tell her."

"Misra—take my coat and go back and tell her." To

me he adds, "She wouldn't believe I'm the captain. Misra makes a very good captain with his gray hair. Where is my bloody ice water?"

"Yes, Captain. Right away, Captain."

Moments later we are taxiing down the runway, gathering speed and lifting steeply over Paris. The Seine, Eiffel Tower, Notre Dame, all clear from the wraparound windows. And, for the first time, my palms aren't sweating. Competence in the cockpit, the delicate fingers of Captain Mukherjee, the mathematical genius of Navigator Misra, the radar below, the gauges above. I settle back and relax. Below, the radar stations check in: Metz, Luxembourg, Rüdesheim, Mainz. I recognize the Rhine, see the towns I once hitchhiked through, and bask in the strangeness of it all, the orbits of India and my early manhood intersecting.

We descend, we slow, and Frankfurt appears. We turn, we drop still lower, slower, 200 miles per hour as we touch down. Everything perfect, my palms are dry again. It's been years since I felt such confidence in another person. The silence in the cockpit is almost worshipful.

The ground-crew chief, a gray-bearded Sikh, comes aboard and gives the captain his instructions for takeoff, which the captain already knows. The weather conditions in Kuwait: 120° with sandstorms. Mukherjee nods, smiles. I ease out silently; *namaste*-ing to the captain and crew, thanking them all as they go about their chores.

12

Within an hour we are farther East than I've ever been. Down the coast of Yugoslavia, then over the Greek islands, across the Holy Land. What if the Israelis open fire? Those SAM missile sites, Iraqi MIGs scrambling to bring us down. Trials in Bagdad, hanging of the Jewish passengers. India is officially pro-Arab, an embarrassment which might prove useful.

This was the shortest day of my life. The east is

darkening, though it's only noon by New York time. An hour later the stars are out; we eat our second lunch, or is it dinner? Wiener schnitzel or lamb curry. Ananda sleeps; Anjali eats her curry, I my Wiener schnitzel.

"After Kuwait things will deteriorate," she says. "The food, the service, the girls—they always do."

We've been descending, and suddenly the seat-belt sign is on. Kuwait: richest country in the world. City lights in the middle of the desert, and an airfield marked by permanent fires. Corridors of flames flapping in a sandstorm, and Captain Mukherjee eases his way between them. Sand stings the window, pings off the wings like Montreal ice.

"The ground temperature is forty-five degrees Centigrade" the hostess announces, and I busily translate: 113°F.

"The local time is ten p.m."

I whisper to Anjali, " 'I will show you fear in a handful of dust. . . .' "

"Through passengers ticketed on Air-India to Bombay and New Delhi will kindly remain in the aircraft. We shall be on the ground for approximately forty-five minutes."

I can feel the heat through the plastic windows. Such heat, such inhuman heat and dryness. I turn to Anjali and quote again:

Here is no water but only rock
Rock and no water and the sandy road. . . .

A ground crew comes aboard. Arab faces, one-eyed, hunched, followed by a proud lieutenant in the Kuwaiti uniform. These are my first Moslems, first Arabs. They vacuum around our feet, pick up the chocolate wrappers, clear the tattered London papers from the seats. It's all too fast, this "voyage out," as they used to call it. We need a month on a steamer, shopping in Italy, in Cairo, bargaining in the bazaars, passing serenely from the Catholic south to the Moslem heartland, thence to holy, Hindu India. The way they did it in the old novels. In Forster, where friendship and tolerance were still

possible. No impressions of the Wasteland in a Forster
novel. No one-eyed, menacing Arabs. But Forster is almost ninety, and wisely, he remains silent. The price
we pay for the convenience of a single day's flight is
the simple diminishment of all that's human. Just as
Europe is changed because of India, so India is
lessened because of the charter flight. I'm bringing a
hard heart to India, dread and fear and suspicion.

13

We are in the final hours over the Persian Gulf and
the Arabian Sea, skimming the coast of Iran then aim-
ing south and east to Bombay. Kuwait gave us children
who play games in the aisles, who spill their Cokes on
my sleeve. Captain Mukherjee, Misra, and the crack
London crew ride with us as passengers; the new stew-
ardess is older, heavier, and a recent blond. No one
sleeps, though we've set our watches on Bombay
time and it is suddenly three o'clock in the morning.

"Daddy will be leaving for the airport now," says
Anjali.

I've never met her parents. They've flown 1,500
miles to meet us tonight, to see us rest a day or two before joining us in the flight back to Calcutta.

"The airport will be a shock," she says. "It always
is."

"Anything to get off this plane."

Three-thirty.

Ananda has taken the window seat; he sits on his
knees with his face cupped to the glass. He's been to
India before, three summers before. He's forgotten his
illness, remembers only an elephant ride and a trip to
the mountains where he chased butterflies up the
slopes.

Twenty minutes to India. I can feel the descent.
Businessmen behind me agree on the merits of military
rule.

"Ladies and gentlemen—"

The lights go on, a hundred seat belts buckle on cue.

Lights suddenly appear beneath us. There are streets, street lamps, cars, bungalows, palm trees. My first palms since Florida—maybe I'll like it here—and we glide to a landing, our fifth perfect landing of the day.

Everyone is standing, pulling down their coats and baggage. I'd forgotten how much we carried aboard (three days ago, by the calendar): a flight bag of clothes for Ananda, camera equipment, liquor and cigars for my father-in-law, my rain hat and jacket, our three raincoats and two umbrellas. We put on everything we can and then line up, facing first the rear and then the front, clutching our passports.

"Ladies and gentlemen, we have landed at Santa Cruz Airport in Bombay. The local time is four a.m. and the temperature is 33° Centigrade...."

"Over ninety," I whisper.

"It's been raining," she says.

As we file to the front and the open door, I can feel the heat. My arms are sweating before I reach the ladder. An open bus is waiting to take us to the terminal. No breeze, SRO. The duty-free bag begins to tear.

I follow our beam of light across the tarmac. A man is sleeping on the edge of the cement, others have built a fire in the mud nearby.

"Tea," Anjali explains.

Other thoughts are coming to me now: not the howling sand of Kuwait—*mud*. Not the empty desert—*people*. Not the wind—*rain*. I want to scream: *"It's four in the bloody morning and I'm soaking with sweat. Somebody do something!"* Even in the open bus as we zip down the runway there's no breeze, no relief. Anjali's hair, cut and set just before we left, has turned dead and stringy, her sari is crushed in a thousand folds. This is how the world will end.

We are dropped in front of the terminal. Families are sleeping on the steps. Children converge on our bus, holding out their hands, making pathetic gestures to their mouth. I have a pocket full of *centimes* and *pfennigs* from this morning's stops, but Anjali frowns as I open my hand. "They're professionals," she says. "If you must give to beggars, wait at least till you get to Calcutta." They pull my sleeve, grab Ananda by the collar of his raincoat, until a man behind us raises his hand. "Wretched little scum," he mutters. They scatter and I find myself half-agreeing.

We have come inside. Harsh lights, overhead fans. Rows of barriers, men in khaki uniforms behind each desk, desks laden with forms and rubber stamps. The bureaucracy. Behind them the baggage, the porters squatting, the customs, more men, more forms. Then the glass, the waiting crowd, the parents, the embraces, the right words, the corridors. *I'm not ready,* I want to scream, *turn this plane around.* I've stopped walking, the passports are heavy in my hand. I've never been so lost.

"Darling, what's the matter?" she asks, but she has already taken my hand, taken the passports, the declarations, and given me the flight bag in their place. Ananda stands before me, the beautiful child in his yellow slicker, black hair plastered to his forehead. I take his hand, he takes Anjali's, and I think again: *I'm not prepared,* not even for the answer which comes immediately: and if you're not, it says, who is?

GETTING ON IN THE WORLD

by *Morley Callaghan*

That night in the tavern of the Clairmont Hotel, Henry Forbes was working away at his piano and there was the usual good crowd of brokers and politicians and sporting men sitting around drinking with their well-dressed women. A tall, good-natured boy in the bond business, and his girl, had just come up to the little green piano, and Henry had let them amuse themselves playing a few tunes, and then he had sat down himself again and had run his hand the length of the keyboard. When he looked up there was this girl leaning on the piano and beaming at him.

She was about eighteen and tall and wearing one of those sheer black dresses and a little black hat with a veil, and when she moved around to speak to him he saw that she had the swellest legs and an eager, straightforward manner.

"I'm Tommy Gorman's sister," she said.

"Why, say . . . you're . . ."

"Sure. I'm Jean," she said.

"Where did you come from?"

"Back home in Buffalo," she said. "Tommy told me to be sure and look you up first thing."

Tommy Gorman had been his chum; he used to come into the tavern almost every night to see him before he got consumption and had to go home. So it did not seem so surprising to see his sister standing there instead. He got her a chair and let her sit beside him. And in no time he saw that Tommy must have made him out to be a pretty glamorous figure. She understood that he knew everybody in town, that big sporting men like Jake Solloway often gave him tips on the horses, and that a man like Eddie Convey, who just about ran the city hall and was one of the hotel owners, too, called him by his first name. In fact, Tommy had even told her that the job playing the piano wasn't much, but that bumping into so many big people every night he was apt to make a connection at any time and get a political job, or something in a stockbroker's office.

The funny part of it was she seemed to have joined herself to him at once; her eyes were glowing, and as he watched her swinging her head around looking at the important clients, he simply couldn't bear to tell her that the management had decided that the piano wouldn't be necessary any more and that he mightn't be there more than two weeks.

So he sat there pointing out people she might have read about in the newspapers. It all came out glibly, as if each one of them was an old friend, yet he actually felt lonely each time he named somebody. "That's

Thompson over there with the horn-rimmed glasses. He's the mayor's secretary," he said. "That's Bill. Bill Henry over there. You know, the producer. Swell guy, Bill." And then he rose up in his chair. "Say, look, there's Eddie Convey," he said. As he pointed he got excited, for the big, fresh-faced, hawk-nosed Irishman with the protruding blue eyes and the big belly had seen him pointing. He was grinning. And then he raised his right hand a little.

"Is he a friend of yours?" Jean asked.

"Sure he is. Didn't you see for yourself?" he said. But his heart was leaping. It was the first time Eddie Convey had ever gone out of his way to notice him. Then the world his job might lead to seemed to open up and he started chattering breathlessly about Convey, thinking all the time, beneath his chatter, that if he could go to Convey and get one little word from him, and if something bigger couldn't be found for him he at least could keep his job.

He became so voluble and excited that he didn't notice how delighted she was with him till it was time to take her home. She was living uptown in a rooming-house where there were a lot of theatrical people. When they were sitting on the stone step a minute before she went in she told him that she had enough money saved up to last her about a month. She wanted to get a job modelling in a department store. Then he put his arm around her and there was a soft glowing wonder in her face.

"It seems like I've known you for years," she said.

"I guess that's because we both know Tommy."

"Oh, no," she said. Then she let him kiss her hard. And as she ran into the house she called that she'd be around to the tavern again.

It was as if she had been dreaming about him without even having seen him. She had come running to him with her arms wide open. "I guess she's about the softest touch that's come my way," he thought, going down the street. But it looked too easy. It didn't require any ambition, and he was a little ashamed of the sudden, weakening tenderness he felt for her.

She kept coming around every night after that and sat there while he played the piano and sometimes sang a song. When he was through for the night, it didn't matter to her whether they went any place in particular, so he would take her home. Then they got into the habit of going to his room for a while. As he watched her fussing around, straightening the room up or maybe making a cup of coffee, he often felt like asking her what made her think she could come bouncing into town and fit into his life. But when she was listening eagerly, and kept sucking in her lower lip and smiling slowly, he felt indulgent with her. He felt she wanted to hang around because she was impressed with him.

It was the same when she was sitting around with him in the tavern. She used to show such enthusiasm that it became embarrassing. You like a girl with you to look like some of the smart blondes who came into the place and have that lazy, half-mocking aloofness that you have to try desperately to break through. With Jean laughing and talking a lot and showing all her straightforward warm eagerness people used to turn and look at her as if they'd like to reach out their hands and touch her. It made Henry feel that the pair of them looked like a couple of kids on a merry-go-round. Anyway, all that excitement of hers seemed to be only something that went with the job, so in the last couple of nights, with the job fading, he hardly spoke to her and got a little savage pleasure out of seeing how disappointed she was.

She didn't know what was bothering him till Thursday night. A crowd from the theater had come in, and Henry was feeling blue. Then he saw Eddie Convey and two middle-aged men who looked like brokers sitting at a table in the corner. When Convey seemed to smile at him, he thought bitterly that when he lost his job people like Convey wouldn't even know him on the street. Convey was still smiling, and then he actually beckoned.

"Gees, is he calling me?" he whispered.

"Who?" Jean asked.

"The big guy, Convey," he whispered. So he

wouldn't make a fool of himself he waited till Convey called him a second time. Then he got up nervously and went over to him. "Yes, Mr. Convey," he said.

"Sit down, son," Convey said. His arrogant face was full of expansive indulgence as he looked at Henry and asked, "How are you doing around here?"

"Things don't exactly look good," he said. "Maybe I won't be around here much longer."

"Oh, stop worrying, son. Maybe we'll be able to fix you up."

"Gee, thanks, Mr. Convey." It was all so sudden and exciting that Henry kept on bobbing his head. "Yes, Mr. Convey."

"How about the kid over there," Convey said, nodding toward Jean. "Isn't it a little lonely for her sitting around?"

"Well, she seems to like it, Mr. Convey."

"She's a nice-looking kid. Sort of fresh and—well ... uh, fresh, that's it." They both turned and looked over at Jean, who was watching them, her face excited and wondering.

"Maybe she'd like to go to a party at my place," Convey said.

"I'll ask her, Mr. Convey."

"Why don't you tell her to come along, see. You know, the Plaza, in about an hour. I'll be looking for her."

"Sure, Mr. Convey," he said. He was astonished that Convey wanted him to do something for him. "It's a pleasure," he wanted to say. But for some reason it didn't come out.

"Okay," Convey said, and turned away, and Henry went back to his chair at the piano.

"What are you so excited about?" Jean asked him.

His eyes were shining as he looked at her little black hat and the way she held her head to one side as if she had just heard something exhilarating. He was trying to see what it was in her that had suddenly joined him to Convey. "Can you beat it!" he blurted out. "He wants you to go up to a party at his place."

"Me?"

"Yeah, you."

"What about you?"

"He knows I've got to stick around here, and, besides, there may be a lot of important people around
there, and there's always room at Convey's parties for a
couple of more girls."

"I'd rather stay here with you," she said.

Then they stopped whispering because Convey was
going out, the light catching his bald spot.

"You got to do things like that," Henry coaxed her.
"Why, there isn't a girl around here who wouldn't give
her front teeth to be asked up to his place."

She let him go on telling her how important Convey
was and when he had finished, she asked, "Why do I
have to? Why can't we just go over to your place?"

"I didn't tell you. I didn't want you to know, but it
looks like I'm through around here. Unless Convey or
somebody like that steps in I'm washed up," he said. He
took another ten minutes telling her all the things Convey could do for people.

"All right," she said. "If you think we have to." But
she seemed to be deeply troubled. She waited while he
went over to the headwaiter and told him he'd be gone
for an hour, and then they went out and got a cab. On
the way up to Convey's place she kept quiet, with the
same troubled look on her face. When they got to the
apartment house, and they were standing on the pavement, she turned to him. "Oh, Henry, I don't want to
go up there."

"It's just a little thing. It's just a party," he said.

"All right. If you say so, okay," she said. Then she
suddenly threw her arms around him. It was a little
crazy because he found himself hugging her tight too.
"I love you," she said. "I knew I was going to love you
when I came." Her cheek, brushing against his, felt
wet. Then she broke away.

As he watched her running in past the doorman that
embarrassing tenderness he had felt on other nights
touched him again, only it didn't flow softly by him
this time. It came like a swift stab.

In the tavern he sat looking at the piano, and his

heart began to ache, and he turned around and looked at all the well-fed men and their women and he heard their deep-toned voices and their lazy laughter and he suddenly felt corrupt. Never in his life had he had such a feeling. He kept listening and looking into these familiar faces and he began to hate them as if they were to blame for blinding him to what was so beautiful and willing in Jean. He couldn't sit there. He got his hat and went out and started to walk up to Convey's.

Over and over he told himself he would go right up to Convey's door and ask for her. But when he got to the apartment house and was looking up at the patches of light, he felt timid. It made it worse that he didn't even know which window, which room was Convey's. She seemed lost to him. So he walked up and down past the doorman, telling himself she would soon come running out and throw her arms around him when she found him waiting.

It got very late. Hardly anyone came from the entrance. The doorman quit for the night. Henry ran out of cigarettes, but he was scared to leave the entrance. Then the two broker friends of Convey's came out, with two loud-talking girls, and they called a cab and all got in and went away. "She's staying. She's letting him keep her up there. I'd like to beat her. What does she think she is?" he thought. He was so sore at her that he exhausted himself, and then felt weak and wanted to sit down.

When he saw her coming out, it was nearly four o'clock in the morning. He had walked about ten paces away, and turned, and there she was on the pavement, looking back at the building.

"Jean," he called, and he rushed at her. When she turned, and he saw that she didn't look a bit worried, but blooming, lazy, and proud, he wanted to grab her and shake her.

"I've been here for hours," he said. "What were you doing up there? Everybody else has gone home."

"Have they?" she said.

"So you stayed up there with him!" he shouted. "Just like a tramp."

She swung her hand and smacked him on the face. Then she took a step back, appraising him contemptuously. She suddenly laughed. "On your way. Get back to your piano," she said.

"All right, all right, you wait, I'll show you," he muttered. "I'll show everybody." He stood watching her go down the street with a slow, self-satisfied sway of her body.

THE WEDDING GIFT

by *Thomas Raddall*

Nova Scotia, in 1794. Winter. Snow on the ground. Two feet of it in the woods, less by the shore, except in drifts against Port Marriott's barns and fences; but enough to set sleigh bells ringing through the town, enough to require a multitude of paths and burrows from doors to streets, to carpet the wharves and the decks of the shipping, and to trim the ships' yards with tippets of ermine. Enough to require fires roaring in the town's chimneys, and blue wood smoke hanging low over the roof tops in the still December air. Enough to squeal under foot in the trodden places and to muffle the step everywhere else. Enough for the hunters, whose snowshoes now could overtake the floundering moose and caribou. Even enough for the always-complaining loggers, whose ox sleds now could haul their cut from every part of the woods. But not enough, not nearly enough snow for Miss Kezia Barnes, who was going to Bristol Creek to marry Mr. Hathaway.

Kezia did not want to marry Mr. Hathaway. Indeed she had told Mr. and Mrs. Barclay in a tearful voice that she didn't want to marry anybody. But Mr. Barclay had taken snuff and said "Ha! Humph!" in the severe tone he used when he was displeased; and Mrs. Barclay had sniffed and said it was a very good match for her, and revolved the cold blue eyes in her fat moon face, and said Kezia must not be a little fool.

There were two ways of going to Bristol Creek. One was by sea, in one of the fishing sloops. But the preacher objected to that. He was a pallid young man lately sent out from England by Lady Huntingdon's connection, and seasick five weeks on the way. He held Mr. Barclay in some awe, for Mr. Barclay had the best pew in the meetinghouse and was the chief pillar of godliness in Port Marriott. But young Mr. Mears was firm on this point. He would go by road, he said, or not at all. Mr. Barclay had retorted "Ha! Humph!" The road was twenty miles of horse path through the woods, now deep in snow. Also the path began at Harper's Farm on the far side of the harbor, and Harper had but one horse.

"I shall walk," declared the preacher calmly, "and the young woman can ride."

Kezia had prayed for snow, storms of snow, to bury the trail and keep anyone from crossing the cape to Bristol Creek. But now they were setting out from Harper's Farm, with Harper's big brown horse, and all Kezia's prayers had gone for naught. Like any anxious lover, busy Mr. Hathaway had sent Black Sam overland on foot to find out what delayed his wedding, and now Sam's day-old tracks marked for Kezia the road to marriage.

She was a meek little thing, as became an orphan brought up as house-help in the Barclay home; but now she looked at the preacher and saw how young and helpless he looked so far from his native Yorkshire, and how ill-clad for this bitter trans-Atlantic weather, and she spoke up.

"You'd better take my shawl, sir. I don't need it. I've got Miss Julia's old riding cloak. And we'll go ride-and-tie."

"Ride and what?" murmured Mr. Mears.

"I'll ride a mile or so, then I'll get down and tie the

horse to a tree and walk on. When you come up to the horse, you mount and ride a mile or so, passing me on the way, and you tie him and walk on. Like that. Ride-and-tie, ride-and-tie. The horse gets a rest between."

Young Mr. Mears nodded and took the proffered shawl absently. It was a black thing that matched his sober broadcloth coat and smallclothes, his black woollen stockings, and his round black hat. At Mr. Barclay's suggestion he had borrowed a pair of moose-hide moccasins for the journey. As he walked a prayerbook in his coat-skirts bumped the back of his legs.

At the top of the ridge above Harper's pasture, where the narrow path led off through gloomy hemlock woods, Kezia paused for a last look back across the harbour. In the morning sunlight the white roofs of the little lonely town resembled a tidal wave flung up by the sea and frozen as it broke against the dark pine forest to the west. Kezia sighed, and young Mr. Mears was surprised to see tears in her eyes.

She rode off ahead. The saddle was a man's, of course, awkward to ride modestly, woman-fashion. As soon as she was out of the preacher's sight she rucked her skirts and slid a leg over to the other stirrup. That was better. There was a pleasant sensation of freedom about it, too. For a moment she forgot that she was going to Bristol Creek, in finery secondhand from the Barclay girls, in a new linen shift and drawers that she had sewn herself in the light of the kitchen candles, in white cotton stockings and a bonnet and shoes from Mr. Barclay's store, to marry Mr. Hathaway.

The Barclays had done well for her from the time when, a skinny weeping creature of fourteen, she was taken into the Barclay household and, as Mrs. Barclay so often said, "treated more like one of my own than a bond-girl from the poorhouse." She had first choice of the clothing cast off by Miss Julia and Miss Clara. She was permitted to sit in the same room, and learn what she could, when the schoolmaster came to give private lessons to the Barclay girls. She waited on table, of course, and helped in the kitchen, and made beds, and dusted and scrubbed. But then she had been taught to spin and to sew and to knit. And she was permitted, indeed encouraged, to sit with the Barclays in the meetinghouse, at the convenient end of the pew, where she could worship the Barclays' God and assist with the Barclay wraps at the beginning and end of the service. And now, to complete her rewards, she had been granted the hand of a rejected Barclay suitor.

Mr. Hathaway was Barclay's agent at Bristol Creek, where he sold rum and gunpowder and corn meal and such things to the fishermen and hunters, and bought split cod—fresh, pickled or dry—and ran a small sawmill, and cut and shipped firewood by schooner to Port Marriott, and managed a farm, all for a salary of fifty pounds, Halifax currency, per year. Hathaway was a most capable fellow, Mr. Barclay often acknowledged. But when after fifteen capable years he came seeking a wife, and cast a sheep's eye first at Miss Julia, and then at Miss Clara, Mrs. Barclay observed with a sniff that Hathaway was looking a bit high.

So he was. The older daughter of Port Marriott's most prosperous merchant was even then receiving polite attentions from Mr. Gamage, the new collector of customs, and a connection of the Halifax Gamages, as Mrs. Barclay was fond of pointing out. And Miss Clara was going to Halifax in the spring to learn the gentle art of playing the pianoforte, and incidentally to display her charms to the naval and military young gentlemen who thronged the Halifax drawing rooms. The dear girls laughed behind their hands whenever long solemn Mr. Hathaway came to town aboard one of the Barclay vessels and called at the big house under the elms. Mrs. Barclay bridled at Hathaway's presumption, but shrewd Mr. Barclay narrowed his little black eyes and took snuff and said "Ha! Humph!"

It was plain to Mr. Barclay that an emergency had arisen. Hathaway was a good man—in his place; and Hathaway must be kept content there, to go on making profit for Mr. Barclay at a cost of only £50 a year. 'Twas a pity Hathaway couldn't satisfy himself with one of the fishermen's girls at the Creek, but there 'twas. If Hathaway had set his mind on a town miss, then a town miss he must have; but she must be the right kind, the sort who would content herself and Hathaway at Bristol Creek and not go nagging the man to remove and try his capabilities elsewhere. At once Mr. Barclay thought of Kezia—dear little Kezzie. A colorless little creature but quiet and well-mannered and pious, and only twenty-two.

Mr. Hathaway was nearly forty and far from handsome, and he had a rather cold, seeking way about him—useful in business of course—that rubbed women the wrong way. Privately Mr. Barclay thought Hathaway lucky to get Kezia. But it was a nice match for the girl, better than anything she could have expected. He impressed that upon her and introduced the suitor from Bristol Creek. Mr. Hathaway spent two or three evenings courting Kezia in the kitchen—Kezia in a quite good gown of Miss Clara's, gazing out at the November moon on the snow, murmuring now and again in the tones of someone in a rather dismal trance, while the kitchen help listened behind one door and the Barclay girls giggled behind another.

The decision, reached mainly by the Barclays, was that Mr. Hathaway should come to Port Marriott aboard the packet schooner on December twenty-third, to be married in the Barclay parlour and then take his bride home for Christmas. But an unforeseen circumstance had changed all this. The circumstance was a ship, "from Mogador in Barbary" as Mr. Barclay wrote afterwards in the salvage claim, driven off her course by gales and wrecked at the very entrance to Bristol Creek. She was a valuable wreck, laden with such queer things as goatskins in pickle, almonds, wormseed, pomegranate skins, and gum arabic, and capable Mr. Hathaway had lost no time in salvage for the benefit of his employer.

As a result he could not come to Port Marriott for a wedding or anything else. A storm might blow up at any time and demolish this fat prize. He dispatched a note by Black Sam, urging Mr. Barclay to send Kezia and the preacher by return. It was not the orthodox note of an impatient sweetheart, but it said that he had moved into his new house by the Creek and found it "extream empty lacking a woman," and it suggested delicately that while his days were full, the nights were dull.

Kezia was no judge of distance. She rode for what she considered a reasonable time and then slid off and tied the brown horse to a maple tree beside the path. She had brought a couple of lamp wicks to tie about her shoes, to keep them from coming off in the snow, and she set out afoot in the big splayed tracks of Black Sam. The soft snow came almost to her knees in places and she lifted her skirts high. The path was no wider than the span of a man's arms, cut out with axes years before. She stumbled over a concealed stump from time to time, and the huckleberry bushes dragged at her cloak, but the effort warmed her. It had been cold, sitting on the horse with the wind blowing up her legs.

After a time the preacher overtook her, riding awkwardly and holding the reins in a nervous grip. The stirrups were too short for his long black-stockinged legs. He called out cheerfully as he passed, "Are you all right, miss?" She nodded, standing aside with her back to a tree. When he disappeared ahead, with a last flutter of black shawl tassels in the wind, she picked up her skirts and went on. The path climbed and dropped monotonously over a succession of wooded ridges. Here and there in a hollow she heard water running, and the creak of frosty poles underfoot, and knew she was crossing a small stream, and once the trail ran across a wide swamp on half-rotten corduroy, wind-swept and bare of snow.

She found the horse tethered clumsily not far ahead, and the tracks of the preacher going on. She had to lead the horse to a stump so she could mount, and when she passed Mr. Mears again she called out, "Please, sir, next time leave the horse by a stump or a rock so I can get on." In his quaint old-country accent he murmured, "I'm very sorry," and gazed down at the snow. She forgot she was riding astride until she had passed him, and then she flushed, and gave the indignant horse a cut of the switch. Next time she remembered and swung her right leg back where it should be, and tucked the skirts modestly about her ankles; but young Mr. Mears looked down at the snow anyway, and after that she did not trouble to shift when she overtook him.

The ridges became steeper, and the streams roared under the ice and snow in the swales. They emerged upon the high tableland between Port Marriott and Bristol Creek, a gusty wilderness of young hardwood scrub struggling up amongst the gray snags of an old forest fire, and now that they were out of the gloomy softwoods they could see a stretch of sky. It was blue-gray and forbidding, and the wind whistling up from the invisible sea felt raw on the cheek. At their next meeting Kezia said, "It's going to snow."

She had no knowledge of the trail but she guessed that they were not much more than halfway across the cape. On this high barren the track was no longer straight and clear, it meandered amongst the meagre hardwood clumps where the path-makers had not bothered to cut, and only Black Sam's footprints really marked it for her unaccustomed eyes. The preacher nodded vaguely at her remark. The woods, like everything else about his chosen mission field, were new and very interesting, and he could not understand the alarm in her voice. He looked confidently at Black Sam's tracks.

Kezia tied the horse farther on and began her spell of walking. Her shoes were solid things, the kind of shoes Mr. Barclay invoiced as "a common strong sort, for women, five shillings"; but the snow worked into them and melted and saturated the leather. Her feet were numb every time she slid down from the horse and it took several minutes of stumbling through the snow to bring back an aching warmth. Beneath her arm she clutched the small bundle which contained all she had in the world—two flannel nightgowns, a shift of linen, three pairs of stout wool stockings—and of course Mr. Barclay's wedding gift for Mr. Hathaway.

Now as she plunged along she felt the first sting of snow on her face and, looking up, saw the stuff borne on the wind in small hard pellets that fell among the bare hardwoods and set up a whisper everywhere. When Mr. Mears rode up to her the snow was thick in their faces, like flung salt.

"It's a nor'easter!" she cried up to him. She knew the meaning of snow from the sea. She had been born in a fishing village down the coast.

"Yes," mumbled the preacher, and drew a fold of the shawl about his face. He disappeared. She struggled on, gasping, and after what seemed a tremendous journey came upon him standing alone and bewildered, looking off somewhere to the right.

"The horse!" he shouted. "I got off him, and before I could fasten the reins some snow fell off a branch—startled him, you know—and he ran off, over that way." He gestured with a mittened hand. "I must fetch him back," he added confusedly.

"No!" Kezia cried. "Don't you try. You'd only get lost. So would I. Oh, dear! This is awful. We'll have to go on, the best we can."

He was doubtful. The horse tracks looked very plain. But Kezia was looking at Black Sam's tracks, and tugging his arm. He gave in, and they struggled along for half an hour or so. Then the last trace of the old footprints vanished.

"What shall we do now?" the preacher asked, astonished.

"I don't know," whispered Kezia, and leaned against a dead pine stub in an attitude of weariness and indifference that dismayed him.

"We must keep moving, my dear, mustn't we? I mean, we can't stay here."

"Can't stay here," she echoed.

"Down there—a hollow, I think. I see some hemlock trees, or are they pines?—I'm never quite sure. Shelter, anyway."

"Shelter," muttered Kezia.

He took her by the hand and like a pair of lost children they dragged their steps into the deep snow of the hollow. The trees were tall spruces, a thick bunch in a ravine, where they had escaped the old fire. A stream thundered among them somewhere. There was no wind in this place, only the fine snow whirling thickly down between the trees like a sediment from the storm overhead.

"Look!" cried Mr. Mears. A hut loomed out of the whiteness before them, a small structure of moss-chinked logs with a roof of poles and birch-bark. It had an abandoned look. Long streamers of moss hung out between the logs. On the roof shreds of birch bark wavered gently in the drifting snow. The door stood half open and a thin drift of snow lay along the split-pole floor. Instinctively Kezia went to the stone hearth. There were old ashes sodden with rain down the chimney and now frozen to a cake.

"Have you got flint and steel?" she asked. She saw in his eyes something dazed and forlorn. He shook his head, and she was filled with a sudden anger, not so much at him as at Mr. Barclay and that—that Hathaway, and all the rest of mankind. They ruled the world and made such a sorry mess of it. In a small fury she began to rummage about the hut.

There was a crude bed of poles and brushwood by the fireplace—brushwood so old that only a few brown needles clung to the twigs. A rough bench whittled from a pine log, with round birch sticks for legs. A broken earthenware pot in a corner. In another some ashwood frames such as trappers used for stretching skins. Nothing else. The single window was covered with a stretched moose bladder, cracked and dry rotten, but it still let in some daylight while keeping out the snow.

She scooped up the snow from the floor with her mittened hands, throwing it outside, and closed the door carefully, dropping the bar into place, as if she could shut out and bar the cold in such a fashion. The air inside was frigid. Their breath hung visible in the dim light from the window. Young Mr. Mears dropped on his wet knees and began to pray in a loud voice. His face was pinched with cold and his teeth rattled as he prayed. He was a pitiable object.

"Prayers won't keep you warm," said Kezia crossly.

He looked up, amazed at the change in her. She had seemed such a meek little thing. Kezia was surprised at herself, and surprisingly she went·on, "You'd far better take off those wet moccasins and stockings and shake the snow out of your clothes." She set the example, vigorously shaking out her skirts and Miss Julia's cloak, and she turned her small back on him and took off her own shoes and stockings, and pulled on dry stockings from her bundle. She threw him a pair.

"Put those on."

He looked at them and at his large feet, hopelessly. "I'm afraid they wouldn't go on."

She tossed him one of her flannel nightgowns. "Then take off your stockings and wrap your feet and legs in that."

He obeyed, in an embarrassed silence. She rolled her eyes upward, for his modesty's sake, and saw a bundle on one of the low rafters—the late owner's bedding, stowed away from mice. She stood on the bench and pulled down three bearskins, marred with bulletholes. A rank and musty smell arose in the cold. She considered the find gravely.

"You take them," Mr. Mears said gallantly. "I shall be quite all right."

"You'll be dead by morning, and so shall I," she answered vigorously, "if you don't do what I say. We've got to roll up in these."

"Together?" he cried in horror.

"Of course! To keep each other warm. It's the only way."

She spread the skins on the floor, hair uppermost, one overlapping another, and dragged the flustered young man down beside her, clutched him in her arms, and rolled with him, over, and over again, so that they became a single shapeless heap in the corner farthest from the draft between door and chimney.

"Put your arms around me," commanded the new Kezia, and he obeyed.

"Now," she said, "you can pray. God helps those that help themselves."

He prayed aloud for a long time, and privately called upon heaven to witness the purity of his thoughts in this strange and shocking situation. He said "Amen" at last; and "Amen," echoed Kezia, piously.

They lay silent a long time, breathing on each other's necks and hearing their own hearts—poor Mr. Mears's fluttering in an agitated way, Kezia's as steady as a clock. A delicious warmth crept over them. They relaxed in each other's arms. Outside, the storm hissed in the spruce tops and set up an occasional cold moan in the cracked clay chimney. The down-swirling snow brushed softly against the bladder pane.

"I'm warm now," murmured Kezia. "Are you?"

"Yes. How long must we stay here like this?"

"Till the storm's over, of course. Tomorrow, probably. Nor'easters usually blow themselves out in a day and a night, 'specially when they come up sharp, like this one. Are you hungry?"

"No."

"Abigail—that's the black cook at Barclay's—gave me bread and cheese in a handkerchief. I've got it in my bundle. Mr. Barclay thought we ought to reach Bristol Creek by suppertime, but Nabby said I must have a bite to eat on the road. She's a good kind thing, old Nabby. Sure you're not hungry?"

"Quite. I feel somewhat fatigued but not hungry."

"Then we'll eat the bread and cheese for breakfast. Have you got a watch?"

"No, I'm sorry. They cost such a lot of money. In Lady Huntingdon's Connection we—"

"Oh well, it doesn't matter. It must be about four o'clock—the light's getting dim. Of course, the dark comes very quick in a snowstorm."

"Dark," echoed young Mr. Mears drowsily. Kezia's hair, washed last night for the wedding journey, smelled pleasant so close to his face. It reminded him of something. He went to sleep dreaming of his mother, with his face snug in the curve of Kezia's neck and shoulder, and smiling, and muttering words that Kezia could not catch. After a time she kissed his cheek. It seemed a very natural thing to do.

Soon she was dozing herself, and dreaming, too; but her dreams were full of forbidding faces—Mr. Barclay's, Mrs. Barclay's, Mr. Hathaway's; especially Mr. Hathaway's. Out of a confused darkness Mr. Hathaway's hard acquisitive gaze searched her shrinking flesh like a cold wind. Then she was shuddering by the kitchen fire at Barclay's, accepting Mr. Hathaway's courtship and wishing she was dead. In the midst of that sickening wooing she wakened sharply.

It was quite dark in the hut. Mr. Mears was breathing quietly against her throat. But there was a sound of heavy steps outside, muffled in the snow and somehow felt rather than heard. She shook the young man and he wakened with a start, clutching her convulsively.

"Sh-h-h!" she warned. "Something's moving outside." She felt him stiffen.

"Bears?" he whispered.

Silly! thought Kezia. People from the old country could think of nothing but bears in the woods. Besides, bears holed up in the winter. A caribou, perhaps. More likely a moose. Caribou moved inland before this, to the wide mossy bogs up the river, away from the coastal storms. Again the sound.

"There!" hissed the preacher. Their hearts beat rapidly together.

"The door—you fastened it, didn't you?"

"Yes," she said. Suddenly she knew.

"Unroll, quick!" she cried. . . . "No, not this way—your way."

They unrolled, ludicrously, and the girl scrambled up and ran across the floor in her stockinged feet, and fumbled with the rotten door bar. Mr. Mears attempted to follow but he tripped over the nightgown still wound about his feet, and fell with a crash. He was up again in a moment, catching up the clumsy wooden bench for a weapon, his bare feet slapping on the icy floor. He tried to shoulder her aside, crying, "Stand back! Leave it to me!" and waving the bench uncertainly in the darkness.

She laughed excitedly. "Silly!" she said. "It's the horse." She flung the door open. In the queer ghostly murk of a night filled with snow they beheld a large dark shape. The shape whinnied softly and thrust a long face into the doorway. Mr. Mears dropped the bench, astonished.

"He got over his fright and followed us here somehow," Kezia said, and laughed again. She put her arms about the snowy head and laid her face against it.

"Good horse! Oh, good, good horse!"

"What are you going to do?" the preacher murmured over her shoulder. After the warmth of their nest in the furs they were shivering in this icy atmosphere.

"Bring him in, of course. We can't leave him out in the storm." She caught the bridle and urged the horse inside with expert clucking sounds. The animal hesitated, but fear of the storm and a desire for shelter and company decided him. In he came, tramping ponderously on the split-pole floor. The preacher closed and barred the door.

"And now?" he asked.

"Back to the furs. Quick! It's awful cold."

Rolled in the furs once more, their arms went about each other instinctively, and the young man's face found the comfortable nook against Kezia's soft throat. But sleep was difficult after that. The horse whinnied gently from time to time, and stamped about the floor. The decayed poles crackled dangerously under his hooves whenever he moved, and Kezia trembled, thinking he might break through and frighten himself, and flounder about till he tumbled the crazy hut about their heads. She called out to him, "Steady, boy! Steady!"

It was a long night. The pole floor made its irregularities felt through the thickness of fur; and because there seemed nowhere to put their arms but about each other the flesh became cramped, and spread its protest along the bones. They were stiff and sore when the first light of morning stained the window. They unrolled and stood up thankfully, and tramped up and down the floor, threshing their arms in an effort to fight off the gripping cold. Kezia undid her bundle in a corner and brought forth Nabby's bread and cheese, and they ate it sitting together on the edge of the brushwood bed with the skins about their shoulders. Outside, the snow had ceased.

"We must set off at once," the preacher said. "Mr. Hathaway will be anxious."

Kezia was silent. She did not move, and he looked at her curiously. She appeared very fresh, considering the hardships of the previous day and the night. He passed a hand over his cheeks and thought how unclean he must appear in her eyes, with this stubble on his pale face.

"Mr. Hathaway—" he began again.

"I'm not going to Mr. Hathaway," Kezia said quietly.

"But—the wedding!"

"There'll be no wedding. I don't want to marry Mr. Hathaway. 'Twas Mr. Hathaway's idea, and Mr. and Mrs. Barclay's. They wanted me to marry him."

"What will the Barclays say, my dear?"

She shrugged. "I've been their bond girl ever since I was fourteen, but I'm not a slave like poor black Nabby, to be handed over, body and soul, whenever it suits."

"Your soul belongs to God," said Mr. Mears devoutly.

"And my body belongs to me."

He was a little shocked at this outspokenness, but he said gently, "Of course. To give oneself in marriage without true affection would be an offense in the sight of heaven. But what will Mr. Hathaway say?"

"Well, to begin with, he'll ask where I spent the night, and I'll have to tell the truth. I'll have to say I bundled with you in a hut in the woods."

"Bundled?"

"A custom the people brought with them from Connecticut when they came to settle in Nova Scotia. Poor folk still do it. Sweethearts, I mean. It saves fire and candles when you're courting on a winter evening. It's harmless—they keep their clothes on, you see, like you and me—but Mr. Barclay and the other Methody people are terrible set against it. Mr. Barclay got old Mr. Mings—he's the Methody preacher that died last year—to make a sermon against it. Mr. Mings said bundling was an invention of the devil."

"Then if you go back to Mr. Barclay—"

"He'll ask me the same question and I'll have to give him the same answer. I couldn't tell a lie, could I?" She turned a pair of round blue eyes and met his embarrassed gaze.

"No! No, you mustn't lie. Whatever shall we do?" he murmured in a dazed voice. Again she was silent, looking modestly down her small nose.

"It's so very strange," he floundered. "This country—there are so many things I don't know, so many things to learn. You—I—we shall have to tell the truth, of course. Doubtless I can find a place in the Lord's service somewhere else, but what about you, poor girl?"

"I heard say the people at Scrod Harbor want a preacher."

"But—the tale would follow me, wouldn't it, my dear? This—er—bundling with a young woman?"

" 'Twouldn't matter if the young woman was your wife."

"Eh?" His mouth fell open. He was like an astonished child, for all his preacher's clothes and the new beard on his jaws.

"I'm a good girl," Kezia said, inspecting her foot. "I can read and write, and know all the tunes in the psalter. And—and you need someone to look after you."

He considered the truth of that. Then he murmured uncertainly, "We'd be very poor, my dear. The connection gives some support, but of course—"

"I've always been poor," Kezia said. She sat very still but her cold fingers writhed in her lap.

He did something then that made her want to cry. He took hold of her hands and bowed his head and kissed them.

"It's strange—I don't even know your name, my dear."

"It's Kezia—Kezia Barnes."

He said quietly, "You're a brave girl, Kezia Barnes, and I shall try to be a good husband to you. Shall we go?"

"Hadn't you better kiss me, first?" Kezia said faintly.

He put his lips awkwardly to hers; and then, as if the taste of her clean mouth itself provided strength and purpose, he kissed her again, and firmly. She threw her arms about his neck.

"Oh, Mr. Mears!"

How little he knew about everything! He hadn't even known enough to wear two or three pairs of stockings inside those roomy moccasins, nor to carry a pair of dry ones. Yesterday's wet stockings were lying like sticks on the frosty floor. She showed him how to knead the hard-frozen moccasins into softness, and while he worked at the stiff leather she tore up one of her wedding bed shirts and wound the flannel strips about his legs and feet. It looked very queer when she had finished, and they both laughed.

They were chilled to the bone when they set off, Kezia on the horse and the preacher walking ahead, holding the reins. When they regained the slope where they had lost the path, Kezia said, "The sun rises somewhere between east and southeast, this time of year. Keep it on your left shoulder awhile. That will take us back toward Port Marriott."

When they came to the green timber she told him to shift the sun to his left eye.

"Have you changed your mind?" he asked cheerfully. The exercise had warmed him.

"No, but the sun moves across the sky."

"Ah! What a wise little head it is!"

They came over a ridge of mixed hemlock and hardwood and looked upon a long swale full of bare hackmatacks.

"Look!" the girl cried. The white slot of the ax path showed clearly in the trees at the foot of the swale, and again where it entered the dark mass of the pines beyond.

"Praise the Lord!" said Mr. Mears.

When at last they stood in the trail, Kezia slid down from the horse.

"No!" Mr. Mears protested.

"Ride-and-tie," she said firmly. "That's the way we came, and that's the way we'll go. Besides, I want to get warm."

He climbed up clumsily and smiled down at her.

"What shall we do when we get to Port Marriott, my dear?"

"Get the New Light preacher to marry us, and catch the packet for Scrod Harbor."

He nodded and gave a pull at his broad hat brim. She thought of everything. A splendid helpmeet for the world's wilderness. He saw it all very humbly now as a dispensation of Providence.

Kezia watched him out of sight. Then, swiftly, she undid her bundle and took out the thing that had lain there (and on her conscience) through the night—the tinderbox—Mr. Barclay's wedding gift to Mr. Hathaway. She flung it into the woods and walked on, skirts lifted, in the track of the horse, humming a psalm tune to the silent trees and the snow.

THE GRAVE OF THE FAMOUS POET

by *Margaret Atwood*

There are a couple of false alarms before we actually get there, towns we pass through that might be it but aren't, uninformative stores and houses edging the road, no signs. Even when we've arrived we aren't sure; we peer out, looking for a name, an advertisement. The bus pauses.

"This has to be it," I say. I have the map.

"Better ask the driver," he says, not believing me.

"Have I ever been wrong?" I say, but I ask the driver anyway. I'm right again and we get off.

We're in a constricted street of gray flat-fronted houses, their white lace curtains pulled closed, walls rising cliff-straight and lawless from the narrow sidewalk. There are no other people, at least it isn't a tourist trap. I have to eat, we've been traveling all morning, but he wants to find a hotel first, he always needs a home base. Right in front of us there's a building labeled HOTEL. We hesitate outside it, patting down our hair, trying to look acceptable. When he finally grits up the steps with our suitcase the doors are locked. Maybe it's a pub.

Hoping there may be a place farther along, we walk down the hill, following the long stone wall, crossing the road when the sidewalk disappears at the corners. Cars pass us, driving fast as if on their way to somewhere else.

At the bottom of the hill near the beach there's a smattering of shops and a scarred, listing inn. Radio music and hilarious voices from inside.

"It seems local," I say, pleased.

"What does 'inn' mean here?" he asks, but I don't know. He goes in to see; then he comes out, dispirited. I'm too tired to think up solutions, I'm scarcely noticing the castle on the hill behind us, the sea.

"No wonder he drank," he says.

"I'll ask," I say, aggrieved: it was his idea, he should do the finding. I try the general store. It's full of people, women mostly, with scarves on their heads and shopping baskets. They say there is no hotel; one woman says her mother has some rooms free though, and she gives me directions while the others gaze pityingly. I'm so obviously a tourist.

The house, when we find it, is eighteenth-century and enormous, a summer residence when the town was fashionable. It offers bed and breakfast on a modest sign. We're glad to have something spelled out for us. The door is open, we go into the hall, and the woman emerges from the parlor as if startled; she has a forties bobby-soxer hairdo with curious frontal lobes, only it's gray. She's friendly to us, almost sprightly, and yes, she has a room for us. I ask, in a lowered voice, if she can tell us where the grave is.

"You can almost see it right from the window," she says, smiling—she knew we would ask that—and offers to lend us a book with a map in it of the points of interest, his house and all. She gets the book, scampers up the wide maroon-carpeted staircase to show us our room. It's vast, chill, high-ceilinged, with floral wallpaper and white-painted woodwork; instead of curtains the windows have inside shutters. There are three beds and numerous dressers and cupboards, crowded into the room as if in storage, a chunky bureau blocking the once-palatial fireplace. We say it will be fine.

"The grave is just up the hill, that way," she says, pointing through the window. We can see the tip of a church. "I'm sure you'll enjoy it."

I change into jeans and boots while he opens and closes the drawers of all the pieces of furniture, searching for ambushes or reading matter. He discovers nothing and we set out.

We ignore the church—he once said it was unremarkable—and head for the graveyard. It must rain a lot: ivy invades everything, and the graveyard is lush with uncut grass, succulent and light green. Feet have beaten animal-trail paths among the tombstones. The graves themselves are neatly tended, most of them have the grass clipped and fresh flowers in the tea-strainer-shaped flower holders. There are three old ladies in the graveyard now, sheaves of flowers in their arms, gladioli, chrysanthemums; they are moving among the graves, picking out the old flowers and distributing the new ones impartially, like stewardesses. They take us for granted, neither approaching nor avoiding us: we are strangers and as such part of this landscape.

We find the right grave easily enough; as the book says, it's the only one with a wooden cross instead of a stone. The cross has been recently painted and the grave is planted with a miniature formal-garden arrangement of moss roses and red begonias; the sweet alyssum intended for a border hasn't quite worked. I wonder who planned it, surely it wouldn't have been her. The old ladies have been here and have left a vase, yellowish glassware of the kind once found in cereal boxes, with orange dahlias and spikes of an unknown pink flower. We've brought nothing and have no ceremonies to perform; we muse for an acceptable length of time, then retreat to the scrollworked bench up the hill and sit in the sun, listening to the cows in the field across the road and the murmur of the ladies as they stoop and potter below us, their print dresses fluttering in the easy wind.

"It's not such a bad place," I say.

"But dull," he answers.

We have whatever it was we came for, the rest of the day is our own. After a while we leave the graveyard and stroll back down the main street, holding hands absentmindedly, looking in the windows of the few shops: an overpriced antique store, a handicrafts place with pottery and Welsh weaving, a nondescript store that sells everything, including girlie joke magazines and copies of his books. In the window, half-hidden among souvenir cups, maps and faded pennants, is a framed photograph of his face, three-quarters profile. We buy a couple of ice-cream bars; they are ancient and soapy.

We reach the bottom of the winding hill and decide to walk along to his house, which we can see, an indistinct white square separated from us by half a mile of rough beach. It's his house all right, it was marked on the map. At first we have no trouble, there's a wide uneven pathway, broken asphalt, the remains of perhaps the beginning of a road. Above us at the edge of the steep leaf-covered cliff, what is left of the castle totters down, slowly, one stone a year. For him, turrets are irresistible. He finds a scrabbly trail, a childrens' entrance up sheer mud.

He goes up sideways, crabwise, digging footholds with the sides of his boots. "Come on!" he shouts down. I'm hesitant but I follow. At the top he reaches his hand to me, but, perpendicular and with the earth beside me, afraid of losing my balance, I avoid it and scramble the last few feet, holding on to roots. In wet weather it would be impossible.

He's ahead, eager to explore. The tunnel through the undergrowth leads to a gap in the castle wall; I follow his sounds, rustlings, the soft thud of his feet. We're in the skeleton of a garden, the beds marked by brick borders now grass-infested, a few rose bushes still attempting to keep order in spite of aphids, nothing else paying any attention. I bend over a rose, ivory-hearted, browning at the edges; I feel like a usurper. He's already out of sight again, hidden by an archway.

I catch up to him in the main courtyard. Everything is crumbling, stairways, ramparts, battlements; so much has fallen it's hard for us to get our bearings, translate this rubbish back into its earlier clear plan.

"That must have been the fireplace," I say, "and that's the main gate. We must have come round from the back." For some reason we speak in whispers; he tosses a fragment of stone and I tell him to be careful.

We go up the remnants of a stairway into the keep. It's almost totally dark; the floors are earth-covered. People must come here though, there's an old sack, an unidentifiable piece of clothing. We don't stay long inside: I'm afraid of getting lost, though it's not likely, and I would rather be able to see him. I don't like the thought of finding his hand suddenly on me unannounced. Besides, I don't trust the castle, I expect it to thunder down on us at the first loud laugh or false step. But we make it outside safely.

We pass beneath the gateway, its Norman curve still intact. Outside is another, larger courtyard, enclosed by the wall we have seen from outside and broken through; it has trees, recent trees not more than a hundred years old, dark-foliaged as etchings. Someone must come here to cut the grass: it's short, hair-textured. He lies down on it and draws me down beside him and we rest on our elbows, surveying. From the front the castle is more complete, you can see how it could once have been lived in by real people.

He lies down, closing his eyes, raising his hand to shade them from the sun. He's pale and I realize he must be tired too, I've been thinking of my own lack of energy as something he has caused and must therefore be immune from.

"I'd like to have a castle like that," he says. When he admires something he wants to own it. For an instant I pretend that he does have the castle, he's always been here, he has a coffin hidden in the crypt, if I'm not careful I'll be trapped and have to stay with him forever. If I'd had more sleep last night I'd be able to frighten myself this way but as it is I give up and lean back on the grass beside him, looking up at the trees as their branches move in the wind, every leaf sharpened to a glass-clear edge by my exhaustion.

I turn my head to watch him. In the last few days he's become not more familiar to me as he should have but more alien. Close up, he's a strange terrain, pores and hairs; but he isn't nearer, he's further away, like the moon when you've finally landed on it. I move back from him so I can see him better; he misinterprets, thinking I'm trying to get up, and stretches himself over me to prevent me. He kisses me, teeth digging into my lower lip; when it hurts too much I pull away. We lie side by side, both suffering from unrequited love.

This is an interval, a truce; it can't last, we both know it, there have been too many differences, of opinion we called it but it was more than that, the things that mean safety for him mean danger for me. We've talked too much or not enough: for what we have to say to each other there's no language, we've tried them all. I think of old science-fiction movies, the creature from another galaxy finally encountered after so many years of signals and ordeals only to be destroyed because he can't make himself understood. Actually it's less a truce than a rest, those silent black-and-white comedians hitting each other until they fall down, then getting up after a pause to begin again. We love each other, that's true whatever it means, but we aren't good at it; for some it's a talent, for others only an addiction. I wonder if they ever came here while he was still alive.

Right now though there's neither love nor anger, no

resentment, it's a suspension, of fear even, like waiting for the dentist. But I don't want him to die. I feel nothing, but I concentrate, somebody's version of God, I will him to exist, right now on the vacant lawn of this castle whose name we don't know in this foreign town we're in only because dead people are more real to him than living ones. Despite the mistakes I want everything to stay the way it is; I want to hold it.

He sits up: he's heard voices. Two little girls, baskets over their arms as if for a picnic or a game, have come into the grounds and are walking toward the castle. They stare at us curiously and decide we're harmless. "Let's play in the tower," one calls and they run and disappear among the walls. For them the castle is ordinary as a backyard.

He gets up, brushing off bits of grass. We haven't visited the house yet but we still have time. We find our break in the wall, our pathway, and slide back down to sea level. The sun has moved, the green closes behind us.

The house is further than it looked from the village. The semi-road gives out and we pick our way along the stony beach. The tide is out; the huge bay stretches as far as we can see, a solid mud-flat except for the thin silty river that cuts along beside us. The dry part narrows and vanishes, we are stranded below the tide line, clambering over slippery masses of purplish-brown rock or squelching through the mud, thick as clotted cream. All around us is an odd percolating sound: it's the mud, drying in the sun. There are gulls too, and wind bending the unhealthy-colored rushes by the bank.

"How the hell did he get back and forth?" he says. "Think of doing this drunk on a dark night."

"There must be a road farther up," I say.

We reach the house at last. Like everything else here it has a wall; this one is to keep out the waves at high tide. The house itself is on stilts, jammed up against the cliff, painted stone with a spindly railed two-decker porch. It hasn't been lived in for many years: one window is broken and the railings are beginning to go. The yard is weed-grown, but maybe it always was.

I sit on the wall, dangling my legs, while he pokes around, examining the windows, the outhouse (which is open), the shed once used perhaps for a boat. I don't want to see any of it. Graves are safely covered and the castle so derelict it has the status of a tree or a stone, but the house is too recent, it's still partly living. If I looked in the window there would be a table with dishes not yet cleared away, or a fresh cigarette or a coat just taken off. Or maybe a broken plate: they used to have fights, apparently. She never comes back and I can see why. He wouldn't leave her alone.

He's testing the railing on the second-story porch, he's going to pull himself up by it.

"Don't do that," I say wearily.

"Why not?" he says. "I want to see the other side."

"Because you'll fall and I don't want to have to scrape you off the rocks."

"Don't be like that," he says.

How did she manage? I turn my head away, I don't want to watch. It'll be such an effort, the police, I'll have to explain what I was doing here, why he was climbing and fell. He should be more considerate. But for once he thinks better of it.

There's another road, we discover it eventually, along the beach and up an asphalt walk beside a neat inhabited cottage. Did they see us coming, are they wondering who we are? The road above is paved, it has a railing and a sign with the poet's name on it, wired to the fence.

"I'd like to steal that," he says.

We pause to view the house from above. There's an old lady in a garden-party hat and gloves, explaining things to an elderly couple. "He always kept to himself, he did," she is saying. "No one here ever got to know him really." She goes on to detail the prices that have been offered for the house: America wanted to buy it and ship it across the ocean, she says, but the town wouldn't let them.

We start back toward our room. Halfway along we

sit down on a bench to scrape the mud from our boots; it clings like melted marshmallow. I lean back; I'm not sure I can make it to the house, whatever reserves my body has been drawing on are almost gone. My hearing is blurred and it's hard to breathe.

He bends over to kiss me, I don't want him to, I'm not calm now, I'm irritated, my skin prickles, I think of case histories, devoted wives who turn kleptomaniac two days a month, the mother who threw her baby out into the snow, it was in *Reader's Digest,* she had a hormone disturbance; love is all chemical. I want it to be over, this long abrasive competition for the role of victim, it used to matter that it should finish right, with grace, but not now. One of us should just get up from the bench, shake hands and leave, I don't care who is last, it would sidestep the recriminations, the totaling up of scores, the reclaiming of possessions, your key, my book. But it won't be that way, we'll have to work through it, boring and foreordained though it is. What keeps me is a passive curiosity, it's like an Elizabethan tragedy or a horror movie, I know which ones will be killed but not how. I take his hand and stroke the back of it gently, the fine hairs rasping my fingertips like sandpaper.

We'd been planning to change and have dinner, it's almost six, but back in the room I have only strength enough to pull off my boots. Then with my clothes still on I crawl into the enormous, creaking bed, cold as porridge and hammock-saggy. I float for an instant in the open sky on the backs of my eyelids, free fall, until sleep rushes up to meet me like the earth.

I wake up suddenly in total darkness. I remember where I am. He's beside me but he seems to be lying outside the blankets, furled in the bedspread. I get stealthily out of the bed, grope to the window and open one of the wooden shutters. It's almost as dark outside, there are no streetlights, but by straining I can read my watch: two o'clock. I've had my eight hours and my body thinks it's time for breakfast. I notice I still have my clothes on, take them off and get back in bed, but my stomach won't let me sleep. I hesitate, then decide it won't do him any harm and turn on the bedside lamp. On the dresser there's a crumpled paper bag; inside it's a Welsh cake, a soft white biscuit with currants in it. I bought it yesterday near the train station, asking in bakeries crammed with English buns and French pastries, running through the streets in a crazed search for local color that almost made us late for the bus. Actually I bought two of them. I ate mine yesterday, this one is his, but I don't care; I take it out of the bag and devour it whole.

In the mirror I'm oddly swollen, as if I've been drowned, my eyes are purple-circled, my hair stands out from my head like a second-hand doll's, there's a diagonal scarlike mark across my cheek where I've been sleeping on my face. This is what it does to you. I estimate the weeks, months it will take me to recuperate. Fresh air, good food and plenty of sun.

We have so little time and he just lies there, rolled up like a rug, not even twitching. I think of waking him, I want to make love, I want all there is because there's not much left. I start to think what he'll do after I'm over and I can't stand that, maybe I should kill him, that's a novel idea, how melodramatic; nevertheless I look around the room for a blunt instrument, there's nothing but the bedside lamp, a grotesque woodland nymph with metal tits and a lightbulb coming out of her head. I could never kill anyone with that. Instead I brush my teeth, wondering if he'll ever know how close he came to being murdered, resolving anyway never to plant flowers for him, never to come back, and slide in among the chilly furrows and craters of the bed. I intend to watch the sun rise but I fall asleep by accident and miss it.

Breakfast, when the time for it finally comes, is shabby, decorous, with mended linens and plentiful but dented silver. We have it in an ornate, dilapidated room whose grandiose mantelpiece now supports only china spaniels and tinted family photos. We're brushed and combed, thoroughly dressed; we speak in subdued voices.

The food is the usual, tea and toast, fried eggs and bacon and the inevitable grilled tomato. It's served by a different woman, gray-haired also but with a corrugated perm and red lipstick. We unfold our map and plan the route back; it's Sunday and there won't be a bus to the nearest railway town till after one, we may have trouble getting out.

He doesn't like fried eggs and he's been given two of them. I eat one for him and tell him to hack the other one up so it will look nibbled at least, it's only polite. He's grateful to me, he knows I'm taking care of him, he puts his hand for a moment over mine, the one not holding the fork. We tell each other our dreams: his of men with armbands, later of me in a cage made of frail slatlike bones, mine of escaping in winter through a field.

I eat his grilled tomato as an afterthought and we leave.

Upstairs in our room we pack; or rather I pack, he lies on the bed.

"What're we going to do till the bus comes?" he says. Being up so early unsettles him.

"Go for a walk," I say.

"We went for a walk yesterday," he says.

I turn around and he's holding out his arms, he wants me to come and lie down beside him. I do and he gives me a perfunctory initial kiss and starts to undo my buttons. He's using only his left hand, the right one is underneath me, he's having trouble. I stand up and take off, reluctantly, the clothes I've so recently put on. It's time for sex, he missed out on it last night.

He reaches up and hauls me in among the tangled sheets. I tense; he throws himself on me with the utilitarian urgency of a man running to catch a train, but it's more than that, it's different, he's biting down on my mouth, this time he'll get blood if it kills him. I pull him into me, wanting him to be with me, but for the first time I feel it's just flesh, a body, a beautiful machine, an animated corpse, he isn't in it anymore, I want him so much and he isn't here. The bedsprings mourn beneath us.

"Sorry about that," he says.

"It's all right."

"No, shit, I really am sorry. I don't like it when that happens."

"It's all right," I say. I smooth his back, distancing him: he's back by the deserted house, back lying on the grass, back in the graveyard, standing in the sun looking down, thinking of his own death.

"We better get up," I say, "she might want to make up the room."

We're waiting for the bus. They lied to me in the general store, there is a hotel, I can see it now, it's just around the corner. We've had our quarrel, argument, fight, the one we were counting on. It was a routine one, a small one comparatively, its only importance the fact that it was the last. It carries the weight of all the other, larger things we said we forgave each other for but didn't. If there were separate buses we'd take them. As it is we wait together, standing a little apart.

We have over half an hour. "Let's go down to the beach," I say, "we can see the bus from there, it has to go the other way first." I cross the road and he follows me at a distance.

There's a wall; I climb it and sit down. The top is scattered with sharp flakes of broken stone, flint possibly, and bleached thumbnail-sized cockleshells, I know what they are because I saw them in the museum two days ago, and the occasional piece of broken glass. He leans against the wall near me, chewing on a cigarette. We say what we have to say in even, conversational voices, discussing how we'll get back, the available trains. I wasn't expecting it so soon.

After a while he looks at his watch, then walks away from me toward the sea, his boots crunching on the shells and pebbles. At the edge of the reed bank by the river he stops, back to me, one leg slightly bent. He holds his elbows, wrapped in his clothes as if in a cape, the storm breaks, his cape billows, thick leather boots sprout up his legs, a sword springs to attention in his hand. He throws his head back, courage, he'll meet them alone. Flash of lightning. Onward.

I wish I could do it so quickly. I sit calmed, frozen, not yet sure whether I've survived, the words we have hurled at each other lying spread in fragments around me, solidified. It's the pause during the end of the world, how does one behave? The man who said he'd continue to tend his garden, does that make sense to me? It would if it were only a small ending, my own. But we aren't more doomed than anything else, it's dead already, at any moment the bay will vaporize, the hills across will lift into the air, the space between will scroll itself up and vanish; in the graveyard the graves will open to show the dry puffball skulls, his wooden cross will flare like a match, his house collapse into itself, cardboard and lumber, no more language. He will stand revealed, history scaling away from him, the versions of him I made up and applied, stripped down to what he really is for a last instant before he flames up and goes out. Surely we should be holding each other, absolving, repenting, saying good-bye to each other, to everything because we will never find it again.

Above us the gulls wheel and ride, crying like drowning puppies or disconsolate angels. They have black rims around their eyes; they're a new kind, I've never seen any like that before. The tide is going out; the fresh wet mud gleams in the sun, miles of it, a level field of pure glass, pure gold. He stands outlined against it, a dark shape, faceless, light catching the edges of his hair.

I turn aside and look down at my hands. They are covered with greyish dust: I've been digging among the shells, gathering them together. I arrange them in a border, a square, each white shell overlapping the next. Inside I plant the flints, upright in tidy rows, like teeth, like flowers.

GHOSTKEEPER

by *Malcolm Lowry*

"What time is it, Tommy?"

"I don't know, sweetheart, have you forgotten I haven't got my watch now?"

"Do you remember the time we took the alarm clock on the picnic?"

"We should have brought the alarm clock along with us on our walk today."

"I guess it's about three. It was about quarter to when we left the apartment."

"Anyhow, we'll be able to see the clock tower in town when we get round the other side of the park."

The two figures, the man and his wife, continued their walk in Stanley Park, in Vancouver, British Columbia. To their right, people were playing tennis, though it was winter; in fact, to be precise, it was February 5, 1952. There was a fine rough wind, steel-blue sea, mountains of rough blue serge topped with snow in the distance. The path they followed had the delicious sense of an English public footpath. Beyond the tennis courts there were dark pines and weeping willows, like fountains of gold thread, when the sun struck them, or bronze harp strings when it didn't. Here at sea level the snow had melted from the ground and early snowdrops were showing faintly under the trees. First they descended to a path that followed the seashore almost on shore level, just under the high bank of the park. There was much driftwood on the beach, evidence of winter storms. One cedar snag seemed scooped out by the sea, as if some Indians had started to make a war canoe out of it.

A woman, skirt tucked up, was sitting on a rock in

the sun and wind. Someone, ahead of them, where the beach was less cluttered with driftwood, was even swimming, then running up and down the beach in the below freezing temperature. (The point of all this is a certain duality of appearance in the picture: which balances the duality within of the theme, and of existence. The picture was wintry, but it is also summery. This is like a nightmare, but it is also extremely pleasant.)

Stepping over winterbournes the man and his wife had to go up on the embankment again. A hoodlum went screeching by in a car: *threat*. The beach reminded the man of his birthplace, New Brighton, England (if this can be done, because one theme is, or should be, rebirth). At frequent intervals steps descended to the beach and a little further on they went down to the beach again. Above, the trees were waving: a soft roaring of trees. Motionless gulls hung in a mackerel sky. The sea now was deserted: one barge, and a far cold lighthouse. (Note: somewhere: his grandfather had been named Henrik Goodhart, had gone down with his ship, a kind of Carlsen.)

And down there now, close under the bank, beneath the softly roaring pines, they found the wrecked boat. But what kind of a boat? On closer inspection it scarcely looked like a boat at all. Nearer, it looked like a wrecked paddlebox. Yet, clearly, it was some sort of boat. Very narrow in the beam, blunt-nosed and blunt-sterned, about fifteen feet long, no paint left on it, salt-gray, battered, pock-marked, and it seemed about a hundred years old. It must have weighed God knows how much. However would they launch such a thing even to lee? A tremendous bilge keel, or bilge piece on both sides, was what made one think of a paddlebox. But this boat was like a solid block, built into the sand, with sand instead of a bottom. A bolted stalwart formidable bottomless hulk, though externally solid and sturdy. On the starboard side at the bow something had been carved: No. 1. For 16 persons. A F 13/2/45, it looked like. And beneath this had been recently written in chalk: H. Ghostkeeper. At this point a wandering Englishman came up; he was wearing dark glasses and was blind, or nearly blind. Some such conversation as this ensues:

"What is it?"

"It's a lifeboat, I think."

"Is it a clinker boat?"

"What's that?"

"The one with the laps." He puts his hands on the boat. "No, it's a carvel. What length is it? Has it got davit hooks?"

"Where would they be?"

"Down in the deadwood at each end. In the forepost and in the stern posts, if it's a lifeboat, there'll be some gudgeons. Generally female gudgeons are on the stern post."

"Why female?"

"Because it's a round hole. The males have a long pintle on them."

"These numbers—would they be the date?"

"No, that'll be cubic capacity."

"Queer it doesn't have a name. Or a port of register."

"Well, it's a lifeboat all right."

Or it strikes me as an alternative idea that the Englishman, instead of being blind, should recognize him, saying, "Haven't I seen you somewhere before, seen your picture in the paper?" It would then devolve that Tom Goodhart's column, "I Walk in the Park," is the Englishman's favorite column and the exposition can be easily handled in this way. But in any event, just as he is leaving, they ask him the time and he says: "That's funny, I lost my watch yesterday."

When he was gone Goodhart makes an entry in his notebook:

Coincidence of the Englishman not having a watch either. The wreck: symbol of something, perhaps bad omen. Or worse—presage of some catastrophe, or death of someone. Then he adds: trouble is, I can't describe it. Once I would have longed to, and gone to endless trouble to find out about the wreck. Now I don't want to bother. How shall I describe it?

(Point is, Goodhart is sick to death of the daily

grind of five hundred words, wants to get out of the city and live in the country and do some creative writing, but can never manage to save up the money.)

Mem: bottle like a grebe below in the bay: the bottle almost had the iridescence of a bird's plumage: ethereal, sea-green, bobbing, swimming.

Mem: also the little turnstones, turning stones.

Mem: Perhaps begin the whole story with a suggestion of the ghostly ballet going on behind the blurred Bon-Ami-ed windows on the old pier used by the Civic Repertory Theatre. Windows like store windows on the disused pier, though it has never been turned properly into a theater and hasn't been used as a pier for twenty years. Packing cases standing about. In the office a notice, a picture of George V and a crown: Keep Calm and Carry On. The hall-echoing sound of an ill-tuned cottage piano. The dimly seen whirling figures and the dismal echoing and trampling of feet.

Now they pass a man reading a Spiritualist newspaper, with a headline saying:

POLICEMEN PURSUE POLTERGEIST

If not use Englishman, then at this point anyhow we must have exposition, perhaps in a dialogue between the Goodharts. Goodhart is a large, bearded man, and is a columnist on a city paper, whose column is entitled "I Walk in the Park." This is full of human-interest stories or observations about nature, etcetera, and is very popular. Goodhart is extremely familiar with this park since he does indeed "walk in the park" to get most of his stories. Goodhart is an Englishman who has emigrated to Canada; his wife is an American, who doesn't think much of Canada and reminds Goodhart on every occasion that he is English. His wife, who is sympathetic in every other respect, and perhaps in this too, has no idea how she wounds Goodhart by these remarks, for her romantic teleologies are the reverse of his and directed toward Europe: for her, England and Europe are romantic and exciting, while to him, the European, it is the frontier, the wild country that is exotic and romantic. Goodhart has been trying to interest an American publisher in a book of short stories to be based on his feuilletons and has finally succeeded. But now, contrarily enough, he suddenly finds he can't write anything, his consciousness is at an agonized standstill; he can hardly write his column. This is at the time of Canada's beginning postwar boom and prosperity, when the Canadian dollar has passed the American dollar in foreign exchange and Americans are taking more interest in Canada. But it is partly this very "boom" which is distressing Goodhart.

Meantime my protagonists have climbed up on the embankment again. Down below the wild ducks are rising and falling on the waves. Mary Goodhart is delighted with the pretty ducks and points them out: "Oh look, darling, scaups, golden eyes, and there's even a pair of buffleheads! Do look!" But Goodhart is obsessed with a sense of tragedy about the lifeboat. It was a sort of nothing, yet it seemed ominous. A sense of something obsolescent, dead.

On the park embankment they are in the forest, and follow a narrow footpath between the huge trees. A few lone men pass them, walking, each with a cloud of smoke blowing over his shoulder, like little lone steamboats. Vancouver is full of lonely men like this and they all go walking along the beach or through the forest in Stanley Park.

Now Tommy Goodhart makes another note in his notebook:

Not sure he has any emotion at all about the lifeboat. Perhaps all he wanted to do was to describe it. Something like a sort of velleity of meaning is trying to possess him. Perhaps he felt like the lifeboat. Were they like the lifeboat? What was like the lifeboat? Was it a symbol of something, or just a lifeboat? To hell with it anyway. Then he added: It was important not to have any fraudulent sincerity about the lifeboat ... as that fake, Barzun, calls it.

Out of the sky came a hushed roaring which was the trees. Now above them the half-moon appeared, and Goodhart made another entry:

The afternoon half-moon like an abstracted reading nun.

Trying to find an image for this moon gave Goodhart so much trouble that he couldn't bear to look at it, and he walked on looking at his feet.

Another man passes with an easel: smell of paints.

Mem: Flying Saucers must come in here: perhaps they pass a man sitting on a bench reading the newspaper: and read over his shoulder, or Mary does: "Vincent Vallach, 1266 Harber Street, was on Strawberry Hill at 10:10 P.M. on Friday night. He saw a spot on the moon, but it started moving across the face of it, and then vanished straight up in the sky, with several other small dots following."

Mrs. Goodhart must be placed as a tiny, pretty woman, all but hidden in your sweet spooky gray costume, Margie dear. She is a very sympathetic character if sometimes tactless, the two have a fine relationship, and she is very interested in nature, flowers, and particularly seabirds and wild ducks.

"A penny for them," Mary said, taking Tom's arm and shaking it gently.

"I'm a Canadian writer, and that's tough."

"Nonsense. You're not a Canadian."

An argument now devolves—as another Englishman goes past, coatless, red-faced, wearing a loud checked vest—on Canada's origins. Mrs. Goodhart is cynical.

"After they'd conquered it from the Indians, they colonized it to a large extent by emptying the jails in England, and picking up the riffraff from the streets and shipping them out, though no Canadian would admit it now."

"Admit it!" Goodhart choked, then said, after a pause: "And what about Virginia?"

"Oh, it's true, to some extent, in America, but not so much. I read that article too, where somebody was very clever debunking the F.F.V.'s. But it doesn't mean what he says is entirely true, any more than all Canadians are descended from convicts."

Goodhart stopped dead for a moment, then said:

"Do you know, you hurt me. I'm English. I'm Canadian. But I'm not descended from a convict."

"Oh Tom, how could you be when you just emigrated—"

"—And if I were descended from a convict and had been shipped out here—and how could I help it if I were—I would resent it."

"So far as I can tell, most Canadians resent the English, no matter how sentimental they may be about England."

Goodhart tried to follow the logic of this, then said: "I know it doesn't mean anything to you, but to me being an Englishman is a serious matter."

"But you always say you're Canadian now—"

"This is absurd! But for me, it's tragic too."

"Ah, tragedy. Why must there always be tragedy?"

"What are we talking about? I'm not English. I'm not Canadian. I am a British Columbian. Ever since I was a kid and collected stamps I have been in love with British Columbia. It had its own stamp once. And I made up my mind to come here, and here I am. I do not recognize confederation. I deplore American influence. But I also deplore Canadian influence. I am unique, the only British Columbian in British Columbia! Keep Calm and Carry On," he added.

They laughed and kissed. They had very tender feelings toward each other and did not pursue this ridiculous argument. He made another note as they walked along:

Perhaps moon is omen too.

They came to Siwash Rock: a lonely storm-beaten pine tree in the rock, beards of grass. He feels an empathy for the lone tree. Gulls are sailing high. Scoters and scaups in the water below. Higher up, on a topped pine, was a kind of tree house, a loggers' contraption or a lookout, perhaps.

"Shall we sit down?"

"For God's sake let us sit upon the ground—" Goodhart said.

But the seat was wet and they walked on. (Perhaps there is a crash, they look round, and the loggers' tree house has fallen bang on to the bench where they thought of sitting.)

Then they came to Prospect Point.

Latitude: 49° 18′ 51″

Longitude: 123° 08′ 24″

Above Sea Level: 220 ft.

—Crown Mountain: 4,931 ft. 7 miles.

—Goat Mountain: 4,587 ft. 6.75 miles.

—Grouse Mountain: 3,974 ft. 5.08 miles.

—Second Narrows: 5.45 miles.

Far below an oil tanker, seemingly as long as the park, is sailing by endlessly into Vancouver. With the scarlet and white paintwork all tiddley, her flags flying, it was like an entire promenade in summer in, say New Brighton, gliding by silently, bandstands, ham and egg walks, flagstaffs and all.

They walked on, through a neck of forest and out into a cleared space. A sign read: *Bears. Rose Garden. Pavilion. Garden of Remembrance. Children's Zoo.* Nearly all the trees in the park were topped, giving them a queer bisected look. A heron, antediluvian, meditated aloft upon one topped tree. Mandarin ducks, as if constructed out of sheets of tin or metal, that fitted into one another, painted with gold, sat about on the grass. Peacocks drowsed in the trees. Squirrels ran about. Pigeons feeding from people's hands. A tame dove. A sense of something unearthly, heavenly, here, like Paradise in a Flemish painting. Pilgrims wandering here and there among the trees.

Mem: Important: Use Margie's note here about the young Frenchman and his watch. (This note follows:)

"—Pardon, but would you like to buy my watch?"

He was very young, nineteen or twenty, tall, thin, blond with hazel or yellow eyes and a meticulously shaven fresh bright face; his smile was clear as a child's except for a certain faint humorous wry curl at the corner of his rather wide but beautifully cut mouth, above a chin that was almost feminine but not weak. His gaze was direct, candid, and sparkling. One liked this boy at once. He wore a belted tan raincoat, of a silky texture, which didn't look very warm. It was a cold frosty day with a rough cold wind, the already low sun was a freezing blurred orange and here, at the waterfront, the streets and the bay were dim and opalescent with cold evening mist. He pushed up his sleeve and showed us a beautiful and expensive gold Swiss watch. Malc, a bit taken aback between his desire to help, lack of money, and imaginative sensitiveness, gave me a swift, baffled, imploring blank look. I said quickly:

"I wish we could, but we're rather broke ourselves this week."

"Next week," said Malc, giving him a beautiful warm smile, which the boy returned, "we'll have some money, but by then, I—"

"Next week," the boy shrugged, "I cannot wait so—"

"Of course, you need it now."

"It is a good watch. I bought in Paris."

"You're French—"

"*Oui.*"

"*Le prochain demain—*"

"*Ah! Vous parlez français!*"

"*Oui. Un peu.*"

"Ah—" His face glowed.

"We were in Paris—how long, Margie?"

"Four years ago. We were there over a year." An instant's silence, then:

"It is a good country, France."

"We love it."

"I am not long in Canada. I am—new."

"You are an immigrant, you are going to stay here, in Canada?" I said.

"*Pardon?—Ah, oui.* I am immigrant. I shall stay. I have been working in a camp, but is closed, when after the New Year I go back."

"Oh, a logging camp."

"*Pardon?—Ah, oui.* They are logs. But I cannot get your insurance for not employment until I am three weeks not employed."

"What will you do?"

"Oh, I will sell my watch." A light Gallic shrug. "And then I will be OK."

"But what a pity!"

Another shrug. Yes it was sad, but then—

We all shook hands warmly. Good luck! Thank you. We admired the watch. One didn't—couldn't—feel any pathos in this, he was obviously too full of adventure and youth and a sort of wry yet open-hearted joyous, light-hearted, casual, Gallic, resigned, active happiness. Off he went, and we the other way.

They walked back to Lost Lagoon through a sort of inside zoo. This on the contrary was a sort of hell. Songbirds in cages. An owl gave a pathetic mew. A hamster, like a minute chipmunk, worked a toy mill furiously in the corner, though he stopped when he thought anyone was watching him. An anteater, with elephant head and long suede nose, in which were shoebutton eyes, walking on the backs of its hands, with a raccoon coat and stiff tail like the backbone of a fish.

"I can't bear to look at that," said Mary Goodhart; but Tom made a mysterious note:

Could get anteater at home. Why go out? Perhaps while he is doing that he returns an almost blind man's watch. The man had been winding it and it had fallen out of his hands and Goodhart picked it up and returned it almost absently, though perhaps he didn't notice the time. But he was thinking of how different this would all look soon, in spring, and the pathetic love of the anteaters for each other.

Then they emerged on the right side of Lost Lagoon. Ducks against the neon lights coming in down-moon to taxi, sunsetward, in Lost Lagoon. An advertisement for Segovia. An advertisement for *The Town Crier* (Tom's paper). Platinum street lamps bloomed. They walked along the edge of the lagoon, remote from the town, into the sunset behind the gold thread of the weeping willows, beyond which was the shore where they had started out for their walk. They kept trying to avoid pools left by the recently melted snow. A man came up behind them and squelched right through the pools, wearing seaboots whose white tops were turned down, looking neither left nor right. To their left, as the day deepened, the ducks were preparing to turn in for the night. Some like sailing ships blown too near a coast in a sou'wester already had their beaks nestled in their plumage. Two little buffleheads—spirit ducks— were doing a little last-minute hunting. And a harmless muskrat cruised peacefully beneath the bank and when they stooped down begged like a puppy. Sense of love between the Goodharts. But also sense of loneliness; of Goodhart, his sense of isolation, partly occasioned by his being an Englishman, from other human beings. Their feeling of love for the ducks. The ducks are indeed their only real companions in British Columbia. There is a notice:

DO NOT MOLEST THE DUCKS

The coots, ivory-billed, squat, awkward and raucous, make a noise like twanging guitar strings (Segovia tuning his guitar), they jerk along, while the mallards sweep easily to their berths. It was touching to see the ducks here, safe and protected in the lagoon, and they wondered how many had come in from the sea where they'd been feeding this afternoon, or were the ones they'd seen earlier. The wind was dropping now at sunset and became a cool, cold, sweet, wet wind. There would be rain tonight, Mary said, sniffing the wind.

The pear-shaped lagoon now narrowed to a kind of rustic canal or neck that connected with the shipless bay beyond, bridged by little arched rustic bridges, exquisitely beautiful. There were still a few chunks of snow to the right in a gulch. A tossed bicycle, like a freak of crumpled ice, pedals, sprockets, by the edge of the lagoon. In this narrower part of the lagoon a whole fleet of ducks were sailing. A magic tin Mandarin duck in the sunset light. On the opposite bank beneath the willows, against the sunset, three children were standing like a threat. Mary was feeding peanuts to the ducks. It took Goodhart some little time to understand why the children had seemed to him like a threat, which was the word that had instantly come to mind. But then he realized they were doing something inconceivable. They had suddenly started to throw stones at the massed ducks.

There were two boys, one short and rather stout—but on the other side of the water, some twenty feet away—one thin and lanky, and a tall girl with red hair wearing blue jeans rolled up to the ankle: none looking more than fifteen. And they were throwing stones at the ducks, massed as for a regatta. The fat boy was skimming stones, and the tall one was throwing them very high, and as Goodhart watched, one dropped on a duck's back; the poor things skimmed and flew in every direction. Bloody murder was in Goodhart's heart but he found he could only gulp, and it was his wife who spoke.

"You boys!" she was saying. "How dare you throw stones at the ducks!"

"Aw."

"Stop it at once!"

"Aw, we just want to see them fly."

"How would you like it if people threw stones at you, just to see you run?"

"Aw, we've heard that one before."

Goodhart was so upset that he was tongue-tied. Anguish trees stood about the suicide lake, apprehension bushes were dotted here and there; and a fear wind rushed through him, depriving him of speech. And that all these emotions were vastly in excess of the situation, which merely demanded a few stern fatherly words—but words which he couldn't deliver—made his anguish worse than ever by frustrating him. A car's horn pealed like cathedral bells for a funeral. Then he just stood there, feeling himself simply like an old buttoned-up overcoat. But meantime, though more aimlessly, the boys went on throwing stones at the ducks. Finally he said:

"Don't you know it's illegal to throw stones at the ducks? Can't you read that sign?"

Flop! For answer the tall boy skied a stone that landed near a mallard and would have killed it had it not missed.

"Aw, we're not hurting them."

"Then what are you throwing stones at them for?" Goodhart heard his overcoat speaking.

"We just want to see them flyyyyy," the boys sneered.

"And anyway, what's it to do with you, you old bastard?" the red-haired girl asked sotto voce, the question followed by giggles.

"If you don't stop throwing stones I'll have you run in, you, taller one," shouted Goodhart, suddenly losing his temper. He did not like being called an old bastard, for he was not old, but perhaps his beard was at fault.

"One more stone and I'll get a policeman," Mary said, shaking with fury. "I won't have anyone hurting the ducks!"

"Aw, go wonn . . ."

"And I'm well known in this town . . ." Goodhart hardly knew what he was saying, "I'm on a newspaper . . ."

"Beaver!" they shouted at him. "Beaver!"

They really stopped throwing stones at the ducks, though they pretended to go on skimming them for a while. Mr. and Mrs. Goodhart now deployed to the right slightly in order to cross the Japanese bridge which brought them abreast of the boys on the same side of the water, Goodhart looking through the trees, trying to make his overcoat appear menacing and himself like a policeman. As the children sidled away Goodhart threw after them:

"God will punish you for this." (I think there should be an almost Lawrentian analysis here, unsentimental, un-SPCA, of what such cruelty *feels* like: it was as if they were throwing stones at them, at their own love, their home, a feeling of "But they don't *understand*.")

Mary Goodhart began to laugh at her husband's portentousness, and so did Tom Goodhart, though a tear had run down his face and in fact they were very upset and hesitant which route to take (for they truly loved the ducks) in case the children should return: whether to continue this path till it crossed the bridle path that came to the stables, or walk through the miniature golf course: either way would bring them back to their apartment. They go by the bridle path and Mrs. Goodhart finds the watch.

(Mem: seagull roosting in the crotch of a tree: Chekhov's *Seagull*—and coincidence and tragic coincidence of this.)

Description of the watch: it seems a very good man's watch, gold, and still running. In fact it said quarter past six. The boys seemed ruled out. There was a boy now walking behind them. Psychological attitude toward watch: Goodhart had no watch (he'd lost his last one and couldn't afford another), also this is a valuable watch, a wristwatch with the clasp broken. The watch had a name on the back though it was difficult to see beneath the trees in the declining day. Goldkipfer, Goalkeeper, it looked like. But it is a man's watch and they do not connect it with the children. As they reach the street:

"Well, we can wait and see if there's an advertisement for it in tomorrow night's paper. Or tomorrow morning. Then, if nobody puts an advertisement in, you've got a watch."

It was certainly a temptation. Moreover the watch was clearly worth a hundred dollars.

"Oughtn't *we* to put an advertisement in the paper?" Goodhart said.

"We can't afford to. We haven't got five dollars to pitch away on an advertisement. If anybody wants it back enough they'll advertise."

"And you mean that we should hang on to the watch? Isn't that being a bit unscrupulous? By gad, aren't you a bit of a hypocrite, Mary? Here a while ago you were accusing us Canadians of being criminals and now you're proposing to steal a watch."

"Steal it! Must you exaggerate everything?"

A minor quarrel ensues, during which Goodhart feels that he's being a bit of a hypocrite because it had been in his mind to keep the watch himself and even perhaps pawn it, which would have temporarily gotten him out of a hole.

Outside their apartment door the Vancouver *Town*

Crier is waiting for them on the floor in the hall. And inside there is a dramatic moment when, in the better light, they see the name on the watch is Henrik Ghostkeeper.

Then, though it seems a bit absurd to do so, they leaf through the *Crier* looking at the Lost and Found ... Mr. Haythornthwaite asked in the legislature what the government intended to do to prevent "use of the knout by mounted cossacks on peaceful residents of Vancouver and to protect constitutional rights to peaceable assemblage and free speech." But that was forty years ago. (Now such things were unknown: that is to say free speech was almost unknown, and of course they order twenty strokes of the lash instead of the knout.)

Under a heading, WHAT RIGHT?, Mother of Two asked:

May a Vancouver-born mother tell "Irish" just what she thinks of a so-called "uncivilized Easterner"? We think the majority of complaining, boasting, insulting people we have in Vancouver must be Easterners. How dare he call our children monsters? Perhaps "Irish" has had the misfortune to run up against one or two badly behaved children. But just what right does that give him to call our children monsters? Mother of Two.

And that was today all right.

Bill Kath and family gone. Am very sick, all alone. Please come and see me, Skinny. And that was today too, but not in the Lost column, or not the right kind of Lost. But here it was: a twelve-foot discharge hose with down pipe and coupling, lost, a brindle bulldog with red harness, a female Boxer pup (anyone harboring after Feb. 15 will be prosecuted), a front pillar-shaped piece of wardrobe 5 ft. long, and a wine bedroom slipper, lost between bus terminal and Richards. And no less than three watches reported lost.

Lady's gold oblong wristwatch, gold expansion bracelet, lost in Woodward's dept. store Friday. Reward. FA 3411R.

Lady's Bulova watch inscribed "Vida" Saturday night. Reward. TA 2221.

And another watch lost in their neighborhood

cinema theatre, the Bay Theatre. Apart from that the only thing of interest was that Segovia had objected to a publicity story that a guitar he was playing in Coblenz had broken at the exact moment that its maker had died in Granada.

But the name on the watch, Ghostkeeper, caused Goodhart to recall the name Ghostkeeper carved on the wreck, and also to recall that the Englishman who'd spoken to them by the wreck had also mentioned that he'd lost his watch. A certain terror also was occasioned by the name, Ghostkeeper. Goodhart privately decided if he returned the watch it will take the curse off the name. Goodhart now decides to try and telephone. So he looks in the telephone book for the strange name, meanwhile remarking the names he encounters are anything but English, save for his own, though it is important that the real reason he is phoning is a compassionate one: he has now decided, from the small span of the strap as it is clasped, that the owner must be a child. But Ghostkeeper was an unlikely name: but then so are these other names unlikely. So was Goodhart.

Zsomber, Zingg, Zero, Pe (Ralph G.), Poffenroth, Peckinpaugh, Pennycuick, Stilborn, Soderroos, Overho, Ovens, Snowball, Shelagh, Snodgrass, Smuck, Smout (he has ceased really looking, being fascinated by these names), Smook, Smitten, Stojcic, Shish, Order of Perceptive Praetorians, Orangecrush, Goodhart, Golf, Goggin, Goranko, Gooselaw, Gathercole—but here we were:

Ghostkeeper, Sigrid, Mrs. r 4942 Ruby. DExter 1576R.
Ghostkeeper, B. H. r 3655 W. 2nd. CEdar 7762.

He phones the second Ghostkeeper and this part is dramatized much as it happened, i.e., it is a female voice, who disclaims any ownership of the watch, but says that the Ghostkeepers must all be related, and that she has read in the paper that a Mrs. Ghostkeeper has "arrived from the East with her small boy." (Mem: this ties in with "Mother of Two.").

Before he phones the second Ghostkeeper they examine the watch again and Mary agrees that the owner must be a child. Suddenly it is as if Goodheart realizes for the first time that perhaps the owner of the watch really was the child who had been throwing stones at the duck, or one of the children, which is a dramatic moment, and he remembers how he has said portentously, "God will punish you." But Mary now says no, it is far too expensive a watch to be entrusted to a young child. Then Tom thinks well, damn it, it may be a girl.

Now they look at the watch: Lilliputian universe, jeweled orrery, miniscule planetarium, it now said quarter past seven. And Mary remarked how it's very compact, very busy, very efficient, in a fussy kind of way: so important, miniscule order, dragging along time with it. (mem: work in ambiguous word *escapement* which is also part of a watch) It is a 21-jewel watch, comes from the U.S., not Canadian at all. Perhaps it belonged to yet another Ghostkeeper, an American, who'd come across the border . . . But the real point is, as they open it, that the reader feels that is the *thing*, the machine—

So now Goodhart rings up the first Ghostkeeper, Sigrid, who turns out also a woman, but who sounds somewhat older. This conversation is dramatized, as it occurred, punctuated by Mrs. Goodhart's interpolations from the kitchen, where she is getting dinner— "Don't tell them what kind of watch it is—" "Don't tell *them*, you ninny—" "Make them tell *you*—"

But the scene should be beautifully funny and so unlikely that it has the unerring stamp of truth, viz: the husband is deaf. The woman is obviously not the widow with the small child, but a watch *is* involved here. The woman has to keep leaving the phone to relay the conversation to her husband, whose name is, to confound matters worse still, Henrik Ghostkeeper. This man says that there is yet another Ghostkeeper to whom he has given a watch when he was overseas. He had it overseas, says Mrs. Ghostkeeper, but she gives the impression that this other Ghostkeeper is about nineteen.

Goodhart says he feels the owner is a child, which is why he's rung up, for the child must be grieving, or even being punished. Goodhart is now reproaching himself for not having walked back to the children with the watch, he feels now that one of the children is the owner, and had he done so it would have been both more dramatic and more of a lesson, should he have said: "Is there anyone here by the name of Henrik Ghostkeeper?" "Yes, that's me." "Have you lost anything? I told you not to throw stones at the ducks." And then to have returned the watch. How salutary that would have been!

But it is relayed via the deaf Ghostkeeper that his nephew's name *is* Henrik Ghostkeeper, so Goodhart is convinced that he has his man, though his picture of him is a pretty weird one, that of an attenuated or hypertrophied unman of nineteen who had apparently been fighting overseas at the age of twelve.

"Does he have a phone?"

"No, I don't think so. But there's a phone in the house."

"Can you get hold of them then."

Mrs. Ghostkeeper promises to find the nephew and have him call the Goodharts. Tom leaves his address and phone number and Mrs. Ghostkeeper tells them that the nephew lives at 33 East 7th Street.

There now follows a slight description of the scene outside our apartment: the terricular solid house opposite, now a hotel, sense of old order changeth, and—it is snowing lightly again—the chicken croquettes covered with powdered sugar in the blooming lamplight, the antediluvian monkey tree that still kept up its liaison with the prehistoric era. This little realistic beautiful description possibly combined with a description of the scene through the Venetian blinds with the street lamps and the snow is important contrast.

The Goodharts now decide to try and discover the phone number of 33 East 7th. They do so, but whoever answers the phone disclaims all knowledge of the Ghostkeepers. In fact they're irritated, and suspect some sort of joke.

The Goodharts are now slightly fed up by the whole thing, so after dinner they seek relaxation at their local cinema, the Bay, where there is an English film playing called *The Magnet*. They greet the box office girl and manager as neighbors and good acquaintances.

But as soon as they enter the cinema Tommy Goodhart thinks he has gone to the next world, is having a dream within a dream, or suffering from some extraordinary hallucination.

For the scene before his eyes seems at first to be the very scene along the beach this afternoon: then he realizes that the scene is taking place in New Brighton, his own birthplace, on the sands where he played as a boy. And the scene that is playing is that which deals with the exchange of the invisible watch!

There follows a short description of the film which is continually interrupted—for Mary Goodhart—by Tommy saying, "There's the cathedral! That's Seacombe pier! That's New Brighton pier! There used to be a tower only they knocked it down. That's the old prom—called that the Ham and Egg Parade. Birkenhead Ales, my God! That's the place where I saw the Lion-faced Lady. The tunnel had not quite been completed when I left England though it was already in use," etcetera. Finally they stand up while the recording of "God Save the King" plays.

But the kid imagining that he is being chased by the cops about the magnet has given Goodhart a sense of guilt about having pretended to be a cop to the kids this afternoon in the park and he wonders if his harshness has frightened them. He has now more or less ceased to think that the wristwatch actually belongs to one of these children—unless for purposes of a hypothetical short story for his column—because of the second Ghostkeeper's story, but he now is possessed by a purely humane feeling and anxiety to return the watch that he feels is valuable to its owner. And there is something pathetic about the watch ticking away in the kitchen. It is like a symbolic band or nexus relating him to humanity.

Mrs. Goodhart is tired and goes to bed when they return, but Goodhart finds his consciousness and inspiration seething to the boiling point and can't sleep at all. New Brighton—rebirth—it is all like a symbol of rebirth, and this is the point where he thinks, "Well, now I really can write! What a marvelous story this is, right under my nose." etcetera etcetera. So he gets pencil and paper and in a frenzy of inspiration sits down to write. First, out with all subjectivity, and tell the story just as it happened, or rather the story, just as it has not yet completely happened. But what happens to him as he tries to write is peculiar. He had been worrying himself sick over lack of material, but now he finds he had far too much. (Perhaps the earlier part of this in dialogue, excitedly and enthusiastically to Mary.)

Nor was it that exactly. Every journalist works on a basis of a plethora of material and selects from it, and he himself had long disciplined himself to turning out his five hundred words a day. Moreover the short-story writers he admired most, the early Flaherty, Chekhov, Sodeborg, Jensen, Pontoppidan, the Irishman James Stern, Herman Bang, Flaubert in his tales, Maugham, Pyeskov, Kataev, even one or two of Faulkner's, James Thurber, Bunin, Saroyan, Hofmannsthal, the author of Job, God knows who, all these writers, even if they did not always succeed, aimed at economy of words. (Mem: find early poem of Conrad Aiken's about a watch and quote from it.) Even Joseph Conrad, hard though it evidently was for him, leaned over backwards to try and keep things shipshape. But here Goodhart found himself confronted with something different, something wholly unprecedented in his experience of "plethora of material." His first instinct was to cut the first part of their walk this afternoon altogether, and start at the pond in the sunset light. *Lex Talionis* would be, he thought, a good title for the story. Boy stones ducks. Man warns boy, tells him he'll be punished. Man finds watch. Man discovers, rounda-

bout, that watch is property of boy—though this would
be swinging the lead, for it obviously wouldn't prove so
in fact—man returns watch. Boy has lesson. God
moves in a mysterious way would be the moral, and
the result a concise heartwarming little story. But in
how much more a mysterious way did God, if it was
God—oh God!—seem to move in fact? (All this ties in
with the kaleidoscope of life, the complexity, flying saucers, the impossibility of writing good short stories.)
For where did Ghostkeeper come in? Perhaps he
wouldn't be able to use the name Ghostkeeper at all,
which was an uncommon name, just as he wouldn't be
able to use his own name, Goodhart, that was too
much like *Pilgrim's Progress*. But without the name
Ghostkeeper, where was the point of the story? Even
though it was the name Ghostkeeper that seemed to de-
prive it of all point. But what was the relation between
the owner of the watch and the name on the wreck?
Why should the Englishman he'd spoken to by the wreck
have lost his watch too? And what was the relation
between this and the watch he'd restored to the blind
man by the anteater's cage? Why had the wreck seemed
a bad omen? And then the tree house had to fall on the
seat where the two of them, but for sheer luck, might
have been sitting at that moment, which suggested a
kind of "on borrowed time" theme. And what was the
relation between all these watches in general and the
invisible watch in the movie, and why did the movie
have to be set in New Brighton which was his birthplace when he had been thinking of his birthplace this
afternoon, just prior to having seen the children? And
the French boy who wanted to sell *his* watch. And now
he thought of a thousand other things. In fact, no sooner did poor Goodhart come to some sort of decision
as to what line his story should take than it was as if a
voice said to him: "But you see, you can't do it like
that, that's not the meaning at all, or rather it's only one
meaning—if you're going to get anywhere near the
truth you'll have twenty different plots and a story no
one will take." And as a matter of fact this was sadly
true. For how could you write a story in which it's main

symbol was not even reasonably consistent, did not even have consistent ambiguity? Certainly the watch did not seem to mean the same thing consistently. It had started by being a symbol of one thing, and ended up—or rather had not yet ended up—by being a symbol of something else. And how after all could you expect the story to mean anything without at least using the name Ghostkeeper. But even as he set down the name Ghostkeeper in desperation, it was as if he seemed to see or hear yet another Ghostkeeper, sitting as it were halfway up in the air like Ezekiel's wheel, smiling broadly and saying: "Wheels within wheels, Mr. Goodhart," or again, "Wheels within wheels within wheels, my dear Mr. Goodhart." Yes, and controlling the escapement. (Perhaps some of this is a little previous and should take place the next day when the story has further developed.)

Finally Goodhart is so confused that he decides there's nothing to do but wait and see how the story develops in real life—for one thing, the very material world seems against him, table rattling, etcetera—and tired to death but still unable to sleep he goes to bed and tries to read himself into somnolence with an article in the *Town Crier* entitled:

BRITISH COLUMBIA, PROVINCE OF MYSTERIES

"Never," he read, "has any place had a tighter tie-up with the supernatural. From the Yukon border to Washington, from the Rockies to the coast, we found them . . . tales that would make the stoutest heart beat faster . . ." etcetera etcetera. Tales that would make the stoutest watch run faster. There was even a little filler about watches: "Finely engraved watches were made in the shape of skulls, little books, octagons, crosses, purses, dogs, and sea shells in olden days."

The next morning Goodhart, despite good resolutions to get up early, etcetera, is very tired, gets up late, finds his wife cleaning house, finds watch has stopped at ten o'clock, so he winds it up again. Nothing is wrong with the watch and it begins ticking merrily. It is a mild cloudy day, the night's snow already melted and outside the shadow of smoke, as if from a steamer's funnel on deck (actually from their own apartment chimney) was pouring somewhat menacingly over the green lawn before the chicken croquettes, streaming over the lawn and flowing up the monkey tree. Finally he goes out to buy some cigarettes and post a letter for his wife. First thing he sees is that all flags are at half-mast. Then, buying cigarettes, he sees the headlines at the newsstand:

THE KING IS DEAD

He feels shocked, and after a while something like crying. He does not however buy the paper, since he's waiting for it to be delivered at the apartment. Death of King makes him very melancholy. Then he remembers that last night in the Bay theatre was a historic occasion, the last time "God Save the King" was sung. He wanders along the promenade: he glances at the octopus and the piteous horrible wolf eel: people are still rehearsing on the pier, the ghostly ballet behind the Bon-Ami-ed windows. Somebody swimming. People still playing tennis despite the cold. But all the time he seems to be hearing the ghostly voice saying, "Do you remember yesterday, when you said, For God's sake let us sit upon the ground and tell—" Strange stories of the death of kings. Wheels within wheels, Mr. Goodhart. Deciding against having another look at the octopus in the aquarium, he goes back to the apartment where the *Town Crier* has arrived with the news of the death of the King.

Mary is very sympathetic about the death of the King. In the paper, however, it says that the King has died at about ten o'clock. This reminds Goodhart of something else, though he can't remember what it is. (Of course it is that the wristwatch has stopped at ten o'clock, which he remembers later.) But all it now suggests is Segovia—perhaps this in dialogue—the story about Segovia in yesterday's paper which he has forgotten and he hunts all through yesterday's paper looking for the bit about Segovia which he feels he should put in his story but can't find it, meantime feeling he's going completely cuckoo. Then they look at tonight's paper again, and feel gloomy with its report of people—the King's neighbors and friends—already in mourning clothes. "Queen Mother Elizabeth and Princess Margaret remained in seclusion during the day. At dusk, as rain began to fall, lights burned in only one room of the house." Then he looks out of the window and sees a newsboy passing with the headline:

LONG LIVE QUEEN ELIZABETH

This suggested to Goodhart that, writer or not, he was now an Elizabethan, and he thought that this remark: "Writer or not, nothing could prevent Gooselaw Goggins from being an Elizabethan," would make a good end to the story, so he made a note to that effect, feeling more cuckoo than ever. Then suddenly he remembered the watch again and looked in the Lost section of Wednesday's paper.

There was no report of flying saucers in today's paper, though there was a guarded editorial warning against guided missiles, something about "braced for disaster," and "well-balanced people," and "the situation calls for a little pulling up of reason's socks." And "Almost every age has seen things in the sky it could not explain."

In the Lost and Found, the same black and white cat, part Persian, was missing; the same wine bedroom slipper remained lost between the bus terminal and Richards Street, the same front pillar-shaped piece of wardrobe 5 feet long was missing, nor had the one 12 ft 2 inch discharge hose off Harrington Motors tank truck between Boston Bar and Vancouver yet been recovered. The other watches were still missing, and so was the wallet or watch reported missing in the local theater, the Bay, where he'd seen the film about New Brighton and the invisible watch. But here it was:

Man's Gold Bulova wristwatch
vicinity Riding Academy, Stanley
Park, FAirmost 1869. Reward.

Goodhart now phones this number, and the exchange is dramatized as it happened. The phone is answered by a girl, who laughs excitedly, "Mummy, I
think they've found the watch," and then by another
woman.

Their conversation is important, you must help me,
Margie, with it, but I can't see quite how to dramatize
it at the moment, Goodhart does not want to speak to
the woman, thinks that he should talk to the watch's
owner. Her description of the watch with Henrik
Ghostkeeper engraved on it is perfectly correct however: on the other hand Mrs. Ghostkeeper insists that
the owner is a minor, "I'm his mother and have to handle all this for him," etcetera. Goodhart is now convinced that he has found the owner of the watch at last
and moreover now feels sure for some reason, though it
is a million-to-one chance, and though it contradicts
what the other Ghostkeeper said, that the boy actually
is the boy, one of the boys, who had been throwing
stones at the ducks, but feeling somewhat exhausted by
this time he turns the telephone over to Mary.

"Tell her to bring the boy with him," he says, "so he
can see who we are."

"Why?"

"So that he can see we're the people who told him
not to throw stones at the ducks."

It is decided she will come about seven, and try to
bring the boy. For some reason the King's death has
made Goodhart feel ten times more isolated and lonely
than ever. At the same time the solemn stately occasion
makes him feel very formal, even prefectorial, and he
dresses very carefully, putting on his old school tie.
What is worrying him now is how to make plain to the
boy the lesson about the ducks. On the other hand this
has to be done subtly without letting the mother know,

for ethically speaking it would be unsporting to give away the boy in front of his mother. In any case the death of the King seems to have called forth an added obligation to behave in every way like a very chivalrous Englishman indeed. But at the same time Goodhart is furiously making up further endings for his story. One of these was somewhat sinister: They would refuse the reward. "No, no. You can buy us a drink some time." "I will. I'll be seeing you," said Mrs. Ghostkeeper, and as she and her child departed a tree fell on them.

This scene of Goodhart dressing carefully for this interview should be done realistically and is important and should be exciting for the very good reason that although this is simply a short story, Goodhart, so far as I can see, is in the kind of *philosophical* situation (although on one plane it is absurd) of the highest dramatic order. That this situation must be in some sense a universal one (even though it is not generally recognized) is what I count on to provide the excitement. What we need too—or rather therefore—is not merely imagination, but hard-boiled logical thinking. If this logical thinking is as good as the reasoning in one of your detective stories, Margie, it should more than suffice. In any case Goodhart is now standing *within the possibilities* of his own story and of his own life—something like Sigbjorn in relation to the Volcano, though this is both more complex and of course less serious. The point seems to be that all these possibilities of his story (as of his own life) wish in some way to fulfill themselves, but what makes it terrifying is that the mind or intelligence that controls these things, or perhaps does not control them, is outside Goodhart and not within. In this intelligence (that which we mean when we say "they're on the job") the *name* Henrik Ghostkeeper is the symbol. In himself (or themselves) of course Ghostkeeper is many things at once, and many persons, including a child, and so is incomprehensible to human thought.

Perhaps what happens is something like this. The

minute an artist begins to try and shape his material—
the more especially if that material is his own life—
some sort of magic lever is thrown into gear, setting
some celestial machinery in motion producing events or
coincidences that show him that this shaping of his is
absurd, that nothing is static or can be pinned down,
that everything is evolving or developing into other
meanings, or cancellations of meanings, quite beyond
his comprehension. There is something mechanical
about this process, symbolized by the watch: on the
other hand the human mind or will or consciousness or
whatever, of which the owner knows nothing at all yet,
which has a will of its own, becomes automatically at
such moments in touch as it were with the control
tower of this machinery. (This brings me to Ortega—
"A man's life is like a work of fiction, that he makes up
as he goes along: he becomes an engineer for the sake
of giving it form etcetera.") I don't think any of the
above should appear in the story—or do I?—of course,
and indeed now I've written it I scarcely know what it
means. But that I am on the right track I am certain—
at least to the extent that the *lies*, literal falsehoods in
this story, such as the name Ghostkeeper on the wreck,
the falling tree house, seem valid, as produced by my
unconscious. They merely parallel other coincidences
we haven't space for, such as Dylan Thomas etcetera.
In any case the average short story is probably a very
bad image of life, and an absurdity, for the reason that
no matter how much action there is in it, it is static, a
piece of death, fixed, a sort of butterfly on a pin; there
are of course some flaws in this argument—it is a pity I
have no philosophical training for I unquestionably
have some of the major equipment of a philosopher of
sorts. But the attempt should be—or should be here—
at least to give the illusion of things—appearances,
possibilities, ideas, even resolutions—in a state of
perpetual metamorphosis. Life is indeed a sort of delir-
ium, perhaps that should be contemplated, however, by
a sober "healthy" mind. By sober and healthy I mean, of

necessity, limited. The mind is not equipped to look at the truth. Perhaps people get inklings of that truth on the lowest plane when they drink too much or go crazy and become delirious but it can't be stomached, certainly not from that sort of upside-down and reversed position. Not that the truth is "bad" or "good": it simply *is*, is incomprehensible, and though one one is part of it, there is too much of it to grasp at once, or it is ungraspable, being perpetually protean. Hense a final need probably for an acceptance of one's limitations, and of the absurd in oneself. So finally even this story is absurd, which is an important part of the point, if any, since that it should have none whatsoever seems part of the point too.

In any case Goodhart dresses carefully, rehearsing: on plane (a) what he is going to say to Mrs. and Master Ghostkeeper, (b) the possible endings for his story. Activity (b) begins to make him feel as if he is going cuckoo again, nor is this feeling mitigated when halfway through shaving his eye falls on a phrase in an article by Karl Jaspers on Nietzsche in an American magazine: "He himself corrected his ideas in new ideas," he reads, "without explicitly saying so. In altered states he forgot conclusions formerly arrived at." This seems to have some bearing on the situation though Goodhart can't make out quite what it is. "For Nietzsche leads us into realms of philosophy which are anterior to clear logical thought, but which strive toward it." H'm. "Not long before his madness he declared that for a number of years he wished only to be quiet and forgotten, for the sake of something that is striving to ripen." Shortly before the end he wrote: 'I have never gone beyond attempts and ventures, preludes and promises of all sorts.' " I'll say I haven't, thinks Goodhart. "There remains to be sure a residue of insoluble absurdities—" I'll say there is, thinks Goodhart, tying his tie.

Finally he is ready for Mrs. and Master Ghostkeeper's arrival, and this part should be dramatized with considerable feeling of tension and sus-

pense, though quietly and realistically, as it were *New
Yorker*-style. On the other hand I think by this time
one should be afraid of the onset of the Ghostkeepers,
almost as if on one plane Ghostkeeper is a symbol of
death. At the same time the numerous channels of the
story now narrow for the moment into one main one
(or at least not more than three or four!). Mr. and
Mrs. Goodhart now emerge as if integrated, kindly,
wise characters, very much in love with each other,
their attitude toward the boy largely parental in character. Their ethics will not allow them—should the boy
prove to be the one that was throwing stones at the
ducks—to give him away in front of his mother. However, can Goodhart take the boy aside? Would the boy
laugh at him? *Would he see the point?* Or spoil the
whole thing. At the same time perhaps Goodhart wonders if the mother is going to prove to be a pretty girl
and perhaps he is wishing in advance to impress her.
(Absolutely disregarding the novelist's touch, and the
usual laws of selection, the story is preparing to end
therefore in a manner not remotely suggested by its beginning or indeed having very much to do with it.) At
the same time fact is so confounded with fiction in
Goodhart's mind that he is sometimes not sure that he
is experiencing any valid emotion and has the sense—
even while we draw him and Mary realistically—that
he is now a character in a story of which perhaps another or that other Henrik Ghostkeeper is the author,
though perhaps Henrik Ghostkeeper hasn't yet made
up his mind either what to do with him. Goodhart feels
as though in short—in Aiken's words—"the whole
buzzing cosmic telephone exchange" were going on in
his head. Every now and then he walks nervously to the
door to see if their visitors are arriving and the Goodharts have a slight dissension about whether to take
the reward or not. Finally Tom clairvoyantly opens the
door just as Mrs. Ghostkeeper is coming down the corridor. She is of course alone, and not pretty. What happened in fact is now dramatized briefly in neutral entertaining fashion. They do not disclaim the reward
perhaps but accept half of it. "We can make a lot of

money that way," Goodhart could say. Nor does he say, "You can buy us a drink sometime," and Mrs. Ghostkeeper replies sinisterly, "I'll be seeing you." Of course the child *is* the child who'd been throwing stones at the ducks, this must be firmly established (and of course he could have, and has, written his name on the wrecked boat), and all during the conversation Goodhart is trying to work in his little prefectorial spiel, while remaining chivalrous.

"Just tell him we were the people who spoke to him about the ducks," he tries to say several times.

"Just tell him that we—"

"Just say we saw him with the ducks—"

But he never manages any real message at all for the boy, and a feeling of frustration becomes so strong he is confused and the incident ends in complete absurdity. And Goodhart looks out the window after she leaves. Secretly he is wondering whether a tree is going to fall on her after all.

Then, feeling completely frustrated and irritated that the boy will *never know,* but on the whole a sense of pleasure and satisfaction that they had managed to do good, he sits down to write his story (in which the boy does find out), sipping away at a glass of milk. Already he has decided that the shorter version is the one he must write. *Lex Talionis.* But in this he has to leave out the name Ghostkeeper altogether, which even if he could use it would perhaps involve a libel suit, etcetera. And naturally his own name in real life he couldn't use anyhow. Finally he decides to give his protagonist no name at all. First he is "I" then he changes it to "he." The man and his wife. The name on the watch—the boy—must, he decides, be a perfectly neutral name like Smithers or Miller—but then he wouldn't be able to find them in the phone book. There is no mention of the falling tree house, the other coincidences of the watches, the invisible watch, or the death of the King, or the feeling that the protagonist is now an Elizabethan. Everything was selection, concision, the storywriter's touch. The protagonist himself was not a journalist nor any sort of writer in any kind of crisis about writing. In fact you would never realize what he was. Well, at least this story was touching, Goodhart thinks, compassionate, simple, on the side of "goodness." And having the advantage of a lowly and unpretentious theme it could scarcely offend the Almighty Spirit. The only trouble was it wasn't "true," that is to say, that though it seemed true that the stoning of the ducks had brought upon the child the immediate retribution of the losing of the watch, so much other material that seemed mysteriously relevant had to be tailored away for the sake of art (or cash) that the result was the same: it was a touching little conte perhaps, but by trimming the whole down to what seemed its bare essentials, what was left did not seem even a synecdoche of the events of the last two days, as their seemingly almost insane series affected him.

But as he thought these things it was as if he seemed to hear, as if from on high, a certain divine assent, nodding, as if to say: "Yes, yes, that is very nice, very touching, Mr. Goodhart, it is just as you say," he seemed to hear yet another voice, as from halfway up in the air, saying, "No, no, Mr. Goodhart, that is very lousy, what did I tell you? What about the King? What about Canada? What about the blind man? What about Segovia? What about the invisible watch? And the young Frenchman? What about the wheels within wheels, Mr. Goodhart, and not merely the wheels within wheels, but the wheels within wheels within wheels, Mr. Goodhart, that are even now still turning and evolving newer, yet more wonderful and more meaningless meanings—"

And yet within himself he knew there was a meaning and that it was not meaningless.

Goodhart laid his pencil aside. He had finished his story but his mind was still sorely troubled. That Ghostkeeper! And "I Walk in the Park." But who else walks in the park? Who else, up there, was writing? Suddenly before his eyes the tree house crashed down on the bench again. And tell strange stories of—Who else was writing, up there, about Kings dying, Elizabethans, invisible watches, flying saucers, blind men,

Mandarin ducks ... Henrik Ghostkeeper! If only one could be sure he were playing a game!

What did we know? And into his mind again came a vision of the ghostly ballet, seen through the half-cleaned windows, on the pier at the entrance to the park. If one could only be sure!

But suddenly his fear was transformed into love, love for his wife, and that meaningless, menacing fear was transformed into a spring wood bearing with it the scent of peach blossoms and wild cherry blossoms.

Pray for them!

THAT YELLOW PRAIRIE SKY

by *Robert Kroetsch*

I was looking at the back of a new dollar bill, at that scene of somewhere on the prairies, and all of a sudden I was looking right through it and I wasn't in Toronto at all anymore—I was back out west. The clouds were moving overhead as if we were traveling and I pointed to that fence that's down and I said, "Look't there, Julie, that must be Tom's place. He hasn't fixed that piece of fence these thirty years." And then I noticed the elevator wasn't getting any closer.

It never does.

My brother Tom, he was quite a guy for women. I'll bet he was the worst for twenty miles on either side of the Battle River. Or the best, whichever way you look at it. I guess I wasn't far behind. Anyway, we spent the winter courting those two girls.

The way it happened, we met them in the fall while we were out hunting. I mean, we knew them all our lives. But you know how it is,. eh? You look at some girl all your life, and then one day you stop all of a sudden and take another look and you kind of let out a low whistle.

Well, Tom was twenty-three then, with me a year younger, and we'd grown up together. He taught me how to play hockey and how to snare rabbits and anything new that came along. Out on the prairies you don't have neighbours over your head and in your back yard, and a brother really gets to be a brother.

When it rained that fall and the fields got too soft for threshing we decided to go out and take a crack at some of the ducks that were feeding on our crop. We built a big stook that would keep us out of view, facing the slough hole and the setting sun, and we crawled inside. I can still see it all in my mind . . . .

A thousand and a 'thousand ducks were milling black against the yellow sky. Like autumn leaves from the tree of life they tumbled in the air; a new flock coming from the north, a flock circling down, a flock tremulous above the water, reluctant to wet a thousand feet. And silhouetted on the far horizon was a threshing machine with a blower pointed at a strawpile, and nearer was the glint of the sun on the slough, and then a rush of wings from behind, overhead, going into the sun, and with a sudden jolt the autumn-sharp smell of a smoking gun.

I let go with both barrels at a flock that was too high up, and before I could reload there was a scream that left my jaw hanging as wide open as the breech of my old 12-gauge.

"I swear," Tom said, "now ain't that the prettiest pair of mallards that ever came close to losing their pinfeathers?"

I pushed my way out of the stook, and Tom was right.

I guess they didn't see us. I mean, Kay and Julie.

They were standing back of our stook, looking scared, with their skirts tucked into—tucked up—and nobody thought of it in the excitement, or at least they didn't.

"Are you trying to kill us?" Julie asked, pushing

back a blond curl and pretending she was only mad and not scared at all.

"Can't you see we're shooting ducks?" Tom said.

"I can't by the number that fell," she said.

That's when I spoke up. "They were too high and I was too anxious."

Julie looked at me and my gun and she blushed. "I didn't mean to insult your shooting. I've heard folks say you're one of the best shots around."

Funny thing. I was pretty good, but just about then I could've told a battalion of the Princess Pat's to back up and drop their guns.

It was then that the redhead, Kay, spoke up. "Really, I'm glad you missed. I hate to see things get killed."

Tom looked up at the distant ducks for a minute, and then said, "As a matter of fact, I hate it myself." It was the first time I ever heard Tom say a thing like that. Most of the time you couldn't hold him.

There was a kind of a loss for words. Then Kay explained, "We're making boxes for the box social in the church hall tonight, and we're taking the short cut over to Rittner's place to borrow four little wheels that the Rittners have left over from the little toy wagon that Halberg's new automobile ran into."

"We're in a terrible hurry," Julie said, "so instead of going around by the road we're going to wade across Rittner's slough—"

And then they noticed it too, and before Tom could say he figured as much, they were in the slough wading above their knees.

"A nice pair of shafts," Tom commented.

"A dandy pair," I said. But I soon found out I was talking about a different pair.

That night at the box social Tom paid three dollars and a half for the lunch box that looked like a pink Red River oxcart with toy wagon wheels on it. He figured it was Kay's because she had red hair, and in a pinch we could make a switch.

Some religious fellow caught on to me and ran me up to five and a quarter on the yellow one. It was a great help to the church committee, and it looked like a fair enough investment otherwise. Sure enough, I got Kay's and I wanted Julie's, so Tom and I switched and the girls never caught on; or at least they never let on that they did.

Through the rest of the fall and during the winter Dad had to do the chores quite a few times by himself. Tom and I didn't miss a dance or a hayride or a skating party within trotting range of the finest team of dapple grays in the country. We didn't have all the fancy courting facilities that folks here in the east have, but we had lots of space and lots of sky. And we didn't miss much on a frosty night, the old buffalo robe doing whatever was necessary to keep warm. . . .

The northern lights in the winter sky were a silent symphony: flickering white, fading red and green, growing and bursting and dying in swirls and echoes of swirls, in wavering angel-shadows, in shimmering music. And on one edge of the wide white prairie shone a solitary light, and toward it moved a sleigh with the jingle of harness, the clop of hoofs, the squeak of runners on the snow; and the jingling, clopping, squeaking rose up like the horses' frozen breath to the silent music in the sky.

I guess we did pretty well. I remember the night we were driving home from a bean supper and dance, and Julie said, "You're getting pretty free with your behavior."

"Well, you're going to be my wife soon enough," I said.

"It can't be soon enough," she whispered, and she pushed my arm away. Women are always contrary that way.

Tom and Kay were curled up at the back of the sleigh and they couldn't hear us.

"Let's get out and run behind for a ways," I said. "My feet are getting cold. And I can clap my hands."

"My feet are warm," she said.

"But mine aren't."

"You're just making that up because you're mad."

"Why would I be mad?"

"You're mad because I stopped you."

"Stopped me what?"

She didn't want to say it. "Nothing," she said.

"I think I'll get out and run behind by myself," I said. "Should I?"

She reached up and kissed me right on the mouth, cold and yet warm, and that was that as far as the running behind went.

"Let's talk," she said. "We've only been engaged since midnight, and here you want to act like we're married already."

"Who, me?" I said, trying to sound like I didn't know what she was talking about.

"Let's talk," she said.

"Talk," I said. "I'm all ears."

"Don't you want to talk?"

"Sure I want to talk. If I can get a word in edgewise."

"I can't get used to being engaged," she said. "I want to talk."

"What'll we talk about?" I said. "It seems to me we've done nothing but talk since last fall."

"Let's plan," she said.

That was the end of my plans.

"We're going to get married, remember?" she went on. "You asked me and I said yes before you had hardly asked the second time."

"You weren't so sure I'd ask a third time."

She soon changed that subject. "Kay said that she and Tom are going to build a house this fall."

"It's a good idea. Living on the home place is no good for them and no good for Ma and Dad."

"Why can't we build a house?"

"We got a shack on our place."

"Shack is right. One room and a lean-to."

"It's a roof."

"Kay and Tom are going to get a new bedroom suite and a new stove, and Kay is going to start making new curtains. I could start making new curtains too if we were going to have a new house with lots of windows."

"If we get a good crop, okay. But I got enough stashed away to get married on and put a crop in, and that's it."

"I want to make a nice home for you. We'll have a family."

"We might," I said. "But things'll have to pick up."

"Promise," she said.

"Sure enough," I said.

"I mean promise we'll have a new house."

"Don't you think it would be better to wait and see?"

She didn't answer.

"We might flood out or dry out or freeze out. How do I know?"

She still didn't answer.

"What if it's a grasshopper year? What about wireworms and wild oats and rust and buckwheat?"

"Promise me," she said. "I don't even think you love me."

That was her final word.

I talked for another ten minutes about wireworms and rust, and after that things got quiet. We sat in that sleigh for an hour, our breath freezing in our scarves (twenty-seven below, it was), wrapped in a buffalo robe and in each other's arms and never once did she speak. To a young fellow twenty-two years old it didn't make much sense. But I didn't push her away. She was soft and warm and quiet; and I thought she had fallen asleep.

"Okay," I said, finally. "Okay okay okay. I promise."

She snuggled closer.

We had a double wedding in the spring.

Tom's father-in-law fixed up two granaries near the house and we held the reception at his place. Everybody was there. My cousin had trouble with the pump, and while everybody was watching him trying to tap the keg, Tom came over to where I was watching the sky for a nice day and he shook my hand.

"We're the luckiest pair of duck hunters this side of

the fourth meridian," he said. "We've each got a half section that's almost paid for, we've got a big crop to put in that'll put us on our feet, and we've each got the prettiest girl in the country. How do you like being a married man?"

"Yes, sir," I said. I had one eye on a couple of my old sidekicks who were kissing the bride for the second time. "This here love business is the clear McCoy."

I remember that my cousin drew the first pitcherful just then, and it was all foam. But we were only just married. . . .

The sky was the garment of love. It was a big sky, freckled with the stars of the universe; a happy sky, shrouding all the pain. It was the time of spring, and spring is love, and in the night sky arrow after arrow of honking geese winged across the yellow moon, driving winter from the world.

Right after the wedding we moved into the shack and really went to work. I was busy from morning till night putting in a big crop, while Julie helped with the chores and looked after her little chicks and put in a big garden. When the crop was in we started on the summer fallow, and before that was done it was haying time.

At noon she brought dinner out to me in the field, out in the sun and the wind, and we sat side by side and talked and laughed, and the dust from my face got on hers sometimes, and sometimes I didn't get started quite on time. And the weather was good too. . . .

In the evening a black cloud towered up in the west and tumbled over the land, bringing lightning and rain and hope. In the morning there was only a fragment of cloud; the dot worn on a woman's cheek beside a pair of beautiful eyes, and the beautiful sun in the fair blue sky sent warmth and growth into the earth, and the rain and the sun turned the black fields green, the green fields yellow.

I remember one Sunday we went over to Tom's for a chicken supper. Tom and Dad and I talked about the way the crops were coming along and where to get bind-er repairs, and we made arrangements to help each other with the cutting and stooking.

The womenfolk talked about their gardens and their chickens until Julie mentioned the drapes she was sewing.

"I'm going to have one of those living room parlors," she said, "one of those living room parlors with lots of windows, like in the magazines, and I'm making drapes for that kind of window."

"I think I will too," Kay said. "Tom cut some of the nicest plans out of last week's *Free Press*. I hope the fall stays nice."

"My husband is even getting enthusiastic," Julie said, giving me a teasing smile. "I caught him holding up the drapes one day and looking at them."

Ma said she was crocheting some new pillow covers for all the pillows and easy chairs that seemed to be coming up, and she thought they all better get together and do some extra canning. Entertaining takes food.

Kay said, "Ma," meaning her mother-in-law, "you'll soon have your house all to yourself again. And since Tom is afraid he'll have to help with the washing, he's going to get me a new washing machine."

"We might pick up a secondhand car," Julie said, "if the crop on our breaking doesn't go down because it's too heavy."

I had mentioned it'd be something to tinker on during the winter.

It wasn't long before Julie was talking about the washing machine and Kay was talking about a secondhand car. Wheat was a good price that year.

We menfolk laughed at the women and we found a few things in the Eaton's catalog that we could use ourselves. It seemed that somebody was always coming up with something new that we couldn't possibly do without.

After supper we all walked out to have a look at Tom's crop. Tom could even make a gumbo patch grow wheat.

I guess it happened a week later. I mean, the storm. Julie was working on her drapes. It was a hot day, too hot and too still, and in the afternoon the clouds began to pile up in the west. . . .

The storm came like a cloud of white dust high in the sky: not black or gray like a rain cloud, but white; and now it was rolling across the heavens with a brute unconcern for the mites below, and after awhile came the first dull roar. The hot, dead air was suddenly cool, stirring to a breeze, and then a white wall of destruction bridged earth and sky and moved across the land and crashed across the fields of ripening grain.

Old man Rittner saw it coming west of us, and he went out and drove his ax in the middle of the yard, figuring to split her. But she didn't split.

In fifteen minutes it was all over and the sun was shining as pretty as you please. Only there was no reason for the sun to shine. Our garden and our fields were flat, and the west window was broken, and half the shingles were gone from the shack. The leaves were half stripped from the trees, and the ground was more white than black and, I remember, the cat found a dead robin.

My wife didn't say a word.

I hitched up old Mag to the buggy and Julie and I drove over to Tom's place.

Tom was sitting on the porch steps with his head in his hands, and Kay was leaning on the fence, looking at her garden. It looked like they hadn't been talking much either.

I got out and walked over to Tom, and Julie stayed in the buggy.

"A hundred percent," I said.

"The works," he said. "And all I got is enough insurance to feed us this winter or to buy a ticket to hell out of here."

"The same with me," I said.

We couldn't think of much to say.

All of a sudden Tom almost shouted at Kay: "Say it and get it over with. If you want we'll go to the city and I'll get a job. I can get on a construction gang. They're paying good now. We'll get a washing machine and a secondhand car." He looked at his wheat fields, beaten flat. "We'll make a payment and get our own house."

He kicked at a hailstone.

"A house with big windows for my new drapes," Kay added.

Tom got up and he walked to the gate where Julie sat in the buggy. Kay and I, we stood there watching him, almost afraid of the storm in his eyes, and Kay looked at me as if I should stop him before he went and grabbed a pitchfork or something.

"Tom, I was joking," Kay said. "I don't need fancy curtains and a washing machine. And we never needed a car before. Did we, Tom? We got enough for us and Ma and Dad. Haven't we, Tom? And we got next year."

Tom snorted at that idea. He kicked open the gate and walked out toward the barn. There was so much helpless anger in him he couldn't talk.

Kay called after him. "We still got this, Tom." She was kind of crying. She was pointing at the black dirt that showed through the broken grass. "Look, Tom, we still got this."

Tom, he stopped in the middle of the yard and he turned around. For a long time he was only looking at Kay's empty hand.

All of a sudden he bent down like he was going to say a prayer or something. And he scooped up a handful of hailstones, and he flung them back at the sky.

Like I say, my wife; she didn't say a word.

THE GREAT ELECTRICAL REVOLUTION

by *Ken Mitchell*

I was only a little guy in 1937, but I can still remember Grandad being out of work. Nobody had any money to pay him and as he said, there wasn't much future in brick-laying as a charity. So mostly he just sat around in his suite above the hardware store listening to his radio. We *all* listened to it when there was nothing else to do, which was most of the time unless you happened to be going to school like me. Grandad stuck right there through it all—soap operas, weather reports and quiz shows—unless he got a bit of cash from somewhere. Then he and Uncle Fred would go downtown to the beer parlor at the King William Hotel.

Grandad and Grandma came from the old country long before I was born. When they arrived in Moose Jaw, all they had was three children: Uncle Fred, Aunt Thecla, and my Dad; a trunk full of working clothes; and a 26-pound post mall for putting up fences to keep "rogues" off Grandad's land. Rogues meant Indians, Orangemen, cattle rustlers and capitalists. All the way out on the train from Montreal, he glared out the Pullman window at the endless flat, saying to his family:

"I came out here for land, b'Christ, and none of 'em's going to sly it on me."

He had sworn to carve a mighty estate from the raw Saskatchewan Prairie, although he had never so much as picked up a garden hoe in his whole life before leaving Dublin.

So when he stepped off the train at the C.P.R. station in Moose Jaw, it looked like he was thinking of tearing it down and seeding the site to oats. It was two o'clock in the morning, but he kept striding up and down the lobby of the station, dressed in his good wool suit with the vest, as cocky as a bantam rooster in a chicken run. My Dad and Uncle Fred and Aunt Thecla sat on the trunk, while Grandma nagged at him to go and find them a place to stay. (It was only later they realized he was afraid to step outside the station.) He finally quit strutting long enough to get a porter to carry their trunk to a hotel down the street.

The next morning they went to the government land office to secure their homestead. Then Grandad rented a democrat and took my Dad and Uncle Fred out to see the land they had come halfway around the world to find. Grandma and Aunt Thecla were told to stay in the hotel room and thank the Blessed Virgin for deliverance. They were still offering their prayers some three hours later, when Grandad burst into the room, his eyes wild and his face pale and quivering.

"Sweet Jesus Christ!" he shouted at them. "There's too much of it! There's just too damn much of it out there." He ran around the room several times in circles knocking against the walls. "Miles and miles of nothing but miles and miles!" He collapsed onto one of the beds, and lay staring at the ceiling.

"It 'ud drive us all witless in a week," he moaned.

The two boys came in and told the story of the expedition. Grandad had started out fine, perhaps just a little nervous. But the further they went from the town, the more agitated and wild-eyed he got. Soon he stopped urging the horse along and asked it to stop. They were barely ten miles from town when they turned around and came back, with Uncle Fred driving. Grandad could only crouch on the floor of the democrat, trying to hide from the enormous sky, and whispering hoarsely at Fred to go faster. He'd come four thousand miles to the wide open spaces—only to discover he suffered from agoraphobia.

That was his last real excursion onto the open prairie. He gave up forever the idea of a farm of his own. (He did make one special trip to Mortlach in 1928 to fix Aunt Thecla's chimney, but that was a family favor. Even then Uncle Fred had to drive him in an enclosed Ford sedan in the middle of the night, with newspapers taped to the windows so he couldn't see out.) There was nothing left for him to do but take up his old trade of brick-laying in the town of Moose Jaw, where there were trees and tall buildings to protect him from the vastness. Maybe it was a fortunate turn of fate; certainly he prospered from then until the Depression hit, about the time I was born.

Yet—Grandad always felt guilty about not settling on the land. Maybe it was his conscience that prompted him to send my Dad out to work for a cattle rancher in the hills, the day after he turned eighteen. Another point: he married Aunt Thecla off to a Lutheran wheat farmer at Mortlach who actually threshed about five hundred acres of wheat every fall. Uncle Fred was the eldest and closer to Grandad (he had worked with him as an apprentice brick-layer before they immigrated) so he stayed in town and lived in the suite above the hardware store.

I don't remember much about my father's cattle ranch, except whirls of dust and skinny animals dragging themselves from one side of the range to the other. Finally there were no more cattle, and no money to buy more, and nothing to feed them if we did buy them, except wild foxtails and Russian Thistles. So we moved into Moose Jaw with Grandad and Grandma, and went on relief. It was better than the ranch where there was nothing to do but watch tumbleweeds roll through the yard. We would have had to travel into town every week to collect the salted fish and government pork, anyway. Grandad was very happy to have us, because when my Dad went down to the railway yard to get our ration, he collected Grandad's too. My Dad never complained about waiting in line for the handout, but Grandad would've starved to death first. "The goddamned government drives us all to the edge," he would say. "Then they want us to queue up for the goddamned swill they're poisoning us with."

That was when we spent so much time listening to Grandad's radio. It came in a monstrous slab of black walnut cabinet he had swindled, so he thought, from a second hand dealer on River Street. An incandescent green bulb glowed in the center to show when the tubes were warming up. There was a row of knobs with elaborate-looking initials and a dial with the names of cities like Tokyo, Madrid, and Chicago. Try as we might on long winter evenings to tune the needle into those stations and hear a play in Japanese or Russian, all we ever got was CHMJ Moose Jaw, The Buckle of the Wheat Belt. Even so, I spent hours lying on the floor, tracing the floral patterns on the cloth-covered speaker while I listened to another world of mystery and fascination.

When the time came that Grandad could find no more bricks to lay, he set a kitchen chair in front of the radio and stayed there, not moving except to go to the King William, where Uncle Fred now spent most of his time. My Dad had managed to get a job with the city, graveling streets for fifty cents a day. But things grew worse. The Moose Jaw Light and Power Company came around one day in the fall of 1937 and cut off our electricity for nonpayment. It was very hard on Grandad not to have his radio. Not only did he have nothing to do, but he had to spend all his time thinking about it. He stared out the parlor window, which looked over the alley running behind the hardware store. There was a grand view of the back of the Rainbow Laundry.

That was what he was doing the day of his discovery, just before Christmas. Uncle Fred and my Dad were arguing about who caused the Depression—R. B. Bennett or the C.P.R. Suddenly Grandad turned from the window. There was a new and strange look on his face.

"Where does that wire go?" he said.

"Wire?" said Uncle Fred, looking absentmindedly around the room. He patted his pockets looking for a wire.

"What wire?" my Dad said.

Grandad nodded toward the window. "This wire running right past the window."

He pointed to a double strand of power line that ran from a pole in the back alley to the side of our building. It was a lead-in for the hardware store.

"Holy Moses Cousin Harry. Isn't that a sight now!" Grandad said, grinning like a crazy man.

"You're crazy," Uncle Fred told him. "You can't never get a tap off that line there. They'd find you out in nothing flat."

Grandma, who always heard everything that was said, called from the kitchen: "Father, don't you go and do some foolishness will have us all electrinated."

"By God," he muttered. He never paid any attention to a word she said. "Cut off *my* power, will they?"

That night, after they made me go to bed, I listened to him and Uncle Fred banging and scraping as they bored a hole through the parlor wall. My Dad wouldn't have anything to do with it and took my mother to the free movie at the co-op. He said Grandad was descending to the level of the Moose Jaw Light and Power Company.

Actually, Grandad knew quite a bit about electricity. He had known for a long time how to jump a wire from one side of the meter around to the other, to cheat the power company. I had often watched him under the meter, stretched out from his tiptoes at the top of a broken stepladder, yelling at Grandma to lift the goddamned Holy Candle a little higher so he could see what the Christ he was doing.

The next day, Grandad and Uncle Fred were acting like a couple of kids, snorting and giggling and jabbing each other in the ribs. They were waiting for the King William beer parlor to open so they could go down and tell their friends about Grandad's revenge on the power company. They spent the day like heroes down there, telling over and over how Grandad had spied the lead-in, and how they bored the hole in the wall, and how justice had finally descended on the capitalist leeches. The two of them showed up at home for supper, but as soon as they ate they headed back to the King William where everybody was buying them free beer.

Grandma didn't seem to think much of their efforts, although now that she had electricity again, she could spend the evenings doing her housework if she wanted to. The cord came through the hole in the wall, across the parlor to the hall and the kitchen. Along the way, other cords were attached which led to the two bedrooms. Grandma muttered when she had to sweep around the black tangle of wires and sockets. With six of us living in the tiny suite, somebody was forever tripping on one of the cords and knocking things over.

But we lived with all that because Grandad was happy again. We might *all* have lived happily if Grandad and Uncle Fred could have kept quiet about their revenge on the power company. One night about a week later we were in the parlor listening to Fibber McGee and Molly when somebody knocked at the door. It was Mrs. Pizak, who lived next door in a tiny room.

"Goot evening," she said, looking all around. "I see your power has turnt beck on."

"Ha," Grandad said. "We turned it on *for* 'em. Damned rogues."

"Come in and sit down and listen to the show with us," Grandma said. Mrs. Pizak kept looking at the black wires running back and forth across the parlor, and at Grandad's radio. You could tell she wasn't listening to the show.

"Dey shut off my power, too," she said. "I always like listen de *Shut-In*. Now my radio isn't vork."

"Hmmmm," Grandad said, trying to hear Fibber and the Old-Timer. Grandma and my Dad watched him, not listening to the radio any more either. Finally he couldn't stand it.

"All right, Fred," he said. "Go and get the brace and bit."

They bored a hole through one of the bedroom walls into Mrs. Pizak's cubicle. From then on, she was on Grandad's power grid, too. It didn't take long for everybody else in the block to find out about the free power, and they all wanted to hook up. There were two floors of suites above the hardware store, and soon the walls and ceiling of Grandad's suite were as full of holes as a colander, with wires running in all directions. For the price of a bottle of whiskey, people could run their lights twenty-four hours a day if they wanted. By Christmas Day, even those who *paid* their bills had given notice to the power company. It was a beautiful Christmas in a bad year—and Grandad and Uncle Fred liked to take a lot of credit for it. Nobody blamed them, either. There was a lot of celebration up and down the halls, where they always seemed to show up as guests of honor. There was a funny feeling running through the block, like being in a state of siege, or a revolution, with Uncle Fred and my Grandad leading it.

One late afternoon just before New Year's, I was lying on the floor of the front parlor, reading a second-hand Book of Knowledge I had got for Christmas. Grandma and my mother were knitting socks, and all three of us were listening vaguely to the *Ted Mack Amateur Hour*. Suddenly, out of the corner of my eye, I thought I saw Grandad's radio move. I blinked and stared at it, but the big console just sat there talking about Geritol. I turned a page. Again, it seemed to move in a jerk. What was going on?

"Grandma," I said. "The radio—"

She looked up from her knitting, already not believing a word I might have to say. I gave it up, and glared spitefully at the offending machine. While I watched, it slid at least six inches across the parlor floor.

"Grandma!" I screamed. "The radio's moving! It was sitting there—and it moved over here. All by itself!"

She looked calmly at the radio, then the tangle of wires spread across the floor, and out the front parlor window.

"Larry-boy, you'd best run and fetch your grandfather. He's over at McBrides'. Number eight."

McBrides' suite was down the gloomy hall and across. I dashed down the corridor and pounded frantically at the door. Someone opened it the width of a crack.

"Is my Grandad in there?" I squeaked. Grandad stepped out into the hall with a glass in his hand, closing the door behind him.

"What is it, Larry?"

"Grandma says for you to come quick. The radio! There's something—"

"My radio!" Grandad was not a large man, but he had the energy of a buzz saw. He started walking back up the hall, breaking into a trot, then a steady gallop, holding his glass of whiskey out in front at arm's length so it wouldn't spill. He burst through the door and screeched to a stop in front of the radio, which sat there, perfectly normal except that it stood maybe a foot to the left of the chair.

"By the holy toenails of Moses—what is it?"

Grandma looked up ominously and jerked her chin toward the window. Her quiet firmness usually managed to calm him, but now, in two fantastic bounds, Grandad stood in front of the window, looking out.

"Larry," he said, glaring outside, "fetch your Uncle Fred." I tore off down the hall again to number eight and brought Uncle Fred back to the suite. The two women were still knitting on the other side of the room. Grandma was doing her stitches calmly enough, but my mother's needles clattered like telegraph keys, and she was throwing terrified glances around the room.

"Have a gawk at this, will you, Fred?"

Uncle Fred and I crowded around him to see out. There, on a pole only twenty feet from our parlor window, practically facing us eye-to-eye, was a lineman from the power company. He was replacing broken glass insulators; God knows why he was doing it in the dead of winter. Obviously, he hadn't noticed our homemade lead-in, or he would have been knocking at the door. We could only pray he wouldn't look at the wire too closely. Once, he lifted his eyes toward the lighted window where we all stood gaping out at him in the growing darkness. He grinned at us, and raised his hand in a salute. He must have thought we were admiring his work.

"Wave back!" Grandad ordered. The three of us waved frantically at the lineman, to make him think we appreciated his efforts, although Grandad was muttering some very ugly things about the man's ancestry.

Finally, to our relief, the lineman finished his work and got ready to come down the pole. He reached out his hand for support—and my heart stopped beating as his weight hung on the contraband wire. Behind me, I could hear the radio slide another foot across the parlor floor. The lineman stared at the wire he held. He tugged experimentally, his eyes following it up to the hole through our wall. He looked at Grandad and Uncle Fred and me standing there in the lit-up window, with

our crazy horror-struck grins and our arms frozen
above our heads in grotesque waves. Understanding
seemed to spread slowly across his face.

He scrambled around to the opposite side of the pole
and braced himself to give a mighty pull on our line.
Simultaneously, Grandad leaped into action, grabbing
the wire on our side of the wall. He wrapped it around
his hands, and braced his feet against the baseboard.
The lineman gave his first vicious yank, and it almost
jerked Grandad smack against the wall. I remember
thinking what a powerful man the lineman must be to
do that to my Grandad.

"Fred, you feather-brained idiot!" he shouted. "Get
over here and haul on this line before the black-hearted
son-of-a-bitch pulls me through the wall."

Uncle Fred ran to the wire just in time, as the man
on the pole gave another, mightier heave. At the window, I could see the lineman stiffen with rage and determination. The slender wire sawed back and forth
through the hole in the wall for at least ten minutes,
first one side, and then the other, getting advantage.
The curses on our side got very loud and bitter. I
couldn't hear the lineman, of course, but I could see
him—with his mouth twisted in an awful snarl,
throwing absolutely terrible looks at me in the window,
and heaving on the line. I know he wasn't praying to
St. Jude.

Grandad's cursing would subside periodically when
Grandma warned: "Now, now, Father, not in front of
the boy." Then she would go back to her knitting and
pretend the whole thing wasn't happening, as Grandad's violent language would soar to a new high.

That lineman must have been in extra-good condition, because our side very quickly began to play out.
Grandad screamed at Grandma and my mother, and
even at me, to throw ourselves on the line and help.
But the women refused to leave their knitting, and they
wouldn't let me be corrupted. I couldn't leave my viewpoint at the window, anyway.

Grandad and Uncle Fred kept losing acreage. Gradually the huge radio had scraped all the way across the floor and stood at their backs, hampering their efforts.

"Larry!" Grandad shouted. "Is he weakenin' any?"

He wanted desperately for me to say yes, but it was useless. "It doesn't look like it," I said. Grandad burst out in a froth of curses I'd never heard before. A fresh attack on the line pulled his knuckles to the wall and barked them badly. He looked tired and beaten. All the slack in the line was taken up and he was against the wall, his head twisted looking at me. A light flared up in his eyes.

"All right, Fred," he said. "If he wants the god-damned thing so bad—let him have it!" They both jumped back—and nothing happened.

I could see the lineman, completely unaware of his impending disaster, almost literally winding himself up for an all-out assault on our wire. I wanted out of human kindness to shout a warning at him. But it was too late. With an incredible backward lunge, he disappeared from sight behind the power pole.

A shattering explosion of wild noises blasted my senses, like a bomb had fallen in Grandad's suite. Every appliance and electric light that Grandma owned flew into the parlor, bounding off the walls and smashing against each other. A table lamp from the bedroom caromed off Uncle Fred's knee. The radio collided against the wall and was ripped off its wire by the impact. Sparking and flashing like lightning, all of Grandma's things hurled themselves against the parlor wall. They were stripped like chokecherries from an electric vine as it went zipping through the hole. A silence fell—like a breath of air to a drowning man. The late afternoon darkness settled through the room.

"Sweet Jesus Christ!" Grandad said. He had barely got it out, when there came a second uproar: a blood-curdling barrage of bangs and shouts, as our neighbors in the block saw all their lamps, radios, irons and toasters leap from their tables and collect in ruined piles of junk around the "free power" holes in their walls. Uncle Fred turned white as a sheet.

I looked out the window. The lineman sat on the

ground at the foot of his pole, dazed. He looked up at me with one more hate-filled glare, then deliberately snipped our wire with a pair of cutters. He taped up the end and marched away into the night.

Grandad stood in the midst of the ruined parlor, trying in the darkness to examine his beloved radio for damage. Grandma sat in her rocking chair, knitting socks and refusing to acknowledge the disaster.

It was Grandad who finally spoke first. "They're lucky," he said. "It's just goddamned lucky for them they didn't scratch my radio."

THE ACCIDENT

by *Mavis Gallant*

I was tired and did not always understand what they were asking me. I borrowed a pencil and wrote:

PETER HIGGINS
CALGARY 1935—ITALY 1956

But there was room for more on the stone, and the English clergyman in this Italian town who was doing all he could for me said: "Is there nothing else, child?" Hadn't Pete been my husband, somebody's son? That was what he was asking. It seemed enough. Pete had renounced us, left us behind. His life-span might matter, if anyone cared, but I must have sensed even then that no one would ever ask me what he had been like. His father once asked me to write down what I remembered. He wanted to compose a memorial booklet and distribute it at Christmas, but then his wife died, too, and he became prudent about recollections. Even if I had wanted to, I couldn't have told much— just one or two things about the way Pete died. His mother had some information about him, and I had some, but never enough to describe a life. She had the complete knowledge that puts parents at a loss, finally: she knew all about him except his opinion of her and how he was with me. They were never equals. She was a grown person with part of a life lived and the habit of secrets before he was conscious of her. She said, later, that she and Pete had been friends. How can you be someone's friend if you have had twenty years' authority over him and he has never had one second's authority over you?

He didn't look like his mother. He looked like me. In Italy, on our wedding trip, we were often taken for brother and sister. Our height, our glasses, our soft myopic stares, our assurance, our sloppy comfortable clothes made us seem to the Italians related and somehow unplaceable. Only a North American could have guessed what our families were, what our education amounted to, and where we had got the money to spend on traveling. Most of the time we were just pie-faces, like the tourists in ads—though we were not as clean as those couples, and not quite as grown-up. We didn't seem to be married: the honeymoon in hotels, in strange beds, the meals we shared in cheap, bright little restaurants, prolonged the clandestine quality of love before. It was still a game, but now we had infinite time. I became bold, and I dismissed the universe: "It was a rotten little experiment," I said, "and we were given up long ago." I had been brought up by a forcible, pessimistic, widowed mother, and to be able to say aloud "we were given up" shows how far I had come. Pete's assurance was natural, but mine was fragile, and recent, and had grown out of love. Traveling from another direction, he was much more interested in his parents than in God. There was a glorious treason in all our conversations now. Pete wondered about his parents, but I felt safer belittling Creation. My mother had let me know about the strength of the righteous; I still thought the skies would fall if I said too much.

What struck me about these secret exchanges was how we judged our parents from a distance now, as if they were people we had known on a visit. The idea that he and I could be natural siblings crossed my mind. What if I, or Pete, or both, had been adopted? We had been raised in different parts of Canada, but we were only children, and neither of us resembled our supposed parents. Watching him, trapping him almost in mannerisms I could claim, I saw my habit of sprawling, of spreading maps and newspapers on the ground. He had a vast appetite for bread and pastries and sweet desserts. He was easily drunk and easily sick. Yes, we were alike. We talked in hotel rooms, while we drank the drink of the place, the *grappa* or wine or whatever we were given, prone across the bed, the bottle and glasses and the ashtray on the floor. We agreed to live openly, without secrets, though neither of us knew what a secret was. I admired him as I could never have admired myself. I remembered how my mother, the keeper of the castle until now, had said that one day—one treeless, sunless day—real life would overtake me, and then I would realize how spoiled and silly I had always been.

The longest time he and I spent together in one place was three days, in a village up behind the Ligurian coast. I thought that the only success of my life, my sole achievement, would be this marriage. In a dream he came to me with the plans for a house. I saw the white lines on the blue paper, and he showed me the sunny Italian-style loggia that would be built. "It is not quite what we want," he said, "but better than anything we have now." "But we can't afford it, we haven't got the capital," I cried, and I panicked, and woke: woke safe, in a room of which the details were dawn, window, sky, first birds of morning, and Pete still sleeping, still in the dark.

The last Italian town of our journey was nothing—just a black beach with sand like soot, and houses shut and dormant because it was the middle of the afternoon. We had come here from our village only to change trains. We were on our way to Nice, then Paris, then home. We left our luggage at the station, with a porter looking after it, and we drifted through empty, baking streets, using up the rest of a roll of film. By now we must have had hundreds of pictures of each other in market squares, next to oleanders, cut in two by broomstick shade, or backed up, squinting, against scaly noonday shutters. Pete now chose to photograph a hotel with a cat on the step, a policeman, and a souvenir stand, as if he had never seen such things in Canada—as if they were monuments. I never once heard him say anything was ugly or dull; for if it was, what were we doing with it? We were often stared at, for we were out of our own background and did not fit into the new. That day, I was eyed more than he was. I was watched by men talking in dark doorways, leaning against the façades of inhospitable shops. I was traveling in shorts and a shirt and rope-soled shoes. I know now that this costume was resented, but I don't know why. There was nothing indecent about my clothes. They were very like Pete's.

He may not have noticed the men. He was always on the lookout for something to photograph, or something to do, and sometimes he missed people's faces. On the steep street that led back to the railway station, he took a careful picture of a bakery, and he bought crescent-shaped bread with a soft, pale crust, and ate it there, on the street. He wasn't hungry; it was a question of using time. Now the closed shutters broke out in the afternoon, and girls appeared—girls with thick hair, smelling of jasmine and honeysuckle. They strolled hand in hand, in light stockings and clean white shoes. Their dresses—blue, lemon, the palest peach—bloomed over rustling petticoats. At home I'd have called them cheap, and made a face at their cheap perfume, but here in their own place, they were enravishing, and I thought Pete would look at them and at me and compare; but all he remarked was "How do they stand those clothes on a day like this?" So real life, the grey noon with no limits, had not yet begun. I distrusted real life, for I knew nothing about it. It was the middle-aged world without feeling, where no one was loved.

Bored with his bread, he tossed it away and laid his hands on a white Lambretta propped against the curb. He pulled it upright, examining it. He committed two crimes in a second: wasted bread and touched an adored mechanical object belonging to someone else. I knew these were crimes later, when it was no use knowing, no good to either of us. The steering of the Lambretta was locked. He saw a bicycle then, belonging, he thought, to an old man who was sitting in a kitchen chair out on the pavement. "This all right with you?" Pete pointed to the bike, then himself, then down the hill. With a swoop of his hand he tried to show he would come straight back. His pantomime also meant that there was still time before we had to be on the train, that up at the station there was nothing to do, that eating bread, taking pictures of shops, riding a bike downhill and walking it back were all doing, using up your life; yes, it was a matter of living.

The idling old man Pete had spoken to bared his gums. Pete must have taken this for a smile. Later, the old man, who was not the owner of the bike or of anything except the fat sick dog at his feet, said he had cried "Thief!" but I never heard him. Pete tossed me his camera and I saw him glide, then rush away, past the girls who smelled of jasmine, past the bakery, down to the corner, where a policeman in white, under a parasol, spread out one arm and flexed the other and blew hard on a whistle. Pete was standing, as if he were trying to coast to a stop. I saw things meaningless now—for instance that the sun was sifted through leaves. There were trees we hadn't noticed. Under the leaves he seemed under water. A black car, a submarine with Belgian plates, parked at an angle, stirred to life. I saw sunlight deflected from six points on the paint. My view became discomposed, as if the sea were suddenly black and opaque and had splashed up over the policeman and the road, and I screamed, "He's going to open the door!" Everyone said later that I was mistaken, for why would the Belgian have started the motor, pulled out, and *then* flung open the door? He had stopped near a change office; perhaps he had forgotten his sunglasses, or a receipt. He started, stopped abruptly, hurled back the door. I saw that, and then I saw him driving away. No one had taken his number.

Strangers made Pete kneel and then stand, and they dusted the bicycle. They forced him to walk—where? Nobody wanted him. Into a pharmacy, finally. In a parrot's voice he said to the policeman, "Don't touch my elbow." The pharmacist said, "He can't stay here," for Pete was vomiting, but weakly—a weak coughing, like an infant's. I was in a crowd of about twenty people, a spectator with two cameras around my neck. In kind somebody's living room, Pete was placed on a couch with a cushion under his head and another under his dangling arm. The toothless old man turned up now, panting, with his waddling dog, and cried that we had a common thief there before us, and everyone listened and marveled until the old man spat on the carpet and was turned out.

When I timidly touched Pete, trying to wipe his face with a crumpled Kleenex (all I had), he thought I was one of the strangers. His mouth was a purple color, as if he had been in icy water. His eyes looked at me, but he was not looking out.

"Ambulance," said a doctor who had been fetched by the policeman. He spoke loudly and slowly, dealing with idiots.

"Yes," I heard, in English. "We must have an ambulance."

Everyone now inspected me. I was, plainly, responsible for something. For walking around the streets in shorts? Wasting bread? Conscious of my sweaty hair, my bare legs, my lack of Italian—my nakedness—I began explaining the true error of the day: "The train has gone, and all our things are on it. Our luggage. We've been staying up in that village—oh, what's the name of it, now? Where they make the white wine. I can't remember, no, I can't remember where we've been. I could find it, I could take you there; I've just forgotten what it's called. We were down here waiting for the train. To Nice. We had lots of time. The porter took our things and said he'd put them on the train for us.

He said the train would wait here, at the border, that it waited a long time. He was supposed to meet us at the place where you show your ticket. I guess for an extra tip. The train must have gone now. My purse is in the dufflebag up at the . . . I'll look in my husband's wallet. Of course that is my husband! Our passports must be on the train, too. Our traveler's checks are in our luggage, his and mine. We were just walking round taking pictures instead of sitting up there in the station. Anyway, there was no place to sit—only the bar, and it was smelly and dark."

No one believed a word of this, of course. Would you give your clothes, your passport, your traveler's checks to a porter? A man you had never seen in your life before? A bandit disguised as a porter, with a stolen cap on his head?

"You could not have taken that train without showing your passport," a careful foreign voice objected.

"What are you two, anyway?" said the man from the change office. His was a tough, old-fashioned movie-American accent. He was puffy-eyed and small, but he seemed superior to us, for he wore an impeccable shirt. Pete, on the sofa, looked as if he had been poisoned, or stepped on. "What are you?" the man from the change office said again. "Students? Americans? No? What, then? Swedes?"

I saw what the doctor had been trying to screen from me: a statue's marble eye.

The tourist who spoke the careful foreign English said, "Be careful of the pillows."

"What? What?" screamed the put-upon person who owned them.

"Blood is coming out of his ears," said the tourist, halting between words. "That is a bad sign." He seemed to search his memory for a better English word. "An *unfortunate* sign," he said, and put his hand over his mouth.

Pete's father and mother flew from Calgary when they had my cable. They made flawless arrangements by telephone, and knew exactly what to bring. They had a sunny room looking onto rusty palms and a strip of beach about a mile from where the accident had been. I sat against one of the windows and told them what I thought I remembered. I looked at the white walls, the white satin bedspreads, at Mrs. Higgins' spotless dressing case, and finally down at my hands.

His parents had not understood, until now, that ten days had gone by since Pete's death.

"What have you been doing, dear, all alone?" said Mrs. Higgins, gently.

"Just waiting, after I cabled you." They seemed to be expecting more. "I've been to the movies," I said.

From this room we could hear the shrieks of children playing on the sand.

"Are they orphans?" asked Mrs. Higgins, for they were little girls, dressed alike, with soft pink sun hats covering their heads.

"It seems to be a kind of summer camp," I said. "I was wondering about them, too."

"It would make an attractive picture," said Pete's mother, after a pause. "The blue sea, and the nuns, and all those bright hats. It would look nice in a dining room."

They were too sick to reproach me. My excuse for not having told them sooner was that I hadn't been thinking, and they didn't ask me for it. I could only repeat what seemed important now. "I don't want to go back home just yet" was an example. I was already in the future, which must have hurt them. "I have a girl friend in the embassy in Paris. I can stay with her." I scarcely moved my lips. They had to strain to hear. I held still, looking down at my fingers. I was very brown, sun streaks in my hair, more graceful than at my wedding, where I knew they had found me maladroit—a great lump of a Camp Fire Girl. That was how I had seen myself in my father-in-law's eyes. Extremes of shock had brought me near some ideal they had of prettiness. I appeared now much more the kind of girl they'd have wanted as Pete's wife.

So they had come for nothing. They were not to see

him, or bury him, or fetch home his bride. All I had to show them was a still unlabeled grave.

When I dared look at them, I saw their way of being was not Pete's. Neither had his soft selective stare. Mr. Higgins' eyes were a fanatic blue. He was thin and sunburned and unused to nonsense. Summer and winter he traveled with his wife in climates that were bad for her skin. She had the fair, papery coloring that requires constant vigilance. All this I knew because of Pete.

They saw his grave at the best time of day, in the late afternoon, with the light at a slant. The cemetery was in a valley between two plaster towns. A flash of the sea was visible, a corner of ultramarine. They saw a stone wall covered with roses, pink and white and near-white, open, without secrets. The hiss of traffic on the road came to us, softer than rain; then true rain came down, and we ran to our waiting taxi through a summer storm. Later they saw the station where Pete had left our luggage but never come back. Like Pete—as Pete had intended to—they were traveling to Nice. Under a glass shelter before the station I paused and said, "That was where it happened, down there." I pointed with my white glove. I was not as elegant as Mrs. Higgins, but I was not a source of embarrassment. I wore gloves, stockings, shoes.

The steep street under rain was black as oil. Everything was reflected upside down. The neon signs of the change office and the pharmacy swam deeply in the pavement.

"I'd like to thank the people who were so kind," said Mrs. Higgins. "Is there time? Shirley, I suppose you got their names?"

"Nobody was kind," I said.

"Shirley! We've met the doctor, and the minister, but you said there was a policeman, and a Dutch gentleman, and a lady—you were in this lady's living room."

"They were all there, but no one was kind."

"The bike's paid for?" asked Mr. Higgins suddenly.

"Yes, I paid. And I paid for having the sofa cushions cleaned."

What sofa cushions? What was I talking about? They

seemed petrified, under the glass shelter, out of the rain. They could not take their eyes away from the place I had said was *there*. They never blamed me, never by a word or a hidden meaning. I had explained, more than once, how the porter that day had not put our bags on the train after all but had stood waiting at the customs barrier, wondering what had become of us. I told them how I had found everything intact—passports and checks and maps and sweaters and shoes. . . . They could not grasp the importance of it. They knew that Pete had chosen me, and gone away with me, and they never saw him again. An unreliable guide had taken them to a foreign graveyard and told them, without evidence that now he was there.

"I still don't see how anyone could have thought Pete was stealing," said his mother. "What would Pete have wanted with someone's old bike?"

They were flying home from Nice. They loathed Italy now, and they had a special aversion to the sunny room where I had described Pete's death. We three sat in the restaurant at the airport, and they spoke quietly, considerately, because the people at the table next to ours were listening to a football match on a portable radio.

I closed my hand into a fist and let it rest on the table. I imagined myself at home, saying to my mother, "All right, real life has begun. What's your next prophecy?"

I was not flying with them. I was seeing them off. Mrs. Higgins sat poised and prepared in her linen coat, with her large handbag, and her cosmetics and airsickness tablets in her dressing case, and her diamond maple leaf so she wouldn't be mistaken for an American, and her passport ready to be shown to anyone. Pale gloves lay folded over the clasp of the dressing case. "You'll want to go to your own people, I know," she said. "But you have a home with us. You mustn't forget it." She paused. I said nothing, and so she continued, "What are you going to do, dear? I mean, after you have visited your friend. You mustn't be lonely."

I muttered whatever seemed sensible. "I'll have to get a job. I've never had one and I don't know anything much. I can't even type—not properly." Again they gave me this queer impression of expecting something more. What did they want? "Pete said it was no good learning anything if you couldn't type. He said it was the only useful thing he could do."

In the eyes of his parents was the same wound. I had told them something about him they hadn't known.

"Well, I understand," said his mother, presently. "At least, I think I do."

They imagine I want to be near the grave, I supposed. They think that's why I'm staying on the same side of the world. Pete and I had been waiting for a train: now I had taken it without him. I was waiting again. Even if I were to visit the cemetery every day, he would never speak. His last words had not been for me but to a policeman. He would have said something to me, surely, if everyone hadn't been in such a hurry to get him out of the way. His mind was quenched, and his body out of sight. "You don't love with your soul," I had cried to the old clergyman at the funeral—an offensive remark, judging from the look on his face as he turned it aside. Now I was careful. The destination of a soul was of no interest. The death of a voice—now, that was real. The Dutchman suddenly covering his mouth was horror, and a broken elbow was true pain. But I was careful; I kept this to myself.

"You're our daughter now," Pete's father said. "I don't think I want you to have to worry about a job. Not yet." Mr. Higgins happened to know my family's exact status. My father had not left us well off, and my mother had given everything she owned to a sect that did not believe in blood transfusions. She expected the end of the world, and would not eat an egg unless she had first met the hen. That was Mr. Higgins' view. "Shirley must work if that's what she wants to do," Mrs. Higgins said softly.

"I do want to!" I imagined myself, that day, in a river of people pouring into subways.

"I'm fixing something up for you, just the same,"

said Mr. Higgins hurriedly, as if he would not be interrupted by women.

Mrs. Higgins allowed her pale forehead to wrinkle, under her beige veil. Was it not better to struggle and to work, she asked. Wasn't that real life? Would it not keep Shirley busy, take her mind off her loss, her disappointment, her tragedy, if you like (though "tragedy" was not an acceptable way of looking at fate), if she had to think about her daily bread?

"The allowance I'm going to make her won't stop her from working," he said. "I was going to set something up for the kids anyway."

She seemed to approve: she had questioned him only out of some prudent system of ethics.

He said to me, "I always have to remember I could go any minute, just like that. I've got a heart." He tapped it—tapped his light suit. "Meantime you better start with this." He gave me the envelope that had been close to his heart until now. He seemed diffident, made ashamed by money, and by death, but it was he and not his wife who had asked if there was a hope that Pete had left a child. No, I had told him. I had wondered, too, but now I was sure. "Then Shirley is all we've got left," he had said to his wife, and I thought they seemed bankrupt, having nothing but me.

"If that's a check on a bank at home, it might take too long to clear," said his wife. "After all Shirley's been through, she needs a fair-sized sum right away."

"She's had that, Betty," said Mr. Higgins, smiling.

I had lived this: three round a table, the smiling parents. Pete had said, "They smile, they go on talking. You wonder what goes on."

"How you manage everything you do without a secretary with you all the time I just don't know," said his wife, all at once admiring him.

"You've been saying that for twenty-two years," he said.

"Twenty-three, now."

With this the conversation came to an end and they sat staring, puzzled, not overcome by life but suddenly lost to it, out of touch. The photograph Pete carried of his mother, that was in his wallet when he died, had been taken before her marriage, with a felt hat all to one side, and an organdie collar, and Ginger Rogers hair. It was easier to imagine Mr. Higgins young—a young Gary Cooper. My father-in-law's blue gaze rested on me now. Never in a million years would he have picked me as a daughter-in-law. I knew that; I understood. Pete was part of him, and Pete, with all the girls he had to choose from, had chosen me. When Mr. Higgins met my mother at the wedding, he thanked God, and was overheard being thankful, that the wedding was not in Calgary. Remembering my mother that day, with her glasses on her nose and a strange borrowed hat on her head, and recalling Mr. Higgins' face, I thought of words that would keep me from laughing. I found, at random, "threesome," "smother," "gambling," "habeas corpus," "sibling."

"How is your mother, Shirley?" said Mrs. Higgins.

"I had a letter. . . . She's working with a pendulum now."

"A pendulum?"

"Yes. A weight on a string, sort of. It makes a diagnosis—whether you've got something wrong with your stomach, if it's an ulcer, or what. She can use it to tell when you're pregnant and if the baby will be a girl or a boy. It depends whether it swings north-south or east-west."

"Can the pendulum tell who the father is?" said Mr. Higgins.

"They are useful for people who are afraid of doctors," said Mrs. Higgins, and she fingered her neat gloves, and smiled to herself. "Someone who won't hear the truth from a doctor will listen to any story from a woman with a pendulum or a piece of crystal."

"Or a stone that changes color," I said. "My mother had one of those. When our spaniel had mastoids it turned violet."

She glanced at me then, and caught in her breath, but her husband, by a certain amount of angry fidgeting, made us change the subject. That was the one mo-

ment she and I were close to each other—something to
do with quirky female humor.

Mr. Higgins did not die of a heart attack, as he had
confidently expected, but a few months after this Mrs.
Higgins said to her maid in the kitchen, "I've got a terrible pain in my head. I'd better lie down." Pete's father wrote, "She knew what the matter was, but she
never said. Typical." I inherited a legacy and some
jewelry from her, and wondered why. I had been care-
less about writing. I could not write the kind of letters
she seemed to want. How could I write to someone I
hardly knew about someone else who did not exist?
Mr. Higgins married the widow of one of his closest
friends—a woman six years older than he. They traveled to Europe for their wedding trip. I had a temporary
job as an interpreter in a department store. When my
father-in-law saw me in a neat suit, with his name, HIG-
GINS fastened to my jacket, he seemed to approve. He
was the only person then who did not say that I was
wasting my life and my youth and ought to go home.
The new Mrs. Higgins asked to be taken to an English-speaking hairdresser, and there, under the roaring
dryer, she yelled that Mr. Higgins may not have been
Pete's father. Perhaps he had been, perhaps he hadn't,
but one thing he was, and that was a saint. She came
out from under the helmet and said in a normal voice,
"Martin doesn't know I dye my hair." I wondered if he
had always wanted this short, fox-colored woman. The
new marriage might for years have been in the maquis
of his mind, and of Mrs. Higgins' life. She may have
known it as she sat in the airport that day, smiling to
herself, touching her unstained gloves. Mr. Higgins had
drawn up a new way of life, like a clean will with everyone he loved cut out. I was trying to draw up a will,
too, but I was patient, waiting, waiting for someone to
tell me what to write. He spoke of Pete conventionally,
in a sentimental way that forbade any feeling. Talking
that way was easier for both of us. We were both responsible for something—for surviving, perhaps. Once

he turned to me and said defiantly, "Well, she and Pete are together now, aren't they? And didn't they leave us here?"

THE ART OF KISSING

by *Mordecai Richler*

I wasn't quite eight years old when I first got into trouble over a girl. Her name was Charna, she lived upstairs from me, and we had played together without incident for years. Then, one spring afternoon, it seemed to me that I'd had enough of marbles and one-two-three-RED LIGHT!

"I've got it. We're going to play hospital. I'm the doctor, see, and you're the patient. Is anybody home at your place?"

"No. Why?"

"It's more of an indoors game, like. Come on."

I had only begun my preliminary examination when Charna's mother came home. My punishment was twofold. I had to go to bed without my supper and my mouth was washed out with soap. "You'd better speak to him," my mother said. "It's a lot worse when they pick up that kind of knowledge on the streets."

"It looks like he's very well-informed already," my father said.

If I wasn't it was clearly my mother's fault. Some years earlier she had assured me that babies came from Eaton's, and whenever she wanted to terrify me into better behavior she would pick up the phone and say, "I'm going to call Eaton's right this minute and have you exchanged for a girl."

My sister would compulsively add to my discomfort. "Maybe Eaton's won't take him back. This isn't bargain basement week, you know."

"I'll send him to Morgan's, then."

"Morgan's," my father would say, looking up from his evening paper, "doesn't hire Jews."

Duddy Kravitz cured me of the department store myth. He was very knowing about how to make babies. "You do it with a seed. You plant it, see."

"Where, but?"

"*Where?* Jesus H. Christ!"

Duddy was also a shrewd one for making it with the girls. When we were both twelve, just starting to go out on dates, he asked me, "When you to go a social, what do you do first?"

"Ask the prettiest girl for a dance."

"Prick."

Duddy explained that everybody went to the dance with the same notion. The thing to do, he said, was to make a big play for the *third* prettiest girl while all the others were hovering around number one. To further my education, he sold me a copy of The Art of Kissing for a dollar. "When you're through with it," he said, "and if it's still in good condition, you bring it back, and for another fifty cents I'll lend you a copy of How to Make Love. Okay?"

The first chapter I turned to in *The Art of Kissing* was called HOW TO APPROACH A GIRL.

In kissing a girl whose experience with osculation is limited, it is a good thing to work up to the kissing of the lips. Only an arrant fool seizes hold of such a girl, when they are comfortably seated on the sofa, and suddenly shoves his face into hers and smacks her lips. Naturally, the first thing he should do is arrange it so that the girl is seated against the arm of the sofa while he is seated at her side. In this way, she cannot edge away from him when he becomes serious in his attentions.

"Hey," my sister yelled, "how long are you going to be in there?"

"Hay is for horses."

"I've got to take a bath. I'm late."

If she flinches, don't worry. If she flinches and makes an outcry, don't worry. If she flinches, makes an outcry and tries to get up from the sofa, don't worry. Hold her, gently but firmly, and allay her fears with reassuring words.

"When you come out of there I'm going to break your neck."
"You, and what army?"

. . . then your next step is to flatter her in some way. All women like to be flattered. They like to be told they are beautiful even when the mirror throws the lie right back in their ugly faces.
Flatter her!
Ahead of you lies that which had been promised in your dreams, the tender, luscious lips of the girl you love. But don't sit idly by and watch her lips quiver.
Act!

"Why did you stuff the keyhole?"
"Because I've heard of snoopers like you before."
"Oh, *now* I get it. Now I know what you're doing in there. Why you filthy little thing, you'll stop growing."

. . . there has been raised quite a fuss in regard to whether one should close one's eyes while kissing or while being kissed. Personally, I disagree with those who advise closed eyes. To me, there is an additional thrill in seeing, before my eyes, the drama of bliss and pleasure as it is played on the face of my beloved.

"Awright," I said, opening the door, it's all your'n."
Our parties were usually held at a girl's house and it was the done thing to bring along the latest hit parade record. Favorites at the time were, *"Besame Mucho,"* *"Dance Ballerina, Dance,"* and *"Tico-Tico."* We would boogie for a while and gradually insist on more and more slow numbers, fox trots, until Duddy would leap

up, clear his throat, and say, "Hey, isn't the light in here hurting your eyes?"

Next, another boy would try a joke for size.

"Hear what happened to Barbara Stanwyck? Robert Taylor."

"What?"

"Robert Tayl'der, you jerk."

"Yeah, and what about Helena Rubenstein?"

"So?"

"Max Factor."

But with the coming of the party-going stage complications set in for me, anyway. Suddenly, my face was encrusted with pimples. I was also small and puny for my age. And, according to the author of *The Art of Kissing,* it was essential for the man to be taller than the woman.

> He must be able to sweep her into his strong arms, and tower over her, and look down into her eyes, and cup her chin in his fingers and then, bend over her face and plant his eager, virile lips on her moist, slightly parted, inviting ones. And, all of these are impossible when the woman is taller than he is. For when the situation is reversed the kiss becomes a ludicrous banality, the physical mastery is gone, everything is gone, but the fact that two lips are touching two other lips. Nothing can be more disappointing.

I had difficulty getting a second date with the same girl and usually the boys had to provide for me. Duddy would get on the phone, hustling some unsuspecting girl, saying, "There's this friend of mine in from Detroit. Would you like to go to a dance with him on Saturday night?"

Grudgingly, the girl would acquiesce, but afterward she would complain "Why didn't you tell me he was such a runt?"

So Duddy took me aside. "Why don't you try body-building or something?"

I wrote to Joe Weider, the Trainer of Champions,

and he promptly sent me a magazine called *How to Build* A STRONG MUSCULAR BODY *with* WEIDER *as Your Leader*.

Be MASCULINE!
Be DESIRED!
Look in the mirror—ARE YOU
really attractive to LOVE?

What does the mirror reveal? A sickly, pimply stringbean of a fellow—OR—a VIBRANT, masculine-looking, romance-attracting WEIDER MAN? If you were a vivacious, lovely, young woman, which would YOU choose? the tired, listless, drab chap, or the strong, energetic, forceful MAN—able to protect his sweetheart and give her the best things in life?

Alas, I couldn't afford the price of making Weider my leader. I tried boxing at the Y instead and was knocked out my second time in the gym ring. I would have persevered, however, if not for the fact that my usual sparring partner, one Herkey Samuels, had a nasty trick of blowing his nose on his glove immediately before he punched me. Besides, I wasn't getting any taller. I wasn't exactly stunted, but a number of the other boys had already begun to shave. The girls had started to use lipstick and high heels, not to mention brassieres.

Arty, Stan, Hershey, Gas, and I were drifting through high school at the time, and there we got a jolt. All at once the neighborhood girls, whom we had been pursuing loyally for years, dropped us for older boys. Boys with jobs, McGill boys—anybody—so long as he was eighteen and had the use of a car.

"They think it's such a big deal," Arty said, "because suddenly they've begun to sprout tits."

"Did you see the guy who came to pick up Helen? The world's number one *shmock*."

"What about Libby's date?"

Disconsolate, we would squat on the outside steps on

Saturday nights and watch the girls come tripping out in their party dresses, always to settle into a stranger's car, and swim off into the night without even a wave for us. Obviously, a double-feature at the Rialto, a toasted tomato sandwich and a Coke afterwards, no longer constituted a bona fide date. That, one of the girls scathingly allowed, was okay "for children" like us, but nowadays they went to fraternity dances or nightclubs and, to hear them tell it, sipped Singapore Slings endlessly.

"Let them have their lousy little fling," Arty advised. "Soon they'll come back crawling for a date. You wait."

We waited and waited until, disheartened, we shunned girls altogether for a period. Instead, we took to playing blackjack on Saturday nights.

"Boy, when I think of all the *mezuma* I blew on Gitel."

"Skip it. I'd rather lose money to friend, a real friend," Duddy said, scooping up another pot, "than spend it on a girl any time."

"They're getting lousy reps, those whores, running around with strange guys in cars. You know what they do? They park in country lanes. . . ."

"I beg your hard-on?"

"I'd just hate to see a sweet kid like Libby getting into trouble. If you know what I mean?"

Duddy told us about Japanese girls and how they jiggled themselves in swinging hammocks. Nobody believed him.

"I've got the book it's written in," he insisted, "and I'm willing to rent it out."

"Hey," Stan said, "you know why Jewish girls have to wear two-piece bathing suits?"

Nobody knew.

"Mustn't mix the milk with the meat."

"Very funny," Duddy said. "Now deal the cards."

"I'll tell you something that's a fact," Arty said. "Monks never go out with dames. For all their lives—"

"Monks are Catholics, you jerk."

Once poker palled on us, we began to frequent St.

Catherine Street on Saturday nights, strutting up and down the neon-lit street in gangs, stopping here for a hot dog and there to play the pinball machines, but never forgetting our primary purpose, which was to taunt the girls as they came strolling past. We tried the Palais d'Or a couple of times, just to see what we could pick up. "Whatever you do," Duddy warned us beforehand, "never give them your right name." But most of the girls shrugged us off. "Send round your older brother, sonny." So we began to go to Belmont Park, hoping to root out younger, more available girls. We danced to the music of Mark Kenny and His Western Gentlemen and at least had some fun in the horror houses and on the rides. We took to playing snooker a good deal.

"A poolroom bum," my father said. "Is that why I'm educating you?"

Then I fell in love.

Zelda was an Outremont girl with a lovely golden head and long dark lashes. The night before our first date I consulted The Art of Kissing on HOW TO KISS GIRLS WITH DIFFERENT SIZES OF MOUTHS.

Another question which must be settled at this time concerns the size of the kissee's mouth. Where the girl's mouth is of the tiny rosebud type, then one need not worry about what to do. However, there are many girls whose lips are broad and generous, whose lips are on the order of Joan Crawford's, for instance. The technique in kissing such lips is different. For, were one to allow his lips to remain centered, there would be wide expanses of lips untouched and, therefore, wasted. In such cases, instead of remaining adhered to the center of the lips, the young man should lift up his lips a trifle and begin to travel around the girl's lips, stopping a number of times to drop a firm kiss in passing. When you have made a complete round of the lips, return immediately to the center bud and feast there. Sip the kissee's honey.

I took Zelda to a Y dance and afterward, outside her house, I attempted to kiss her broad and generous lips.

"I thought," Zelda said, withdrawing stiffly, "you were a more serious type."

And so once more Duddy had to find me dates. One or another of his endless spill of girls always had a cousin with thick glasses—"She's really lots of fun, you know,"—or a kid sister—"Honestly, with high heels she looks sixteen."

THE YELLOW SWEATER

by *Hugh Garner*

He stepped on the gas when he reached the edge of town. The big car took hold of the pavement and began to eat up the miles on the straight, almost level, highway. With his elbow stuck through the open window he stared ahead at the shimmering grayness of the road. He felt heavy and pleasantly satiated after his good small-town breakfast, and he shifted his bulk in the seat, at the same time brushing some cigar ash from the front of his salient vest. In another four hours he would be home—a day ahead of himself this trip, but with plenty to show the office for last week's work. He unconsciously patted the wallet resting in the inside pocket of his jacket as he thought of the orders he had taken.

Four thousand units to Slanders . . . his second-best line too . . . four thousand at twelve percent . . . four hundred and eighty dollars! He rolled the sum over in his mind as if tasting it, enjoying its tartness like a kid with a gumdrop.

He drove steadily for nearly an hour, ignorant of the smell of spring in the air, pushing the car ahead with his mind as well as with his foot against the pedal. The success of his trip and the feeling of power it gave him carried him along toward the triumph of his homecoming.

Outside a small village he was forced to slow down for a road repair crew. He punched twice on the horn as he passed them, basking in the stares of the yokels who looked up from their shovels, and smiling at the envy showing on their faces.

A rather down-at-heel young man carrying an army kitbag stepped out from the office of a filling station and gave him the thumb. He pretended not to see the gesture, and pressed down slightly on the gas so that the car began to purr along the free and open road.

It was easy to see that the warm weather was approaching, he thought. The roads were becoming cluttered up once more with hitchhikers. Why the government didn't clamp down on them was more than he could understand. Why should people pay taxes so that other lazy bums could fritter away their time roaming the country, getting free rides, going God knows where? They were dangerous too. It was only the week before that two of them had beaten up and robbed a man on this very same road. They stood a fat chance of *him* picking them up.

And yet they always thumbed him, or almost always. When they didn't he felt cheated, as a person does when he makes up his mind not to answer another's greeting, only to have them pass by without noticing him.

He glanced at his face in the rear-view mirror. It was a typical middle-aged businessman's face, plump and well-barbered, the shiny skin stretched taut across the cheeks. It was a face that was familiar to him not only from his possession of it, but because it was also the face of most of his friends. What was it the speaker at that service club luncheon had called it? "The physiognomy of success."

As he turned a bend in the road he saw the girl about a quarter of a mile ahead. She was not on the pavement, but was walking slowly along the shoulder of the highway, bent over with the weight of the bag she was carrying. He slowed down, expecting her to turn and thumb him, but she plodded on as though impervious to his approach. He sized her up as he drew near. She was young by the look of her back . . . stocking seams straight . . . heels muddy but not rundown. As he passed he stared at her face. She was a good-looking kid, probably eighteen or nineteen.

It was the first time in years that he had slowed down for a hiker. His reasons evaded him, and whether it was the feel of the morning, the fact of his going home, or the girl's apparent independence, he could not tell. Perhaps it was a combination of all three, plus the boredom of a long drive. It might be fun to pick her up, to cross-examine her while she was trapped in the seat beside him.

Easing the big car to a stop about fifty yards in front of her he looked back through the mirror. She kept glancing at the car, but her pace had not changed, and she came on as though she had expected him to stop. For a moment he was tempted to drive on again, angered by her indifference. She was not a regular hitchhiker or she would have waited at the edge of town instead of setting out to walk while carrying such a heavy bag. But there was something about her that compelled him to wait—something which aroused in him an almost forgotten sense of adventure, an eagerness not experienced for years.

She opened the right rear door, saying at the same time, "Thank you very much, sir," in a frightened little voice.

"Put your bag in the back. That's it, on the floor," he ordered, turning towards her with his hand along the back of the seat. "Come and sit up here."

She did as he commanded, sitting very stiff and straight against the door. She was small, almost fragile, with long dark hair that waved where it touched upon the collar of her light-colored topcoat. Despite the warmth of the morning the coat was buttoned, and she held it to her in a way that suggested modesty or fear.

"Are you going very far?" he asked, looking straight

ahead through the windshield, trying not to let the question sound too friendly.

"To the city," she answered, with the politeness and eagerness of the recipient of a favor.

"For a job?"

"Well, not exactly—" she began. Then she said, "Yes, for a job."

As they passed the next group of farm buildings she stared hard at them, her head turning with her eyes until they were too far back to be seen.

Something about her reminded him of his eldest daughter, but he shrugged off the comparison. It was silly of him to compare the two, one a hitchhiking farm skivvy and the other one soon to come home from finishing school. In his mind's eye he could see the photograph of his daughter Shirley that hung on the wall of the living room. It had been taken with a color camera during the Easter vacation, and in it Shirley was wearing a bright yellow sweater.

"Do you live around here?" he asked, switching his thoughts back to the present.

"I was living about a mile down the road from where you picked me up."

"Sick of the farm?" he asked.

"No." She shook her head slowly, seriously.

"Have you anywhere to go in the city?"

"I'll get a job somewhere."

He turned then and got his first good look at her face. She was pretty, he saw, with the country girl's good complexion, her features small and even. "You're young to be leaving home like this," he said.

"That wasn't my home," she murmured. "I was living with my Aunt Bernice and her husband."

He noticed that she did not call the man her uncle.

"You sound as though you don't like the man your aunt is married to?"

"I hate him!" she whispered vehemently.

To change the subject he said, "You've chosen a nice day to leave, anyhow."

"Yes."

He felt a slight tingling along his spine. It was the

same feeling he had experienced once when sitting in the darkened interior of a movie house beside a strange yet, somehow, intimate young woman. The feeling that if he wished he had only to let his hand fall along her leg . . .

"You're not very talkative," he said, more friendly now.

She turned quickly and faced him. "I'm sorry. I was thinking about—about a lot of things."

"It's too nice a morning to think of much," he said. "Tell me more about your reasons for leaving home."

"I wanted to get away, that's all."

He stared at her again, letting his eyes follow the contours of her body. "Don't tell me you're in trouble?" he asked.

She lowered her eyes to her hands. They were engaged in twisting the clasp on a cheap black handbag. "I'm not in trouble like that," she said slowly, although the tone of her voice belied her words.

He waited for her to continue. There was a sense of power in being able to question her like this without fear of having to answer any questions himself. He said, "There can't be much else wrong. Was it boy trouble?"

"Yes, that's it," she answered hastily.

"Where's the boy? Is he back there or in the city?"

"Back there," she answered.

He was aware of her nearness, of her young body beside him on the seat. "You're too pretty to worry about one boy," he said, trying to bridge the gap between them with unfamiliar flattery.

She did not answer him, but smiled nervously in homage to his remark.

They drove on through the morning, and by skillful questioning he got her to tell him more about her life. She had been born near the spot where he had picked her up, she said. She was an orphan, eighteen years old, who for the past three years had been living on her aunt's farm. On his part he told her a little about his job, but not too much. He spoke in generalities, yet let her see how important he was in his field.

They stopped for lunch at a drive-in restaurant outside a small town. While they were eating he noticed that some of the other customers were staring at them. It angered him until he realized that they probably thought she was his mistress. This flattered him and he tried to imagine that it was true. During the meal he became animated, and he laughed loudly at his *risqué* little jokes.

She ate sparingly, politely, not knowing what to do with her hands between courses. She smiled at the things he said, even at the remarks that were obviously beyond her.

After they had finished their lunch he said to her jovially, "Here, we've been traveling together for two hours and we don't even know each other's names yet."

"Mine's Marie. Marie Edwards."

"You can call me Tom," he said expansively.

When he drew out his wallet to pay the check he was careful to cover the initials G.G.M. with the palm of his hand.

As they headed down the highway once again, Marie seemed to have lost some of her timidity and she talked and laughed with him as though he were an old friend. Once he stole a glance at her through the corner of his eye. She was staring ahead as if trying to unveil the future that was being overtaken by the onrushing car.

"A penny for your thoughts, Marie," he said.

"I was just thinking how nice it would be to keep going like this forever."

"Why?" he asked, her words revealing an unsuspected facet to her personality.

"I dunno," she answered, rubbing the palm of her hand along the upholstery of the seat in a gesture that was wholly feminine. "It seems so—safe here, somehow." She smiled as though apologizing for thinking such things. "It seems as if nothing bad could ever catch up to me again."

He gave her a quick glance before staring ahead at the road once more.

The afternoon was beautiful, the warm dampness of the fields bearing aloft the smell of uncovered earth and budding plants. The sun-warmed pavement sang like muted violins beneath the spinning tires of the car. The clear air echoed the sound of life and growth and the urgency of spring.

As the miles clicked off, and they were brought closer to their inevitable parting, an idea took shape in his mind and grew with every passing minute. Why bother hurrying home, he asked himself. After all he hadn't notified his wife to expect him, and he wasn't due back until tomorrow.

He wondered how the girl would react if he should suggest postponing the rest of the trip overnight. He would make it worth her while. There was a tourist camp on the shore of a small lake about twenty miles north of the highway. No one would be the wiser, he told himself. They were both fancy free.

The idea excited him, yet he found himself too timid to suggest it. He tried to imagine how he must appear to the girl. The picture he conjured up was of a mature figure, inclined to stoutness, much older than she was in years but not in spirit. Many men his age had formed liaisons with young women. In fact it was the accepted thing among some of the other salesmen he knew.

But there remained the voicing of the question. She appeared so guileless, so—innocent of his intentions. And yet it was hard to tell; she wasn't as innocent as she let on.

She interrupted his train of thought. "On an afternoon like this I'd like to paddle my feet in a stream," she said.

"I'm afraid the water would be pretty cold."

"Yes, it would be cold, but it'd be nice too. When we were kids we used to go paddling in the creek behind the schoolhouse. The water was strong with the spring freshet, and it would tug at our ankles and send a warm ticklish feeling up to our knees. The smooth pebbles on the bottom would make us twist our feet, and we'd try to grab them with our toes. . . . I guess I must sound crazy," she finished.

No longer hesitant he said, "I'm going to turn the car

into one of these side roads, Marie. On a long trip I usually like to park for a while under some trees. It makes a little break in the journey."

She nodded her head happily. "That would be nice," she said.

He turned the car off the highway and they traveled north along the road that curved gently between wide stretches of steaming fields. The speed of the car was seemingly increased by the drumming of gravel against the inside of the fenders.

It was time to bring the conversation back to a more personal footing, so he asked. "What happened between you and your boyfriend, Marie?" He had to raise his voice above the noise of the hurtling stones.

"Nothing much," she answered, hesitating as if making up the answer. "We had a fight, that's all."

"Serious?"

"I guess so."

"What happened? Did he try to get a little gay maybe?"

She had dropped her head, and he could see the color rising along her neck and into her hair behind her ears.

"Does that embarrass you?" he asked, taking his hand from the wheel and placing it along the collar of her coat.

She tensed herself at his touch and tried to draw away, but he grasped her shoulder and pulled her against him. He could feel the fragility of her beneath his hand and the trembling of her skin beneath the cloth of her coat. The odor of her hair and of some cheap scent filled his nostrils.

She cried, "Don't, please!" and broke away from the grip of his hand. She inched herself into the far corner of the seat again.

"You're a little touchy, aren't you?" he asked, trying to cover up his embarrassment at being repulsed so quickly.

"Why did you have to spoil it?"

His frustration kindled a feeling of anger against her. He knew her type all right. Pretending that butter wouldn't melt in her mouth, while all the time she was secretly laughing at him for being the sucker who picked her up, bought her a lunch, and drove her into town. She couldn't fool him; he'd met her type before.

He swung the car down a narrow lane, and they flowed along over the rutted wheel tracks beneath a flimsy ceiling of budding trees.

"Where are we going?" she asked, her voice apprehensive now.

"Along here a piece," he answered, trying to keep his anger from showing.

"Where does this road lead?"

"I don't know. Maybe there's a stream you can paddle in."

There was a note of relief in her voice as she said, "Oh! I didn't mean for us—for you to find a stream."

"You don't seem to know *what* you mean, do you?"

She became silent then and seemed to shrink farther into the corner.

The trees got thicker, and soon they found themselves in the middle of a small wood. The branches of the hardwoods were mottled green, their buds flicking like fingers in the breeze. He brought the car to a stop against the side of the road.

The girl watched him, the corners of her mouth trembling with fear. She slid her hand up the door and grabbed the handle. He tried to make his voice matter-of-fact as he said, "Well, here we are."

Her eyes ate into his face like those of a mesmerized rabbit watching a snake.

He opened a glove compartment and pulled out a package of cigarettes. He offered the package to her, but she shook her head.

"Let's get going," she pleaded.

"What, already? Maybe we should make a day of it."

She did not speak, but the question stood in her eyes. He leaned back against the seat, puffing on his cigarette. "There's a tourist camp on a lake a few miles north of here. We could stay there and go on to the city tomorrow."

She stifled a gasp. "I can't. I didn't think—I had no idea when we—"

He pressed his advantage. "Why can't you stay? Nobody'll know. I may be in a position to help you afterward. You'll need help, you know."

"No. No, I couldn't," she answered. Her eyes filled with tears.

He had not expected her to cry. Perhaps he had been wrong in his estimation of her. He felt suddenly bored with the whole business, and ashamed of the feelings she had ignited in him.

"Please take me back to the highway," she said, pulling a carefully folded handkerchief from her handbag.

"Sure. In a few minutes." He wanted time to think things out; to find some way of saving face.

"You're just like he was," she blurted out, her words distorted by her handkerchief. "You're all the same."

Her outburst frightened him. "Marie," he said, reaching over to her. He wanted to quiet her, to show her that his actions had been the result of an old man's foolish impulse.

As soon as his hand touched her shoulder she gave a short cry and twisted the door handle. "No. No, please!" she cried.

"Marie, come here!" he shouted, trying to stop her. He grabbed her by the shoulder, but she tore herself from his grasp and fell through the door.

She jumped up from the road and staggered back through the grass into the belt of trees. Her stockings and the bottom of her coat were brown with mud.

"Don't follow me!" she yelled.

"I'm not going to follow you. Come back here and I'll drive you back to the city."

"No you don't! You're the same as he was!" she cried. "I know your tricks!"

He looked about him at the deserted stretch of trees, wondering if anybody could be listening. It would place him in a terrible position to be found with her like this. Pleading with her he said, "Come on, Marie. I've got to go."

She began to laugh hysterically, her voice reverberating through the trees.

"Marie, come on," he coaxed. "I won't hurt you."

"No! Leave me alone. Please leave me alone!"

His pleas only seemed to make things worse. "I'm going," he said hurriedly, pulling the car door shut.

"Just leave me alone!" she cried. Then she began sobbing, "Bernice! Bernice!"

What dark fears had been released by his actions of the afternoon he did not know, but they frightened and horrified him. He turned the car around in the narrow lane and let it idle for a moment as he waited, hoping she would change her mind. She pressed herself deeper into the trees, wailing at the top of her voice.

From behind him came a racking noise from down the road, and he looked back and saw a tractor coming around a bend. A man was driving it and there was another one riding behind. He put the car in gear and stepped on the gas.

Before the car reached the first turn beneath the trees he looked back. The girl was standing in the middle of the road beside the tractor and she was pointing his way and talking to the men. He wondered if they had his license number, and what sort of a story she was telling them.

He had almost reached the highway again before he remembered her suitcase standing on the floor behind the front seat. His possession of it seemed to tie him to the girl; to make him partner to her terror. He pulled the car to a quick stop, leaned over the back of the seat and picked the suitcase up from the floor. Opening the door he tossed it lightly to the side of the road with a feeling of relief. The frail clasp on the cheap bag opened as it hit the ground and its contents spilled in the ditch. There was a framed photograph, some letters and papers held together with an elastic band, a comb and brush, and some clothing, including a girl's yellow sweater.

"I'm no thief," he said, pushing the car into motion again, trying to escape from the sight of the opened bag. He wasn't to blame for the things that had happened to her. It wasn't his fault that her stupid little life was spilled there in the ditch.

"I've done nothing wrong," he said, as if pleading his case with himself. But there was a feeling of obscene guilt beating his brain like a reiteration. Something of hers seemed to attach itself to his memory. Then suddenly he knew what it was—the sweater, the damned yellow sweater. His hands trembled around the wheel as he sent the car hurtling towards the safe anonymity of the city.

He tried to recapture his feelings of the morning, but when he looked at himself in the mirror all he saw was the staring face of a fat frightened old man.

TO SET OUR HOUSE IN ORDER

by *Margaret Laurence*

When the baby was almost ready to be born, something went wrong and my mother had to go to the hospital two weeks before the expected time. I was wakened by her crying in the night, and then I heard my father's footsteps as he went downstairs to phone. I stood in the doorway of my room, shivering and listening, wanting to go to my mother, but afraid to go lest there be some sight there more terrifying than I could bear.

"Hello, Paul?" my father said, and I knew he was talking to Doctor Cates. "It's Beth. I'm only thinking of what happened the last time, and another like that would be— Yes, I think that would be the best thing. Okay, make it as soon as you can."

He came back upstairs, looking bony and disheveled in his pajamas, and running his fingers through his sand-colored hair. At the top of the stairs he came face to face with Grandmother MacLeod, who was standing there in her quilted black-satin dressing gown, her light figure held straight and poised, as though she was unaware that her hair was bound grotesquely like white-feathered wings in the snare of her coarse nighttime hairnet.

"What is it, Ewen?"

"It's all right, Mother. Beth's having . . . a little trouble. I'm going to take her to the hospital. You go back to bed."

"I told you," Grandmother MacLeod said in her clear voice, never loud, but distinct and ringing like the tap of a silver spoon on a crystal goblet, "I did tell you, Ewen, did I not, that you should have got a girl in to help her with the housework? She should have rested more."

"I couldn't afford to get anyone in," my father said. "If you thought she should've rested more, why didn't you ever . . . Oh, God, I'm out of my mind tonight. Just go back to bed, Mother, please. I must get back to Beth."

When my father went down to open the front door for Doctor Cates, my need overcame my fear and I slipped into my parents' room. My mother's black hair, so neatly pinned up during the day, was startlingly spread across the white pillowcase. I stared at her, not speaking, and then she smiled, and I rushed from the doorway and buried my head upon her.

"It's all right, Vanessa," she said. "Honey, the baby's just going to come a little early, that's all. You'll be all right. Grandmother MacLeod will be here."

"How can she get the meals?" I wailed, fixing on the first thing that came to mind. "She never cooks. She doesn't know how."

"Yes, she does," my mother said. "She can cook as well as anyone when she has to. She's just never had to very much, that's all. Don't worry, she'll keep everything in order, and then some."

My father and Doctor Cates came in, and I had to go, without saying anything I had wanted to say. I went back to my own room and lay with the shadows all around me, listening to the night murmurings that always went on in that house, sounds that never had a source—rafters and beams contracting in the dry air, perhaps, or mice in the walls, or a sparrow that had flown into the attic through the broken skylight there. After a while, although I would not have believed it possible, I slept.

The next morning, though summer vacation was not quite over, I did not feel like going out to play with any of the kids. I was very superstitious and felt that if I left the house, even for a few hours, some disaster would overtake my mother. I did not, of course, mention this to Grandmother MacLeod, for she did not believe in the existence of fear, or if she did, she never let on.

I spent the morning morbidly, seeking hidden places in the house. There were many of these—odd-shaped nooks under the stairs, and dusty tunnels and forgotten recesses in the heart of the house where the only things actually to be seen were drab oil paintings stacked upon the rafters and trunks full of outmoded clothing and old photograph albums. But the unseen presences in these secret places I knew to be those of every person, young or old, who had ever belonged to the house and had died, including Uncle Roderick, who got killed on the Somme, and the baby, who would have been my sister if only she had come to life. Grandfather MacLeod, who had died a year after I was born, was present in the house in a more tangible form. At the top of the main stairs hung a mammoth picture of a darkly uniformed man riding a horse whose prancing stance and dilated nostrils suggested the battle was not yet over, that it might continue until Judgment Day. The stern man was the Duke of Wellington, but at the time I believed him to be my Grandfather MacLeod, still keeping an eye on things.

We had moved in with Grandmother MacLeod when the depression got bad and she could no longer afford a housekeeper; yet the MacLeod house never seemed like home to me. Its dark-red brick was grown over at the front with Virginia creeper that turned crimson in the fall until you could hardly tell brick from leaves. It boasted a small tower in which Grandmother MacLeod kept a weedlike collection of anemic ferns. The veranda was embellished with a profusion of wrought-iron scrolls, and the circular rose window upstairs contained many-colored glass that permitted an outlooking eye to see the world as a place of absolute sapphire or emerald or, if one wished to look with a jaundiced eye, a hateful yellow. In Grandmother MacLeod's opinion, these features gave the house style. To me, they seemed fascinating, but rather as the paraphernalia of an alchemist's laboratory might be, things to be peered at curiously but with caution, just in case.

Inside, a multitude of doors led to rooms where my presence, if not actually forbidden, was not encouraged. One was Grandmother MacLeod's bedroom, with its stale and old-smelling reek of medicines and lavender sachets. Here resided her monogrammed dresser silver —brush and mirror, nail buffer and button hook and scissors—none of which must even be fingered by me now, for she meant to leave them to me in her will and intended to hand them over in their original flawless and unused condition. Here, too, were the silver-framed photographs of Uncle Roderick—as a child, as a boy, as a man in his army uniform. The massive walnut spool bed had obviously been designed for queens or giants, and my tiny grandmother used to lie within it all day when she had migraines, contriving somehow to look like a giant queen.

The day my mother went to the hospital, Grandmother MacLeod called me at lunchtime, and when I appeared, smudged with dust from the attic, she looked at me distastefully.

"For mercy's sake, Vanessa, what have you been doing with yourself? Get washed this minute. Not that way. Use the back stairs, young lady. Get along now. Oh, your father phoned."

I swung around. "What did he say? How is she? Is the baby born?"

"Curiosity killed the cat," Grandmother MacLeod said, frowning. "I cannot understand Beth and Ewen telling you all these things at your age. What sort of vulgar person you'll grow up to be, I dare not think. No, it's not born yet. Your mother's just the same. No change."

I looked at my grandmother, not wanting to appeal to her, but unable to stop myself. "Will she—will she be all right?"

Grandmother MacLeod straightened her already straight back. "If I said definitely yes, Vanessa, that would be a lie, and the MacLeods do not tell lies, as I have tried to impress upon you before. What happens is God's will. 'The Lord giveth, and the Lord taketh away.'"

Appalled, I turned away so she would not see my face. Surprisingly, I heard her sigh and felt her papery white and perfectly manicured hand upon my shoulder.

"When your Uncle Roderick got killed," she said, "I thought I would die. But I didn't die, Vanessa."

At lunch she chatted animatedly, and I realized she was trying to cheer me in the only way she knew. "When I married your Grandfather MacLeod, he said to me, 'Eleanor, don't think because we're going to the prairies that I expect you to live roughly. You're used to a proper house, and you shall have one.' He was as good as his word. Before we'd been in Manawaka three years, he'd had this place built. He earned a good deal of money in his time, your grandfather. He soon had more patients than either of the other doctors. We ordered our dinner service and all our silver from Birks in Toronto. We had resident help in those days, of course, and never had less than twelve guests for dinner parties. When I had a tea, it would always be twenty or thirty. Never any less than half a dozen different kinds of cake were ever served in this house. Well, no one seems to bother much these days. Too lazy, I suppose."

"Too broke," I suggested. "That's what Dad says."

"I can't bear slang," Grandmother MacLeod said. "If you mean hard up, why don't you say so? It's mainly a question of management, anyway. My accounts were always in good order, and so was my house. No unexpected expenses that couldn't be met, no fruit cellar running out of preserves before the winter was over. Do you know what my father used to say to me when I was a girl?"

"No," I said. "What?"

" 'God loves order,' " Grandmother replied with emphasis. "You remember that, Vanessa, 'God loves order.' He wants each one of us to set our house in order. I've never forgotten those words of my father's. I was a MacInnes before I got married. The MacInnes is a very ancient clan, the lairds of Morven and the constables of the Castle of Kinlochaline. Did you finish that book I gave you?"

"Yes," I said. Then, feeling additional comment was called for, I added, "It was a swell book, Grandmother."

This was somewhat short of the truth. I had been hoping for her cairngorm brooch on my tenth birthday and had received instead the plaid-bound volume entitled *The Clans and Tartans of Scotland*. Most of it was too boring to read, but I had looked up the motto of my own family and those of some of my friends' families. *Be then a wall of brass. Learn to suffer. Consider the end. Go carefully*. I had not found any of these slogans reassuring. What with Mavis Duncan learning to suffer, and Laura Kennedy considering the end, and Patsy Drummond going carefully, and I spending my time in being a wall of brass, it did not seem to me that any of us were going to lead very interesting lives. I did not say this to Grandmother MacLeod.

"The MacInnes motto is *Pleasure arises from work*," I said.

"Yes," she agreed proudly. "And an excellent motto it is, too. One to bear in mind."

She rose from the table, rearranging on her bosom the looped ivory beads that held the pendant on which a full-blown ivory rose was stiffly carved.

"I hope Ewen will be pleased," she said.

"What at?"

"Didn't I tell you?" Grandmother MacLeod said. "I hired a girl this morning for the housework. She's to start tomorrow."

When my father got home that evening, Grandmother MacLeod told him her good news. He ran a hand distractedly across his forehead.

"I'm sorry, Mother, but you'll just have to unhire her. I can't possibly pay anyone."

"It seems odd," Grandmother MacLeod snapped, "that you can afford to eat chicken four times a week."

"Those chickens," my father said in an exasperated voice, "are how people are paying their bills. The same with the eggs and the milk. That scrawny turkey that arrived yesterday was for Logan MacCardney's appendix, if you must know. We probably eat better than any family in Manawaka, except Niall Cameron's. People can't entirely dispense with doctors or undertakers. That doesn't mean to say I've got any cash. Look, Mother, I don't know what's happening with Beth. Paul thinks he may have to do a Caesarean. Can't we leave all this? Just leave the house alone. Don't touch it. What does it matter?"

"I have never lived in a messy house, Ewen," Grandmother MacLeod said, "and I don't intend to begin now."

"Oh, Lord," my father said. "Well, I'll phone Edna, I guess, and see if she can give us a hand, although God knows she's got enough, with the Connor house and her parents to look after."

"I don't fancy having Edna Connor in to help," Grandmother MacLeod said.

"Why not?" my father shouted. "She's Beth's sister, isn't she?"

"She speaks in such a slangy way," Grandmother MacLeod said. "I have never believed she was a good influence on Vanessa. And there is no need for you to raise your voice to me, Ewen, if you please."

I could barely control my rage. I thought my father would surely rise to Aunt Edna's defense. But he did not.

"It'll be all right," he soothed her. "She'd only be here for part of the day, Mother. You could stay in your room."

Aunt Edna strode in the next morning. The sight of

her bobbed black hair and her grin made me feel better at once. She hauled out the carpet sweeper and the weighted polisher and got to work. I dusted while she polished and swept, and we got through the living room and front hall in next to no time.

"Where's her royal highness, kiddo?" she inquired.

"In her room," I said. "She's reading the catalog from Robinson and Cleaver."

"Good glory, not again?" Aunt Edna cried. "The last time she ordered three linen tea cloths and two dozen napkins. It came to fourteen dollars. Your mother was absolutely frantic. I guess I shouldn't be saying this."

"I knew anyway," I assured her. "She was at the lace-handkerchief section when I took up her coffee."

"Let's hope she stays there. Heaven forbid she should get onto the banqueting cloths. Well, at least she believes the Irish are good for two things—manual labor and linen-making. She's never forgotten Father used to be a blacksmith, before he got the hardware store. Can you beat it? I wish it didn't bother Beth."

"Does it?" I asked and immediately realized this was a wrong move, for Aunt Edna was suddenly scrutinizing me.

"We're making you grow up before your time," she said. "Don't pay any attention to me, Nessa. I must've got up on the wrong side of the bed this morning."

But I was unwilling to leave the subject. "All the same," I said thoughtfully, "Grandmother MacLeod's family were the lairds of Morven and the constables of the Castle of Kinlochaline. I bet you didn't know that."

Aunt Edna snorted. "Castle, my foot. She was born in Ontario, just like your Grandfather Connor, and her father was a horse doctor. Come on, kiddo, we'd better shut up and get down to business here."

We worked in silence for a while.

"Aunt Edna," I said at last, "what about Mother? Why won't they let me go and see her?"

"Kids aren't allowed to visit maternity patients. It's tough for you, I know. Look, Nessa, don't worry. If it doesn't start tonight, they're going to do the operation. She's getting the best of care."

I stood there, holding the feather duster like a dead bird in my hands. I was not aware that I was going to speak until the words came out. "I'm scared," I said.

Aunt Edna put her arms around me, and her face looked all at once stricken and empty of defenses.

"Oh, honey, I'm scared, too," she said.

It was this way that Grandmother MacLeod found us when she came stepping lightly down into the front hall with her order for two dozen lace-bordered handkerchiefs of pure Irish linen.

I could not sleep that night, and when I went downstairs, I found my father in the den. I sat down on the hassock beside his chair, and he told me about the operation my mother was to have the next morning. He kept saying it was not serious nowadays.

"But you're worried," I put in, as though seeking to explain why I was.

"I should at least have been able to keep from burdening you with it," he said in a distant voice, as though to himself. "If only the baby hadn't got twisted around—"

"Will it be born dead, like the little girl?"

"I don't know," my father said. "I hope not."

"She'd be disappointed, wouldn't she, if it was?" I said, wondering why I was not enough for her.

"Yes, she would," my father replied. "She won't be able to have any more, after this. It's partly on your account that she wants this one, Nessa. She doesn't want you to grow up without a brother or sister."

"As far as I'm concerned, she didn't need to bother."

My father laughed. "Well, let's talk about something else, and then maybe you'll be able to sleep. How did you and Grandmother make out today?"

"Oh, fine, I guess. What was Grandfather MacLeod like, Dad?"

"What did she tell you about him?"

"She said he made a lot of money in his time."

"Well, he wasn't any millionaire," my father said, "but I suppose he did quite well. That's not what I associate with him, though." He reached across to the bookshelf, took out a small leather-bound volume and opened it. On the pages were mysterious marks, like doodling, only much neater and more patterned.

"Greek," my father explained. "This is a play called *Antigone*. See, here's the title in English. There's a whole stack of them on the shelves there. *Oedipus Rex. Electra. Medea.* They belonged to your Grandfather MacLeod. He used to read them often."

"Why?" I inquired, unable to understand why anyone would pore over those undecipherable signs.

"He was interested in them," my father said. "He must have been a lonely man, although it never struck me that way at the time. Sometimes a thing only hits you a long time afterward."

"Why would he be lonely?" I wanted to know.

"He was the only person in Manawaka who could read these plays in the original Greek," my father said. "I don't suppose many people, if anyone, had even read them in English translation. Maybe he once wanted to be a classical scholar—I don't know. But his father was a doctor, so that's what he was. Maybe he would have liked to talk to somebody about these plays. They must have meant a lot to him."

It seemed to me that my father was talking oddly. There was a sadness in his voice that I had never heard before, and I longed to say something that would make him feel better, but I could not, because I did not know what was the matter.

"Can you read this kind of writing?" I asked hesitantly.

My father shook his head. "Nope. I was never very intellectual, I guess. Your Uncle Rod was always brighter than I, in school, but even he wasn't interested in learning Greek. Perhaps he would've been later, if he'd lived. As a kid, all I ever wanted to do was go into the merchant marine."

"Why didn't you?"

"Oh, well," my father said, "a kid who'd never seen the sea wouldn't have made much of a sailor. I might have turned out to be the seasick type."

I had lost interest, now that he was once more speaking like himself.

"Grandmother MacLeod was pretty cross today about the girl," I said.

"I know," my father said. "Well, we must be as nice as we can to her, Nessa, and after a while she'll be all right."

Suddenly I did not care what I said.

"Why can't she be nice to *us* for a change?" I burst out. "We're always the ones who have to be nice to her."

My father put his hand down and tilted my head until I was forced to look at him. "Vanessa," he said, "she's had troubles in her life which you really don't know much about. That's why she sometimes gets migraines and has to go to bed. It's not easy for her these days. The house is still the same, so she thinks other things should be, too. It hurts her when she finds they aren't."

"I don't see——" I began.

"Listen," my father said, "you know we were talking just now about what people are interested in, like Grandfather MacLeod being interested in Greek plays? Well, your grandmother was interested in being a lady, Nessa, and for a long time it seemed to her that she was one."

I thought of the Castle of Kinlochaline and of horse doctors in Ontario.

"I didn't know——" I stammered.

"That's usually the trouble with most of us," my father said. "Now you go on up to bed. I'll phone tomorrow from the hospital as soon as the operation's over."

I did sleep at last, and in my dreams I could hear the caught sparrow fluttering in the attic and the sound of my mother crying and the voices of dead children.

My father did not phone until afternoon. Although Grandmother MacLeod said I was being silly, for you could hear the phone ringing all over the house, I refused to move out of the den. I had never before examined my father's books, but now, at a loss for something to do, I took them out one by one and read snatches here and there. After several hours, it dawned on me that most of the books were of the same kind. I looked again at the titles.

Seven League Boots. Travels in Arabia Deserta. The Seven Pillars of Wisdom. Travels in Tartary, Tibet and China. Count Luckner, the Sea Devil. And a hundred more. On a shelf by themselves were copies of the *National Geographic Magazine.* I had looked at these often enough, but never with the puzzling compulsion which I felt now, as though I was on the verge of some discovery, something which I had to find out and yet did not want to know. I riffled through the picture-filled pages. Hibiscus and wild orchids grew in soft-petaled profusion. The Himalayas stood lofty as gods, with the morning sun on their peaks of snow. Leopards snarled from the depth of a thousand jungles. Schooners buffeted their white sails like the wings of giant angels against the sea winds.

"What on earth are you doing?" Grandmother Mac-Leod inquired waspishly, from the doorway. "You've got everything scattered all over the place. Pick it all up this minute, Vanessa, do you hear?" So I picked up the books and magazines and put them neatly away.

When the telephone finally rang, I was afraid to answer it. At last I did. My father sounded far away, and the relief in his voice made it unsteady.

"It's okay, honey. Everything's fine. The boy was born alive and kicking after all. Your mother's pretty weak, but she's going to be all right."

I could hardly believe it. I did not want to talk to anyone. I wanted to be by myself, to assimilate the presence of my brother, toward whom, without even having seen him, I felt such tenderness and such resentment.

That evening, Grandmother MacLeod approached my father, who at first did not take her seriously when she asked what they planned to call the child.

"Oh, I don't know. Hank, maybe, or Joe. Fauntleroy, perhaps."

She ignored his levity. "Ewen, I wish you would call him Roderick."

His face changed. "I'd rather not."

"I think you should," Grandmother MacLeod insisted, in a voice as pointed and precise as her silver nail scissors.

"Don't you think Beth ought to decide?" my father asked.

"Beth will agree if you do."

My father did not bother to deny something that even I knew to be true. He did not say anything. Then Grandmother MacLeod's voice, astonishingly, faltered a little. "It would mean a great deal to me," she said.

I remembered what she had told me: *When your Uncle Roderick got killed, I thought I would die. But I didn't die.* All at once her feeling for that unknown dead man became a reality for me. And yet I held it against her, as well, for I could see that she was going to win now.

"All right," my father said. "We'll call him Roderick."

Then, alarmingly, he threw back his head and laughed. "Roderick Dhu!" he cried. "That's what you'll call him, isn't it? Black Roderick. Like before. Don't you remember? As though he was a character out of Sir Walter Scott, instead of an ordinary kid who—"

He broke off and looked at her with a kind of desolation in his face.

"God, I'm sorry, Mother," he said. "I had no right to say that."

Grandmother MacLeod did not flinch, or tremble, or indicate that she felt anything at all. "I accept your apology, Ewen," she said.

My mother had to stay in bed for several weeks after she arrived home. The baby's crib was kept in my parents' room, and I could go in and look at the small creature who lay there with his tightly closed fists and his feathery black hair. Aunt Edna came in to help each morning, and when she had finished the housework, she would have coffee with my mother. They kept the door closed, but this did not prevent me from eavesdropping, for there was an air register in the floor of the spare room that was linked somehow with the register in my parents' room. If you put your ear to the iron grille, it was almost like a radio.

"Did you mind very much, Beth?" Aunt Edna was saying.

"Oh, it's not the name I mind," my mother replied. "It's just that Ewen felt he had to. You knew that Rod only had the sight of one eye, didn't you?"

"Sure, I knew. So what?"

"There was only a year and a half between Ewen and Rod," my mother said, "so they often went around together when they were youngsters. It was Ewen's air rifle that did it."

"Oh, Lord," Aunt Edna said. "I suppose she always blamed him?"

"No, I don't think it was so much that, really. It was how he felt himself. I think he even used to wonder sometimes if—but people shouldn't let themselves think like that, or they'd go crazy. Accidents do happen, after all. When the war came, Ewen joined up first. Rod should never have been in the army at all, but he couldn't wait to get in. He must have lied about his eyesight. It wasn't so very noticeable unless you looked at him closely, and I don't suppose the medicals were very thorough in those days. He got in as a gunner, and Ewen applied to have him in the same company. He thought he might be able to watch out for him, I guess, Rod being at a disadvantage. They were both only kids. Ewen was nineteen and Rod was eighteen when they went to France. And then the Somme. I don't know, Edna, I think Ewen felt that if Rod had had proper sight, or if he hadn't been in the same outfit and had been sent somewhere else—you know how people always think these things afterward, not that it's ever a bit of use. Ewen wasn't there when Rod got hit. They'd lost each other somehow, and Ewen was looking for him, not bothering about anything else, you know, just frantically looking. Then he stumbled across him quite by chance. Rod was still alive, but—"

"Stop it, Beth," Aunt Edna said. "You're only upsetting yourself."

"Ewen never spoke of it to me," my mother went on,

"until his mother showed me the letter he'd written to her at the time. It was a peculiar letter, almost formal, saying how gallantly Rod had died, and all that. I guess I shouldn't have, but I told him she'd shown it to me. He was very angry that she had. And then, as though for some reason he was terribly ashamed, he said, 'I had to write something to her, but men don't really die like that, Beth. It wasn't that way at all.' It was only after the war that he decided to study medicine and go into practice with his father."

"Had Rod meant to?" Aunt Edna asked.

"I don't know," my mother said. "I never felt I should ask Ewen that."

Aunt Edna was gathering up the coffee things, for I could hear the clash of cups and saucers being stacked on the tray. "You know what I heard her say to Vanessa once, Beth? *The MacLeods never tell lies.*' Those were her exact words. Even then, I didn't know whether to laugh or cry."

"Please, Edna." My mother sounded worn out now. "Don't."

"Oh, glory," Aunt Edna said, "I've got all the delicacy of a two-ton truck. I didn't mean Ewen, for heaven's sake. That wasn't what I meant at all. Here, let me plump up your pillows for you."

Then the baby began to cry, so I could not hear anything more of interest. I took my bike and went out beyond Manawaka, riding aimlessly along the gravel highway. It was late summer, and the wheat had changed color, but instead of being high and bronzed in the fields, it was stunted and desiccated, for there had been no rain again this year. Yet on the bluff where I stopped and crawled under the barbed-wire fence and lay stretched out on the grass, the plentiful poplar leaves were turning to a luminous yellow and shone like church windows in the sun. I put my head down very close to the earth and looked at what was going on there. Grasshoppers with enormous eyes ticked and twitched around me, as though the dry air was perfect for their purposes. A ladybug labored mightily to climb a blade of grass, fell off and started all over again, seeming to be unaware that she possessed wings and could have flown up.

I thought of the accidents that might easily happen to a person—or, of course, might not happen, might happen to somebody else. I thought of the dead baby, my sister, who might as easily have been I. Would she, then, have been lying here in my place, the sharp grass making its small toothmarks on her brown arms, the sun warming her to the heart? I thought of the leather-bound volumes of Greek, and of the six different kinds of iced cakes that used to be offered always in the MacLeod house, and of the pictures of leopards and green seas. I thought of my brother, who had been born alive after all, and now had been given his life's name.

I could not really comprehend these things, but I sensed their strangeness, their disarray. I felt that whatever God might love in this world, it was certainly not order.

HE HAD A DOG ONCE

by *Jean-Guy Carrier*

It was a spotted dog, black and white, with a pencil tail. Joseph got him free from Ernest Barrière, on a whim. Thought, upon seeing the dog in the litter, that William might like such a pet.

Joseph strode up the hill toward home with the dog under his arm. Walked past the houses with elderly folk on the porches and nodded when he caught their eyes.

"Hello, Mrs. Tessier," he called and waved, for she was hard of hearing. Mrs. Tessier returned a broad smile. He knew from the way she inclined toward him that she hadn't caught his words.

The dog under his arm fidgeted. Joseph shifted it to

the other arm. It licked his face and he pushed the snout away, pleased.

Eugénie was in the kitchen when he arrived.

"Is William in?" he asked. She was bent double, fussing with something in the oven. Without looking up from her work she extended an arm toward the stairs. "Upstairs," she said. Joseph decided not to interrupt her; he would surprise her later.

At the top of the stairs he called for the boy. "William." He flinched, for it rang more loudly than he meant it to.

He called again "William," more softly, and when there was no answer went searching down the hallway. He stepped cautiously into the boy's bedroom, expecting to find him asleep there.

The bed was unkempt but empty. Then he heard a sound that he knew was the sliding of wood upon wood. It ended with a screech. Joseph knew instantly it came from his bedroom.

He hurried to it and as he entered saw William rigid beside the dresser. Outraged, Joseph saw that his private drawer was ajar. The key lay on the dresser.

The boy was paralyzed, his ears boiling red. Joseph dropped the dog and instantly was upon the boy, who fell back instinctively to avoid the first slap of his father's hand. The dog scrambled across the wooden floor, confused, tail wagging.

Joseph seized William by the back of his neck. "Get out of here," he raged, thrusting the boy ahead of him, slapping him about the ears.

William gasped for air. His feet flailed beneath him, seeking firm ground, as he was dragged and battered down the hall, his father's voice roaring in his ears.

In his terror, he didn't hear the yelp the dog let loose when Joseph kicked it out of his way, sent it thudding against the wall. It fell and scrambled on slippery paws to escape.

"Get in there," Joseph yelled and pushed the boy into his room. William slipped to the floor but Joseph was immediately upon him again. Yanking him up by the hair and an arm, he hurled him onto the bed.

William scrambled up against the far wall, pressed himself against it, breathless. "If I catch you in there again I'll kill you, you bastard," his father screamed, a fist held up trembling at William. The boy, gasping tears, crushed himself still harder against the wall.

"What is it?" Eugénie cried as she dashed in, distraught and breathless from the stairs.

"Your damned whelp there, that sneaking little bastard, was in my things again." The muscles of Joseph's throat contracted, thrusting out the words.

Her eyes glistened confusion. "What was he doing?"

"I'll kill him next time," Joseph yelled. "I'll kill your damned sweetheart."

"No," she screamed and threw herself at Joseph, clasped her arms around him, pressing herself to him, screaming at him to stop.

"Damn you," Joseph raged and spun to rid himself of her. Eugénie was tossed from him and reeled back against the wall.

He stood in the door, glowering at them. "I'll kill you both someday," he said, shaking his fist at them. "God help me, I'll kill you both," he shouted and stormed away down the stairs and out the kitchen door. They heard it slam shut and bounce.

William crumpled to the bed, heaving great sobs. Eugénie went to him. She pulled him to her, cradled his tremulous body in her lap and pressed her own contorted features to his back.

The dog poked his head around the corner and saw the figures huddled on the bed. He backed away. The little paws clattered down the corridor, back to safety in the other room.

On the dresser in the bedroom lay an envelope. The creased corner of a photograph protruded from its ragged opening. It was of a young man in a striped suit, face all bright, and a pretty woman dressed in pleated silk.

Both smiled out from the photograph, their arms around each other in a clasp so tentative they seemed to be seated near each other rather than with each other.

That picture fascinated William. He had returned to it often, scrutinized the two figures for long moments. He was drawn by them, and by the warmth they made him feel, as if he were contained within the circle of their arms.

He'd risked his father's anger again and again to search those faces, and each time wondered what changes these two had endured to become his parents.

There were other things in the drawer. Lapel pins cast in heavy metal were tucked in a small box. He wished he could wear one for a badge. In the corners there were papers, pressed and folded into piles and held together by rubber bands. The words printed on them he understood vaguely, and thought they might have to do with his father's business dealings.

There was a small brass compass, and a mouth organ he dreamed of blowing sounds from, but he never dared. Things to be touched in secret moments—their value balanced against the risk of discovery. The lies and secrecy left the boy with a taste of guilt. But it never deterred him.

He was still sobbing when Eugénie laid him under the blankets. Sleep would overcome him soon, she thought, as she wiped away the last of her own tears.

She tucked the blankets in around him and left quietly. In the bathroom, before the mirror, she dabbed her swollen eyes with a moist cloth, then turned away quickly.

The bedroom floor was strewn with objects from the dresser. Eugénie gathered them up and put them back where they belonged. She didn't look at the picture on the dresser, merely tucked it into its envelope and laid it in the drawer. She patted everything into place and slid the drawer shut. Locked it and put away the key.

Eugénie's resolve weakened for a moment and she sat on the bed, suddenly exhausted. The despair that tightened in her throat nearly engulfed her, nearly bent her head to her open hands. But she refused the moment of weakness, held herself instead to thoughts of things that needed doing, and remembered the oven.

She pushed her hair back into place, smoothed her

clothing free of creases and hurried down to the kitchen.

William lay asleep, breathing in spasms. The dog crawled out from under the large bed, where he had been hiding, and padded over to William's bedroom. He looked around the corner and seeing no one proceeded cautiously across the floor.

He raised himself on his hind legs against William's bed, his nose over the edge. But the person sleeping there didn't stir.

He turned to leave but changed his mind. He crawled under William's bed and stretched out on a mat there. He rested his muzzle on his forelegs and waited.

The next day he was gone and was never spoken of. And never a question was raised.

THE FLOOD

by *Jacques Ferron*

A habitant and good farmer, who had managed to obtain from his wife thirteen children, all well-grown though of unequal size, lived with his family in a farmhouse which was a strange kind of house, for every year in winter it would float on the snow for forty days or more; yet in spring it would become a house like any other, returning to the very spot it had occupied before, in Fontarabie *rang*, Sainte-Ursule de Maskinongé. This house had two doors; the front door opened onto the King's Highway, the back door onto the habitant's land. Now one spring the eldest son went out the back door and began to help his father, whose heir he subsequently became. That door was never used again. Every spring from then on the children went out by the front door; boys and girls in the flower of youth, they set out one by one on the King's Highway to sow their seeds elsewhere. The habitant shook hands with each and every one, saying: "Bon voyage, my pigeon, bon voyage, my dove. Come and see me at Christmas; I'll be expecting you." But these children bore more resemblance to the crow: they never came back. With the exception of one. When he appeared in Fontarabie, having failed to found a family elsewhere, the old man was sitting on his front steps, his beard bristling, his stick between his knees, raising himself up from time to time to get a better look at any creature that happened by. When he saw his son he asked himself whose offspring this runt could be, for he looked familiar. He started with the most distant families, then, having no success, worked closer and with some apprehension began to go through local names and names of relatives. "You don't understand," said the runt, "I'm your son." The old man did not deny it; it was quite possible.

"Have you come to see your mother?" he asked.

"Yes," replied the son.

"Well, you're out of luck: your mother's dead and buried."

The runt took the news very well; he had been away for a long time.

"I haven't married again," added the old habitant; but so saying he raised himself up with the help of his stick, peering into the distance to see if there were not by chance a woman in sight.

"What about you, son; have you got any children?"

"No," the poor devil replied.

The old man grew thoughtful.

"And your wife, what's she like?" he asked, without getting up, but tightening his grip on the stick, his beard flashing sparks. He was thinking that his runt of a son might invite him to his house, where he would be alone all day with a young daughter-in-law. The answer shattered his hopes.

"Have you at least been to the city?"

"Yes," replied the son.

Then the old man, who knew perfectly well, having

seen it in the papers, that in the city there were hundreds and hundreds of girls gathered together in an enclosure, raised himself up on his stick, filled with the greatest indignation:

"Stay here," he shouted, "I'll go in your place!"

And off he went. Winter was not far away. Soon the snow came down and the strange house broke loose from Fontarabie and began to float; it floated slowly over the lost generation, an absurd ark, raft of the helpless; it floated over the old man, who, from the depths of the flood, brandished his terrible stick.

THE MILITARY HOSPITAL

by *Phyllis Gotlieb*

The helicopter moved through the city in the airlane between skyscrapers. It was on autopilot, preset course, and there was no one to squint down the canyons of the streets where the life-mass seethed. Children looked up at it with dull eyes; if it had come lower they would have stoned or shot at it. The armored cars that burrowed among them were scratched and pocked from their attacks.

Fresh and smooth, dressed in crisp white, DeLazzari came into the Control Room at the top of the hospital. He had had a week off, he was on for three; he ran the hospital, supervised nurse-patient relationships, directed the sweepers in the maintenance of sterility, and monitored the pile. He took over this function wherever he was told to go, but he particularly liked the Military Hospital because it was clean, roomy, and had very few patients. He was a stocky man with thick black hair, broad wings of moustache, and skin the color of baked earth; he had the blood of all nations in him. "The bad blood of all nations," he would add with a laugh if he felt like impressing one of the trots Mama Rakosy sent up to the apartment, though it was rare he felt like impressing anyone. He was sworn to forgo women, drugs and liquor for three weeks, so he switched on the big external screen and dumped out of his bag the cigars, candy and gum that would sustain him, while he watched the course of the helicopter over the city.

A trasher's bomb went off in one of the buildings; daggers of glass blew out singing, and sliced at the scalps and shoulders of a knot of demonstrators clumped at its base; a fragment of concrete hurled outward and grazed the helicopter, then fell to dent a fiberglass helmet and concuss the bike rider who fell from his machine and lay unconscious under the bruising feet; the wounded demonstrators scattered or crawled, leaving their placards, and others took their places, raising neon-colored cold-light standards of complicated symbols; they camped in the table-sized space, oblivious to bloody glass, hardhats with crossbows, skinheads with slingshots, longhairs, freaks, mohicans, children, and above all the whoop and howl of police sirens coming up.

The helicopter moved north and away; the armored cars butted their way through, into less crowded streets where merchants did business across wickets in iron cages in which one touch of a floor button dropped steel shutters and made a place impregnable fast enough to cut a slice off anyone who got in the way. Farther north the City Hospital and the Central Police Depot formed two wings of a great moth-shaped complex webbed about by stalled paddy wagons and ambulances.

DeLazzari grinned. In City Hospital twelve directors manned the control room, endlessly profane and harried. Shop was always depleted: the sweepers rusted and ground down from lack of parts and the nurses were obsolete and inefficient. Only the doctors moved at great speed and in Olympian calm.

He switched on his own O.R. screen. Doctors were already closing around the operating table, waiting.

They were silver, slab-shaped, featureless. They drew power from a remote source, and nobody he knew had any idea where it was. They had orders and carried them them out—or perhaps they simply did what they chose. He had never been in their physical presence, nor wanted to be.

The helicopter was passing between blank-walled buildings where the dead were stored in very small vaults, tier upon tier upon tier; at street level the niches reserved for floral tributes were empty except for wire frames to which a few dried leaves and petals clung trembling in the down draft from the rotors. North beyond that in the concrete plaza the racers were heating up for the evening, a horde endlessly circling.

But the city had to end in the north at the great circle enclosing the Military Hospital. It had no wall, no road, no entrance at ground level. What it had was a force field the helicopter had to rise steeply to surmount. Within, for a wall it had a thicket of greenery half a mile deep going all the way around; outside the field there was a circuit of tumbled masonry pieces, stones, burnt sticks, as if many ragged armies had tried to storm it and retreated, disgusted and weary.

Inside there was no great mystery. The Military Hospital healed broken soldiers from distant and ancient wars; the big circular building had taken no architectural prizes, and on its rolling greens two or three stumbling patients were being supported on their rounds by nurses. Like all directors DeLazzari tended to make himself out a minor Dracula; like all the rest his power lay in the modicum of choice he had among the buttons he pushed.

The helicopter landed on its field and discharged its cell, a Life Unit in which a dying soldier lay enmeshed; it took on another cell, containing another soldier who had been pronounced cured and would be discharged germ-free into his theatre of war; it was also boarded by the previous director, pocket full of credits and head full of plans for a good week.

The hospital doors opened, the cell rolled through

them down a hall into an anteroom where it split, a wagon emerged from it carrying the patient and his humming, flickering life-system, the anteroom sealed itself, flooded with aseptic sprays and drained, washing away blood traces; the O.R. sweeper removed the wet packs from the ruined flesh and dropped them on the floor, which dissolved them. In the operating room the TV system was pumping, the monitors pulsed, the doctors activated their autoclaves in one incandescent flash and then extruded a hundred tentacles, probes, knives, sensors, and flexed them; their glitter and flash was almost blinding in the harsh light. DeLazzari was obliged to watch them; he hated it, and they needed no light. It was provided on demand of the supervisors' and directors' union, though if machines chose to go renegade there was very little the supervisors and directors could say or do.

Doctors had never gone renegade. Neither had sweepers or nurses; it was a delicious myth citizens loved to terrify themselves with, perhaps because they resented the fact that madness should be reserved for people. DeLazzari thought that was pretty funny and he was scared too.

The O.R. sweeper sprayed himself (DeLazzari thought of it as delousing), the doors opened, the sweeper pushed in the body, still housing its low flicker of life, removed the attachments and set it on the table. The doctors reattached what was needed; the sweeper backed into a corner and turned his own power down. DeLazzari flicked a glance at the indicator and found it correct.

One doctor swabbed the body with a personal nozzle and began to remove steel fragments from belly and groin, another slit the chest and reached in to remove bone slivers from the left lung, a third trimmed the stump of the right forefinger and fitted a new one from the Parts Bank, a fourth tied off and removed torn veins from the thighs, all without bumping head, shoulders or elbows because they had none, a fifth kept the throat clear, a sixth gave heart massage, the first opened the belly and cut out a gangrened bowel section, the third sewed and sealed the new right forefinger and as an afterthought trimmed the nail, the fifth, still watching every breath, peeled back sections of the scalp and drilled holes in the skull. All in silence except for the soft clash and ringing of sensors, knives and probes. Blood splashed; their body surfaces repelled it in a mist of droplets and the floor washed it away.

The sweeper turned his power up on some silent order and fetched a strange small cage of silver wires. The fifth doctor took it, placed it over the soldier's head, and studied its nodes as coordinates in relation to the skull. Then he spoke at last. "Awaken," he said.

DeLazzari gave a hoarse nervous laugh and whispered, *Let there be light*. The boy's eyelids flickered and opened. The eyes were deep blue; the enlarged pupils contracted promptly and at an equal rate. DeLazzari wondered, as always, if he were conscious enough to be afraid he was lying in an old cemetery among the gravestones. Silver graves.

"Are you awake?" The voice was deep, God-the-Father-All-Powerful. The doctor checked the nose tube and cleared the throat. "Max, are you awake?"

"Yes . . . yes . . . yes. . . ."

"Can you answer questions?"

"Yes."

"Recording for psychiatric report." He extruded a fine probe and insterted it into the brain. "What do you see? Tell me what you see."

"I see . . . from the top of the ferris wheel I can see all the boats in the harbor, and when I come down in a swoop all the people looking up. . . ."

The probe withdrew and reentered. "What do you see now, Max?"

"My father says they're not sweet peas but a wild-flower, like a wild cousin of the sweet pea, toadflax, some people call them butter-and-eggs. . . . 'Scrophulariaceae Linaria vulgaris is the big name for them, Max, and that *vulgaris* means common, but they're not so common anymore. . . .'"

Probe.

". . . something like the fireworks I used to watch when I was a kid, but they're not fireworks, they're the real thing, and they turn the sky on fire. . . ."

"Area established."

Probe.

"One eye a black hole and the kid lying across her with its skull, with its skull, with its skull, I said Chrissake, Yvon, why'd you have to? Yvon? why'd you have to? Why? he said ohmigod Max how was I to know whether they were? Max? How was I to know whether?"

The probe tip burned, briefly.

"Yes, Max? He said: how was I to know whether what?"

"Know what? Who's he? I don't know what you're talking about."

DeLazzari watched the probes insinuate the cortex and withdraw. The doctors pulled at the associations, unraveling a tangled skein; they didn't try to undo all the knots, only the most complicated and disturbing. Was the act, he wondered, a healing beneficence or a removal of guilt associated with killing?

After four or five burns the cage was removed and the scalp repaired. Surprised, DeLazzari punched O.R. Procedures, Psych Division, and typed:

WHY SURGEONS OMIT DEEP MIL. INDOCTRINATION?

NEW RULING ONE WEEK PREVIOUS, the computer said.

WHOSE AUTHORITY?

BOARD OF SUPERVISORS.

And who ordered them around? He switched off and turned back to the doctors.

After their duties had been completed they followed some mysteriously-developed ritual that looked like a laying on of hands. All probes and sensors extended, they would go over a body like a fine-tooth comb, slicing off a wart, excising a precancerous mole, straightening a twisted septum. DeLazzari switched off and lit a cigar. There were no emergencies to be expected in the next ten minutes. He blinked idly at a small screen recording the flat encephalogram of a dead brain whose body was being maintained for Parts.

The doctors had other customs that both annoyed and amused him by their irrationality. Tonight they had been quiet, but sometimes one of them, sectioning a bowel, might start a running blue streak of chatter like a Las Vegas comic while another, probing the forebrain, would burst out in a mighty organ baritone, "Nearer My God to Thee." On the rare but inevitable occasions when an irreparable patient died with finality they acted as one to shut down the life system and retract their instruments; then stood for five minutes in a guardian circle of quietness, like the great slabs of Stonehenge, around the body before they would allow the sweeper to take it away.

The big external screen was still on and DeLazzari looked down into the city, where a torchlight procession was pushing its flaming way up the avenue and the walls to either side wavered with unearthly shadows. He shut off and called Shop. He peered at the fax sheet on Max Vingo clipped to his notice board and typed:

YOU GOT A CAUCASIAN TYPE NURSE APPROX FIVE-SEVEN FAIR HAIR QUIET VOICE NOT PUSHY MILD-TO-WARM AND FIRST RATE?

2482 BEST QUALITY CHECKED OUT LIGHT BROWN WE CAN MAKE IT FAIR HAIR.

LIGHT BROWN OK HEALING UNIT 35.

He yawned. Nothing more for the moment. He dialed supper, surveyed the sleeping alcove and bathroom, all his own, with satisfaction, checked the pill dispenser which allowed him two headache tablets on request, one sleeping pill at 11 P.M. and one laxative at 7:30 A.M. if required. He was perfectly content.

All nurses looked about twenty-five years old, unutterably competent but not intimidating unless some little-boy type needed a mother. 2482 was there when Max Vingo first opened his eyes and stirred weakly in his mummy wrappings.

"Hello," she said quietly.

He swallowed; his throat was still sore from the respirator. "I'm alive."

"Yes, you are, and we're glad to have you."

"This is a hospital."

"It is, and I'm your nurse, 2482."

He stared at her. "You're a—a mechanical—I've heard about you—you're a mechanical—"

"I'm a Robonurse," she said.

"Huh . . . it sounds like some kind of a tank."

"That's a joke, baby—God help us," said DeLazzari, and turned her dial up half a point.

She smiled. "I'm not at all like a tank."

"No." He gave it a small interval of thought. "No, not at all."

It was the third day. DeLazzari never bothered to shave or wash on duty where he didn't see another human being; his face was covered with gray-flecked stubble. Outside he was vain, but here he never glanced into a mirror. The place was quiet; no new patients had come in, no alarms had sounded, the walking wounded were walking by themselves. Besides 2482 there were only two other nurses on duty, one with a nephritis and another tending the body soon to be frozen for Parts. Still, he did have 2482 to control and he watched with weary amusement as she warmed up under the turn of his dial.

"You're getting better already." She touched Max Vingo's forehead, a nonmedical gesture since the thermocouple already registered his temperature. Her fingers were as warm as his skin. "You need more rest. Sleep now." Narcotic opened into his bloodstream from an embedded tube, and he slept.

On the fifth day the people of the city rose up against their government and it fell before them. Officers elected themselves, curfews were established, the torchlight parades and demonstrations stopped; occasionally a stray bomb exploded in a callbox. Packs of dogs swarmed up the avenue, pausing to sniff at places where the blood had lain in puddles; sometimes they met a congregation of cats and there were snarling yelping skirmishes. DeLazzari eyed them on his screen, devoutly thankful that he was not stationed in City Hospital. He filled City's requests for blood, plasma and parts as far as regulations required and didn't try to contact their control room.

At the Military Hospital the nephritis got up and walked out whole, the deadhead was cut up and frozen in Parts, an interesting new malaria mutation came in and was assigned a doctor to himself in Isolation. 2482 peeled away the bandages from Max Vingo's head and hand.

He asked for a mirror and when she held it before him he examined the scars visible on his forehead and scalp and said, "I feel like I'm made up of spare parts." He lifted his hand and flexed it. "That's not so funny." The forefinger was his own now, but it had once belonged to a black man and though most of the pigment had been chemically removed it still had an odd bluish tinge. "I guess it's better than being without one."

"You'll soon be your old handsome self."

"I bet you say that to all the formerly handsome guys."

"Of course. How would you get well otherwise?"

He laughed, and while she was wiping his face with a soft cloth he said, "2482, haven't you ever had a name?"

"I've never needed one."

"I guess if I get really familiar I can call you 2 for short."

"Hoo, boy, this is a humorist." DeLazzari checked the dial and indicator and left them steady on for the while. The malaria case went into convulsions without notice and he turned his attention elsewhere.

She rubbed his scalp with a cream to quicken regrowth of hair.

"What does that do for a bald guy?"

"Nothing. His follicles no longer function.'"

He flexed his new finger again and rubbed the strange skin with the fingertips of his other hand. "I hope mine haven't died on me."

By day 7 DeLazzari was beginning to look like a debauched beachcomber. His hospital whites were grimy and his moustache ragged. However, he kept a clean desk, his sweeper cleared away the cigar stubs and the ventilators cleaned the air. Two badly scarred cases of yaws came in from a tropical battleground and two doctors called for skin grafts and whetted their knives. In the city a curfew violator was shot and killed, and next morning the first of the new demonstrators appeared. One of the doctors took the chance of visiting Max for the first time when he was awake.

The soldier wasn't dismayed; he answered questions readily enough, showed off his growing hair, and demonstrated his attempts to use the grafted finger, but he kept looking from the doctor to 2482 and back in an unsettling way, and DeLazzari turned up the nurse's dial a point.

When the doctor was gone she said, "Did he disturb you?"

"No." But his eyes were fixed on her.

She took his hand. "Does that feel good?"

"Yes," he said. "That feels good." And he put his other hand on top of hers.

DeLazzari ate and slept and monitored the screens and supervised the duties of nurses and sweepers. Sometimes he wiped his oily face with a tissue and briefly considered rationing his cigars, which he had been smoking excessively because of boredom. Then three cases of cholera came in from the east; one was dead on arrival and immediately incinerated, the other two occupied him. But he still had time to watch the cure of Max Vingo and by turns of the dial nourish his relationship with 2482. He thought they were a pretty couple.

Max got unhooked from his TV, ate solid food with
a good appetite, and got up and walked stiffly on his
scarred legs, now freed of their bandages. His hair grew
in, black as DeLazzari's but finer, and the marks on his
skin were almost invisible. He played chess sometimes
with 2482 and didn't make any comments when she let
him win. But there was an odd sadness about him,
more than DeLazzari might have guessed from his
psych report. Although the ugliest of his memories had
been burned away the constellations of emotion attached to them had remained and the doctors would
never be able to do anything about those during the
short time he stayed in the hospital.

So that often at night, even sometimes when he fell
into a light doze, he had sourceless nightmares he
couldn't describe, and when he flailed his arms in terrified frustration 2482 took his hands and held them in
her own until he slept at peace.

DeLazzari watched the TV news, followed the
courses of battles over the world and on Moonbase and
Marsport, and made book with himself on where his
next casualties would be coming from. Not from the
planets, which had their own hospitals, or from the
usual military base establishments. His own hospital
(he liked to think of it as his own because he was so
fond of its conveniences and so full of respect for its
equipment) was one of the rare few that dealt with the
unusual, the interesting and the hopeless. Down in the
city the fire marchers were out and the bombs were ex-
ploding again. He knew that soon once more the people
of the city would rise against their government and it
would fall before them, and he kept check of blood and
parts and ordered repairs on old scuppered nurses.

Max Vingo dressed himself now and saw the scars
fade on his newly exposed torso. Because he was so far
away from it he didn't think of the battle he might be
going into. It was when he had stood for a long time at
the window looking out at the rain, at how much

greener it made the grass, that 2482 said to him, "Max, is there something you're afraid of?"

"I don't know."

"Is it the fighting?"

"I don't even remember much of that."

"The doctors took those memories away from you."

"Hey!" DeLazzari growled, hand poised over the control. "Who said you could say a thing like that?"

"I don't mind that," Max said.

DeLazzari relaxed.

"Don't you want to know why?"

"If you want to tell me."

"I'm not sure . . . but I think it was because the doctors knew you were a gentle and loving man, and they didn't want for you to be changed."

He turned and faced her. "I'm the same. But I'm still a man who has to dress up like a soldier—and I don't know when that will ever change. Maybe that's why I'm frightened."

DeLazzari wondered for a moment what it would be like to be sick and helpless and taken care of by a loving machine in the shape of a beautiful woman. Then he laughed his hoarse derisive crow and went back to work. He had never been sick.

On the eighteenth day five poison cases came in from a bloodless coup in a banana republic; DeLazzari sent a dozen nurses with them into the Shock Room and watched every move. He was hot and itchy, red-eyed and out of cigars, and thinking he might as well have been in City Hospital. They were having their troubles over there, and once again he sent out the supplies. By the time he had leisure for a good look at Max Vingo, 2482's dial was all the way up and Max was cured and would be going out next day: day 21, his own discharge date. He listened to their conversation for a while and whistled through his teeth. "End of a beautiful interlude," he said.

That evening Max ate little and was listless and depressed. 2482 didn't press him to eat or speak, nor did DeLazzari worry. The behaviour pattern was normal for situation and temperament.

Max went to sleep early but woke about eleven and lay in the darkness without calling or crying out, only stared toward the ceiling; sometimes for a moment he had a fit of trembling.

2482 came into the room softly, without turning on the light. "Max, you're disturbed."

"How do you know?" he said in an expressionless voice.

"I watch your heartbeat and your brainwaves. Are you feeling ill?"

"No."

"Then what is the matter? Do you have terrible thoughts?"

"It's the thoughts I can't think that bother me, what's behind everything that got burned away. Maybe they shouldn't have done that, maybe they should have let me become another person, maybe if I knew, really knew, really knew what it was like to hurt and kill and be hurt and be killed and live in filth for a lifetime and another lifetime, ten times over, I'd get to laugh at it and like it and say it was the way to be, the only way to be and the way I should have been. . . ."

"Oh no, Max. No, Max. I don't believe so."

Suddenly he folded his arms over his face and burst out weeping, in ugly tearing sobs.

"Don't, Max." She sat down beside him and pulled his arms away. "No, Max. Please don't." She pulled apart the fastenings of her blouse and clasped his head between her tender, pulsing and unfleshly breasts.

DeLazzari grinned lasciviously and watched them on the infrared scanner, chin propped on his hand. "Lovely, lovely, lovely," he whispered. Then he preset

2482's dial to move down three points during the next four hours, popped his pill and went to bed.

The alarm woke him at four. "Now what in hell is that?" He staggered groggily over to the console to find the source. He switched on lights. The red warning signal was on over 2482's dial. Neither the dial nor the indicator had moved from UP position. He turned on Max Vingo's screen. She had lain down on the bed beside him and he was sleeping peacefully in her arms. DeLazzari snarled. "Circuit failure." The emergency panel checked out red in her number. He dialed Shop.

REROUTE CONTROL ON 2482.

CONTROL REROUTED, the machine typed back.

WHY DID YOU NOT REROUTE ON AUTO WHEN FAILURE REGISTERED?

REGULATION STATES DIRECTOR AUTONOMOUS IN ALL ASPECTS NURSE-PATIENT RELATIONSHIP NOW ALSO INCLUDING ALTERNATE CIRCUITS.

WHY WAS I NOT TOLD THAT BEFORE?

THAT IS NEW REGULATION. WHY DO YOU NOT REQUEST LIST OF NEW REGULATIONS DAILY UPDATED AND READILY AVAILABLE ALL TIMES?

"At four o'clock in the morning?" DeLazzari punched off. He noted that the indicator was falling now, and on the screen he could see 2482 moving herself away from Max and smoothing the covers neatly over him.

DeLazzari woke early on the last day and checked out the cholera, the yaws and the poison. The choleras were nearly well; one of the yaws needed further work on palate deformity; one of the poisons had died irrevocably, he sent it to Autopsy; another was being maintained in Shock, the rest recovering.

While he ate breakfast he watched the news of battle and outrage; growing from his harshly uprooted childhood faith a tendril of thought suggested that Satan was plunging poisoned knives in the sores of the world. "DeLazzari the metaphysician!" He laughed. "Go on, you bastards, fight! I need the work." The city seemed to be doing his will, because it was as it had been.

Max Vingo was bathing himself, depilating his own face, dressing himself in a new uniform. A sweeper brought him breakfast. DeLazzari, recording his director's report, noted that he seemed calm and rested, and permitted himself a small glow of satisfaction at a good job nearly finished.

When the breakfast tray was removed, Max stood up and looked around the room as if there was something he might take with him, but he had no possessions. 2482 came in and stood by the door.

"I was waiting for you," he said.

"I've been occupied."

"I understand. It's time to go, I guess."

"Good luck."

"I've had that already." He picked up his cap and looked at it. "2482—Nurse, may I kiss you?"

DeLazzari gave her the last downturn of the dial.

She stared at him and said firmly, "I'm a machine, sir. You wouldn't want to kiss a machine." She opened the top of her blouse, placed her hands on her chest at the base of her neck and pulled them apart, her skin opened like a seam. Inside she was the gold and silver gleam of a hundred metals threaded in loops, wound on spindles, flickering in minute gears and casings; her workings were almost fearsomely beautiful, but she was not a woman.

"Gets 'em every time." DeLazzari yawned and waited for the hurt shock, the outrage, the film of hardness coming down over the eyes like a third eyelid. Max Vingo stood looking at her in her frozen posture of display. His eyelids twitched once, then he smiled. "I would have been very pleased and grateful to kiss a machine," he said and touched her arm lightly. "Good-bye, Nurse." He went out and down the hall toward his transportation cell.

DeLazzari's brows rose. "At least that's a change." 2482 was still standing there with her innards hanging out. "Close it up, woman. That's indecent." For a wild moment he wondered if there might be an expression trapped behind her eyes, and shook his head. He called down Shop and sent her for post-patient diagnostic with special attention to control system.

He cleaned up for the new man. That is, he evened up the pile of tape reels and ate the last piece of candy. Then he filched an ID plate belonging to one of the poison cases, put everything on Auto, went down a couple of floors and used the ID to get into Patients' Autobath. For this experience of hot lather, stinging spray, perfume and powder he had been saving himself like a virgin.

When he came out in half an hour he was smooth, sweet-smelling and crisply clothed. As the door locked behind him five doctors rounded a corner and came down the corridor in single file. DeLazzari stood very still. Instead of passing him they turned with a soft whirr of their lucite castors and came near. He breathed faster. They formed a semicircle around him; they were featureless and silver, and smelt faintly of warm metal. He coughed.

"What do you want?"

They were silent.

"What do you want, hey? Why don't you say something?"

They came nearer and he shrank against the door, but there were more machines on the other side.

"Get away from me! I'm not one of your stinking zombies!"

The central doctor extruded a sensor, a slender shining limb with a small bright bulb on the end. It was harmless, he had seen it used thousands of times from the control room, but he went rigid and broke out into a sweat. The bulb touched him very lightly on the forehead, lingered a moment, and retracted. The doctors, having been answered whatever question they had asked themselves, backed away, resumed their file formation, and went on down the hall. DeLazzari burst into hoarse laughter and scrubbed with his balled fist at the place the thing had touched. He choked on his own

spit, sobered after a minute, and walked away very
quickly in the opposite direction, even though it was a
long way around to where he wanted to go. Much later
he realized that they had simply been curious and per-
plexed in the presence of an unfamiliar heartbeat.

He went out in the same helicopter as Max Vingo,
though the soldier in his sterile perimeter didn't know
that. In the control room the new director, setting out
his tooth cleaner, depilatory and changes of underwear,
watched them on the monitor. Two incoming helicop-
ters passed them on the way; the city teemed with fires
and shouting and the children kicked at the slow-mov-
ing cars. In the operating theater the silver doctors
moved forward under the lights, among the machines,
and stood motionless around the narrow tables.

FLYING A RED KITE

by *Hugh Hood*

The ride home began badly. Still almost a stranger to
the city, tired, hot and dirty, and inattentive to his sur-
roundings, Fred stood for ten minutes, shifting his parcels from arm to arm and his weight from one leg to
the other, in a sweaty bath of shimmering glare from
the sidewalk, next to a grimy yellow-and-black bus
stop. To his left a line of murmuring would-be passengers lengthened until there were enough to fill any vehicle that might come for them. Finally an obese brown
bus waddled up like an indecent old cow and stopped
with an expiring moo at the head of the line. Fred was
glad to be first in line, as there didn't seem to be room
for more than a few to embus.

But as he stepped up he noticed a sign in the window which said *Côte des Neiges—Boulevard* and he

recoiled as though bitten, trampling the toes of the woman behind him and making her squeal. It was a Sixty-six bus, not the Sixty-five that he wanted. The woman pushed furiously past him while the remainder of the line clamored in the rear. He stared at the number on the bus stop: Sixty-six, not his stop at all. Out of the corner of his eye he saw another coach pulling away from the stop on the northeast corner, the right stop, the Sixty-five, and the one he should have been standing under all this time. Giving his characteristic weary put-upon sigh, which he used before breakfast to annoy Naomi, he adjusted his parcels in both arms, feeling sweat run around his neck and down his collar between his shoulders, and crossed Saint Catherine against the light, drawing a Gallic sneer from a policeman, to stand for several more minutes at the head of a new queue, under the right sign. It was nearly four-thirty and the Saturday shopping crowds wanted to get home, out of the summer dust and heat, out of the jitter of the big July holiday weekend. They would all go home and sit on their balconies. All over the suburbs in duplexes and fourplexes, families would be enjoying cold suppers in the open air on their balconies; but the Calverts' apartment had none. Fred and Naomi had been ignorant of the meaning of the custom when they were apartment hunting. They had thought of Montreal as a city of the Sub-Arctic and in the summers they would have leisure to repent the misjudgment.

He had been shopping along the length of Saint Catherine between Peel and Guy, feeling guilty because he had heard for years that this was where all those pretty Montreal women made their promenade; he had wanted to watch without familial encumbrances. There had been girls enough but nothing outrageously special so he had beguiled the scorching afternoon making a great many small idle purchases, the kind one does when trapped in a Woolworth's. A ball-point pen and a note-pad for Naomi, who was always stealing his and leaving it in the kitchen with long, wildly-optimistic, grocery lists scribbled in it. Six packages of cigarettes, some legal-size envelopes, two Dinky-toys, a long-playing record, two parcels of second-hand books, and the lightest of his burdens and the unhandiest, the kite he had bought for Deedee, two flimsy wooden sticks rolled up in red plastic film, and a ball of cheap thin string—not enough, by the look of it, if he should ever get the thing into the air.

When he'd gone fishing, as a boy, he'd never caught any fish; when playing hockey he had never been able to put the puck in the net. One by one the wholesome outdoor sports and games had defeated him. But he had gone on believing in them, in their curative moral values, and now he hoped that Deedee, though a girl, might sometime catch a fish; and though she obviously wouldn't play hockey, she might ski, or toboggan on the mountain. He had noticed that people treated kites and kite-flying as somehow holy. They were a natural symbol, thought Fred, and he felt uneasily sure that he would have trouble getting this one to fly.

The inside of the bus was shaped like a boxcar with windows, but the windows were useless. You might have peeled off the bus, as you'd peel the paper off a pound of butter, leaving an oblong yellow lump of thick solid heat, with the passengers embedded in it like hopeless bread crumbs.

He elbowed and wriggled his way along the aisle, feeling a momentary sliver of pleasure as his palm rubbed accidentally along the back of a girl's skirt— once, a philosopher—the sort of thing you couldn't be charged with. But you couldn't get away with it twice and anyway the girl either didn't feel it, or had no idea who had caressed her. There were vacant seats toward the rear, which was odd because the bus was otherwise full, and he struggled toward them, trying not to break the wooden struts which might be persuaded to fly. The bus lurched forward and his feet moved with the floor, causing him to pop suddenly out of the crowd by the exit, into a square well of space next to the heat and stink of the engine. He swayed around and aimed himself at a narrow vacant seat, nearly dropping a parcel of books as he lowered himself precipitately into it.

The bus crossed Sherbrooke Street and began, intolerably slowly, to crawl up Côte des Neiges and around the western spur of the mountain. His ears began to pick up the usual melange of French and English and to sort it out; he was proud of his French and pleased that most of the people on the streets spoke a less correct, though more fluent, version than his own. He had found that he could make his customers understand him perfectly—he was a book salesman—but that people in the street were happier when he addressed them in English.

The chatter in the bus grew clearer and more interesting and he began to listen, grasping all at once why he had found a seat back here. He was sitting next to a couple of drunks who emitted an almost overpowering smell of beer. They were cheerfully exchanging indecencies and obscure jokes and in a minute they would speak to him. They always did, drunks and panhandlers, finding some soft fearfulness in his face which exposed him as a shrinking easy mark. Once in a railroad station he had been approached three times in twenty minutes by the same panhandler on his rounds. Each time he had given the man something, despising himself with each new weakness.

The cheerful pair sitting at right angles to him grew louder and more blunt and the women within earshot grew glum. There was no harm in it; there never is. But you avoid your neighbor's eye, afraid of smiling awkwardly, or of looking offended and a prude.

"Now, this Pearson," said one of the revelers, "he's just a little short-ass. He's just a little fellow without any brains. Why, some of the speeches he makes ... I could make them myself. I'm an old Tory myself, an old Tory."

"I'm an old Blue," said the other.

"Is that so, now? That's fine, a fine thing." Fred was sure he didn't know what a Blue was.

"I'm a Balliol man. Whoops!" They began to make monkeylike noises to annoy the passengers and amuse themselves. "Whoops," said the Oxford man again, "hoo, hoo, there's one now, there's one for you." He was talking about a girl on the sidewalk.

"She's a one, now, isn't she? Look at the legs on her, oh, look at them now, isn't that something?" There was a noisy clearing of throats and the same voice said something that sounded like "Shaoil-na-baig."

"Oh, good, good!" said the Balliol man.

"Shaoil-na-baig," said the other loudly, "I've not forgotten my Gaelic, do you see, shaoil-na-baig," he said it loudly, and a woman up the aisle reddened and looked away. It sounded like a dirty phrase to Fred, delivered as though the speaker had forgotten all his Gaelic but the words for sexual intercourse.

"And how is your French, Father?" asked the Balliol man, and the title made Fred start in his seat. He pretended to drop a parcel and craned his head quickly sideways. The older of the two drunks, the one sitting by the window, examining the passing legs and skirts with the same impulse that Fred had felt on Saint Catherine Street, was indeed a priest, and couldn't possibly be an impostor. His clerical suit was too wellworn, egg-stained, and blemished with candle droppings, and fit its wearer too well, for it to be an assumed costume. The face was unmistakably a southern Irishman's. The priest darted a quick peek into Fred's eyes before he could turn them away, giving a monkey-like grimace that might have been a mixture of embarrassment and shame but probably wasn't.

He was a little gray-haired bucko of close to sixty, with a triangular sly mottled crimson face and uneven yellow teeth. His hands moved jerkily and expressively in his lap, in counterpoint to the lively intelligent movements of his face.

The other chap, the Balliol man, was a perfect type of English-speaking Montrealer, perhaps a bond salesman or minor functionary in a brokerage house on Saint James Street. He was about fifty with a round domed head, red hair beginning to go slightly white at the neck and ears, pink porcine skin, very neatly barbered and combed. He wore an expensive white shirt with a fine blue stripe and there was some sort of ring around his tie. He had his hands folded fatly on the knob of a stick, round face with deep laugh lines in the cheeks, and a pair of cheerfully darting little blue-blood-shot eyes. Where could the pair have run into each other?

"I've forgotten my French years ago," said the priest carelessly. "I was down in New Brunswick for many years and I'd no use for it, the work I was doing. I'm Irish, you know."

"I'm an old Blue."

"That's right," said the priest, "John's the boy. Oh, he's a sharp lad is John. He'll let them all get off, do you see, to Manitoba for the summer, and bang, BANG!" All the bus jumped. "He'll call an election on them and then they'll run." Something caught his eye and he turned to gaze out the window. The bus was moving slowly past the cemetery of Notre Dame des Neiges and the priest stared, half-sober, at the graves stretched up the mountainside in the sun.

"I'm not in there," he said involuntarily.

"Indeed you're not," said his companion, "lots of life in you yet, eh, Father?"

"Oh," he said, "oh, I don't think I'd know what to do with a girl if I fell over one." He looked out at the cemetery for several moments. "It's all a sham," he said, half under his breath, "they're in there for good." He swung around and looked innocently at Fred. "Are you going fishing, lad?"

"It's a kite that I bought for my little girl," said Fred, more cheerfully than he felt.

"She'll enjoy that, she will," said the priest, "for it's grand sport."

"Go fly a kite!" said the Oxford man hilariously. It amused him and he said it again. "Go fly a kite!" He and the priest began to chant together, "Hoo, hoo, whoops," and they laughed and in a moment, clearly, would begin to sing.

The bus turned lumberingly onto Queen Mary Road. Fred stood up confusedly and began to push his way toward the rear door. As he turned away, the priest grinned impudently at him, stammering a jolly good-bye. Fred was too embarrassed to answer but he smiled uncertainly and fled. He heard them take up their chant anew.

"Hoo, there's one for you, hoo. Shaoil-na-baig. Whoops!" Their laughter died out as the bus rolled heavily away.

He had heard about such men, naturally, and knew that they existed; but it was the first time in Fred's life that he had ever seen a priest misbehave himself publicly. There are so many priests in the city, he thought, that the number of bum ones must be in proportion. The explanation satisfied him but the incident left a disagreeable impression in his mind.

Safely home he took his shirt off and poured himself a Coke. Then he allowed Deedee, who was dancing around him with her terrible energy, to open the parcels.

"Give your Mummy the pad and pencil, sweetie," he directed. She crossed obediently to Naomi's chair and handed her the cheap plastic case.

"Let me see you make a note in it," he said, "make a list of something, for God's sake, so you'll remember it's yours. And the one on the desk is mine. Got that?" He spoke without rancor or much interest; it was a rather overworked joke between them.

"What's this?" said Deedee, holding up the kite and allowing the ball of string to roll down the hall. He resisted a compulsive wish to get up and rewind the string.

"It's for you. Don't you know what it is?"

"It's a red kite," she said. She had wanted one for weeks but spoke now as if she weren't interested. Then all at once she grew very excited and eager. "Can you put it together right now?" she begged.

"I think we'll wait till after supper, sweetheart," he said, feeling mean. You raised their hopes and then dashed them; there was no real reason why they shouldn't put it together now, except his fatigue. He looked pleadingly at Naomi.

"Daddy's tired, Deedee," she said obligingly, "he's had a long hot afternoon."

"But I want to see it," said Deedee, fiddling with the flimsy red film and nearly puncturing it.

Fred was sorry he'd drunk a Coke; it bloated him and upset his stomach and had no true cooling effect.

"We'll have something to eat," he said cajolingly, "and then Mummy can put it together for you." He turned to his wife. "You don't mind, do you? I'd only spoil the thing." Threading a needle or hanging a picture made the normal slight tremor of his hands accentuate itself almost embarrassingly.

"Of course not," she said, smiling wryly. They had long ago worked out their areas of uselessness.

"There's a picture on it, and directions."

"Yes. Well, we'll get it together somehow. Flying it ... that's something else again." She got up, holding the notepad, and went into the kitchen to put the supper on.

It was a good hot-weather supper, tossed greens with the correct proportions of vinegar and oil, croissants and butter, and cold sliced ham. As he ate, his spirits began to percolate a bit, and he gave Naomi a graphic sketch of the incident on the bus. "It depressed me," he told her. This came as no surprise to her; almost anything unusual, which he couldn't do anything to alter or relieve, depressed Fred nowadays. "He must have been sixty. Oh, quite sixty, I should think, and you could tell that everything had come to pieces for him."

"It's a standard story," she said, "and aren't you sentimentalizing it?"

"In what way?"

"The 'spoiled priest' business, the empty man, the man without a calling. They all write about that. Graham Greene made his whole career out of that."

"That isn't what the phrase means," said Fred laboriously. "It doesn't refer to a man who actually *is* a priest, though without a vocation."

"No?" She lifted an eyebrow; she was better educated than he.

"No, it doesn't. It means somebody who never became a priest at all. The point is that you *had* a vocation but ignored it. That's what a spoiled priest is. It's an Irish phrase, and usually refers to somebody who is a failure and who drinks too much." He laughed shortly. "I don't qualify, on the second count."

"You're not a failure."

"No, I'm too young. Give me time!" There was no reason for him to talk like this; he was a very productive salesman.

"You certainly never wanted to be a priest," she said positively, looking down at her breasts and laughing, thinking of some secret. "I'll bet you never considered it, not with your habits." She meant his bedroom habits, which were ardent, and in which she ardently acquiesced. She was an adept and enthusiastic partner, her greatest gift as a wife.

"Let's put that kite together," said Deedee, getting up from her little table, with such adult decision that her parents chuckled. "Come on," she said, going to the sofa and bouncing up and down.

Naomi put a tear in the fabric right away, on account of the ambiguity of the directions. There should have been two holes in the kite, through which a lugging string passed; but the holes hadn't been provided and when she put them there with the point of an icepick they immediately began to grow.

"Scotch tape," she said, like a surgeon asking for sutures.

"There's a picture on the front," said Fred, secretly cross but ostensibly helpful.

"I see it," she said.

"Mummy put holes in the kite," said Deedee with alarm. "Is she going to break it?"

"No," said Fred. The directions were certainly ambiguous.

Naomi tied the struts at right angles, using so much string that Fred was sure the kite would be too heavy. Then she strung the fabric on the notched ends of the struts and the thing began to take shape.

"It doesn't look quite right," she said, puzzled and irritated.

"The surface has to be curved so there's a difference

of air pressure." He remembered this, rather unfairly, from high-school physics classes.

She bent the crosspiece and tied it in a bowed arc, and the red film pulled taut. "There now," she said.

"You've forgotten the lugging string on the front," said Fred critically, "that's what you made the holes for, remember?"

"Why is Daddy mad?" said Deedee.

"I'M NOT MAD!"

It had begun to shower, great pear-shaped drops of rain falling with a plop on the sidewalk.

"That's as close as I can come," said Naomi, staring at Fred, "we aren't going to try it tonight, are we?"

"We promised her," he said, "and it's only a light rain."

"Will we all go?"

"I wish you'd take her," he said, "because my stomach feels upset. I should never drink Coca-Cola."

"It always bothers you. You should know that by now."

"I'm not running out on you," he said anxiously, "and if you can't make it work, I'll take her up tomorrow afternoon."

"I know," she said, "come on, Deedee, we're going to take the kite up the hill." They left the house and crossed the street. Fred watched them through the window as they started up the steep path hand in hand. He felt left out, and slightly nauseated.

They were back in half an hour, their spirits not at all dampened, which surprised him.

"No go, eh?"

"Much too wet, and not enough breeze. The rain knocks it flat."

"O.K.!" he exclaimed with fervor. "I'll try tomorrow."

"We'll try again tomorrow," said Deedee with equal determination—her parents mustn't forget their obligations.

Sunday afternoon the weather was nearly perfect, hot, clear, a firm steady breeze but not too much of it,

and a cloudless sky. At two o'clock Fred took his
daughter by the hand and they started up the mountain
together, taking the path through the woods that led up
to the university parking lots.

"We won't come down until we make it fly," Fred
swore, "that's a promise."

"Good," she said, hanging on to his hand and letting
him drag her up the steep path, "there are lots of bugs
in here, aren't there?"

"Yes," he said briefly—he was being liberally bitten.

When they came to the end of the path, they saw
that the campus was deserted and still, and there was
all kinds of running room. Fred gave Deedee careful
instructions about where to sit, and what to do if a car
should come along, and then he paid out a little string
and began to run across the parking lot toward the
main building of the university. He felt a tug at the
string and throwing a glance over his shoulder he saw
the kite bobbing in the air, about twenty feet off the
ground. He let out more string, trying to keep it filled
with air, but he couldn't run quite fast enough, and in a
moment it fell back to the ground.

"Nearly had it!" he shouted to Deedee, whom he'd
left fifty yards behind.

"Daddy, Daddy, come back," she hollered apprehensively. Rolling up the string as he went, he retraced his
steps and prepared to try again. It was important to
catch a gust of wind and run into it. On the second try
the kite went higher than before but as he ran past the
entrance of the university he felt the air pressure lapse
and saw the kite waver and fall. He walked slowly
back, realizing that the bulk of the main building was
cutting off the air currents.

"We'll go up higher," he told her, and she seized
his hand and climbed obediently up the road beside
him, around behind the main building, past ash barrels
and trash heaps; they climbed a flight of wooden steps,
crossed a parking lot next to L'Ecole Polytechnique
and a slanting field further up, and at last came to a
pebbly dirt road that ran along the top ridge of the
mountain beside the cemetery. Fred remembered

the priest as he looked across the fence and along the broad stretch of cemetery land rolling away down the slope of the mountain to the west. They were about six hundred feet above the river, he judged. He'd never been up this far before.

"My sturdy little brown legs are tired," Deedee remarked, and he burst out laughing.

"Where did you hear that," he said, "who has sturdy little brown legs?"

She screwed her face up in a grin. "The gingerbread man," she said, beginning to sing, "I can run away from you, I can, 'cause I'm the little gingerbread man."

The air was dry and clear and without a trace of humidity and the sunshine was dazzling. On either side of the dirt road grew great clumps of wildflowers, yellow and blue, buttercups, daisies and goldenrod, and cornflowers and clover. Deedee disappeared into the flowers—picking bouquets was her favorite game. He could see the shrubs and grasses heave and sway as she moved around. The scent of clover and of dry sweet grass was very keen here, and from the east, over the curved top of the mountain, the wind blew in a steady uneddying stream. Five or six miles off to the southwest he spied the wide intensely gray-white stripe of the river. He heard Deedee cry: "Daddy, Daddy, come and look." He pushed through the coarse grasses and found her.

"Berries," she cried rapturously, "look at all the berries! Can I eat them?" She had found a wild raspberry bush, a thing he hadn't seen since he was six years old. He'd never expected to find one growing in the middle of Montreal.

"Wild raspberries," he said wonderingly, "sure you can pick them, dear; but be careful of the prickles." They were all shades and degrees of ripeness from black to vermilion.

"Ouch," said Deedee, pricking her fingers as she pulled off the berries. She put a handful in her mouth and looked wry.

"Are they bitter?"

"Juicy," she mumbled with her mouth full. A trickle of dark juice ran down her chin.

"Eat some more," he said, "while I try the kite again." She bent absorbedly to the task of hunting them out, and he walked down the road for some distance and then turned to run up toward her. This time he gave the kite plenty of string before he began to move; he ran as hard as he could, panting and handing the string out over his shoulders, burning his fingers as it slid through them. All at once he felt the line pull and pulse as if there were a living thing on the other end and he turned on his heel and watched while the kite danced into the upper air currents above the treetops and began to soar up and up. He gave it more line and in an instant it pulled high up away from him across the fence, two hundred feet and more above him up over the cemetery where it steadied and hung, bright red in the sunshine. He thought flashingly of the priest saying, "It's all a sham," and he knew all at once that the priest was wrong. Deedee came running down to him, laughing with excitement and pleasure and singing joyfully about the gingerbread man, and he knelt in the dusty roadway and put his arms around her, placing her hands on the line between his. They gazed, squinting in the sun, at the flying red thing, and he turned away and saw in the shadow of her cheek and on her lips and chin the dark rich red of the pulp and juice of the crushed raspberries.

A FEW NOTES FOR ORPHEUS

by *Don Bailey*

I was sitting in my room when the phone rang.
"Hello."
"It's me," she said. Mother. I was almost glad to

hear her. But something must be wrong. She never phoned me.

"Is something wrong?"

"Your father," she said. "The doctor called yesterday and told me."

"What! What did he tell you?" Why did she have to turn everything into one of those serial mysteries? Each episode yanked from her in between commercials.

"I've been telling him for years," she said.

"Never mind that. What did the doctor say?"

"Cancer. It's in his lungs. I've been telling him for years but he'd never listen. Stubborn. Smoking his damn cigarettes like a train. I told him. . . ."

Her voice broke. She was crying. It made me angry to hear her crying for herself. She never once mentioned cigarettes that I could remember.

"Will you come up to the cottage this weekend?"

"Why? What's the point?"

"He's going to die!" she said, back to her favorite soap opera. "He's your father, Jake. You're his only son."

And you're his wife, I felt like saying; his only wife, but what was the point; it would be like taking away her bingo card with one number to go.

"Come," she said.

"All right. Tomorrow. I'll drive up in the afternoon."

"In the morning," she said. "Or tonight, Jake. Come up tonight. I'm scared. When I'm alone with him I don't know what to say."

"I'll be up tomorrow."

"Early," she said.

"Yeah." And I hung up. It was crazy, her being scared after all these years of being alone with him. But it scared me too in a way. It was like suddenly now that he was going to die we had to face the fact that he was alive.

I sat staring at the telephone for a long time and thought about statues. I hated them. Statues were the way other people made you stand still. Like dying. People loved you, made you their hero and killed you so they could build a monument to their feelings. Statues. And now in my mother's mind I could see the old man turning to stone. She would buy the biggest and best headstone. Bingo! A perfect card. A prize.

I picked up the phone and called my wife.

"It's me," I said. My mother's son.

"You sound like the ghost of somebody I used to know. . . ."

The father, the son, the holy ghost. Yes the holy ghost was the rattling skeleton in my closet.

"I haven't got this month's check yet," she said.

"It's in the mail," I lied. I'd drunk it the weekend before with some girl from Baltimore who was in Toronto for a hairdresser's convention. You might say she clipped me, but I didn't mind, I needed a trim.

I like to make jokes to myself. It's a good cover for all the laughing I do.

"So how are things," she said. "Selling lots of cars?"

"Great, but I'm thinking of going into another field. Selling headstones."

"You make money at that?"

"People keep dying."

"I suppose. . . ."

I could see her, face pulled in like an accordion to squeeze her thoughts into a recognizable tune. Everything has to be familiar to her before she can accept it. I guess I never became familiar enough. And when I left she kept expecting me to come back. Like Eurydice waiting and I didn't even look back.

"Is this a social call or what?" she said. "I haven't heard anything from you for months."

"Sort of business," I said. "How's the kid?"

"Great. She even mentioned you a couple of days ago; the man that used to live with us."

"I was wondering if it'd be okay for me to take her away for the weekend."

"Where?"

"Up to my parents' cottage."

"Since when did you get chummy with them?"

"Look Edith, it's just a thing. The old lady asked me up, the old man's sick and I said I'd come. I thought it'd be nice for the kid. Fresh air, swimming, the whole thing."

"What about me? I'm supposed to sit in this lousy sweat box while you and her go gallivanting off."

If she'd been in my room I would have punched her. It made me sick, the petty talk that led to this kind of thought. It was a way of chiseling at you, a reforming. My wife, the reformer.

"She hasn't even met your father," she continued. "I can't understand why you'd want her to get involved with them now. You never did before. You hardly saw them yourself."

"Forget it, then," I said. "I just thought she might enjoy the outing."

"I don't want to forget it, I want to know why all of a sudden you want to be nice to everybody. You know how often I've asked you to take her for a weekend so I could get away by myself, but you were always too busy. Now all of a sudden you're the good samaritan."

"Edith, my old man's sick. I want the kid to meet him at least once before he dies. At least once."

I was tired of this and sorry I had called. It had been a stupid idea and only proved how scared I was too. Frightened to go up there alone.

"Is he that bad?"

"Yeah."

"I never met him either," she said and began to cry. I began to wish that the hairdressers' convention hadn't been the week before and that it would happen this weekend. Or that my phone was disconnected; I felt the same way from the calls being made to me and the ones I made too.

"I'm sorry," I said. And I was. I was sorry that that was all I could be. There was nothing I could change or would if I could, except maybe to never have had a phone installed.

"What time did you want her?" she asked.

"Whatever time's best for you."

"I'll send her over about ten," she said. "She can ride the streetcar by herself now."

She sounded proud. "That's great," I said. "I'll have her back Sunday after supper. Okay?"

"Take care of her."

"I will. Good-bye."

"Good-bye, Jake."

I hung up and spent another long time staring at the phone. It was black like the night was becoming outside my windows. The phone could brighten up the night; one call to someone. A name somewhere in a directory.

I walked out to the balcony. The stars were like tiny animals' eyes. A coldness out there. "This is the winter of the world; and here we die." Did Shelley mean that? I'd have liked to have been on the moon with an endless supply of light bulbs; wire the moon to shine away the night.

I dreamed awhile. Night dream of people I'd lost long ago in a daylight somewhere.

The old man was dying and I preferred to be seen in the dark. It was as though I was preparing myself for a sudden departure. Cutting myself off except for the phone. And telling myself I liked my privacy.

I went to bed early without even one drink.

A knock woke me. The room was full of light. A beam of dust particles formed a moving mural in one corner. In a way it was more of a picture than the posters I had pasted on the walls. Art should always be elusive. Somebody said that, I'm sure.

"Come in," I said. "It's not locked." I never lock the door. Locking anything defeats its own purpose.

"It's me," she said, and stood in the doorway with a brown shopping bag and a brown face split like a potato with a jagged grin.

"Com'on in," I said again. "Close the door."

She closed it and discreetly held her back to me while I fumbled around for my pants. They were on the floor and in a minute I was up and jamming the blankets from the studio couch into the closet.

"You look great," I said. "How's school?" Standard question.

"It's holidays," she said.

"Oh yeah. I forgot."

"You always forget," she said softly so I almost didn't hear her.

"You're starting to sound like your mother."

"I'm sorry. I didn't mean that. But you do forget. All the time when I see you, you always say you forgot this or you forgot that. All the time you say that."

It's true. And it's strange because I really want to be remembered. But not as a statue. I want to be remembered in an unclear way. Like a stranger that you see some night on the subway and never forget.

"Let's forget it," I said.

She laughed. "See!"

I laughed too. "I'm just lazy," I said.

She continued to laugh in the nervous way my wife has. An unnatural sound from a ten-year-old. But maybe not. I don't know any other ten-year-olds. Maybe they all end up sounding like that.

I shaved and came back to find her asleep. It frightened me.

"Hey, com'on, sleepy-head, time to go. Didn't you get any sleep last night?"

"I couldn't," she said. "I was too excited."

At least she's still honest enough to admit what she feels.

"Let's go, then. You got all your stuff?"

"Right here. I put my bathing suit in too."

Because my living is made selling cars I always have a road-worthy vehicle at my disposal. My boss believes that as I zoom along the highway in one of his red convertibles, people will flag me down and make wild offers to buy the thing from me. So far the only person who's flagged me down was a hitchhiker headed for the east coast. Another dreamer. But still it's pleasant to have a nice car waiting for you at the curb. And the kid liked it.

"Can you put the top down?" she asked.

"Sure," I said.

The drive took less than two hours. Just over a hundred miles from Toronto. The old man had bought the cottage years back when I was still a kid and prices were on a level that only demanded a man's right arm stopping at the first joint. Now they wanted the shoulder and both legs.

With the top down it was difficult to talk and after a few distorted questions to each other that the wind blew around we gave up. When I pulled off the highway onto the dirt road that led to the lake she asked me something she seemed to have been saving for a long time.

"Do you have any girl friends?"

It startled me. Was she a spy? My wife liked to know things like that, but the kid had never sought information to take back with her before. Not that I could remember. Maybe I hadn't noticed. I didn't want to have to be cautious with her.

"Sometimes," I said.

"What do you mean?"

"I mean sometimes women are my friends but sometimes they won't leave me alone. You know what I mean?"

"Like mommy when she calls you?"

"Yeah, like that." But you're my friend, I wanted to say, but perhaps that wasn't true either. An infiltrator.

The old lady was sitting in a lawn chair when I pulled in the lane. Waiting. She got up slowly as though unwilling to admit we had arrived.

"I thought you'd be coming up on your own," she said when we got out.

"Thought I'd surprise you," I said. "You remember Berniee."

"I should say, my only grandchild. And how you've grown."

She didn't touch the kid. Standard policy. She hadn't seen her for over two years, since the separation, and she still didn't even put a hand out. Some families grow like trees, each separate but the branches touching from one to another and intertwining. Our family was like a series of telephone poles strung along a highway without even the wires to link us up. We are not a close family. I mean that as a kind of joke.

"What a lovely outfit," my mother said. "I'll bet your father got you that."

"My mother."

"Oh, wasn't that nice? And yellow too. You look so nice in yellow."

"Thank you," the kid said. I could tell it was killing her, this crap, and I was glad. All she had to do was one of those curtsies and the old lady would've been all over her, but the kid held back. No fancy dog tricks to get a bone and a pat on the head.

"Could you run along and play, Bernice? I want to talk to your daddy for a minute."

The kid fluttered around and took off into the trees behind the cottage; her yellow skirt like a windborne kite.

"What was the idea of bringing her up?"

"It was just an idea. You don't like it we can leave."

"You don't think I've got enough to worry about with him in that condition? And what's he going to think? He hasn't even met the girl."

"That's not my fault," I said. "And he can think what he wants. I figured it was time he met her. Where is he anyway?"

"Down at the dock," she said, and began to smile her secret scorn.

"What's he doing down there?"

The dirty pool look was there now. She was out to get him. She would have her revenge before she bought the statue. Her rule.

"When I told him you were coming, he decided you'd like to go fishing. He's down at the dock now getting the boat ready."

"That sounds like a hell of an idea. I haven't been fishing for years. We can take the kid too. She's never been."

"Crazy foolishness, in his condition." She was disappointed. She wanted me to join her in lashing out at the crazy old bastard. She was right, he probably wasn't in any condition to fish, but maybe he was looking for revenge too. It was hard to say and I wondered where I'd fit in, if I did, and the kid too.

"He even took a case of beer down too," she said, as if this were some final proof of his unbalanced state.

"I'll go down and see him," I said. "Has he got the rods and stuff with him?"

"Everything. It's all gone down. He carried it all. If he'd've died on the path it's me that would've had to drag him back. He doesn't care. It's just too bad."

"Stop it, will you? Just leave the guy alone. We'll be back later."

She muttered something at my back that I didn't hear, but I'd heard it all before.

I found the kid sitting on a stump along the path to the lake. She faced the trail as though she'd been waiting. Sure I'd come. That felt nice for some reason.

"Is he really my grandfather?" she asked.

"Sure. My father, your grandfather."

She took my hand and hers was warm and wet and I molded its gentle roughness like an autumn apple. She knew the gestures that lead me to standing still. For statue making. To become a hero. But it was only for today, I thought. I could afford it for one day at least.

"Mommy's father is dead," she said. "He was my grandfather too."

"I know."

"How come your father never came to see us. Mommy's did sometimes."

"He's pretty busy," I said. "I hardly ever see him myself."

"Like you," she said. "Always busy too."

"Not like that. I mean . . ." I couldn't assemble the words to build the picture the way it really was. Maybe someday.

"He's been sick a lot," I said.

"Oh." It was a wounded sound. A moan. Orpheus looking back and regretting it in his throat.

We passed out of the trees and could see the water now. The sight, sheared from our full view by more trees, left the shape of an orchestra pit. It shone in the sun like a blue fuzz blanket. And the old man was there in front of us loading something in the boat.

"That's him," I said.

"I see. He's smaller than you."

She was right. I had always thought of him as being bigger, but he was tiny and shriveled in an old-dog kind of way. I hadn't seen him in over two years and it was like I had forgotten what he looked like.

"This is a surprise," he said. "Who've we got here?"

"This is my daughter Bernice. This is my father, Bernice, your grandfather."

"Well," he said, and took her hand smoothly. They walked away, he holding her hand and talking. "I was just gettin' the boat ready to do a bit of fishin'. You ever been fishin'?"

She shook her head. The long brown strands of hair reflecting gold in the sharply focused sun. Her mother's hair. It had reflected like that two summers ago in this very spot. Nothing changes.

"It okay to bring her along, Jake?"

His tone was polite but we all knew the question had been settled. He was already helping her into the boat.

"Sure," I said. "You got an extra rod?"

"She can use mine."

He'd done it again. I stood there feeling awkward, the way I had so often in the past. Like I was a kid again and didn't know what to do with my hands or feet, or the words in my mouth.

"You comin', Jake?" He was behind the motor tugging at the cord, as thin as the cord himself and looking frail in a tough way with an old raggedy wine-colored sweater dropping from his shoulders. So often in the past when he had offered things in that tone I'd refused. Now I jumped into the boat before he left without me.

He had the kid sitting across from him helping steer the boat as it plowed through the water making miniature rainbows in the spray. He was talking to her but I couldn't make out the words above the sound of the engine.

Once he had taken me to a baseball game at Maple Leaf Stadium. In the eighth inning I had to go to the bathroom, and he didn't want to miss any of the game so he let me go by myself. I was seven or eight. I got lost and he didn't find me until an hour after the place was cleared out. He wasn't angry. Disappointed maybe. And I was ashamed. Always when I was around him I did things to make me ashamed.

The motor slowed, gurgled, stopped. He dropped the paint can full of stones he used for an anchor.

"Is this the place where you catch the fish?" the kid asked. She was excited now, on the brink of some new discovery. Animated face like her mother.

"This is it," he said, "but don't forget what I said, fish can hear, so you've gotta be real quiet."

She put her hand to her mouth and ssshed.

"Right," he said.

So easy for her to get his approval. Was it easier now than it had been for me? He baited the hook for her as she watched intently. He plunked the line in the water and looked up to see me watching him.

"I was just remembering the first time you showed me how to put a worm on a hook," I said. "You remember?"

He laughed drowsily and coughed quietly. He was a quiet man, I thought. A quiet, polite man. He was sitting four feet away dying the same way he had lived.

"You were worse than a girl," he said.

"Yeah," and I tried to smile politely too, but I had always resented that about him; his attitude to my ... what did the old lady call it? My frailness.

"Sssh, Daddy, the fish'll hear," Bernice cautioned, her face serious.

The old man smiled. He had a way. Maybe I was jealous. I was a sickly kid, lousy at sports, anything physical, but he had a way of making it harder for me. Just stand there politely smiling at my attempts. He never laughed. Just that damn polite smile. And sometimes, now that I remembered, not even that. He wasn't always around when I tried my stunts; the day I finally made the hockey team and actually scored a goal. The second-place medal for swimming. He was busy playing golf, a game he was so good at different people encouraged him to turn pro. That made me proud when I heard that. I had daydreams of caddying for him in the big tournaments, but he just smiled his polite smile and said no.

I watched him put together a cigarette. He rolled his own and his hands moved quickly like a woman knitting.

"Nothin' bitin'," he said.

"No, not today by the look of it. Could be too hot. Maybe we should go in. The kid's got no hat, she might get sunstroke."

"I'm okay, Daddy. This is fun."

She kept standing up when she thought she had a bite. It made me nervous but the old man was right beside her. She was okay. Just my nerves.

"A beer?" he said.

"Yeah. Okay." He handed me a bottle and it was warm in the clammy way of a fish. I drank it quickly. I like beer, it reminds me of my mother: from hand to mouth, that's the way she describes the way I live, from hand to mouth. The beer being lifted, sucked at, the liquid measuring out my life. Like Hemingway, I thought with a sudden fright. From hand to mouth; his hand taking the gun to his mouth because he had nothing left to say and no reason to go on living. His statue molded and waiting for his death.

My trouble is I want to be remembered so much and yet I spend my time trying to forget. That's what my life is about these days; trying to forget. My wife. The kid. Mother. Everyone including the old man, and I never wanted to be spending this weekend with him in a boat supposedly fishing. I've dreaded the thought of such a weekend all my life.

"Surprised you're up this way," he said.

"Mom invited me."

"Probably told you about the business," he said.

So like him; business, his death.

"Yeah, she mentioned you weren't well."

"She gets excited."

Not like you with your polite smile.

"Daddy, you guys are gonna scare all the fish."

The old man puffed on his cigarette and grinned, his mouth unsealing like a steamed envelope. What was be-

hind the flap? What songs had found their way out, or
had any? Had the old man ever made music somewhere with someone? I'd have liked to have known.
Somehow I felt it would make me feel better if he had.
More hopeful. Something.

And suddenly the kid was standing, jerking forward
like a Buddhist monk in prayer falling to his knees.

"There's something . . ." she yelled, and splashed
into the water.

It was a short distance to fall from her position at
the back of the boat, and I watched the bright yellow
dress congeal into a dish rag. It was all so strange: once
I had fallen off the end of the dock when I was five. I
may even have done it on purpose and I kept my eyes
open in the water as I sank and I saw the eerie arm of
my father reach down and grab me. He used a fish gaff
to hook me. I still have the scars on my shoulder. The
proof. Of something.

The old man was right beside her. All he had to do
was reach over the side and pull her in. It would be
easy for him.

He yelled at me. Something was wrong. He never
yelled. A quiet polite man.

"Get her, Jake! Move, you stupid bugger!"

Me.

I plunged in. The water turned my clothes into a
smothering blanket. It was cold. I couldn't see her. I
had to go up. I couldn't breathe. I didn't want to
drown. I didn't want to die. I really didn't.

Oh God! Everything was ending. God. God. God.
Damn. And then I saw her. She was upside down, her
dress over her head. She seemed to be spinning slowly
and I grabbed a leg. I pawed upward with my hand,
not knowing any longer that there was anything
beyond. The surface was a spot in my mind that had
receded to a soft blur. Like a memory of long-ago pain.

But it was there waiting. I punched into the air, my
arm clawing for something to hold but the boat was
several yards away. I saw the old man still seated. He
spotted me and leaned forward, yelled something and I
was under again. I fought to turn the girl around. She

was like a shot deer. Stiff feeling. Her head was up and I cupped her under the chin and swam back to the boat just the way I'd been taught in the Red Cross life-saving course. The old man hadn't been around when I got the certificate either.

He was waiting and held her arms while I crawled in the boat. Everything was clear now. Pull her aboard, put her on the bottom of the boat with his sweater under her head. Check her mouth for obstructions. Head to one side. Arms in position. Pushing down gently. Pulling back. Counting. And repeating the whole thing over and over again.

The old man watched. He rolled a cigarette and coughed politely several times. He didn't smile and I saw he was sweating.

She began to cough. And then she was sick. That was good. It was okay. She began to cry. And then louder, screaming. Shock. The old man handed me his sweater and I wrapped her in it. Soon it was reduced to a sob.

"Daddy, the fish tried to take me away."

"It's okay, baby. Everything's okay. I've got you now."

And as suddenly as the tears had come, she fell asleep in my arms.

We sat there for a few minutes and then the old man spoke.

"I'm sorry, Jake. I just didn't have the strength. She was right there but I didn't have the strength to get her. She could've drowned."

"She didn't," I said. "That's the main thing. Everything's all right now."

"We'd better go back," he said.

He turned and started the motor. The girl slept huddled against me, and I thought of the phone in my room, the receiver in its cradle. And I thought of all the nights when I had almost called so many people like the girl I was holding. After today I would have to begin to make some of those calls or have the phone removed. I wasn't sure why, but something had changed, and I'd have to face it.

At the dock he helped me lift her out of the boat.

"Careful," I said.

"I'm fine now," he said. "Just sometimes my strength goes all out of me."

"You shouldn't've gone to all this trouble with the boat," I said.

He smiled. Polite again. We began walking back to the cottage, the girl asleep still in my arms.

"See, Jake," he said, when we reached the trees, "I'm a selfish man."

"We all are," I said.

"Yeah, but with me it was different in some way. Sometimes I feel like I missed something. I always figured the most important thing to a man was his privacy. A man's got to have his privacy. I always lived that way, Jake."

It may have been an explanation or even an apology but whatever it was, it was enough. He'd had his polite smile all his life and I had my telephone. You could hide behind either one or use it to reach out. I could learn a lot from the old man. If only he'd tell me. Maybe, though I had to ask. And maybe privacy was another way of saying lonely.

The old lady was waiting for us on the path. He walked straight toward her voice. I felt the pinch of her words and fell behind. The man walked straight ahead and didn't look back.

HUNTING

by *W. D. Valgardson*

In his prime, Sonny Brum had been 280 pounds of muscle that angled sharply from broad, straight shoulders to a narrow waist, but years of sitting around a display room drinking coffee and eating jelly busters as he waited for customers had thickened him. The muscle had diminished but his appetite had not and a heavy roll of flesh sagged over his belt. His head was square, his skin swarthy, and his nose, which was large and hooked, had been broken so many times that it was permanently bent to the left. A white scar curved like a third eyebrow in the middle of his forehead. When he walked, he did so with a hesitating limp.

If he had been older, he could have been a casualty of some foreign war, one of those who don blue blazers and lay wreaths once a year, but he was not. His facial scars had been gathered in the vicious struggles of semi-pro football and his knee cap had been smashed during the first game he played for the Winnipeg Blue Bombers. Although his first game as a pro had been his last, he had, on the wall of his office, a 24- by 18-inch photograph of himself in uniform with the rest of the team and he always carried a wallet-size duplicate along with his birth certificate and his driver's license.

Although it was only seven o'clock, he had been awake since five. First, he lay in bed and worried. Then, when he couldn't stand to be inactive any longer, he dressed and paced through the cold rooms of the house. Because it was Sunday and there was no hunting, he was afraid that Buzz Anderson and Roger Charleston, having nothing to keep them entertained, would want to return home. Not having shot their deer right away had made them discontented. Even though they had not complained, he could tell that it wouldn't take much for them to decide to leave. Since he was unable to think of anything else to keep them happy, he had decided to take them to the bootlegger's.

They had meant to use the entire house but they couldn't get the furnace to work so they had moved three cots into the kitchen and were heating the room with a catalytic heater.

Sonny swung open the kitchen door and let it bang closed behind him. Roger sat up and dug the knuckles of his index fingers into his eyes. He kicked himself free of his blankets and swung his feet over the edge of the cot. His legs, like the rest of him, were pale and flat

looking. All he had on were jockey shorts as he saun-
tered over to the counter and bent down to peer outside.

"We're going to get some snow," he said.

The sky was dull grey and the distant sun was small
and pale. On the horizon there was a ridge of pewter
cloud.

"Good," Sonny replied. "That'll make tracking
easier. You wound a deer and he'll leave a trail nobody
can miss. Blood on the snow's the best thing you can
have."

Roger stood on one leg, then the other, to pull on his
pants. "We've got to see them before we shoot them."
His voice carried a hint of irritation. He tucked in his
shirt, then went back to standing on one leg to pull on
his white coveralls.

"Hey, Buzz, what do you want for breakfast?"
Sonny lit the Coleman stove and put on the coffee pot.

Buzz groaned and sat up. He had on an orange
toque and a matching scarf. He was constantly afraid
of catching a cold or getting laryngitis and not being
able to host his morning radio show for housewives.
"Bacon, eggs, coffee, whiskey," he said. "In that
order." With a sigh, he dropped back onto the bed.

The kitchen smelled stale. The house was solid and
large, with five bedrooms upstairs, four rooms downstairs and a full basement, but it had been empty for so
long that the front yard was overgrown with young
poplars.

After breakfast, when Sonny led the way outside, the
air was sharp. The Russian thistle, touched by frost,
drooped blackly. In the muted light the branches of the
trees were stark and brittle looking. Huddled together
on the porch, the three of them studied the dark edge
of forest that gaped toward them, then turned to study
the yellows and browns of the fields which staggered
toward the horizon.

"See there!" Sonny called out, punching his large red
fist in the air. His two companions squinted and
strained to see what had excited him but there was
nothing except the trees and weeds.

Keeping his left leg stiff, he awkwardly descended the stairs and with his massive arms moving before him in a breast stroke, swept the saplings out of his way. The other two followed him uncertainly. He snapped off the stem of a poplar and held it out for their inspection. The top had been bitten off and the tender outer bark nibbled away.

"Look at that," he said. "There were deer in here last night. Tomorrow morning we can get up early and shoot one or two from the doorway."

Buzz and Roger's interest had risen sharply and, for the moment, Sonny's worry eased. Their good will was crucial to him. After recuperating from a series of operations on his knee, he had become a salesman with a Ford dealership next to the stadium. He hated every minute of his fifteen years of working for someone else but by saving every cent possible and buying and selling used cars out of his back yard, he finally managed to gather enough for a down payment on a dealership. At the same time, he moved his wife and daughter into a new house in a good neighborhood. Then, a series of small reverses combined with too little capital, squeezed him into a position where he had to have more money or lose his business.

During his two years in his new neighborhood, he had assiduously cultivated his neighbors in the hope of turning them into customers. When they did buy, he gave them the best possible price so that they would bring him other customers. Now, pressed for cash, and unable to obtain further credit, he had invited Roger and Buzz on a hunting trip.

Neither of them had been deer hunting before but both had said they would like to go hunting. That, and the fact that they both had steered customers his way in return for a bottle of whiskey or a pair of football tickets, made him choose them. As well, he knew from a credit check he had had run on them, that they had a fair amount of money salted away. What he intended to do was wait until they both had a deer and a few drinks and then offer to make them silent partners. He already had the papers made up.

Buzz quit studying the chewed stems and started for the car. His low, gentle voice drew women to his program in large numbers but he never allowed himself to be photographed if he could help it. He was barely five feet tall and his face—round and smooth, with slightly bulging eyes, a small, nearly bridgeless nose, red hair and freckles—made him look like a mildly retarded child.

They set off in Buzz's car, a maroon Cadillac he had bought for two hundred dollars. It was not much to look at. The left rear door was caved in, its window held together with a black spiderweb of electrician's tape. The fenders were so rusted that their edges resembled brown lace, but the motor ran well and the tires still had half a penny's width of rubber. Its major fault was that the steering was so loose that Buzz had a hard time keeping it under control.

The area they were driving through had, at one time, been the bottom of a lake. Now, a series of gravel ridges marked the successive shores. In the hollows, swamp grass that was the same pale brown as a red squirrel's ruff, rose as high as the car windows and willow clustered in dark, impenetrable thickets. The crests were crowded with scrub oak, hazel and black poplar.

It was on the crest of a ridge that they saw a buck standing in a hazel thicket.

"Lookit that!" Roger hollered, startling Buzz so badly that he jammed on the brakes. Sonny was sitting in the back. The sudden stop nearly pitched him into the front seat.

"Look at that rack," Buzz sighed, thinking of the family room in his basement. "He's got seven points."

"I told you," Sonny jubilantly said. "I told you the way it was."

"We don't have our rifles," Roger reminded them. He had a long tubular face and the minute he was unhappy, he looked like an undertaker. He pressed as close as possible to the windshield.

"I put my .22 into the trunk, remember," Sonny answered. "Give me the keys."

Buzz handed him the keys and Sonny slipped outside. Without taking his eyes off the buck, he crept to the rear of the car. Easing the trunk up slowly, he reached past the spare wheel and lifted out a rifle wound in burlap. He unwrapped it, raised it to his shoulder and squeezed the trigger. There was a sharp click.

Cursing under his breath, he tip-toed along the driver's side of the car. "Bullets," he whispered urgently. "I left them in the glove compartment."

The buck was so close that Sonny could have hit it with a rock. It stood at an angle to them, shoulder deep in brush, its head turned sideways. The curving antlers looked polished.

"Here," Buzz said, shoving the box out of the window upside down. As Sonny snatched the box, the lid popped open and the cartridges cascaded to the ground. Sonny stood stupefied, then flung the empty box aside and scooped up a handful of cartridges and gravel. Before he could get a bullet into the chamber, the buck trotted across the road and disappeared with a bound.

Sonny fumbled a moment longer then bitterly snapped, "Son-of-a-bitch!" He restrained an impulse to smash the car window.

As Roger and Buzz joined him, Sonny handed Roger the rifle. Then he and Buzz picked up the spilled cartridges.

"I couldn't get a bullet into the gun," Sonny explained defensively. The incident had shaken him. The buck seemed symbolic. Everything, his house, his business, his independence, seemed ready to slip away while he stood and watched helplessly.

"It was Sunday anyway," Buzz replied.

"Mounties." Roger warned. A black car had topped the adjacent ridge and was racing toward them. As Buzz and Sonny ran to the side of the road, Roger stood stupefied, then, as his long legs scissored beneath him, carrying him to safety, he flung the rifle into the bush.

Seconds later, a black Ford rocketed past, spraying them with gravel. The driver was an old woman with a green, wide-brimmed hat jammed over her ears.

With a sigh of relief, Buzz sat on a tree stump. Dramatically, he felt his heart. "You shouldn't do that, Roger. If my sponsors ever found out that I had been arrested for hunting illegally . . ." He left the rest unsaid.

"Where's my rifle?" Sonny asked.

Wordlessly, Roger scurried into the bush and began flailing about like a wounded duck. When he found the rifle, he waved it over his head.

To be certain the rifle was not damaged, Sonny loaded it, then fired three times. A hundred feet away, on the edge of the road, gravel flew into the air and a tin can jumped and spun on its rim before falling back. With a grunt of satisfaction, he rewrapped the rifle and stuffed it under the front seat.

Buzz brought back the can. It was pitted with rust but the edges of the bulletholes were bright and shiny. Where a hollow-nosed slug had entered, the hole was smaller than the end of a little finger. Where it exited, the hole was larger than a nickle and the edges were bent back like the sepals of a rose after the petals have fallen.

As they drove, they passed some farmhouses that, except for the television aerials on the roofs, looked abandoned. Frequently, they saw people working among the roadside bushes. Buzz slowed down.

"What are they doing?" he asked.

"Collecting hazelnuts," Sonny answered. "They husk them and sell them to the wholesale in Winnipeg."

A man and woman were working close to the road. Each held a gunny sack. The man wore rubber boots, overalls, a brown jacket and cap. The woman wore a red *babushka*, a brown jacket and a faded dress with men's pants underneath. Two boys, dressed exactly like their father, emerged to stare at the car. Like their parents, they might have been part of the weathered landscape. From a short distance, they were nearly indistinguishable from the trees.

Buzz pulled away. "They can't get much for their work."

"They don't." Sonny was glad they were moving

again. The sight of the children had been like a thrust of pain. He had been like that once. Suddenly, he could feel the weight of the scoop shovel. The stink of manure clogged his nostrils and the car seemed filled with the restless shifting of cattle.

Every morning from the time he was eight, he had shoveled out the barn. In the evenings and on weekends, he hauled or pitched hay or cut wood or staggered behind the stone boat, drunk with tiredness, as he attempted the hopeless task of trying to clear the fields of their yearly crop of stone.

"What keeps people here?" Roger asked.

"Stupidity. They don't know nothing and they don't want to know nothing."

On either side, the ditches were clogged with bulrushes. Behind the ditches were hay fields, then thin lines of trees marking the edges of the fields and more trees.

"Slow down," Sonny said. "It should be along here." He was puzzled, apologetic. He had Buzz turn at the next crossroads but after 200 yards, the road trailed away to a grassy path.

A farmhouse with the wreckage of three cars littering its front yard appeared on their right. Someone had tarpapered the outside walls and tacked on laths and chicken wire but had never put on stucco. Tattered plastic from the previous winter clung to the window frames. The yard was adrift with chickens.

Sonny could hear the steady one-stroke beat of a small engine so he braved a black mongrel which rushed up to bare his teeth and glare malevolently from pus-stained eyes.

Behind the house, a rawboned woman in a grey shapeless dress that came to her ankles was washing clothes in a gasoline washing machine. She looked no friendlier than her dog but when Sonny motioned to her, she moved close enough to hear what he had to say. Her face was haggard, her eyes sunken and suspicious and her hair was pinned in an untidy bun at the back of her neck. Sonny forced a smile while he tried to keep an eye on the dog which constantly twisted out of sight.

"We've got lost. We're looking for Joe Luprypa's place," he explained.

"Down the road one mile, then turn west." Her teeth were rotted to brown stumps.

He had not recognized her face but he remembered her voice. He looked at her more carefully. In the lined, coarse skin there was nothing to guide him but then she said, thinking he had not understood. "It's that way. See. Go down to the mile road."

Annie, sprang into his mind.

He nodded and said, "Thank you. Thank you," as he backed away. Except for the voice, he was unable to see any resemblance between the girl who had sat in front of him at school and the woman with the ravaged face and raw, rough hands folded across drooping breasts.

As Sonny opened the car door, the dog lunged for his ankle but he was ready and caught it in the ribs with his foot.

Joe Luprypa's driveway was deeply rutted and only wide enough for one car. It twisted down a gentle slope through a meadow of uncut hay and disappeared into a dense grove of poplars. The trees stopped at the beginning of a marsh. The car, caught by the twin ruts, was locked as securely to its path as any train. As a joke, Buzz took both hands from the wheel and clasped them behind his head. As the car bumped and rocked along the grooves in the dark earth, the wheel seemed to take on a life of its own.

In the center of the grove there was a large patch of rutted dirt. They bounced toward a small house covered in plastic panelling which was supposed to look like natural stone. At the back of the house there was a summer kitchen that had been painted bright purple. Permanently marching across the brown grass of the side yard to their diamond mine were plywood cutouts of the seven dwarves. An elderly blue pickup was parked to one side.

"No one's home," Buzz said. He sounded relieved. He could listen for hours to someone else's escapades but when he became involved in one, his enthusiasm quickly cooled. "We might as well go." He studied the house apprehensively.

Sonny shoved open his door and stepped away from the car. "They're just waiting to see who we are."

The back door cracked open but they could not see who had opened it. Then the door was flung back and a short, fat man in charcoal gray suit pants, a white shirt and a red flowered tie, waddled over, threw his arms around Sonny and beat him on the back. "Sonny! Long time no see. I wouldn't have recognized you except for that nose. It's still traveling in a different direction."

"We've come for a drink," Sonny waved his arm in a half-circle. "I thought there'd be no place to park."

Joe was studying Buzz and Roger closely.

"It's OK," Sonny reassured him, "they're next-door neighbors. Roger's in medicine and Buzz is in communications. Have you anything to drink?"

Joe nodded. Each time he ducked his head, he accumulated three more chins. "A little." He waved them inside. "Go in," he urged. "What do you want? Government or homebrew? My brother, Alec, made the homebrew."

"Homebrew," Sonny replied. "I haven't had any for years."

The house smelled strongly of cabbage. Joe's wife, a dried-out woman with a disapproving look frozen to her face, cleared the table and set out three beer glasses.

The kitchen was smaller and shabbier than Sonny remembered it. It was painted bright yellow. Flowers and birds cut from magazines had been glued to the cupboards and shellacked. The windows were crammed with geraniums in red clay pots. Over the doorway to the living room there was a plaster crucifix. The blood on it had been brightened with purple paint. From his place at the kitchen table, all Sonny could see of the living room was a high-backed brown chesterfield layered with scalloped pink and orange doilies. Above the chesterfield in an ornate gilt frame was a paint-by-number picture of a collie.

Joe scraped his feet and locked the door behind him. "We've just come from church," he explained. He was carrying a 26-ounce bottle which was smeared with mud and grass. He held the bottle to the light and grimaced with distaste.

"We sterilize our bottles. But on the outside it's like this because of the mounties' dogs. I have to tie the bottles with a string and throw them into the marsh." He made a pulling motion with his hands. "Then I go fishing."

He rinsed the bottle under the tap. "Five dollars for this. Sixty-five cents for tomato juice." After he pocketed Sonny's six dollars, Joe handed over the bottle and punched holes in a can. The tomato juice and homebrew swirled together like oil and water.

The homebrew was as raw as the cheapest bourbon. Joe brought a glass to the table and half-filled it with tomato juice but his wife said, "No. His liver's bad. He's just home from the hospital," when Sonny went to add liquor.

Joe laughed to cover his embarrassment. "It must be great to be in the city. I heard you on radio once, in a football game. Since then I heard you're doing good at cars. It's a good business. Everybody needs cars."

"It's a great business," Sonny enthusiastically agreed. He watched Roger and Buzz. "You can make a lot of money. Right now I'm ready to expand. Profits are going to be even bigger. For $10,000 I'd make someone a one-quarter partner."

Joe shook his head. "That's big money."

"It's a good investment," Sonny added. "Anybody buys in and from then on they collect while I work. No headaches, no problems, just profits."

Joe raised his glass at Roger. "Doctors always make lots of money. Somebody's always sick. That's the deal for your retirement fund."

Roger laughed off the suggestion. "Not me," he protested. "I like to put it in a nice safe bank."

"Me, too," Buzz agreed. "No risk." He gently felt his

throat. "You never know when a delicate instrument might lose its tone."

Quickly, Sonny asked, "How's business for you, Joe?"

"Not good. The mounties are a problem."

"The mounties are always a problem."

Joe was downcast. He made rings on the table with the bottom of his glass. "Not like now. On weekends, in good weather, they park at the end of my driveway and sit all day. Nobody dares come. Last time, the judge said no more fines. From now on, jail. I'm too old for that."

As Joe complained, Sonny could see how much he had changed. It was not just the new lines on his face or his thinning hair. He looked worn. At one time he had been prosperous. On weekends, fifty, a hundred people came and he dispensed homebrew from a water pitcher. Then, Joe's was the place to get drunk, pick a fight or pick up a woman.

They drank steadily. At noon, Joe's wife made them roast pork sandwiches with lots of salt and thick slices of Spanish onion. Sonny bought another bottle. By two o'clock, Roger and Buzz were very drunk. Their conversation had become so loud that they were nearly shouting.

Sonny kept his glass full of tomato juice. He wanted to stay sober so that he could lead the conversation back to his dealership when the time was right. He tried to follow the conversation but could not because Annie kept forcing her way into his thoughts. Once he had had a crush on her. She had been pretty with large dark eyes and a soft mouth. Now, his wife, with her trips to the health spa and the clothing stores and beauty parlor looked like an adolescent compared to Annie. Poverty had done that. It could still do it to his wife and daughter. If he lost his dealership, the ballet, music and figure-skating lessons would be the first to go. Then the house. He was forty-one and no one would want him when they could get college kids fresh out of school.

The more he brooded about it, the worse his situation seemed. The others were so involved in their storytelling that they ignored him. Then Roger started to tell Joe about the deer. As Roger demonstrated how he got rid of the rifle, his glass slipped and crashed into the cupboard. Joe brought him a new one.

"Shooting a deer on Sunday," Joe frowned. "That's bad."

Buzz laughed and slopped his drink down the front of his coveralls. "Never mind. Sonny couldn't have hit it anyway." He stumbled from his chair and began scrambling around in a circle as he imitated Sonny's attempts to pick up the cartridges. Roger and Joe were shouting with laughter. As he turned faster and faster, like a dog chasing its tail, he shouted, "A deer. Bullets. Help. A deer."

Sonny was offended. He could see the story being told back home. Angrily, he said, "You think I can't hunt? Come on, I'll show you." He grabbed the bottle by the neck and marched outside. "I'll get a deer the way we used to."

Buzz and Roger staggered after him. A heavy, wet snow was starting to fall. Buzz drove the car to the main road. Sonny crouched in the back with the rifle sticking out the window.

"I'll show you some shooting," he said.

They swerved wildly on the slick clay. The first thing Sonny shot was a stop sign. They halted to inspect it.

"See that," he said, jabbing at the hole with his finger. "Roger couldn't do that."

"Sure, I could. Give me that rifle." Roger grabbed the barrel.

"You're in no condition." Sonny held onto the butt.

"I said give it to me." Roger's voice was belligerent. He jerked the rifle out of Sonny's hands.

The snow was beginning to fall so heavily that the countryside was blurred. They started up again and Buzz had even more difficulty controlling the car. Roger leaned so far out the car window that he looked like he was going to fall out.

"Turn left," Sonny ordered. "That's the best way. There's always deer there."

The road was so slick that they were reduced to a crawl. The snow covered the back window and clogged the windshield wipers.

"Turn here," Sonny directed. "We'll try along here."

They followed the road for over a mile, then Buzz said excitedly, "A deer."

Roger emptied the rifle as Buzz skidded to a stop.

"Did you see it?" Buzz asked. Both he and Roger started down the road. Both had difficulty keeping their balance and they walked with exaggerated care, their legs stiffly spread. With a yelp, Buzz slipped backward and sat down in the mud. Sonny stayed in the car.

"Sonny!" Roger screamed in a high, frightened voice. "Sonny!"

When Buzz and Sonny reached Roger, he was kneeling beside a middle-aged woman in a faded brown coat with a fur collar. A man's felt cap was tied under her chin and her face was lined and shrunken. It looked like a small, dark leaf: She was an average-sized woman but lying on the ground, her legs drawn up so that only the toes of her black rubbers showed, she seemed a grotesque dwarf. Tightly gripped in her left hand was a gunnysack.

Sonny shook Roger's shoulder. "Do something. You're a doctor."

"No, I'm not." Roger replied. "I'm an optometrist."

The woman was lying on her side and a red stain was spreading over the snow at her back. The stain was as scarlet as lipstick.

"You shot her," Buzz accused him.

"You said it was a deer." Roger's voice trembled.

The woman's slack mouth tightened, then, as her lips drew back over her teeth, she gave a low, harsh cry.

"Maybe she isn't hurt bad," Roger said.

Behind them, Buzz gagged and threw up. Roger began to cry. "Lady," he said, his face stricken. "I didn't mean it."

"You shot her," Buzz repeated.

Sonny turned on him. "Shut up," he ordered. "You said she was a deer."

Snow was gathering along the woman's nose and in

the folds of her coat. Except for her harsh breathing and the muted throbbing of the car's exhaust, there was no sound. They stayed absolutely still, watching the blood spread outward, becoming pink at its edge.

Just then, the woman's eyes, which had been nearly shut, opened wide and fixed fiercely upon them. Her body tensed and, for a moment, it seemed as if she would rise and strike them. Instead, her body was shaken with a violent convulsion and she rolled onto her back. After that, she was still.

"It was an accident," Roger mumbled.

"Manslaughter," Sonny replied harshly. "You were both drunk."

"We've got to get her out of here." As Buzz spoke, he began to back away. Roger hesitated, then he rose. Together, they rushed for the car. Buzz tried to open the front door on the passenger's side but his hands were trembling so violently he could not control them. Sonny yanked open the rear door and shoved Buzz, then Roger, inside.

The snow was falling heavily. The nearby woods were dark and endless. The air was filled with an impenetrable whiteness that isolated them in a landscape without familiar landmarks. There were no signs, not even the sun, by which to take their bearing.

"Joe," Buzz said. "He'll know."

"Joe," Sonny replied, "won't know anything. He doesn't want to go to jail." He put the car into gear.

In the back seat, Roger and Buzz stared through the windows but there was nothing except the endless whiteness. The world was blurred and indistinct and as dangerous as an uncharted coast in dense fog. Even the road was gradually disappearing.

"Where are we going?" Roger cried, his hands gripping the back of the front seat. Buzz, his arms wrapped tightly around himself, sat hunched and mute.

Expertly, Sonny steered the car to the crest of the ridge. Roger repeated his plaintive question but Sonny, having already started them down the side of the ridge into the next hollow, was too busy to reply.

A CYNICAL TALE

by *Ray Smith*

Sweet William was a very successful fag couturier who lived in a refulgent fag apt. that had cost him five figures. He had a boyfriend named George. Life was very good for Sweet William & indeed he had often been heard to exclaim: "Everything is George!" (one of his loudest clangers). Sweet William was in his thirties.

But then there moved into the apt. next door to Sweet William's an ultrafeminist of undeniable beauty named Barbary Ellen. Barbary Ellen owned a string of health spas, a ritzy speed reading course for execs. & a language school. Hardly a month had gone by when Babsie had insinuated herself into the good graces of Sweet William. She did this by buying his clothes and sending him cases of plum cordial which was his and George's favorite drink. However, George did not like Barbary Ellen. Barbary Ellen was herself in her thirties & George had made it to his twentieth yr.

One night Swt. Wlm. took George to a cocktail party and what happened was they didn't like it and went home for a plum cordial. (*It should be noted here that Barbary Ellen in fact knew they were going out.*)

When they got home again they found Barbary Ellen had insinuated herself into their apt.

"I thaid she wath a nathty bitch!" This from Grg.

"Goodness gracious!" cried Sweet Wlm.

"Vithious prying creature!" He thereupon scurried off to protect his protector's lingerie.

"Shit." So saying, Babs E. proceeded to pull a neat little automatic fromst out her garter holster.

(A NOTE OF EXPL.: *All was not what it might have seemed. Sweet William was in fact a Russian*

*spy—having been subverted whilst in Moskva to view
the spring collections ("All the sprightly charm of a
pre-war tractor")—and Barbary Ellen was in the employ of counterespionage.)*

Well!

(Note: *a frail swoon approacheth.*)

Sweet William sank to the Bokhara with a groan &
all might have transpired A-OK had it not been for
George who came scampering in at this moment and
tried to strangle our lush Barbie Doll with a taupe ny-
lon. Of course she had to shoot him. (THE FATAL
FLAW! THE TURN OF THE SCREW! THE LAST
TRUMP! *et al.: for B. E. was no less than a latent les-
bian & hated all fags & thus, stupidly, let old George
have the full magazine of twelve rounds in the forehead, viz: fitfitfitfitfitfitfitfitfitfitfitfit! The "fit" being
caused by the silencer. So.*) Then she put the corpse in
the fridge and went on looking for the microfilm which
was indeed the very object of her visit.

But! Sweetie W. was not so silly as some of us think
fags to be. Not a bit of it! He had craftily secreted
about his apt. various and sundry deadly devices of
devious but innocent-seeming nature. Thusly, while
Barbary Ellen's svelte St. Laurent suited back (*this being the final insult to Swt. W.*) was turned toward his
supposedly swooned bod, Sweet William plucked a sprig
of briar from a fag floral arrangement nearby and drove
the stem (*previously dipped in a deadly poison by himself*) right the way through Babs's skirt, half-slip &
chaste Lycra panty girdle into her right buttock.

"Fag creep!" screeched Barbary Eln. with somewhat
less than her usual aplomb, then lamented as follows:
"Me, Barbary Ellen, beaten by a lousy fag creep:
Arrgh!"

So saying, she plucked from the same floral arngmt.
an equally poisoned rose clipping and this no less
deadly *fleur* she thrust through S. W.'s shot-silk fag
trousers and through his Lycra panty girdle into his left
buttock.

Ah! Irony!

Anyway, they both of them died and their cadavers

just stayed there on the floor, one beside t'other. And by some shoddy admin. oversight on the part of their superiors in the spy game, and because the legal eagles conducting their businesses were straight folk thus in love with lucre, the persons of Barbary Ellen and Sweet William (*and of George on ice if it come to that*) were not missed. And they didn't live in France so there was no concierge to twig & rat.

The briar & the rose, strange though it seem to us of the routine, day-to-day world, took root in the bodies of Sweet Willie and Barbie E. & flowered & intertwined (*symbolic of the love which might have united them in life had not nature played a cruel jest upon their hormonal balances before birth*) & mingled, thus adding a piquant touch to this gruesome tableau, etc.

SPRINGTIME

by *Claire Martin*

The neighbors laughed when Miss Amelia went by. The women would shrug their shoulders, which set their bountiful breasts bouncing under their flowered housecoats. The children, repeating what they had heard their parents say, would shout after her, "Crazy old maid! Crazy old maid!"

Miss Amelia wouldn't even deign to lift an eyelid. Stiffly, in her black dress, she would pass on by.

Poor Amelia. It's true she was still a maid, but she wasn't old. Thirty-five, thirty-eight maybe. In the prime of life. And not ugly either. But her face was always ravaged by rage.

From the back she was enticing enough to be followed frequently. By men who were strangers to the neighborhood, it should be noted. Anger, her daily

bread, kept her as thin as a gartersnake, gave a spring
to her step, and an extraordinary toss to her head.
Compared to the old housefraus on the block, she
made you think of an unbroken mare in a field of fat
cows.

The follower, being attracted to nervous women,
would trot along behind. Drawing abreast, he would
stop dumbfounded, then hurry right on by. There
wasn't a single one who ever thought of anything but
escape, followed by the laughter of the natives.

She had a look like a bull whip, did Miss Amelia.
You really had to be a stranger not to know its devastating effects.

There was only one person, the lady who lived on
the third floor left, who tried to be kind to her. It
wasn't easy, yet she didn't give up trying. She was the
persevering sort, a woman who followed her notions
right through to the end.

Since she was going through her third husband, Miss
Amelia's case seemed triply pathetic to her. "The poor
thing," she would sigh. "Just put yourself in her shoes.
Have you seen those red hot coals in her eyes? She's
burning up, she is! It's all very well to say, better
marry than burn. But Saint Paul doesn't say what to do
when you're only a woman and no husband comes forward."

With that she would pull a little pout for the misogy-
nist saint and then dissolve in pretty smiles and confusion. In her case, husbands flocked forward like indi-
gents to a soup kitchen.

It was mainly her brother Charles, lately come to the
neighborhood, whom the wife from the third floor left
chose as confidant for her compassion. Charles was for-
tyish, a shoemaker, and a good-looking man. And like
his sister he had a heart that was tender and understanding.

The day he saw the old maid come into his shop
with her offended face, he couldn't resist the sudden
urge to be a little bit nice to her, just to see. A compli-
ment is quickly made, doesn't cost anything, and can't
lead very far. As he was a shoemaker, he looked at her

foot, quickly saw that it was slender and nicely arched, and told her as much.

Now it so happened that Miss Amelia had always been quite proud of her feet. Perhaps she had always been waiting for someone to say something nice about them. Perhaps that was all she held against the human race, their ignorance of the fact that her feet existed. Her expression softened. She inclined her head gently and gave a little laugh as fresh as a schoolgirl's upon leaving the convent at the end of term.

Down she sat, took off her shoe, and put her foot up on the low stool. Charles felt impelled to rush forward, he knew he should have, but he stood there like a simpleton. The sparkle of her teeth, the curve of her foot, the caress of her laugh, had gone straight to his heart, and he was filled with a kind of fearful joy.

When the worst of his emotion had passed, he got out his finest shoes, shoes that were supple and soft as a girl's cheek. He could see how his trembling hands gave him away, but he didn't care. If a man doesn't speak, you can't slap him for trembling, can you? And apart from a slap he was ready for anything.

Courage! The moment had come. He seized her foot with just the right degree of warmth and slipped it into the shoe. "It fits like a glove! And you notice I didn't even ask your size." It was true. This happy stroke seemed to lend the whole affair a flavor of predestination that was troublesome indeed.

He stayed there holding the narrow foot closely in his hand. She felt the burn through the leather. Silently she savored this unknown happiness, thinking all the while that the other foot was cold too. He let her have the shoes at cost. For him she was already almost the boss. At cost price. And he blushed when he took the money.

Miss Amelia's romance left the neighborhood stunned and bewildered. The news dominated the conversations of the local gossips. Doors and windows filled with heads as she passed by.

That the old maid was loved and in love was already grist to their mill, but even more astounding was her new physical appearance. Each day that went by put a little more velvet in her look, a little more satin to her skin, and a sort of abandon in the roll of her hips. Now her ankles betrayed her and she would stumble when she walked out under Charles' admiring gaze. Her knees buckled under the miracle.

The grocer's wife, who had been chosen by her husband because she was solidly built and could stay on her feet behind the counter twelve hours at a stretch without grumbling, and who had accepted because the grocery business is the most serious of all commercial enterprises, followed this metamorphosis with an astonished eye and sighed all day long.

Charles' sister came close to believing that there must be a strain of sorcery in the family. She talked to her third husband at great length about it. So much so that the poor man began to get shivers down his spine whenever she looked at him, as she often did now with a mildly haggard expression as if seeing through him. He couldn't help feeling that the spell hadn't been exhausted yet and that it was a fourth chance at happiness his wife was watching as it advanced through the promise-laden fog of the future.

When Amelia and Charles announced their marriage, the neighborhood breathed a sigh of relief. At last things were going to return to normal. Everyone had managed to survive the courtship, but it would be nice to get back to preoccupations a little less torrid. By the wedding day, interest was already on the wane. The lovers were turning out just like everyone else.

A month hadn't passed before a little of the old Miss Amelia—just a trifle—began to show through. At first just a slight tensing of the nostrils. A few weeks later and it had spread to her mouth. After six months she had got back the two furrows between her eyebrows. Nobody noticed because nobody was particularly interested anymore. From time to time they would size up the state of her belly, but when that showed no signs of change they thought about something else.

It wasn't till months later that two old cronies, whiling away their time pinching lettuce heads, were struck by a sense of *déjà vu* when Miss Amelia walked by. She had completely recovered her prancing gait, her furious face, and her whiplash look.

The two old women burst out laughing and began slapping their thighs. After all, nobody expected that dreamy mood to last a lifetime, did they?

Poor Amelia, would she ever remember anything about that spring, that gentle madness, that brief blossoming?

THE LAMP AT NOON

by *Sinclair Ross*

A little before noon she lit the lamp. Demented wind fled keening past the house: a wail through the eaves that died every minute or two. Three days now without respite it had held. The dust was thickening to an impenetrable fog.

She lit the lamp, then for a long time stood at the window motionless. In dim, fitful outline the stable and oat granary still were visible; beyond, obscuring fields and landmarks, the lower of dust clouds made the farmyard seem an isolated acre, poised aloft above a sombre void. At each blast of wind it shook, as if to topple and spin hurtling with the dust-reel into space.

From the window she went to the door, opening it a little, and peering toward the stable again. He was not coming yet. As she watched there was a sudden rift overhead, and for a moment through the tattered clouds the sun raced like a wizened orange. It shed a soft, diffused light, dim and yellow as if it were the light from the lamp reaching out through the open door.

She closed the door, and going to the stove, tried the

potatoes with a fork. Her eyes all the while were fixed and wide with a curious immobility. It was the window. Standing at it, she had let her forehead press against the pane until the eyes were strained apart and rigid. Wide like that they had looked out to the deepening ruin of the storm. Now she could not close them.

The baby started to cry. He was lying in a homemade crib over which she had arranged a tent of muslin. Careful not to disturb the folds of it, she knelt and tried to still him, whispering huskily in a singsong voice that he must hush and go to sleep again. She would have liked to rock him, to feel the comfort of his little body in her arms, but a fear had obsessed her that in the dust-filled air he might contract pneumonia. There was dust sifting everywhere. Her own throat was parched with it. The table had been set less than ten minutes, and already a film was gathering on the dishes. The little cry continued, and with wincing, frightened lips she glanced around as if to find a corner where the air was less oppressive. But while the lips winced the eyes maintained their wide, immobile stare. "Sleep," she whispered again. "It's too soon for you to be hungry. Daddy's coming for his dinner."

He seemed a long time. Even the clock, still a few minutes off noon, could not dispel a foreboding sense that he was longer than he should be. She went to the door again—and then recoiled slowly to stand white and breathless in the middle of the room. She mustn't. He would only despise her if she ran to the stable looking for him. There was too much grim endurance in his nature ever to let him understand the fear and weakness of a woman. She must stay quiet and wait. Nothing was wrong. At noon he would come—and perhaps after dinner stay with her awhile.

Yesterday, and again at breakfast this morning, they had quarreled bitterly. She wanted him now, the assurance of his strength and nearness, but he would stand aloof, wary, remembering the words she had flung at him in her anger, unable to understand it was only the dust and wind that had driven her.

Tense, she fixed her eyes upon the clock, listening.

There were two winds: the wind in flight, and the wind that pursued. The one sought refuge in the eaves, whimpering, in fear; the other assailed it there, and shook the eaves apart to make it flee again. Once as she listened this first wind sprang into the room, distraught like a bird that has felt the graze of talons on its wing; while furious the other wind shook the walls, and thudded tumbleweeds against the window till its quarry glanced away again in fright. But only to return—to return and quake among the feeble eaves, as if in all this dust-mad wilderness it knew no other sanctuary.

Then Paul came. At his step she hurried to the stove, intent upon the pots and frying pan. "The worst wind yet," he ventured, hanging up his cap and smock. "I had to light the lantern in the tool shed, too."

They looked at each other, then away. She wanted to go to him, to feel his arms supporting her, to cry a little just that he might soothe her, but because his presence made the menace of the wind seem less, she gripped herself and thought, "I'm in the right. I won't give in. For his sake, too, I won't."

He washed, hurriedly, so that a few dark welts of dust remained to indent upon his face a haggard strength. It was all she could see as she wiped the dishes and set the food before him: the strength, the grimness, the young Paul growing old and hard, buckled against a desert even grimmer than his will. "Hungry?" she asked, touched to a twinge of pity she had not intended. "There's dust in everything. It keeps coming faster than I can clean it up."

He nodded. "Tonight, though, you'll see it go down. This is the third day."

She looked at him in silence a moment, and then as if to herself muttered broodingly, "Until the next time. Until it starts again."

There was a dark timbre of resentment in her voice now that boded another quarrel. He waited, his eyes on her dubiously as she mashed a potato with her fork. The lamp between them threw strong lights and shadows on their faces. Dust and drought, earth that betrayed alike his labor and his faith, to him the struggle had given sternness, an impassive courage. Beneath the whip of sand his youth had been effaced. Youth, zest, exuberance—there remained only a harsh and clenched virility that yet became him, that seemed at the cost of more engaging qualities to be fulfillment of his inmost and essential nature. Whereas to her the same debts and poverty had brought á plaintive indignation, a nervous dread of what was still to come. The eyes were hollowed, the lips pinched dry and colorless. It was the face of a woman that had aged without maturing, that had loved the little vanities of life, and lost them wistfully.

"I'm afraid, Paul," she said suddenly. "I can't stand it any longer. He cries all the time. You will go, Paul—say you will. We aren't living here—not really living—"

The pleading in her voice now, after its shrill bitterness yesterday, made him think that this was only another way to persuade him. Evenly he answered, "I told you this morning, Ellen; we keep on right where we are. At least I do. It's yourself you're thinking about, not the baby."

This morning such an accusation would have stung her to rage; now, her voice swift and panting, she pressed on, "Listen, Paul—I'm thinking of all of us— you, too. Look at the sky—and your fields. Are you blind? Thistles and tumbleweeds—it's a desert, Paul. You won't have a straw this fall. You won't be able to feed a cow or a chicken. Please, Paul, say that we'll go away—"

"No, Ellen—" His voice as he answered was still remote and even, inflexibly in unison with the narrowed eyes, and the great hunch of muscle-knotted shoulder. "Even as a desert it's better than sweeping out your father's store and running his errands. That's all I've got ahead of me if I do what you want."

"And here—" She faltered. "What's ahead of you here? At least we'll get enough to eat and wear when you're sweeping out his store. Look at it—look at it, you fool. Desert—the lamp lit at noon—"

"You'll see it come back," he said quietly. "There's good wheat in it yet."

"But in the meantime—year after year—can't you understand, Paul? We'll never get them back—"

He put down his knife and fork and leaned toward her across the table. "I can't go, Ellen. Living off your people—charity—stop and think of it. This is where I belong. I've no trade or education. I can't do anything else."

"Charity!" she repeated him, letting her voice rise in derision. "And this—you call this independence! Borrowed money you can't even pay the interest on, seed from the government—grocery bills—doctor bills—"

"We'll have crops again," he persisted. "Good crops—the land will come back. It's worth waiting for."

"And while we're waiting, Paul!" It was not anger now, but a kind of sob. "Think of me—and him. It's not fair. We have our lives, too, to live."

"And you think that going home to your family—taking your husband with you—"

"I don't care—anything would be better than this. Look at the air he's breathing. He cries all the time. For his sake, Paul. What's ahead of him here, even if you do get crops?"

He clenched his lips a minute, then, with his eyes hard and contemptuous, struck back, "As much as in town, growing up a pauper. You're the one who wants to go, Ellen—it's not for his sake. You think that in town you'd have a better time—not so much work—more clothes—"

"Maybe—" She dropped her head defenselessly. "I'm young still. I like pretty things."

There was silence now—a deep fastness of it enclosed by rushing wind and creaking walls. It seemed the yellow lamplight cast a hush upon them. Through the haze of dusty air the walls receded, dimmed, and came again. Listlessly at last she said, "Go on—your dinner's getting cold. Don't sit and stare at me. I've said it all."

The spent quietness in her voice was harder even

than her anger to endure. It reproached him, against his will insisted that he see and understand her lot. To justify himself he tried, "I was a poor man when you married me. You said you didn't mind. Farming's never been easy, and never will be."

"I wouldn't mind the work or the skimping if there was something to look forward to. It's the hopelessness—going on—watching the land blow away."

"The land's all right," he repeated. "The dry years won't last forever."

"But it's not just dry years, Paul!" The little sob in her voice gave way suddenly to a ring of exasperation. "Will you never see? It's the land itself—the soil. You've plowed and harrowed it until there's not a root or fibre left to hold it down. That's why the soil drifts—that's why in a year or two there'll be nothing left but the bare clay. If in the first place you farmers had taken care of your land—if you hadn't been so greedy for wheat every year—"

She had taught school before she married him, and of late in her anger there had been a kind of disdain, an attitude almost of condescension, as if she no longer looked upon the farmers as equals. He sat still, his eyes fixed on the yellow lamp flame, and seeming to know how her words had hurt him, she went on softly, "I want to help you, Paul. That's why I won't sit quiet while you go on wasting your life. You're only thirty—you owe it to yourself as well as me."

Still he sat, with his lips drawn and white and his eyes on the lamp flame. It seemed indifference now, as if he were ignoring her, and stung to anger again she cried, "Do you ever think what my life is? Two rooms to live in—once a month to town, and nothing to spend when I get there. I'm still young—I wasn't brought up this way."

Stolidly he answered, "You're a farmer's wife now. It doesn't matter what you used to be, or how you were brought up. You can get enough to eat and wear. Just now that's all that I can do. I'm not to blame that we've been dried out five years."

"Enough to eat!" she laughed back shrilly, her eyes

all the while fixed expressionless and wide. "Enough salt pork—enough potatoes and eggs. And look—" Springing to the middle of the room, she thrust out a foot for him to see the scuffed old slipper. "When they're completely gone, I suppose you'll tell me I can go barefoot—that I'm a farmer's wife—that it's not your fault we're dried out—"

"And look at these—" He pushed his chair away from the table now to let her see what he was wearing. "Cowhide—hard as boards—but my feet are so callused I don't feel them anymore."

Then hurriedly he stood up, ashamed of having tried to match her hardships with his own. But frightened now as he reached for his smock she pressed close to him. "Don't go yet. I brood and worry when I'm left alone. Please, Paul—you can't work on the land anyway."

"And keep on like this?" Grimly he buttoned his smock right up to his throat. "You start before I'm through the door. Week in and week out—I've troubles enough of my own."

"Paul—please stay—" The eyes were glazed now, distended a little as if with the intensity of her dread and pleading. "We won't quarrel anymore. Hear it! I can't work—I just stand still and listen—"

The eyes frightened him, but responding to a kind of instinct that he must withstand her, that it was his self-respect and manhood against the fretful weakness of a woman, he answered unfeelingly, "I'm here safe and quiet—you don't know how well off you are. If you were out in it—fighting it—swallowing it—"

"Sometimes, Paul, I wish I were. I'm so caged—if I could only break away and run. See—I stand like this all day. I can't relax. My throat's so tight it aches—"

Firmly he loosened his smock from the clutch of her hands. "If I stay we'll only keep on like this all afternoon. Tomorrow when the wind's down we can talk over things quietly."

Then, without meeting her eyes again he swung outside, and doubled low against the buffets of the wind, fought his way slowly toward the stable. There was a deep hollow calm within, a vast darkness engulfed beneath the tides of moaning wind. He stood breathless a moment, hushed almost to a stupor by the sudden extinction of the storm and the incredible stillness that enfolded him. It was a long, far-reaching stillness. The first dim stalls and rafters led the way into cavernlike obscurity, into vaults and recesses that extended far beyond the stable walls. Nor in these first quiet moments did he forbid the illusion, the sense of release from a harsh, familiar world into one of immeasurable peace and darkness. The contentious mood that his stand against Ellen had roused him to, his tenacity and clenched despair before the ravages of wind, it was ebbing now, losing itself in the cover of darkness. Ellen and the wheat seemed remote, unimportant. At a whinny from the bay mare, Bess, he went forward and into her stall. She seemed grateful for his presence, and thrust her nose deep between his arm and body. They stood a long time thus, comforting and assuring each other.

For soon again the first deep sense of quiet and peace was shrunken to the battered shelter of the stable. Instead of release or escape from the assaulting wind, the walls were but a feeble stand against it. They creaked and sawed as if the fingers of a giant hand were tightening to collapse them; the empty loft sustained a pipelike cry that rose and fell but never ended. He saw the dust-black sky again, and his fields blown smooth with drifted soil.

But always, even while listening to the storm outside, he could feel the tense and apprehensive stillness of the stable. There was not a hoof that clumped or shifted, not a rub of halter against manger. And yet, though it had been a strange stable, he would have known, despite the darkness, that every stall was filled. They, too, were all listening.

From Bess he went to the big gray gelding, Prince. Prince was twenty years old, with rib-grooved sides, and high, protruding hipbones. Paul ran his hand over the ribs, and felt a sudden shame, a sting of fear that Ellen might be right in what she said. For wasn't it true—nine years a farmer now on his own land, and still he couldn't even feed his horses? What, then, could he hope to do for his wife and son?

There was much he planned. And so vivid was the future of his planning, so real and constant, that often the actual present was but half felt, but half endured. Its difficulties were lessened by a confidence in what lay beyond them. A new house for Ellen, new furniture, new clothes. Land for the boy—land and still more land—or education, whatever he might want.

But all the time was he only a blind and stubborn fool? Was Ellen right? Was he trampling on her life, and throwing away his own? The five years since he married her, were they to go on repeating themselves, five, ten, twenty, until all the brave future he looked forward to was but a stark and futile past?

She looked forward to no future. She had no faith or dream with which to make the dust and poverty less real. He understood suddenly. He saw her face again as only a few minutes ago it had begged him not to leave her. The darkness around him now was as a slate on which her lonely terror limned itself. He went from Prince to the other horses, combing their manes and forelocks with his fingers, but always still it was her face, its staring eyes and twisted suffering. "See, Paul—I stand like this all day. I just stand still— My throat's so tight it aches—"

And always the wind, the creak of walls, the wild lipless wailing through the loft. Until at last as he stood there, staring into the livid face before him, it seemed that this scream of wind was a cry from her parched and frantic lips. He knew it couldn't be, he knew that she was safe within the house, but still the wind persisted as a woman's cry. The cry of a woman with eyes like those that watched him through the dark. Eyes that were mad now—lips that even as they cried still pleaded, "See, Paul—I stand like this all day. I just stand still—so caged! If I could only run!"

He saw her running, pulled and driven headlong by the wind, but when at last he returned to the house, compelled by his anxiety, she was walking quietly back and forth with the baby in her arms. Careful, despite his concern, not to reveal a fear or weakness that she might think capitulation to her wishes, he watched a moment through the window, and then went off to the tool shed to mend harness. All afternoon he stitched and riveted. It was easier with the lantern lit and his hands occupied. There was a wind whining high past the tool shed too, but it was only wind. He remembered the arguments with which Ellen had tried to persuade him away from the farm, and one by one he defeated them. There would be rain again—next year or the next. Maybe in his ignorance he had farmed his land the wrong way, seeding wheat every year, working the soil till it was lifeless dust—but he would do better now. He would plant clover and alfalfa, breed cattle, acre by acre and year by year restore to his land its fiber and fertility. That was something to work for, a way to prove himself. It was ruthless wind, blackening the sky with his earth, but it was not his master. Out of his land it had made a wilderness. He now, out of the wilderness, would make a farm and home again.

Tonight he must talk with Ellen. Patiently, when the wind was down, and they were both quiet again. It was she who had told him to grow fibrous crops, who had called him an ignorant fool because he kept on with summer fallow and wheat. Now she might be gratified to find him acknowledging her wisdom. Perhaps she would begin to feel the power and steadfastness of the land, to take a pride in it, to understand that he was not a fool, but working for her future and their son's.

And already the wind was slackening. At four o'clock he could sense a lull. At five, straining his eyes from the tool shed doorway, he could make out a neighbor's buildings half a mile away. It was over— three days of blight and havoc like a scourge—three days so bitter and so long that for a moment he stood still, unseeing, his senses idle with a numbness of relief.

But only for a moment. Suddenly he emerged from the numbness; suddenly the fields before him struck his eyes to comprehension. They lay black, naked. Beaten and mounded smooth with dust as if a sea in gentle swell had turned to stone. And though he had tried to prepare himself for such a scene, though he had known since yesterday that not a blade would last the storm, still now, before the utter waste confronting him, he sickened and stood cold. Suddenly like the fields he was naked. Everything that had sheathed him a little from the realities of existence: vision and purpose, faith in the land, in the future, in himself—it was all rent now, all stripped away. "Desert," he heard her voice begin to sob. "Desert, you fool—the lamp lit at noon!"

In the stable again, measuring out their feed to the horses, he wondered what he would say to her tonight. For so deep were his instincts of loyalty to the land that still, even with the images of his betrayal stark upon his mind, his concern was how to withstand her, how to go on again and justify himself. It had not occurred to him yet that he might or should abandon the land. He had lived with it too long. Rather was his impulse to defend it still—as a man defends against the scorn of strangers even his most worthless kin.

He fed his horses, then waited. She too would be waiting, ready to cry at him, "Look now—that crop that was to feed and clothe us! And you'll still keep on! You'll still say 'Next year—there'll be rain next year'!"

But she was gone when he reached the house. The door was open, the lamp blown out, the crib empty. The dishes from their meal at noon were still on the table. She had perhaps begun to sweep, for the broom was lying in the middle of the floor. He tried to call, but a terror clamped upon his throat. In the wan, returning light it seemed that even the deserted kitchen was straining to whisper what it had seen. The tatters of the storm still whimpered through the eaves, and in their moaning told the desolation of the miles they had traversed. On tiptoe at last he crossed to the adjoining room; then at the threshold, without even a glance inside to satisfy himself that she was really gone, he wheeled again and plunged outside.

He ran a long time—distraught and headlong as a few hours ago he had seemed to watch her run— around the farmyard, a little distance into the pasture, back again blindly to the house to see whether she had returned—and then at a stumble down the road for help.

They joined him in the search, rode away for others, spread calling across the fields in the direction she might have been carried by the wind—but nearly two hours later it was himself who came upon her. Crouched down against a drift of sand as if for shelter, her hair in matted strands around her neck and face, the child clasped tightly in her arms.

The child was quite cold. It had been her arms, perhaps, too frantic to protect him, or the smother of dust upon his throat and lungs. "Hold him," she said as he knelt beside her. "So—with his face away from the wind. Hold him until I tidy my hair."

Her eyes were still wide in an immobile stare, but with her lips she smiled at him. For a long time he knelt transfixed, trying to speak to her, touching fearfully with his fingertips the dust-grimed cheeks and eyelids of the child. At last she said, "I'll take him again. Such clumsy hands—you don't know how to hold a baby yet. See how his head falls forward on your arm."

Yet it all seemed familiar—a confirmation of what he had known since noon. He gave her the child, then, gathering them up in his arms, struggled to his feet, and turned toward home.

It was evening now. Across the fields a few spent clouds of dust still shook and fled. Beyond, as if through smoke, the sunset smoldered like a distant fire.

He walked with a long dull stride, his eyes before him, heedless of her weight. Once he glanced down and with her eyes she still was smiling. "Such strong arms, Paul—and I was so tired with carrying just him. . . ."

He tried to answer, but it seemed that now the dusk was drawn apart in breathless waiting, a finger on its lips until they passed. "You were right, Paul. . . ." Her voice came whispering, as if she too could feel the hush. "You said tonight we'd see the storm go down. So still now, and the sky burning—it means tomorrow will be fine."

HEIL!

by *Randy Brown*

Bob woke up and listened. He turned to his wife, Carol, but she was still breathing heavily into her pillow. He swung his feet out of bed and walked over to the window. There, standing on the porch below, illuminated by the backdoor light, was a man. He was beckoning to him. Bob bent over and stared. The man seemed to know he was there, for he beckoned even more insistently.

"Carol!" said Bob. She rolled over and raised her head. "There's someone out there, someone's standing on the porch."

Carol lifted herself up on her hands.

"What does he want?" she said.

"I don't know. He seems to be waving at me."

Carol came over beside him.

"Oh, my God!"

"What's the matter?"

"Look at him," replied Carol. Then Bob realized. The man wore only a bathrobe over his pajamas and was in his bare feet. Six inches of snow lay on the ground. Carol clutched his arm. "Don't let him in."

Bob hesitated. It seemed incongruous. Where could he have come from? Their farmhouse was half a mile from the road and a mile from the next house. They spent only occasional weekends there during the winter so it didn't seem possible that a neighbor would come that way for help. Yet a half-dressed man was standing on their porch, freezing to death, beckoning.

"I've got to let him in, Carol," he blurted.

"No, no, don't. He looks too strange. Call the police."

"I've got to let him in. He'd be dead by the time the police got here. Anyway, he's alone. I can handle one man."

"I won't let you! I won't let you! Call the police, oh please, call the police!"

"You stay here," he ordered and started out of the room.

"No! Don't leave me here alone! I'll come with you."

"O.K. Suit yourself, but come on."

Bob turned on the hall lights and headed downstairs to the kitchen with Carol right behind. They could hear the man pounding on the door, a loud, almost panic-stricken sound.

"O.K., O.K., I'm coming!"

"Wait!" called Carol. She pulled open the utensil drawer and lifted out the carving knife. Bob turned. Her hands shook so that she nearly dropped it on the floor.

"Just leave that on the table," he said. The pounding on the door was deafening. Bob hesitated. He could not understand the situation. They led such an ordered life. He had never come across anything that so defied an explanation. Carol had retreated into the far corner of the kitchen, her eyes fixed on him, and between them, on the table, lay the knife, shiny and ominous. He knew he could never use it. Shaking his head, he crossed to the door and pulled back the latch.

The door burst open and the man was on him, pinning his arms to his sides. They crashed to the floor and Bob struggled for his breath amidst the shock of the impact and Carol's piercing scream. He kicked out and the kitchen table went crashing over. Carol's screams faded into the background of his own rasping breath as he struggled to beat the man off. The knife was on the floor only a foot away. He lunged to grasp it and stabbed it into the man's back again and again.

Bob rolled from under the body.

"It's all right," he gasped, staggering up, "It's all right." Carol kept screaming. Following the line of her gaze, he turned around. The back door was crowded with a dozen more of the same men, all in pajamas and bare feet, all babbling and shoving their way into the house.

Bob swung the knife at the figures that seemed only a blur to him. Carol was lifted up bodily and thrown down, her screams stifled. The press of the men forced Bob back into the corner. He could not advance against them. One large figure came out of the blur and Bob stabbed the knife deep into the man's chest. The figure toppled over onto him and he threw it back into the arms grasping at him. Directly behind him was the open cellar door. He darted through and slammed it, then quickly jammed several timbers against it so that it was immovable. The men tried to knock it down, but they could not, and they finally left it alone.

For several hours Bob crouched alone in his sanctuary, listening. He could hear Carol. She tried to scream quite often. Bob thought she couldn't scream because she couldn't get her breath. Mostly, she groaned. At the first she managed to scream about once every five minutes, but after about an hour, she moaned. There were other noises, too, of furniture being pulled over and general destruction going on, but he barely registered those noises. It was Carol he was listening for, and when they threw her around, he knew, because the sound of her body was softer than that of the furniture. He prayed that she would die. He began to curse her, screaming at her to die. Several times he caught himself screaming at the top of his lungs, "Die, die, die, die!"

In the morning, when the search parties arrived, they found Carol's naked, frozen body by the front steps. The madmen were still roaming about the house. The police loaded them into several paddy wagons. They broke down the cellar door. Bob was sitting on the top step, babbling gently to himself and playing with the drawstring of his pajamas.

"I don't know how this one got down here," said the officer, "but take him and throw him into the wagon with the others."

THE CURE

by *E. G. Perrault*

It all began with the stamp album, though the Lord alone knows when it really began. Years and years, maybe, with him carrying on like that whenever her back was turned.

"I threw your stamp album in the furnace, Richard." She told him out of a clear sky after supper one night.

"You shouldn't have done that, Hilda," he said. That was all he said; didn't even raise his voice according to Mrs. Grindley.

"You can't say I haven't warned you time and time again," she told him, " 'snippets' of paper all over the living room table, people tracking through all the mud holes in town and then across my carpets just to look at your stamps. Didn't I warn you now?"

"Many times, dear," he said and walked out of the room and up the stairs as though the whole thing was over and done with.

She says he hadn't been right since he retired from the post office. Always mooning around, looking for something to do. His friends weren't exactly the kind you'd want in the house; mailmen mostly, all of them pipe smokers or tobacco chewers according to her. It didn't seem fair somehow for him to be visiting away at all hours without her so he stayed around the place most of the time doing nothing. The Devil finds work for that kind.

But the fact is she lay half an hour in bed that very same night, waiting for him to come in and turn the light off. Twice she called out, "Richard, come to bed this minute." Her voice is strong for a woman. No answer. So she climbed out of bed and went down the hallway to see what he was up to.

He was in the bathroom. She saw him through a crack in the door standing in front of the mirror looking at himself; preening like a peacock; making clown faces at himself; carrying on like a monkey in a cage.

"Richard," she said, "what do you think you're doing?"

"Shaving," he said, and started to take his shaving tools out of the cupboard.

"You never shaved at night in your life," she told him, "and you don't need to start now. Yesterday was your shaving day." He didn't argue with her; just followed along to bed not saying a word.

That's the first she remembers. Other things fit into the picture now. He became interested in the brass and silver in the house. I saw him with my own eyes many a time sitting at the kitchen table polishing the teaspoons with a chamois cloth.

Mrs. Grindley swears she didn't have a notion until the day she found a looking glass in his trousers pocket. That's nothing, you say? Maybe so but when another one turns up in his vest, and another in his dressing gown and still another one in the hip pocket of his gardening denims you'll be as surprised as she was. Little oblong mirrors they were, the kind you and I would carry in a purse. She waited until suppertime to tell him about it.

"I see you have a new hobby, Richard," she said throwing the mirrors on the table in front of him.

"I often wonder what I got for a husband. Carrying on like a drugstore dandy! What have you got to be proud of," she said. "Twenty years ago you were no beauty and time hasn't done you any favors." My it must have been something to hear her give him his comeuppance. She's got a wonderful tongue, that woman!

He just sat there with his head bent over his teacup and let the words tumble down like brimstone on Sodom and Gomorrah. She thought he was taking it to heart until she noticed that he was smiling into his cup.

It was plain enough what he was up to and she didn't waste any time pouring his tea back into the pot.

"You ought to be ashamed," she said, and broke the mirrors like soda crackers in front of his eyes. "Primping like a movie star actor! You try that sort of thing again and I'll do more than just talk."

She's a woman of her word; you know that as well as I do. Have you seen the place since she done it over? Richard was the reason for that. She threw out everything that could make a reflection; that lovely walnut bookcase they used to have; the brass around the fireplace, vases, silverware. It must have broken her heart to do it, but then she had the house redecorated; new drapes and bric-a-brac, wallpaper in every room. When it was all over she gave him the bills and a good talking to for the trouble he had caused. There was some satisfaction in that.

It seemed she had him beaten. For a week or more she watched his every move. There's no cure like a complete cure, they say. He seemed to come back to normal again and took to sitting in the kitchen in the evenings, staring out into the dark garden, saying never a word. She let him sulk; and then one night coming into the kitchen in a hurry she caught him with his face right up to the window glass, smiling at what he saw there.

I hate to tell it, but she threw the salt cellar across the room and knocked out a pane above his head. He was lucky to get away with a few splinter cuts. You can't blame her altogether. I ask myself what I would have done at a time like that.

She couldn't leave him alone for a minute. It might have looked harmless enough to watch them walking along on a Sunday afternoon, but you should have seen how she steered away from store fronts and weighing scales, and that sort of thing. Poor woman!

She came to my house one day as close to tears as I've ever seen her.

"He was out in the backyard after the shower today," she said. "I caught him behind the tool house kneeling over a puddle of rain water. What can I do with the man?"

"Get his mind off himself," I told her. "Maybe his friends can help."

"You know how I feel about his friends," she said.

"Hasn't he got any interests—besides stamp collecting," I said. "My John spends hours in the basement with his jigsaw."

"Noisy machinery gives me a headache," she said; and I know it's true for a fact; she has a bad time with migraine.

"Take him visiting," I told her. "Let him see how husbands should behave. Bring him over here and we'll have a nice evening together." She agreed to that and they came over one Saturday. I made up sandwiches and things. John and I didn't let on we knew about the trouble.

Richard just sat there saying nothing and Mrs. Grindley had to talk for both of them. I have to hand it to her she carried it off well, until Richard pulled his little surprise.

"Pardon me a moment," he says halfway through the evening; and he was gone before she could open her mouth.

Now what could we say under the circumstances. You can't go following a guest through the house. Mrs. Grindley began to fidget and look over her shoulder in the middle of sentences. John and I suffered along with her; but he was back soon enough smiling and contented.

"I believe I'll have another of your macaroons," he said to me as natural as you please, and from that time on he talked right along with us. You never saw such a change. John thinks he stopped a few minutes in front of the hall mirror. Whatever he did it picked him up like a nip of toddy on a winter's night. Mrs. Grindley didn't take him visiting again. Couldn't run the risk.

Imagine the poor soul with such a responsibility. She couldn't leave the house for more than a few minutes at a time. I phoned her two, three times a day and visited when I could to see how she was making out.

"You can't go on like this," I told her finally. "Someone should be called in, one of those doctor fellows that knows about these things."

"I do believe he's not quite right," she said.

"It's as plain as can be," I said. "What normal healthy man would carry on like that? You talk to a mind doctor about him."

"I believe I will," she said.

That doctor shouldn't be allowed to practice. He started to blame the whole thing on her.

"You don't give him a chance," he told her. "You don't take any interest in what he does or what he wants to do. I really believe you're not in love with the man."

"Nonsense!" she shot right back at him. "I married him didn't I? He's had the best years of my life."

"Why didn't you have a family," he asks her, although the question had nothing to do with Richard.

"On a mailman's wages I could have a dozen children, I suppose," she said.

Oh, he told her a good deal more; and the harder she tried to make him see reason the more confused he got. He had it figured that Richard had no friends, or interests, or recognition. All he had left was himself—which is little enough at that. When Mrs. Grindley explained that Richard was probably trying a new way to aggravate her he wouldn't hear of it. "You give that man a little love," he said, "and he'll be well in no time."

He was wrong as wrong can be, she knew it but she had to clutch at straws. It was terrible the way she tried. I was over there many a time and saw her, fetching his slippers, pouring him a second cup of tea, and smiling at him when there was no need at all to be nice.

The strain showed on her face but she knew her duty and she did it. As for him, I'm sure he didn't understand what was going on. He let her know he was suspicious.

"What do you want from me?" he'd say.

"Nothing, darling, just for you to be happy," she'd say.

"You're working too hard at it," he told her. "I'd rather have you the other way." Oh he said mean, cruel things; flew into rages which was something he'd never done before. But Mrs. Grindley stuck to her guns. The worse he got the nicer she became.

"I'm knitting Richard a pair of socks," she'd say and smile across at him slumped in the window seat. "Hold your foot up 'til I see how this is going to be."

"You know my size," he'd say.

"Green's his favorite color," she'd say, letting on she hadn't heard him.

"Green's your favorite color," he'd snap, "talk about something else."

I wonder now that she didn't leave him; but then neither of them had any place to go. The house is all they have and they're not spring chickens. Mrs. Grindley isn't the kind to run away at any rate. She tried everything she knew to win him over; took to wearing bright flouncy dresses instead of the good practical greys and purples that she's partial to; had her hair curled up a new way and wore a touch of color in her cheeks. She'd walk up to him right in front of me and peck him on his forehead.

"It's Yorkshire pudding for lunch, Richard," she'd say. If she got a growl out of him she was lucky. He just couldn't see what she was up to.

And then overnight everything changed. You've seen them yourself. Remember last week at the bazaar—embracing like newlyweds in front of the fish pond with half the town milling around them? That happened overnight.

"It's a miracle," she said to me over the phone that morning. "He's like a schoolboy with his first lover. Last evening I tried to kiss him good night—he started to push me away and then such a change came over him I couldn't believe it. He pulled me back and squeezed me till I fairly begged for breath."

Oh, I'll tell you she was excited. It's been the same ever since with him playing lovey-dovey every hour of

the day. I don't see how she puts up with it really—
him stepping out of closets when she least expects it to
plant kisses on her that would put Rudolph Valentino
to shame. He gives no thought to who might be
watching.

"Let me look at you," he says, and he gazes at her
with such a tender expression that it sends the shivers
up my spine. It's not fitting in a man his age.

"It's too good to be true!" she tells me. "I'll put up
with any amount of his nonsense so long as he forgets
about his looking glasses."

Too good to be true indeed! I see through his game
plain enough, and I haven't the heart to tell her. I
wouldn't breathe a word of it to you either except I
know you can be trusted to keep it to yourself.

Watch how he gazes at her. Watch how he looks
deep into those big, shiny eyes of hers. What will happen in a year or two when old age dulls them? What
will he do then? Love! He loves what he sees in her
eyes, and he sees himself there, twice over. It's a sin
and a shame the way that man has treated her.

AFTER DINNER BUTTERFLIES

by *Matt Cohen*

They were sitting in the library, drinking coffee. She
noticed that he had a hand in one of his pockets, he
seemed to be fiddling with something.

George?

What?

What have you got there?

Nothing, he said.

Show it to me immediately.

It's nothing, he said. He took his hand out of his

pocket and puffed elaborately on his cigar. Good cigar, he said.

No cigar, she said. Take that thing out of your pocket.

George stood up and leaned against the mantel, still puffing on his cigar. He pulled a rabbit out of a vase. Look at the nice rabbit, he said.

Put it away.

He stuck the rabbit out the window and returned to his chair. He picked up an old newspaper and started reading it. When he was sure she wasn't looking he put his hand back into his pocket.

George!

What.

Let me see it.

There's nothing here.

Oh yes there is. I saw you fiddling with it. Now let me see it.

All right, he said. He reached into his pocket. Then he changed his mind. No, you have to guess.

I'm not playing one of your stupid games.

Okay, George said. Let's forget it then. He relit his cigar and stuck his hand back into his pocket. Time passed. His cigar went out. Mary got another cup of coffee. The fire was going. George kept his hand in his pocket. He got tired of the newspaper. He went over to the library table and sat down to work on the jigsaw puzzle. He was so absorbed in a little bit of orange and green that he didn't hear Mary sneak up on him.

There, she exclaimed. I've got it. Her hand was in his pocket. Then she withdrew it, puzzled. There's nothing there, she said.

They sat back down. A few moments later she noticed that George was working his hand in his pocket. When he looked up he saw her watching him. Do you want to see what's in my pocket?

You don't have anything in your pocket.

Yes I do.

Prove it.

Okay, George said. He reached into his pocket and pulled out a shiny bit of metal. It appeared to be some sort of complicated miniature. He brought it over to her, holding it cupped in the palm of his hand. But when she reached for it, he drew back. Don't touch, he said. You'll break it. He held it out to her again so she could look at it. It was a metal sphere with little red things sticking out of its silver surface.

What is it? she asked.

It's a spaceship.

That's nice.

Watch this. He walked to the side of the room farthest from the fire. Come here, he said. She stood beside him. He threw his metal gizmo into the fire. There was a clicking sound, metal against brickwork.

Well, she said, you could have done that with a firecracker.

Right, George said. They sat back down. After a while Mary noticed that she had, in a very faint way, the same sort of feeling in her stomach that she sometimes got in an elevator.

George, she said.

Yes?

I feel funny. I feel like we're in an elevator.

Or in a spaceship, George said. He walked over to the sideboard and poured himself a glass of sherry. Cheers, he said.

Don't think you can upset me with your silly games.

Oh no, George said.

I was once married to a Hungarian count.

Were there bagpipes at your wedding? Yes there were. I was there. I remember them clearly: they were off key.

Mary crossed her legs and tried to pull her skirt down over her knees. They felt strange, as if something was about to land on them. George, she said, prove to me that we are on a spaceship.

All right, George said. He snapped his fingers. Nothing happened. Then a delicate golden butterfly landed on Mary's right knee. Isn't that beautiful?

Isn't what beautiful? Mary said. She could have sworn that a golden butterfly had landed on her knee.

The music, George said. He turned up the radio so

that the library was filled with sounds. A second golden butterfly landed on Mary's knee.

I don't like it, she said. She got up and turned the radio off. The butterflies followed her, circling her head like a halo. Go on, she said when she sat down, flicking at her shoulders, go sit on someone else. But they just came back.

You'd bettter leave them alone, George said.

Why? I don't like them.

But they like you.

I don't like the feeling of them sitting on my shoulders, watching me.

They're very pretty.

I can't even see them without straining my neck.

I'll get you a mirror, George said.

I don't want a mirror. Let's just forget them and see if they go away.

All right, George said. He lit a new cigar and sipped at his sherry. After a while Mary noticed that he had a hand in his pocket again and seemed to be fiddling with something.

George.

What?

What are you doing now?

Nothing, George said. He took his hand out of his pocket. I'm just trying to get this damned thing turned around.

What thing?

The spaceship.

The butterflies were still perched on Mary's shoulders, waiting patiently. George snapped his fingers again. A white wolf appeared in the middle of the room. Its eyes were as golden as butterflies. It walked over to George's chair, climbed up into it, and licked its paws. Go on, George said. Sit on the floor. The wolf looked up at him and then returned to its paws.

You see? You don't know how to do anything right.

I'm sorry, George said.

What a lovely wolf. Look at its eyes.

I wish it would get off my chair.

It likes you, Mary said. That's why it wants to sit on your chair.

If it really liked me it would get off of my chair and fetch a stick or something. He took a cigar from the mantel and waved it in the air. Fetch, doggie, he said. He threw the cigar across the room. The wolf looked at him, looked over at the cigar, raised its eyebrows, and went back to sleep.

That reminds me, Mary said. Did I ever tell you that I was once married to a Hungarian count?

Yes, George said. You just told me five minutes ago. Do you mind if I sit on the arm of your chair? The butterflies were still perched on her shoulders, waiting patiently.

Yes, she said. I do mind. Why don't you stand at the mantel and try to look unconcerned?

There was a knock at the door. Come in, George shouted. A man wearing gray coveralls and carrying a toolbox entered the room.

Is this the place with the television?

Yes, George said, it's there in the corner. I don't know what's wrong with it.

Probably blew a tube, the repairman said. It often happens. Nice dog.

Yes.

The repairman pushed the television out from the wall and began poking at its innards.

Do you want a glass of sherry?

No thanks, the man said. He reached into the television and pulled out three stuffed camels. Here's your problem, he said. There were three stuffed camels in the back of your television set.

Oh, George said. I was hiding them there for my wife's birthday.

You should've told me. He turned on the set. Works fine now. He pushed the television back against the wall and packed up his tools. I'll send you a bill, he said, and left the room.

The repairman made two more house calls and then went home. His wife was sitting up, waiting for him. He changed out of his coveralls, washed up, and then got his dinner out of the oven and a beer from the refrigerator.

How did it go tonight?

The usual. Is Jimmy asleep?

Yes, he went to bed hours ago.

What else did you do?

Nothing much, she said. She crossed her legs and tried to pull her skirt down over her knees. I watched TV for a while and read Jimmy a story.

Is there anything for dessert?

There's some pie. He went into the kitchen and found a coconut cream pie in the refrigerator. He brought it back into the living room.

Have you ever wanted to throw a pie in my face?

Once, she said. Remember that dance we went to just after we started going out? You put an ice cube down my dress? Well, when you took me home my parents were still up and we had strawberry pie with whipped cream. You were all sitting at the table and I was getting the pie. I could feel the ice water trickling down my skin, and the inside of my dress was wet. I almost dumped the pie right on your head.

He leaned back and lit a cigarette. God, he said, that must have been ten years ago.

Eleven, she said. Eleven years and two months. I remember standing there. I was just about to turn the pie onto your head when I decided to marry you. She crossed the room and sat down beside him on the couch. I don't know why I never told you, she said. I always meant to.

What else didn't you ever tell me?

Did I ever tell you that I was once married to a Hungarian count?

No, he said. And I wouldn't believe you if you did. He was leaning back with his eyes closed. She dipped her hand into the pie and spread it gently over his face. She formed little ridges at the eyebrows, being careful not to get any into his eyes. She spread it on his cheeks with the palms of her hands and then swirled it with her index finger so that his cheeks stood out in spiral puffs. She gave him a moustache and a beard—a nice

pointed Vandyke beard that reminded her of a picture.
When the beard started to drip she pushed it back up
onto his chin and drew a picture of a rose in it. All the
whipped cream was gone. She took a fork and fed him
some of the coconut filling.

How does it taste?

Good, he said.

I should have saved you some of the whipped cream.

That's all right. He stuck out his tongue and licked a
path along his right cheek. Tonight I saw a woman
with two golden butterflies perched on her shoulders.

That's nice, dear.

MAGICIANS

by *Beth Havor*

He was showing her his recent past, slide after slide
of it. She held small views of western streets and Rocky
Mountains and Pacific Ocean up to the kitchen window's light. These were from his last trip. Now he was
off once more, and would soon be bringing back the
east coast for her to squint at—harbor by harbor and
street by street. But now he was getting to the end of
the box. He had saved the best one for the last.

"Here's quite a good one," he said, handing it to her
between forefinger and thumb.

She thought it was good too. An old gray house
down by a waterfront. On one side of the door the pale,
peeling torso of a ship's figurehead—all blues, sick
whites, the nose missing, the hair like badly piled
snakes. The remains of the face were placid; it was a
face that gave distance its due: Also, the paint of the
eyes had flaked off. And on the other side of the doorway, there was a tall narrow window, and behind the
window, behind the smeared glass, a little girl with pale

snaggy hair and a round deprived face. It seemed strange that a face could be so perfectly round and at the same time so perfectly deprived. Just as it seemed strange that she, Clare, should so often be unhappy in quite a different sort of house, in this house, here, where the sun shone on the handsome black-and-white tile floor (superimposing its own squares of light), where she could even look out into a garden while she washed the dishes—a beautiful garden (even as gardens go) and in winter beautiful too, in fact in winter a graphic garden, the black branches, the vertical black boards of the fences, all with their epaulets of snow. She looked at the little girl in her leaning sad beautiful blue-gray and probably smelly harbor house, and felt some guilt that she could find such a picture beautiful. Tourists were said to cope with the same kinds of feelings in places like Naples and in the poorer parts of Rome.

"It really captures the poverty and the fog," she said.

"It does," he said.

"Will you have your tea now then?" she asked him.

He shoved over his cup.

The tea sprang from the spout in a high clear arch.

"Like a little boy seeing how far he can make it go," she said.

"It is," he said. He looked at it down in the cup. "It *looks* like something done by a little boy, too," he said. "You never make it strong enough." He shoved it back to her. "For God's sake, Clare, steep it a little."

She steeped it till it looked like consommé.

"Is it OK now?"

"Better than it *was*, anyway."

From one extreme to the other, was what he was thinking though. He wished she wouldn't wear those oversized sad, sad cardigans. She had no right to look so vulnerable, so sloppy. Her face was very young-looking, her straight hair was pulled back into an elastic band. But her stomach looked three months pregnant. She hadn't had a baby for years, all their children were now in school, and here she slopped around, forever looking three months pregnant. He found he was looking forward to the next lap of the tour and all the airline stewardesses.

"I hardly think about you when you're gone," she said. "I mean, I never worry or wonder about what you're doing in the evenings, or anything."

"I never worry or wonder about what you're doing in the evenings, *either*," he said, "because I know you're never doing anything."

"I have a rich fantasy life," she said.

"I daresay you need it."

"When will you be back then?" she asked him.

"Two weeks."

Now he was gathered together at the door, and stood flanked by matching graduated luggage. His raincoat, on his arm, was folded neat as a flag.

"I love you," he said dutifully.

She couldn't bring herself to say anything one way or the other. So she tenderly patted his face.

He pried his tongue into her mouth when they kissed good-bye. But while he was kissing her she could feel him looking at the clock over her shoulder.

"I love you, I love you, I love you," Clare thought, walking in her high boots along the wet leaf-littered streets. It wasn't her husband she was thinking of, but somebody else's. A man who crawled on his stomach through her blood, kneed his way up and down her system, was on her, in her, night and day, in her mind. A speck of plane flew high overhead, very high up in that sky of stomach-dropping blue. Maybe it was the plane her husband was on, maybe he was at this very moment being lulled by aquamarine music, maybe he was at this very moment being leaned down to, being served airline cookies—little cellophane packs of scalloped circles stuck together with oversweet frosting fill and embossed with maple leaves. He could have them.

While she was making supper her children changed themselves into magicians. They came to the table with long black eyebrows and moustaches that went up into commas, and pointed black beards. They kept making faces at her. "God, you look repulsive," she told them. They were delighted. They couldn't hear it often enough.

"Are we really repulsive?" they kept saying.

"Yes," she kept saying back.

And at bedtime, as she was wiping the black from the face of one of them, from the face of Martin, the oldest one, she was thinking of the husband of her friend. Her desire for him was quite unbearable sometimes. She was thinking of how she loved him, when suddenly, without warning, she said out loud, "I love you." Her son, thinking it was meant for him, smiled at her sweetly. Swept by guilt, she held him to her for a moment, terribly tightly.

Her friend's husband was named Don. An ordinary name. An ordinary person. No! Not an ordinary person! Not even ordinary-*looking* once you got to know him. And *he* had such a way of looking at people. Or at least he had such a way of looking at her. A look that took you in entirely, enclosed you. She remembered being a small child and standing barefoot on a sheet of brown paper while her father held a pencil up close against each foot, and described each foot with the pencil, so that he could take the pictures of her feet out in his pocket and come back bringing new shoes. She had been delighted with those pictures of her feet. The way Don looked at her, she felt he saw her exactly as she was, his look described her, and yet she felt such deep approval in his eyes. He treated her with the gentle courtesy one might show to a beloved child. She remembered she had gone to their house to deliver something, some books, late one raining Sunday afternoon. And she had stood out on their white porch with the sky all dark behind her, and her maroon leather shoes had been rained on till they turned the color of wine, and she had been shaking the rain out of her coat when he had opened the door to her, but she hadn't been able to shake the happiness out of her eyes. She had always felt that he was ten times more interesting and ten times less pretentious than anyone else. And apart from that, and apart from all the sexual feeling, she had always felt that he was *good*. He had held the door open for her and she had preceded him into the summer dimness of his house. And there had been such a curious smell in the interior of that house, a smell of old socks and fallen flowers. His wife was away. She had known that, known that, known that, when she had cunningly come, returning his books. She didn't see any of the old socks, but she saw little collars of fallen petals around all the vases in the living room. In the kitchen there was a little more light. Not much, but a little. Big windows looked out into a garden of soppy tropical greens and the rain dribbled down them while he put on water for tea.

"Which tea will it be?" he had asked her. "Formosa Oolong? Lapsang Souchong? Jasmine? St. John's Wort?"

They had decided on a blend of Jasmine and St. John's Wort.

"St. John's Wort is like a field of hay," he had said. "You're not allergic to hay, are you?"

No, she had assured him, she wasn't allergic to anything. And she had hoped this would raise her stock with him. The Jasmine flowers had floated like bits of discolored paper among the grasses in her cup of tea.

And some time later, walking home in the rain, past all the sopping wet gardens, she had felt that she should think some sobering thoughts and douse the happiness in her face before she got back to her husband and children.

On the porch she had taken off her shoes, squeaky with wet, and had come into the house barefoot. A wet-footed, white-footed, barefooted truant! But her children had been watching television and her husband had been reading the paper. They had hardly looked at her at all, and she had gone into the kitchen to start supper, pirouetting as she had cooked and cleaned up, leaping across the chessboard linoleum floor with a violent silent joy. And the happiness inside her! But now she was safer with it. She could push it out of her face and back onto a secret simmer and make it last for hours and no-one would know it was there. She felt happy the way a child can feel happy—without a reason, without knowing a reason and with no need to know a reason.

And so she had sometimes seen him since. Him and his wife, Frances, who was her friend. Frances appreciated him, anyone could see that. And besides, Frances was a warm and attractive person herself. And so Clare went on, would go on forever, feeling that way about him, feeling that deep submerged bond between them, but nothing would ever come of it.

Now all the magicians were asleep. Their moustaches and beards had been creamed away, their faces were upturned, fair, flushed, flung this way and that. She was getting ready for bed herself, had brushed her hair, had figure-eighted an elastic band around it, and was now standing in front of the bathroom mirror, clowning her face with cream. The nightly circus of the no-longer-young. Next week she was invited to a party where Don and Frances would also be. She would wear her African print dress, and her hair hanging straight, and she would be feeling too happy to need jewelry. She was *that* young, anyway, that she could still get by on clean hair and happiness. Downstairs, the phone rang, making her jump. She ran down into the coldness of the hall. She jerked one of her husband's old raincoats off a hanger and was still working herself into it as she picked up the receiver and said hello.

"May I speak to Clare Stanzel?" A man's voice asked her.

"Clare Stanzel speaking."

"Clare! Is it really you?"

"Yes," she said, "but who's this?"

"Someone who loves you very much."

That narrows the field, she thought, but it was not a voice she recognized.

She said: "There can't be that many people who love me very much."

He said: "There can't be that many people who love you as much as *I* do."

A pause followed this gallant remark.

"Keep saying nice things," she instructed him finally. "Maybe after a while I'll figure out who you are."

He laughed and then she knew him.

"Wilf Dasgupta!"

"Wilf Dasgupta it is," he said, sounding even more delighted than she did.

"Good to hear from you, Wilf."

"It's been too long," he said. "How's Rawge?"

"Rawge is well. Traveling at the moment."

"And the children?"

"Sleeping. But they're fine too. They were magicians at supper tonight."

"Magicians," he said. "And you?"

"Pardon?"

"And how are you?"

"All right," she said. "Fine. Very well, as a matter of fact."

A skeptical silence ensued. She remembered how he used silences to browbeat you into confessing how you *really* felt. She felt a need to quickly pour words into the void.

"It's strange, I was thinking of you just the other night," she said. She knew he would like that. And besides, it was true.

"What were you thinking?"

"Well, you remember that beautiful art book you gave us when we were married?" she asked him. "We still have it," she continued—she was making it sound as if they made a practice of throwing their beautiful art books out with the garbage or something—"and I was just passing by the bookshelf—"; by now she was wishing she had never started on this, for her thought of Wilf as she had passed by the bookshelf had been a feeling of irritation at the tyranny of his love, at his insistence on beauty, and she had even taken the book down and had read the impassioned dedication he had written to her and Roger on their marriage, telling them how beautiful they were, how miraculous it was that these two beautiful people should have found each other and should now be joined together, and she had closed the book with a real slap of anger. "And?" Wilf was saying, pleased as punch, by now certain he sniffed the scent of a beautiful dénouement. "Well, I noticed how it—how the book—was sticking a little out from the shelf—" She paused, by now regretting her whole contribution to this conversation. She wanted quickly to finish it. She finished: "—and so I shoved it back in."

"That's what you do to me," Wilf said in a heavy swinging voice, "shove me back on the shelf."

She couldn't answer this. She could only think of Wilf in his Montreal studio. Of his tender drawings of nude pregnant negresses up high on the walls. Of the dark nipples, sturdy as gumdrops, hung in the gleaming brown slings of the breasts. Of Wilf, standing barefoot, serving, at just the right moment of the day, when the sun lay across the low black table in the strong-smelling studio, the little glasses of apricot brandy that went down the throat with an oversweet slippery sting. Of the holes at the shoulder of his shirt where his pet bird sometimes sat and clawed. Of the free-form bird cage he had made for the bird, but which the bird had never taken to. Of an older black-wire bird cage (which the bird had never taken to either), that Wilf had later converted into a portable liquor cabinet, housing half a dozen tall-necked bottles, and of how he used to swing the cage back and forth in front of them, saying, "What'll you have? Port? Sherry? Madeira?" And then he would sing in a cracked satanic Bengalee falsetto, "Have some Madeira, my dear . . . ," and she remembered too his great bowls of fruit that he washed at the old sink where he apparently also washed himself and mixed his paints, and of how good the fruits always looked when he brought them around, clear-beaded with water. And later, coming down into the suppertime dark and the snow-thickened streets, they had felt their eyes were overtired, overbright, that everything about Wilf and his studio always came on too strong—the dogmatic batiks, the tangled plants, the raucous tyrannical bird. Even the tenderness of the nude pregnant negresses, up there on the walls in small worlds of their own, even that came on too strong. And Wilf had played ragas long before anyone else, long before they had become fashionable in the West, for his father had come from Bombay, and the fact that his mother was a hard-shell Canadian baptist hadn't cancelled this out. In fact, in Wilf, nothing had been cancelled out.

"Clare," Wilf was saying, with a kind of deliberate urgency on the other end of the telephone line.

She hugged the raincoat very tightly around her and waited.

"Clare, you know I care for you and Rawge very much."

"Yes, Wilf."

"But about *you,* Clare, *for you,* Clare, I've always felt something very special, ever since I first met you, ever since you opened the door to me that time when you were staying at the Weinbergs'. . . . How old were you then, Clare? Twenty? You were very beautiful then, you know that, and you also know, and *I* know that *you* know, that I don't mean beauty in any outside ordinary surface sense, I mean *real* beauty." He paused a moment. His voice had begun to sound charged. He said finally: "I felt that you were good."

"But I'm a mixture of good and bad!" she cried. "Like everyone else!"

"I know what I know," he said, in his inscrutable stubborn voice. There was both Bombay and Baptist in that voice.

"I think you tried to put some kind of halo around me," she said.

"No, no! I didn't try to sanctify you, I didn't try to deify you, I just know what I saw! I feel that there's a place in *my heart* for you, just as there is a place in *your heart* for me, that no one else will ever occupy, in either of us; that there is an area, a territory, a *country,* if you like, where only you and I meet. A spiritual bond, if you like."

She didn't know if she liked or not. Still she felt a

need to say, "Wilf, would you care to come over and have some tea or something?"

"Clare, I'm here for the opening of an exhibition of a friend of mine. You remember my good and beautiful friend, Jean-Luc? Yes? Well, he's having a one-man show here at the Wells Gallery, and now here I am at a party in his honor, here at the Cattleys' until I take the train back very late tonight."

There was a pause.

"But to hell with the party!" he cried suddenly. "*You* are more important than a party! I'll come and see you!"

Clare didn't see how a cup of tea could compete with a party. Even a cup of tea with her. Aloud she said: "I don't want to take you away from your party, Wilf." This was the truth.

"But of course I'll come!" he insisted. "One moment. Someone here drives me over. Can you hold the line?"

She could hold the line. She could also suddenly hear a great avalanche of talk in the background, as if double doors had just been opened. Then, after a time, the talk stopped; the double doors must have closed. She heard him pick up the phone again.

"Clare," he said. Now his voice sounded low, confidential. He sounded like some sort of salesman. "There seem to be some complications here, my little one, so I don't think I'll be able to see you this time, but I'm going to be writing to you."

"Fine, Wilf. I look forward to seeing you another time. It's pretty late right now anyway." Again true.

"Why haven't you ever written to me?" he demanded suddenly. His voice was strong with claims.

"But Wilf, I never write to *any*one."

"But that's putting me with everyone else!"

Damnit, he *was* with everyone else. This time she refused to answer.

"Clare," he said, after a silence, "will you do something for me?"

"I'll try," she said warily. She wanted to know what it was first, though.

"Remember that I love you," he said.

"Yes, Wilf, thank you, I'll remember."

"I love you."

"Yes, Wilf, thank you. And thank you for calling."
By now she was feeling very old.

"Good-bye, then, Clare."

"Good-bye, Wilf," she said, and she quickly put
down the phone. And then she fled, actually fled, up the
stairs, pulling the old raincoat off her as she ran, and
pelting it into a pile of dirty laundry at the top of the
stairs. Then she bounced onto her bed, and pulled the
covers up quickly before she had time to get cold. She
snapped out the light, and lay at attention under the
blankets.

But inside her, her heart was beating like a mad bird
in the cage of her ribs. And for a long time she
couldn't get to sleep. She knew Wilf's need to think he
loved people. She knew how he needed to think that
things were beautiful and good. She knew it didn't have
anything to do with her, any more than the fact that his
paintings shone out at you had anything to do with the
canvas they were painted on. But this is what bothered
her, lying there in the bed; if it didn't have anything to
do with her, and if it didn't mean anything, then why
did she feel so angry? And why did she feel as if something had been taken away from her? Why were her
eyes stinging in her cold-creamed face? Why did she
feel as if she had been robbed?

CONTRIBUTORS

Margaret Atwood (1939–   )

In Margaret Atwood's second novel, *Surfacing* (1972), two inept moviemakers shoot nonsense sequences, mistakenly believing that as "new Renaissance men" they can undertake any new technical challenge and carry it off. The novel reveals them both to be doltish failures, but their dreamed-of Renaissance versatility is actually realized in their creator.

Margaret Atwood was born and grew up in Ottawa, took a B.A. degree from the University of Toronto, an A.M. from Radcliffe College, and did further graduate studies in English literature at Harvard. Since then she has held teaching posts at various Canadian universities and spent one year, 1972–73, as writer-in-residence at the University of Toronto. As a writer she has shown remarkable flexibility; she has ranged from market research reports and film scripts to poetry, novels, short stories and literary criticism. Among her volumes of poetry are *The Circle Game* (1966), which won a Governor General's Award, *The Animals in That Country* (1968), *The Journals of Susanna Moodie* (1970), *Power Politics* (1971), and *You Are Happy* (1974). An option for filming has been taken on her first novel, *The Edible Woman* (1969), and her critical work, *Survival: A Thematic Guide to Canadian Literature* (1972), has created more discussion than any recent comparable study.

The narrative voice in "The Grave of the Famous Poet" is a typically disillusioned Atwood "persona." A young woman whose love affair has proved oppressively disappointing gives a present-tense running commentary on what is going on between her and her lover. The flow of sentences suggests an intense, low-voiced monotone, providing an aural setting for images of death and decay that are disturbing, and, in the final stages of the story, even horrifying.

Don Bailey (1942–   )

While in Kingston Penitentiary serving part of a twelve-year sentence for armed robbery, Don Bailey tried to relieve the tedium of confinement by writing a novel—"a really terrible novel I've never shown to anyone." After his transfer to a lesser security prison at Collins Bay, he took English courses offered to inmates there and tried his hand at writing short stories, one of which was printed in the Kingston, Ontario literary magazine, *Quarry*. Since his release from prison Bailey has worked in Winnipeg as the director of three half-way houses for ex-convicts run by the United Church, and has published one collection of short stories, *If You Hum Me a Few Bars I Might Remember the Tune* (1973), and a novel, *In the Belly of the Whale* (1974). So far his fiction has probed the psychology of the self-destructive loser who is down, but who still has a few rounds of fight left in him and is looking up through puffy eyes for an opening that will allow him to get in one good lick against his fearsome opponent—himself.

Clark Blaise (1941–   )

Through his origins and personal history Clark Blaise illustrates the Canadian problem of national identity. He was born in Fargo, North Dakota, of a French-

Canadian father and a Manitoban mother who were constantly at odds with one another. As a child he followed his father's vagrant life as a furniture salesman in the small towns of Florida and the American Middle West. After graduation from Dennison University, Ohio, he did graduate studies at Harvard and at the University of Iowa. In 1966 he moved to Montreal and now teaches creative writing at Concordia University. In 1973 he chose his parents' country and became a Canadian citizen.

His two collections of short fiction, *A North American Education* (1973), and *Tribal Justice* (1974), contain patterns of stories arranged to support an underlying theme, somewhat in the manner of James Joyce's *The Dubliners*. All the stories employ the same first-person narrative technique, and although the fictional identity of the narrator changes from story to story, the tone and outlook of the speaker remains consistent; a strong element of autobiography runs through both books. In each story the central problem is Blaise's own disorientation and need to find out who he really is. Perhaps complicating his search for a national loyalty and personal identity was his marriage to Bharati Mukarjee, a graduate student from India whom he met at the University of Iowa. "Going to India" is a fictional re-creation of his journey to Asia with her to meet her family. The story traces his progressively deepening culture shock through the several stages of the flight, culminating with his cry of, "I've never been so lost," when they arrive at last in Bombay.

Randy Brown (1944–   )

When he graduated from high school in Cobourg, Ontario, Randy Brown, like many of the post-war generation, decided to travel the world instead of finding a steady job or going directly to university. His wanderings as a hitchhiker took him from Mexico to northern British Columbia, and during the 1960s he held jobs as diverse as staking claims for copper mines in the northern Canadian wilderness and teaching English for Berlitz in Heidelberg, Germany. In 1971 he began studies at the University of Toronto and graduated in 1975 with a B.A. degree. His four full-length plays have been produced by university theater groups, and several of his short stories have been published in literary magazines. He considers "Heil!," to be an ironic parable of late twentieth-century North America.

Morley Callaghan (1903–   )

In the same year that he was admitted to the Ontario Bar as a lawyer, Morley Callaghan published the novel, *Strange Fugitive* (1928). From that time onwards he has never practiced law but continually practiced the craft of fiction. His twelve novels include *Such Is My Beloved* (1934), *They Shall Inherit the Earth* (1935), *More Joy in Heaven* (1937), *Luke Baldwin's Vow* (1948), *The Loved and the Lost* (1951), *A Passion in Rome* (1961), and *A Fine and Private Place* (1975). He has also written plays, articles and a memoir of his youthful experience in Europe with Ernest Hemingway and F. Scott Fitzgerald, *That Summer In Paris* (1963), but it is as a writer of short stories that he is most widely admired. These he began writing in the 1920s while working as a reporter with Hemingway on the *Toronto Star*, and in the years since then has had scores of them appear in such magazines as *Maclean's*, *The New Yorker*, *Cosmopolitan*, *The Atlantic Monthly*, and *Esquire*. Fifty-seven of his best stories were published in 1959 under the title, *Morley Callaghan's Stories*.

Because his style is spare and he portrays characters with unsentimental realism, his work has often been compared with Hemingway's. But the differences between the two authors are more significant than their surface similarities. In Hemingway's existential conflicts, men may achieve a vestigial and mortal grace through stoical endurance or the warrior's code of honor. Morley Callaghan writes of a world infused by his Roman Catholic background and conviction, a fallen world of sin and possible redemption. The critic Edmund Wilson said that Callaghan wrote parables which sometimes upset readers because their endings frustrated expectations and enforced thought. "Getting On in the World" is that kind of story.

Jean-Guy Carrier (1945–   )

The cycle of stories in *My Father's House* (1974) spans three generations of the Mercier and Moreau families of the Quebec parish of St. Camille. An actual village lying to the southeast of Quebec city, St. Camille is where Jean-Guy Carrier grew up, but in his stories it becomes a mythical place, a stage for re-enacting the archetypal battle of father against son, wife against husband. Young William in "He Had a Dog Once" is the first-born son of Joseph and Eugénie Moreau, a couple who helplessly relive their own parents' generational nightmare "of seventeen children, of seventeen tortuous birthings and seventeen wet mouths." In the final story of the cycle, William breaks out of this nightmare pattern. Like his creator, Jean-Guy Carrier, who now lives in Ottawa, he leaves rural Quebec and sets out for the cities of Ontario.

The author, an experienced newspaper and broadcast journalist, is at present working for the New Democratic Party and completing his first novel. Although French-Canadian by birth and upbringing, he wrote *My Father's House* in English and has recently translated it into French for publication in Quebec.

Matt Cohen (1942–   )

Matt Cohen attended school in Kingston, Ontario, took a degree at the University of Toronto, taught for awhile at McMaster University, and now lives and writes on his farm near Godfrey, Ontario. Since the appearance in 1968 of *Korsoniloff*, his first novel, he has published three further novels, *Johnny Crackle Sings* (1971), *The Disinherited* (1974), *The Wooden Hunters* (1975), and a collection of short stories, *Columbus and the Fat Lady* (1972).

The first two novels dealt with the turbulent generation of the 1960s: André Korsoniloff, a young teacher, hallucinated toward some schizophrenic perception of self, and Johnny Crackle strummed a febrile guitar into temporary rock stardom. The style of these two early books was as raucously disjunctive as the lives of the disturbed characters they chronicled.

In the two later novels Cohen has returned to the Canadian mainstream of realistic narrative. *The Disinherited* follows the fortunes of three generations of an Ontario farm family, while *The Wooden Hunters* traces the attempt of a disaffected young couple to reassemble their lives on a remote island off the coast of British Columbia. Both novels are logically coherent explorations of character.

"After Dinner Butterflies" represents a transitional stage in Cohen's fiction. The syntax is sane but the events are madly surreal. The mirror that Cohen holds up to male-female domestic relations is like that of E. G. Perrault in "The Cure" but with even more distorting ripples on the glass.

Jacques Ferron (1921–   )

Journalist, medical doctor, politician, novelist, playwright, short story writer—Jacques Ferron's activities have earned him all of these titles. For many years his articles have appeared in the Quebec press where they have done much to awaken French-Canadian national consciousness. During the October crisis of 1970 when the kidnapping of the British diplomat James Cross and the murder of the Quebec cabinet minister Pierre Laporte caused the government of Canada to invoke the War Measures Act, it was Jacques Ferron that Prime Minister Trudeau and the separatist rebels agreed on as an intermediary to arrange the surrender of the separatist Chénier cell.

Since 1948 Ferron has practised medicine in Ville Jacques Cartier, a working-class suburb of Montreal, but his medical practice has not impeded his writing of plays; some of which are *L'Ogre* (1949), *Le Dodu* (1956), *Le Cheval de Don Juan* (1957), and *La Tête du Roi* (1963). In 1974 two of his novels were published in English translation, *Dr. Cotnoir* and *The Saint Elias*. His collection of stories *Contes du Pays Incertain* (1962) won a Governor General's Award for fiction and in 1972 appeared in English translation under the title, *Tales from the Uncertain Country*.

Like Claire Martin's "Springtime," Ferron's "The Flood" is an example of the "conte," the French subspecies of the short story which is a parable or symbolic folk tale. The fantastic ending of this one makes it first cousin to the absurdist pieces by Ray Smith and Matt Cohen, also in this anthology.

Mavis Gallant (1922–   )

Mavis Gallant may fairly be described as an expatriate writer. For more than twenty years she has lived in Europe and written of North America expatriates undergoing a European experience. She was born in Montreal and attended schools in Canada and the United States. For a time she worked at the National Film Board and for a brief period was film critic for the Montreal *Standard*. But in 1951 she left North America for Paris, where she has resided ever since. Shortly before her departure from Canada one of her stories was accepted for publication by *The New Yorker* and most of her stories since then have appeared first in that magazine.

She has written two novels, *Green Water, Green Sky* (1959), and *A Fairly Good Time* (1970). A selection of her short fiction appears in several collections, *The Other Paris* (1956), *My Heart Is Broken* (1964), *The Pegnitz Junction* (1973), and *The End of the World and Other Stories* (1974).

Shirley, the girl narrator in "The Accident" reappears as the central character in Mavis Gallant's more recent novel, *A Fairly Good Time*. At one point in this later work Shirley describes the letters that she and her mother write to each other as "an uninterrupted dialogue of the deaf." The subtle exploration of personal relations in "The Accident" suggests just this failure of communication. The dead boy's parents who have been married for twenty-three years are seen by Shirley to be "out of touch" with one another, as indeed she and Peter had been, even in the last conscious moments of his short life.

Hugh Garner (1913–   )

Hugh Garner's restless life has taken him to a great variety of places and jobs. During the Depression years of the 1930s he was an itinerant harvest hand, a hobo, and a door-to-door salesman. Towards the end of the Depression in 1936 and 1937 his first articles and stories appeared in *Canadian Forum*, a political and literary magazine with socialist sympathies. In 1937, like the main character in his novel, *Cabbagetown* (1950), he fought for the Loyalist cause in the Spanish Civil War, and during World War II he saw action on a corvette in the Royal Canadian Navy, a sea experience which lent authenticity to his war novel, *Storm Below* (1949).

Since the war he has written widely as a journalist and television dramatist, and has continued to produce a flow of novels and short story collections, among which are *Present Reckoning* (1951), *The Yellow Sweater and Other Stories* (1952), *Silence On the Shore* (1962), *Hugh Garner's Best Stories* (1963), *The Sin Sniper* (1970), *A Nice Place to Visit* (1970), and *Death in Don Mills* (1975). In his short stories Garner shows a tough-minded adherence to craftsmanship in the classical short-story tradition which stands in sharp contrast to the experimental short fiction of such writers as Ray Smith and Matt Cohen. Every deft touch of plot and characterization in "The Yellow Sweater" is placed in a realistically plausible sequence to produce a powerful emotional impact.

Phyllis Gotlieb (1926–   )

The career of Phyllis Gotlieb shows an interesting balance between the conventional and the unusual. Conventionality marks her domestic life; she still resides in Toronto where she was born and educated, she has borne three children, and she is the wife of a university professor. Her unusual aspect lies in her literary activities. She has to her credit three volumes of poems, *Who Knows Me?* (1969), *Within the Zodiac* (1964), and *Ordinary Moving* (1969). In addition, she has written two novels, *Sunburst* (1963), *Why Should I Have All the Grief?* (1969), and many short stories.

Of course, other poets have also tried their hand at fiction, but what sets Phyllis Gotlieb apart from the rest is that she specializes in *science* fiction. Her short stories appear not just in academically respectable journals like *Tamarack Review* and *Queen's Quarterly,* but also in such racy magazines as *Amazing, If,* and *Fantastic.* Her first novel, *Sunburst,* set in the twenty-first century, is about a gang of psychopathically gifted children imprisoned by the rest of society in a technological ghetto after a thermonuclear accident has turned them into Frankensteins with monstrously destructive powers. "The Military Hospital" generates a similar chilling atmosphere of a community without a soul.

Beth Harvor (1936–   )

Beth Harvor was born in St. John, New Brunswick, and grew up in the rural Kingston Peninsula region of that province. After high school she became a student nurse but left in her final year before graduation. However, this period of medical training left a strong impression on her; references to hospitals and doctors are frequent in her stories, and one of her recurring characters, Anna, is a drop-out from nursing school. Anna is also the first-person narrator in the novel that Beth Harvor is currently working on, *Monster Baby,* a part of which appears in her collection of stories, *Women and Children* (1973).

Her stories have been published in Canadian and American literary periodicals such as *Canadian Forum, Fiddlehead, Hudson Review* and *Colorado Quarterly,* and several of them have won awards. "Magicians" was one of two of her stories picked as prizewinners to be broadcast on CBC radio. Like many of her sensitively drawn women, Clare in "Magicians" is a young mother in her thirties, disillusioned in her relations with her husband but still hoping to make some sense out of her life through love. The vivid evocation of line and color in this story reflects Beth Harvor's interest in painting.

Hugh Hood (1928–   )

Like Clark Blaise, Hugh Hood is a Canadian of mixed French-Canadian and English-Canadian parentage, and like Blaise he is now teaching English in a Montreal university. But unlike Blaise his experiences of childhood and formal education have been entirely in Canada, and for that reason he writes of Canadian scenes and characters familiarly, from the inside, not as a sensitive outsider trying to feel his way to the psychological interior.

He has written three novels, *White Figure, White Ground* (1964), *The Camera Always Lies* (1967), *A Game of Touch* (1970), and a book of essays about his life in Toronto, *The Governor General's Bridge Is Closed* (1973), but he has been most prolific as a writer of short stories, more than sixty of which have appeared in Canadian and American literary magazines. Three collections of his stories have been published, *Flying A Red Kite* (1962), *Around the Mountain: Scenes from Montreal Life* (1967), and *The Fruit Man, the Meat Man and the Manager* (1970).

In "Flying a Red Kite," Fred Calvert's yearning discontent and need for revelation make him a fairly typical Hugh Hood character. It is interesting to note how unobtrusively the author deploys Fred's acute perceptions of physical sensation to plot his troubled advance toward a moment of spiritual awakening. A seventeen-minute color film (16 m.m.) is available from the National Film Board under the abbreviated title of "The Red Kite."

Robert Kroetsch (1927–   )

Although he now teaches English at the State University of New York in Binghampton, most of Robert Kroetsch's fiction has been set in the Canadian North-West. He was born in Heisler, Alberta, and grew up on a prairie farm nearby. After graduating from the University of Alberta he worked for two years on riverboats plying the Mackenzie River in the North West Territories, the locale for his first novel, *But We Are Exiles* (1965). His three subsequent novels have been set in Alberta: *The Words of My Roaring* (1967), *The Studhorse Man* (1969), for which he won a Governor General's Award, and *Gone Indian* (1973).

From the realism of his early work he has moved toward the creation of archetypal characters and mythical events in his more recent writing. Concerning this shift he says, "I have become somewhat impatient with certain traditional kinds of realism, because I think

there is a more profound kind of truth available to us."
Even in "That Yellow Prairie Sky," his first published
story, the reader can detect those "mythological moments" which Kroetsch wants to recreate from his
remembered prairie youth. The intermittent passages
printed in italics form a poetic counterpoint to the flat,
colloquial voice of the narrator and lift the story out
of his prosaic consciousness to the level of representa-
tive human experience.

Margaret Laurence (1926–   )

In the years following her departure from Neepawa,
Manitoba, first to attend university in Winnipeg, then
to accompany her husband to West Africa where he
worked as a civil engineer, Margaret Laurence thought
that she had said a final goodbye to the small prairie
town of her birth. Her first novel, *This Side Jordan*
(1960), and her first collection of short stories, *The
Tomorrow Tamer* (1963), were both based on her
African experience. However, absence from Canada,
further prolonged by several years spent in England,
made remembered scenes and characters from the
prairies rise to her mind with creative urgency, and her
next four novels, *The Stone Angel* (1964), *A Jest of
God* (1966), *The Fire Dwellers* (1969), and *The Di-
viners* (1974), are all set in the Canadian West.

Like Sinclair Ross whose early novel, *As For Me
and My House,* she deeply admires, she cannot escape
the need to write about the people and places that lie
at the roots of her consciousness. Her major characters
are all women from the same sun-blanched community,
called Manawaka in her fiction, but clearly modelled
on Neepawa. What strikes the reader about these
women is the utter plausibility of their struggle to rise
above the social and sexual bigotry that have marred
their early youth. Hagar Shipley, the formidable old

woman of *The Stone Angel*, has entered the imaginative life of almost every adult Canadian who reads novels, and Rachel Cameron, the ironic spinster in *A Jest of God*, has had blood and fibre enough as a character to survive cinematic transplantation from the Canadian Prairie to New England, the locale of the 1968 film version of the novel, re-entitled *Rachel, Rachel*. Vanessa MacLeod, whose viewpoint we share in "To Set Our House in Order," is the narrator for all the related stories in *A Bird in the House* (1970). Margaret Laurence, who now writes from her home in Lakefield, Ontario, says that the Manawaka experiences of Vanessa in this story cycle are the closest she has come to writing autobiographical fiction.

Malcolm Lowry (1909–1957)

Even though he was born and educated in England and did not come to Canada until he was in his thirties, an important part of Malcolm Lowry's writing is considered to belong to Canadian literature. An urge to travel had led him at the age of seventeen to leave his comfortable middle-class home in Liverpool and sign on as a deckhand on a cargo ship bound for the China Seas. After a year of voyaging he returned to England and entered Cambridge University where he combined formal studies with work on an autobiographical sea novel, *Ultramarine* (1933), which was accepted for publication in his last term before graduation.

In the years that followed, Lowry traveled extensively and during the late 1930s lived for a time in Mexico where he began writing *Under the Volcano* (1947), a novel which is now generally regarded as a masterwork of twentieth-century fiction. In 1939 he arrived in British Columbia and from 1940 until 1954 he and his wife, Margerie, lived in a squatter's cabin in the village of Dollarton on the shore of Burrard Inlet, a few miles east of Vancouver. It was here that he completed *Under the Volcano* and worked on other prose narratives and poems, many of which show how deeply the local people and environment influenced his imaginative life. These fourteen years in Canada were the most productive of his career, although after *Under the Volcano* he actually published little else before his death in 1957. His procedure was to work on several books at the same time, revising endlessly and seldom drawing one to a conclusion that he could regard as satisfactory.

Since his death more of his work has come before the public. *Hear Us O Lord from Heaven Thy Dwelling Place* (1961), a collection of five stories and two novellas published posthumously, won a Governor General's Award for fiction. In the same year his *Selected Poems,* edited by Earle Birney, appeared. Margerie Lowry helped to edit one of his unfinished novels, *Dark Is the Grave Wherein My Friend Is Laid* (1968), and more recently has prepared another one for publication, *October Ferry to Gabriola* (1970).

The uncompleted story, "Ghostkeeper," which first appeared in *American Review 17* (May, 1973), is a further example of Lowry's "fiction in process." He intended it to be a tentative exploration of life's great question: Does the apparently absurd flux of human affairs have a significance which art can interpret? The story's incompleteness is obvious from the memos and parenthetic comments that the writer keeps inserting regarding what a character may say or do, or concerning the levels of signficance of an event; and at one point he even interpolates a note on the story by his wife, Margerie, in which she takes over as narrator and the character, Tom Goodhart, suddenly becomes her own husband, "Malc." Still, "Ghostkeeper" is much more than a set of notes on their way to becoming a story. The various possibilities for dialogue and incident that Lowry leaves unresolved become part of the story's final effect on the reader and embody the author's theory that if a short story is to avoid being "static, a piece of death, fixed, a sort of butterfly on a pin," then it must attempt "at least to give the illusion of things—appearances, possibilities, ideas, even resolutions—in a state of perpetual metamorphosis."

Claire Martin (1914–   )

Claire Martin is the pseudonym of Madame Roland Fauchier, born in Quebec city and educated in convents run by the Ursuline Sisters and Sisters of the Congregation of Notre Dame. Her autobiography, *Dans un Gant de Fer* (1966) translated into English as *In an Iron Glove*, won a Governor General's Award and both Le Prix France—Québec and Le Prix de la Province de Québec. It is a devastating criticism of the narrowness that ruled some convent schools in the 1920s and of the authoritarian cruelty of her own father.

She has also published a collection of short stories, *Avec ou Sans Amour* (1959), and two novels, *Doux-Amer* (1960) and *Quand J'Aurai Paye Ton Visage* (1962). Philip Stratford's translation of "Springtime" provides an example of the "conte," the precise French term for that type of short story which is a symbolic tale or parable. It is also an illustration of Claire Martin's awesome ability to express with ultimate compression her ironic view of romantic love.

Ken Mitchell (1940–   )

As well as writing plays, short stories and a novel, Ken Mitchell teaches in the English department of the University of Saskatchewan, Regina. Perhaps to fertilize his creative potentialities, he chose early occupations that were widely diverse. He has been a newspaper reporter, an ice cream salesman, a house painter, a pressman in a rubber factory, and a pig farmer. That spectrum, and the fact that he was born in a city called Moose Jaw, suggests a comic range, and indeed comedy has been uppermost in most of his writing so far. It energizes his picaresque novel, *Wandering Rafferty* (1972), and it certainly permeates "The Great Electrical Revolution," which first appeared in the spring, 1970 issue of *Prism International.*

In addition to many short stories, Ken Mitchell has written a dozen radio plays for the CBC, and one of his stage plays, *Heroes,* took first prize in the 1971 Ottawa Little Theatre Competition. His ear for dialogue is apparent in the present story, particularly in the salty aphorisms of Grandad.

Alice Munro (1931–)

For more than twenty years Alice Munro has lived with her husband and family in British Columbia, first in Vancouver and more recently in Victoria. But many of her stories continue to be set in a fictitious small town in Western Ontario whose actual prototype may well be Wingham, where she was born and grew up. In her student years she worked as a waitress, house servant, tobacco picker and library clerk, all jobs that developed her writer's skill in observing rural and small-town people and the ways they impinged on each other's lives. Her stories examine these relationships from an intensely feminine point of view, her central characters usually being intelligent, highly sensitive, and troubled women.

Her published collections include *Dance of the Happy Shades* (1968), which won a Governor General's Award for fiction, *Lives of Girls and Women* (1971), a cycle of stories with the same girl protagonist, and *Something I've Been Meaning to Tell You* (1974), from which the selection in this anthology is taken. In his foreword to *Dance of the Happy Shades*, Hugh Garner wrote, "Writers are a dime a dozen, even in Canada, but artists are few and hard to find. Alice Munro belongs among the real ones."

"How I Met My Husbands," which was dramatized for television and broadcast in 1974 by the CBC, confirms Garner's judgment. Her control of tone is flawless. Even though the speaker is a drily practical woman, now stout and middleaged, the reader never forgets the fragile innocence of the fifteen-year-old girl she was, awakening to the false dawn of a first love affair. The blend of voices is unerringly modulated to the irony and pathos of that ambiguous experience.

E. G. Perrault (1925–)

E. G. (Ernie) Perrault lives in Vancouver where he pursues one career during the day—in advertising—and a second one in his spare time late at night or early in the morning—writing "action" and "thriller" fiction. So far he has published three popular novels in this vein, *The Kingdom Carver* (1968), *The Twelfth Mile* (1972), and *Spoil!* (1975). "If this third book takes off and makes me a lot of money," he says, "then I'll write one that's significant and therefore less successful."

His short story, "The Cure," indicates his mastery of a significant type of fiction far removed from the blood-curdling world of cops, spies, and tidal waves. It might be described as domestic satire edging towards fantasy.

Thomas Raddall (1903–)

Thomas Raddall has a solid reputation as both an historian and a writer of fiction. His historical works include two books which won Governor General's Awards for nonfiction, *Halifax, Warden of the North* (1949) and *The Path of Destiny* (1957), and his first published collection of short stories, *The Pied Piper of Dipper Creek* (1943), won a Governor General's Award for fiction.

Born in England, he came to Halifax with his parents in 1913. At the age of fifteen he left school to join the merchant marine as a wireless operator, and from 1918 to 1922 served both at sea and at stations along the Nova Scotia coast. Later he settled in Liverpool, Nova Scotia, working as a bookkeeper, doing private historical research, and contributing short stories to various magazines.

Some of his other collections of short fiction are *The Wedding Gift and Other Stories* (1947), *A Muster of Arms* (1954), and *At the Tide's Turn and Other Stories* (1959). Among his novels are *His Majesty's Yankees* (1942), *The Nymph and the Lamp* (1950), *The Wings of the Night* (1956), *The Governor's Lady* (1960), and *Hangman's Beach* (1966).

"The Wedding Gift" illustrates Raddall's ability to evoke a lively sense of an earlier time and place. Although the story belongs to the genre of historical romance, Kezia Barnes and her reluctant parson seem almost too authentic not to have existed. In 1973 the CBC presented a television dramatization of the story.

Mordecai Richler (1931–   )

Mordecai Richler now lives in Westmount, an affluent suburb of Montreal, but when he was still an expatriate Canadian living in England he wrote, "No matter how long I live abroad, I do feel forever rooted in St. Urbain Street. That was my time, my place, and I have elected myself to get it right." The stories, essays, and novels that record his attempt "to get it right" have spread familiarity with Montreal's St. Urbain Street working-class microcosm far beyond Canada. Richler's books have been translated into French, German, Hebrew, Italian, and Japanese.

When he graduated from Sir George Williams College in Montreal he traveled to Europe, living first in Paris, then London, where he worked as a free-lance journalist and wrote scripts for radio and television and for films such as *Life at the Top*. Although he was also turning out a stream of articles for Canadian, American, and British journals like *Maclean's, The Montrealer, Encounter, and Spectator*, he still found time to work at his major craft, fiction, and during the expatriate years wrote a succession of novels, *The Acrobats* (1954), *Son of a Smaller Hero* (1955), *A choice of Enemies* (1957), *The Apprenticeship of Duddy Kravitz* (1959), *The Incomparable Atuk* (1963), *Cocksure* (1968), and *St. Urbain's Horseman* (1971).

The novel which established his reputation, *The Apprenticeship of Duddy Kravitz*, was made into a movie in 1974 and has been exhibited successfully throughout North America and Europe. Its central character, Duddy, is the child of Jewish immigrants, a ruthless young hustler who uses his keen wits with manic energy to scrabble out of the St. Urbain Street ghetto toward a place in the monied sun. In "The Art of Kissing" Richler shows us Duddy turning a profit on the comically pathetic sexual fantasies of adolescence. The narrator-victim is never named, but he closely resembles Jacob Hersh, the troubled hypochondriac who is the central figure in *St. Urbain's Horseman*.

Sinclair Ross (1908–   )

In his first novel, *As For Me and My House* (1941), Sinclair Ross has his central woman character describe a June day on the prairies during one of the drought years of the 1930s: "The wind keeps on. When you step outside its strong hot push is like something solid pressed against the face. The sun through the dust looks big and red and close. Bigger, redder, closer every day. You begin to glance at it with a doomed feeling that there's no escape." The theme of "no escape" has dominated the vision of Sinclair Ross as a writer. Even though he worked in Montreal as a bank clerk from 1946 until 1968 and has for several years since then been living in Malaga, Spain, nearly all his fiction goes back to those formative years on the prairies. He cannot forget the care-worn men and women whose lives depended on the whim of weather, who for five years running could not harvest a crop from the parched soil.

Born on a north Saskatchewan farm himself, he grew up among homesteaders and spent his young manhood as a bank clerk in a succession of prairie towns until his transfer to Montreal.

In "The Lamp at Noon" he explores not merely the ancient man-versus-nature conflict, but the resulting psychological tensions between a man and woman who must share the ordeal, and whose relationship has frayed to breaking under the constant friction of a struggle they seem doomed to lose. The story, which was adapted for television and broadcast by the CBC in 1968, is the title piece in the collected short fiction of Sinclair Ross, *The Lamp at Noon and Other Stories* (1968). When it first appeared in 1941 *As For Me and My House* created no stir at all; only in recent years has it been acknowledged as a Canadian classic. He has written three subsequent novels, *The Well* (1958), *Whir of Gold* (1970), and *Sawbones Memorial* (1974).

Ray Smith (1941–   )

Ray Smith, who was born in Inverness, Cape Breton, now teaches at Dawson College in Montreal. In between he grew up, took an Honors B.A. from Dalhousie University, Halifax, worked as a systems analyst for an insurance company, read Eric Ambler and Vladimir Nabokov, got married, and developed a lively sense of how crazy life is.

He has published two collections of short stories, *Cape Breton is the Thought Control Centre of Canada* (1969), and *Lord Nelson Tavern* (1974). As the title of the first book hints, its stories are surreal, emphasizing the bizarre and the ironic. Since the world is absurd, their author seems to suggest, then the tales and fables which will reveal its proper image must also be absurd. But there is no denying the exuberance of his characters' symbolic capers in "A Cynical tale." If this be madness, says Smith, let's make the most of it.

W. D. Valgardson (1939–   )

Like many writers today, W. D. Valgardson has teaching as his bread-and-butter occupation. At present he is an assistant professor at Cottey College, Nevada, but he spent his childhood and youth in Winnipeg, Manitoba, where he attended university, taking a B.A. degree from the University of Manitoba in 1961 and a B.Ed. in 1966. Before moving to Nevada he taught English and art in several high schools in his native province.

He has contributed articles and poems to a variety of magazines and journals, but is best known for his short stories, which have appeared in *The Journal of Canadian Fiction, Tamarack Review, Dalhousie Review,* and *Queen's Quarterly.* His story, "Bloodflowers," was selected for inclusion in *The Best American Short Stories 1971* and is the title piece in his collection of short fiction, *Bloodflowers* (1973). Many of his stories probe into the minds of characters who have become entrapped in conditions of physical and psychological isolation. Sonny Brum in "Hunting" is in the company of two other men, but he is insulated from them at the level of real communication, unable to confess his deceitful plans or utter his growing despair. Often Valgardson shows these frustrations issuing in a climax of violence, as they do in this story.

ABOUT THE EDITOR

JOHN STEVENS is a professor of English in the Faculty of Education of the University of Toronto. Prior to that, he was Inspector of Schools for the Ontario Department of Education, and taught in several high schools. He has edited or co-edited numerous anthologies, among them: *Stage One: A Canadian Scenebook,* an anthology of Canadian drama; *The Urban Experience,* an anthology of prose and poetry; and four prose anthologies with Professor Malcolm Ross: *Man and His World, Images of Man, In Search of Ourselves,* and *Eighteen Stories.*

THE SNOW WALKER

FARLEY MOWAT

Chronicler of man against the elements.

In this collection of ten passionate and dramatic stories, Farley Mowat writes of the heroic Eskimo people in the stark and savage Arctic wastes, and of the powerful bonds between that vanishing race and their strange world.

> *"Mowat has often been described as one of Canada's greatest storytellers and his new book is splendid evidence of why he deserves that title... it is engrossing reading."*
>
> —*Vancouver Sun*

AVAILABLE IN PAPERBACK AT ALL GOOD BOOKSTORES THROUGHOUT CANADA

SWFM